S0-ACX-742

The Scorching Flames of Love and Duty

"Och, I'm looking forward to teaching you submission," Darach growled provokingly, pulling the robe over her tousled jet mane as she stood shaking with barely suppressed ire. "Aye, you're a comely wench, and I'm a most fortunate groom," he teased, lowering his dark head and brushing his firm lips across her rebellious mouth. He laughed harshly, avoiding her sharp teeth as she snarled and tried to nip him. "To bed, my little bride. 'Tis time we truly celebrate our marriage in proper Scottish custom by remaining secluded in the privacy of our own chamber for several days and nights . . ."

CHILDREN OF THE MIST

ALEEN MALCOLM

A JOVE BOOK

CHILDREN OF THE MIST

A Jove Book / published by arrangement with
Saxonia Productions, Inc.

PRINTING HISTORY
Jove edition / November 1986

All rights reserved.
Copyright © 1986 by Aleen Malcolm
This book may not be reproduced in whole
or in part, by mimeograph or any other means,
without permission. For information address:
The Berkley Publishing Group,
200 Madison Avenue, New York, N.Y. 10016.

ISBN: 0-515-08750-5

Jove Books are published by The Berkley Publishing Group,
200 Madison Avenue, New York, N.Y. 10016.
The words "A JOVE BOOK" and the "J" with sunburst
are trademarks belonging to Jove Publications, Inc.

PRINTED IN THE UNITED STATES OF AMERICA

part one

Scots are like witches; do but whet your pen,
Scratch till the blood come, they'll not hurt
 you then.
 Now as the martyrs were enforced to take
The shapes of beasts, like hypocrites at stake,
 I'll bait my Scot so, yet not cheat your eyes;
A Scot within a beast is no disguise.
 No more let Ireland brag her harmless
 nation
Fosters no venom since the Scot's plantation:
 Nor can ours feigned antiquity maintain;
Since they came in, England hath wolves
 again.
 Had Cain been Scot, God would have changed his
 doom
Not forced him to wander but confined him home!

—John Cleveland, 1613–1658
from the *Rebel Scot*

chapter 1

Rain lashed at the windows of the small attic room, and the wind skirled and whined through the many cracks and holes of the ramshackle house, guttering the candles that poignantly lit the sorrowful scene. The occupants of the room were frozen in a tableau about a bed where a wasted woman lay with a small boy curled in sleep within the comfort of her skeletal arms. Two young girls sat on each side of their dying mother, the flickering light captured inside the tears that silently streamed down their smooth cheeks and played across their bowed heads. One had hair as fair and fine as spun gold, and the other's was as thickly dark as the sheen on a raven's wing. An old woman stood in the shadows, her pleated lips pursed tightly, trying to smother the sobs that shook her bent body.

"Katrine, 'tis best you go now and find your father," urged the old woman, gently nudging the dark child. Green, tear-filled eyes flashed angrily and the glossy black head was fiercely shaken. "Go on wie you now, wee-an. If you dinna fetch him, there'll be the de'il to pay. *Auld* Simmie has gone for the doctor, so there's just you," she pleaded.

Katrine allowed her old nurse to usher her from the room. She stared at the closed door, trying to stop her torrent of tears. "What if she wakes and needs me?" she asked, sobbing.

"She'll wait till you are back. She might be ill, but Suibhan

3

MacNiall MacGregor has a strong spirit," the old woman returned huskily. "Now, off wie tha' gown and into your trews. Sinfu', it is, tha' a fine, well-born young lady should hae to dress up like a common street urchin and go searching the brothels and taverns," she muttered angrily beneath her breath as the girl stepped out of the ill-fitting, threadbare gown and pulled tight trews over her lithe legs.

"So, I hae to pull my drunken father out of a whore's bed and bring him home to my dying mother?" Katrine spat derisively.

"Bite tha' bitter tongue, my lass. Your puir father has enough hate and fury for the world, so we dinna need more from you!"

"How can you defend him, Aggie? My mother's dying—and he's rutting like some animal! It has been more'n a week since we last saw him, and he knows how ill she is!"

"Keep your voice down! I'll nae hae your thoughtless, unruly mouth upsetting your mother. Your father is a mon, and you are a wee-an of barely twelve. Aye, 'tis a hard life and you should not be knowing aboot a mon's appetites, but you do. And here's a wee bit more to ponder," she hissed, tying back the thick hair with a piece of twine. "Each mon deals wie grief in a different way. There's many a mon who canna deal wie sickness or a woman's weakness, and they hide from it—put their energies to other . . . things . . ."

"Aye, to that wee tail between their legs!"

"Och, Katrine MacGregor," Aggie reproved softly after a stunned silence. She stared into the young girl's face, sadly noting the fury that distorted the exquisite features. "Here's your hat," she added, roughly cramming the black felt over the ebony hair so the shadow of the brim muted the hard rebellious expression.

Katrine hesitated at the top of the steep narrow stairs, hearing the sharp scrambling of hard rats' nails in the darkness below. She was very conscious of the heavy silence behind her mother's door. A terrible shudder shook her slight frame and she turned back to her old nurse.

"Och, Aggie, I maun kiss my mama just one last time," she whispered, her green eyes wide and brimming with pain. Not a trace of the hard bitterness remained. She was a soft, sorrowing little child. Old Aggie held her close for a second, then thrust her toward the door. Kat sidled into the room. Macaree, her fourteen-year-old sister, looked up and frowned at seeing Katrine's masculine attire. Her pale, delicate hand held her mother's.

"What is it, my gentle Macaree? What is it, my wee fairy lady?" whispered Suibhan. Kat froze upon hearing her mother's voice. "Is it my wee Wild Kat?" she asked, her sunken eyes trying to probe the looming, moving shadows.

"Aye, 'tis me," answered Kat, her voice cracking with emotion. She removed her hat and hung back, somehow afraid to approach the bed.

"Come closer," Suibhan said weakly. Macaree exchanged a fearful glance with her younger sister. Afraid that their mother would fret at seeing her dressed as a boy and surmise that once more her errant husband had to be fetched from some sordid place, Kat yanked the confining twine from her hair so that her lustrous raven curls encircled her face. Then she obeyed her mother.

"Here I am," she said, trying to be cheerful but unable to stop the tears.

Suibhan gazed up at her daughter and reached a thin trembling hand to stroke the wet cheeks.

"Aye, here you are, my wee Wild Kitten—my *bardach* Kat. Och, dinna cry for me, my wee warrior. Weep for thyself, for I am leaving you with an awesome task. You are my strong one despite your tender years, and you maun take care of my gentle Macaree and wee Robbie." Her hand clawed painfully, tangling in Kat's hair. "You maun protect them," she repeated urgently.

"Aye, I swear to it." Katrine wept, taking her mother's hands in hers.

"And where's my gentle Macaree? Where's my fairy princess?" asked Suibhan, panic sharpening her voice. She frantically pulled her hands away from Kat's and flailed the air.

"I'm here, Mother." Macaree's soft musical voice and soothing touch calmed Suibhan. "I've not left you."

"You should be dressed in silks and laces, my golden angelchild. Look at you, as perfect as a china doll. Take care of her, Kat, dinna let any stain her pure beauty. Macaree, you maun be mother to wee Rob . . . You and Aggie maun mother him well so he grows to manhood straight and true." Suibhan absently ruffled her sleeping son's flaxen head, and Macaree's gentle tears fell on the faded and much-darned coverlet.

"Go quickly, Katrine," urged Aggie when once again the woman lay motionless, her eyes wide and fixed.

"Is she . . . ?" Macaree asked fearfully.

"She's having herself a wee rest," Aggie said comfortingly. "Take care of Robbie," she ordered as the little boy tossed fretfully. "And you, Miss Katrine . . ." But the girl had already rushed from the room, and her swift feet took the dark rickety stairs two at a time.

The wet night air stung Kat's cheeks. She bent her head against the icy wind as she raced across the shining cobblestones of the winding streets toward the raucous sounds of the tavern. She impatiently pushed her way through the milling crowd of men, not heeding the cuffs and shoves she received in return. She deftly dodged under restraining arms and fled to the small hidden gaming room in the back.

"L'écossais MacGregor n'est pas ici, et s'il était ici, je le donnerais . . ." A brawny arm picked her up and she was carried through the public house, hearing what manner of violence the enormous man would inflict upon the Scot MacGregor if he were there. Katrine was roughly thrown into the street; she scrambled to her feet as other angry voices joined in with suggestions of what havoc to wreak on the man who cheated at cards, robbing honest workers of their hard-earned money. Katrine rubbed her sore ribs and fled from the chorus of drunken yells.

Obviously, her father had been there earlier, and from the anger that had met her at the mention of his name, she surmised that his pockets were well lined. She scampered through the dark, wet streets not daring to slow her pace, although she had a painful stitch in her side. She entered the fashionable district and raced through the wider, cleaner streets, nimbly dodging carriages and elegantly dressed couples, ignoring the shouts as her feet splashed through puddles and doused silks and satins. Gasping for breath, she arrived at an imposing town house, where each pink-laced-draped window was lit and the sounds of laughter and music could be heard.

Wise to the ways of footmen toward uninvited guests, Kat grasped the heavy knocker in both hands and let it fall. She then dodged to one side. The massive door was opened, and when the servant stepped out to see who was there, she ducked behind him and crept into the house. Several rooms led off the large marbled entrance hall; the ornate doors were all wide open and cloying, heavy perfume assailed her small nose. Seductively dressed women were draped across sofas and men's laps.

"Gregor MacGregor!" Kat yelled at the top of her lungs, knowing she had just a few scant seconds to be heard before she would be once again thrown into the street. "Gregor Mac-Gregor!" she screamed again, directing her voice upstairs, hoping he wasn't ensconced out of hearing range in one of the bedrooms. "Gregor MacGregor! Your wife is on her death-bed!" She took advantage of the stunned inaction as many pairs of dazed eyes turned to stare with disbelief at the small ragged urchin. *They're all drugged to the gills!* she thought contemptuously as she recognized the sickly sweet smell of opium mixed with the many perfumes used to cover unwashed bodies. "Gregor MacGregor!" she shrieked as rough hands grabbed her.

"Laissez le garçon!" purred a low voice, and the liveried servant released Kat instantly and stepped back as a heavily painted older woman approached. *"Cherchez l'écossais Mac-Gregor,"* she ordered, waving a gloved hand toward the ceiling.

"Merci, madame," thanked Kat when the servant had swiftly run up the stairs. She stood still, hearing the blood pulse in her ears, biting the insides of her cheeks and trying to ignore the curious stares of the indolent people who clustered in the doorways.

"You are in the employ of the Scot MacGregor?" the painted woman queried softly in English. Kat nodded. "Then you know better than to keep your head covered in front of your superiors, boy." She reached out and snatched the hat from Katrine's head. "Your master may have many inexcus-able faults, but bad manners is not one of them," she added as the lustrous ebony hair settled about the child's poignant face, and fear-filled green eyes gazed at her.

"What a pretty little boy you are," she remarked. "I have many clients who would pay much to taste your sweet in-nocence."

"Gregor MacGregor!" screeched Kat, backing away from the grotesque woman, whose colorless wet tongue licked painted waxed lips, her spittle beading on the bright vermilion.

"What the hell is going on?" a deep voice bellowed, and for the first time in many years Kat was relieved to see her father.

She forgot she was meant to be perceived as his servant. She turned and ran up the stairs toward him, not noticing the disarray of his elegant clothes or the strange angle of his wig.

"Oh, Father, I'm glad I found you. It's Mother . . ." she managed to say before a blow across the face silenced her.

"How dare you!" he roared, propelling her down the stairs by the scruff of her neck and striding purposefully toward the front door.

"That is your son?" the painted woman inquired greedily.

"A bastard . . . a love child," Gregor said dismissively.

"Mother's dying. You must come!" cried Kat, pulling desperately at her father's brocade coat.

"Get awa' from here, you foolish child," hissed Gregor. "And why on earth should I be at the bedside of a pox-ridden slut?" He spoke loudly, for the benefit of the assembled audience.

"Let the *joli petit garçon* stay, MacGregor, and *peut-être* I shall conveniently forget the very large amount of money that you owe me," the painted woman wheedled. Her suggestions were received with enthusiasm by several men. A mighty shove dislodged Kat's grasping hands and propelled her down the hard stone steps. Her already bruised cheekbone smashed on the sharp stones of the street, but she agilely scrambled to her feet as she felt her father's hoarse whisper searing her ear.

"Run, my wee-an, run!" he ordered, and she ran as though her very life depended on it. There had been something so shiny, pink, and evil in the opulence of the high-class brothel, something that made her feel sick. She longed to be back in the poor but cozy comfort of the dim attic, cuddled with her siblings and her mother beneath the ragged quilt, sharing warmth, singing silly songs, and telling funny stories.

"Mother," she sobbed. "Oh, Mother." Unbearable grief welled up inside of her at the realization that very soon such comfort and safety would no longer exist for her. She increased her speed and, blinded by her tears and her wild mop of hair, barreled into a tall, strong figure.

"*Excusez-moi . . . monsieur,*" she managed to choke.

Darach Campbell caught his breath upon seeing the face of the small ragged urchin. Startling green eyes gazed up at him, bewildered and full of pain. Tears spilled down, mixing with blood from a gashed cheek. There was a still, frozen moment, and then the small child fought free of Campbell's steadying hands and whirled away into the wet, windy night. Darach watched until the fleet figure had faded into the inhospitable shadows, a frown creasing his handsome face. Something teased his mind. The boy seemed nightmarishly familiar, yet he couldn't fathom why. Finally, chiding himself for foolishness, he resumed his walk. Paris, like any other city, was full of homeless waifs, and yet a picture of the pain-filled little face nagged at him.

Kat's legs felt like jelly as she ran up the narrow flight of rickety stairs. At the landing she stopped and listened. On hearing the sounds of steady weeping and the shrill unhappy voice of her five-year-old brother, she slumped dejectedly against the wall.

"I want my mama!" was the strident demand. "Mama? Mama? Wake up!"

"I want my mama, too," whispered Kat, sitting on the stairs. The terrible realization of her mother's death dug into her whole being. "I will be strong for you, Mama," she promised, willing her tears away. She sat in the darkness, listening to Macaree's gentle tear-filled voice trying to sing a lullaby.

"She's not dead, she's not! She'd never leave me!" Rob screamed angrily. "Wake up, Mama!"

Kat opened the door and stood numbly watching the small boy try to shake his dead mother awake. Aggie and Macaree stood weeping in each other's arms. Heavy, weary feet trudged slowly up the creaking stairs, and Aggie's husband, Simmie, shuffled in and sorrowfully removed his woollen cap.

"Simmie, Aggie and Caree are telling lies. They say my mama is dead. Help me wake her up, Simmie!" screamed Rob.

"There was none tha' would come," stated Sim, wanting to comfort but not knowing how.

"My mama is not dead! She's not! She's sleeping! Kat, tell Caree and Aggie not to tell lies!" he pleaded.

"There wasna a doctor who'd set foot outside on this raw nicht wie-out seeing the color of my coin," Sim explained brokenly. "I hadna more to sell."

"Dinna *fash*, *auld* mon. 'Twouldna hae made a haepenny's worth of difference. When a person's time has come, it has come." Aggie sniffed, pulling herself together and blowing her nose. "Come to your nanny. Come to your *auld nurreych*, my wee *baichie,*" she coaxed, opening her arms to the small boy. "Come to your *auld* Aggie, master Robbie, and let your puir mother rest in peace."

"I don't want you. I want my mama."

"She's dead!" shouted Kat. "Hear it, Rob MacGregor, your mother is dead and she'll never wake up again, and our father is in a fancy whorehouse lying wie another woman. He wouldna come and called our mother a pox-ridden slut!"

"Shame on you, using such words in front of your puir dead mother," chided Aggie, scooping the little boy into her arms and covering his ears.

"Well, 'tis true," Kat retorted sullenly, feeling guilty when she saw Macaree's terrified, haunted face.

"Whether it be true or not, it shouldna be said aloud," snapped Aggie, rocking the boy against her ample bosom.

"You shouldna speak of our father like that," whispered Macaree. "He's a guid man who does his best. What happened to your face, Katrine?"

"Our guid father hit me . . . called our mother a slut and threw me out of the whorehouse!" Kat spat, angered by her sister's gentle reproach.

"Miss Macaree, take your brother into the kitchen," Aggie said, thrusting the weeping child into the girl's arms. Kat ignored them. She sat sullenly on a stool, staring at her mother. The door shut behind her brother and sister, but their weeping was audible through the thin, water-stained walls.

"Your father was outa his head wie grief, and he dinna ken wha' he was aboot," Aggie ventured to say, reaching out to push the hair away from the girl's injured face. She staggered back in shock when Kat roughly shoved her caring hand away and started to laugh jeeringly.

"You're a fool, Aggie. Och, he knows what he's about, old woman. There lies my mother, dressed in rags, while he's dressed in fine clothes! He's pumping his living seed into a whore—and my mother lies there dead!"

"Child, child, dinna talk like tha'!" cried Sim.

"I'm a child no longer, old mon," Kat interrupted, keeping her eyes pinned to the still features of her mother.

Aggie shook her head with consternation and sucked air through her sparse teeth, making a disapproving, anxious sound before scurrying across the room to cover the dead, staring face. Kat leaped up and savagely flicked back the sheet.

"Soon enough she'll be smothered by earth, all alone in the darkness of a grave, so dinna stop her eyes yet!"

The old couple blindly clasped hands, fretting at the change in the twelve-year-old girl they had known since birth. They had no words, no gestures, nothing to offer as comfort.

"Miss Katrine . . ." Sim struggled to speak.

"Leave me be! I want to be alone wie my mother!"

"But 'tis morbid," protested Aggie.

" 'Twas you who said we all have our different ways to mourn," the girl replied sardonically. Aggie and Sim quietly left the room, and soon their voices joined the younger ones in a low lamenting drone. They not only mourned their dead mistress, Suibhan MacNiall MacGregor, but also the end of Katrine MacGregor's childhood.

Kat sat for several hours tracing the premature lines on her mother's beautiful face, a face that appeared much older than the scant thirty years she had lived. How could her mother have loved her father? How could she have loved him so much that she gave up family, friends, and her native land to follow him into exile? Time and time again Kat had seen the pain her mother had tried valiantly to hide from her, pain caused by her father.

"He's like a little boy. He doesna mean to hurt anyone. He just wants what he wants—love, money, adoration, title, respect—all that he feels was stolen from him. Dinna judge him, my wee Wild Kitten," her mother's gentle voice had chided, echoing through the circles of time. Kat's scalp tingled as she remembered the soothing hands that had patiently attempted to cool her hot rage. "Remember the guid times, Katrine? Remember our beautiful château near Chartres by the river? There'll be guid times again."

Kat sat staring at her mother, thinking back to her first memories when her father had been larger than life, a splendid hero on horseback, a member of the prestigious Garde Ecossais, the Scottish regiment that protected the French royalty. They had lived a beautiful, pampered existence, on an estate with swans and rolling lawns. It seemed almost unreal, like a wonderful dream full of springtime and butterflies. Kat stared about at her present state of squalor. Little by little the beautiful life had crumbled. Little by little the splendid hero on horseback had lost his luster. He grew plump and careless, bringing frightening painted women and lecherous grasping men into their home. Parties would go on for days, and she and her siblings would be confined to the nursery wing. Macaree had been content with her books, her painting, and her needlepoint, but Kat had devised ways to free herself. Curious about her father's guests, she had secreted herself behind voluminous drapes and watched the gambling and ritualistic orgiastic behavior of the rich and bored.

Kat shivered, remembering the nightmarish displays: the sickly sweet smell of opium and cloying perfume; the paint, powder, and patches that masked faces; the brittle voices and tinkling pianofortes; the cards, shuffling and shuffling; and the anger, the accusations, the violence.

They had moved first to a smaller mansion and then to a smaller house, each time nearer to Paris until . . . Kat stared about at the squalid attic.

"Always one step ahead of the creditors." She sighed. "Oh, Mother, how could you have loved him? How could you have allowed him to bring you to this? I shall never let a man hae such power over me," she promised herself.

Dimly, Kat was aware of the staggering, heavy footsteps that shook the dingy house—invading footsteps that stumbled noisily up the stairs, jarring the very rafters and making a mockery of the reverence of death. The door opened and her father fell into the room. Kat didn't move. She just sat on her stool, numbly realizing that she had been waiting for him.

"Och, Suibhan!" lamented Gregor, not noticing his younger daughter. His attention was riveted on the bed, where the frail figure of his dead wife lay. "Och, Suibhan, my sweeting, my heart, my love, you dinna wait for me!" He leaned against the closed door, and then, with an awful cry, sagged to his knees. He crawled across the room, emitting horrible, drunken sobs that racked Kat's nerves. "Forgie me, Suibhan, my sweet, sweet love," he begged, pulling himself on the bed to lie beside his wife.

Kat was repulsed. Her disgust and fury were so intense she was nauseated. She wanted to drag him away from her mother. How dare he defile her with the stench of the whore, the cloying scent of cheap perfume still clinging to his disheveled but elegant clothes? How dare he lie with his head upon her motionless breast!

"How could you leave me, my only true love?" Gregor wept, stroking Suibhan's now serene face.

Many stinging retorts to her father's question bubbled in Kat's mind, but she kept silent. Her hands gripped the splintery sides of the stool as her father gracelessly blubbered, begging his wife to wake up, just as his five-year-old son had done earlier.

"Good-bye, my sweet wife," sniveled Gregor, unnerved by the hollow staring eyes. He recoiled and hastily covered Suibhan's still face, feeling a ghostly reproach emanate.

Kat watched unmoved as her father's seemingly abject grief flowered into a blustering rage, and he swore vengeance on the Campbells, blaming them for all his misfortunes. There ensued an endless list of grievances and accusations against the English and the sons of Diarmid, a list that she had heard from the cradle whenever his pockets were empty or the sun didn't shine.

"I solemnly vow to you, my love, tha' I shall take our *bairns* home to Scotland and reclaim the MacGregor lands from the Campbells!"

"You had to cover her face so she wouldna see the lie in your eyes," Kat snarled, unable to remain silent. Gregor looked at his daughter with a dazed expression, and she saw that his face was wet with tears.

"I had to hit you, wee-an . . ." he stammered after a shocked pause, gesturing drunkenly at her cut cheek. "That *madame* is an evil woman. She wanted me to sell you to her. Thought you were a pretty lad to be sodomized by the court catamites she panders to. These French are a perverted lot, you know. I couldna let them touch my bonny, wee lass—foul your sweet innocence."

"Like one of your friends did to Macaree?" spat Kat.

"You'll never speak of that. Never! It was nothing but a dream! You mind me! It never happened! Never! You'll hae your mother turning in her grave!" Gregor hissed.

"A pauper's grave?"

"What is this ugliness in your sweet voice, Katrine? Och, 'tis that puir battered face. I had to do it, lass. It hurt me more than it hurt you, it hurt my heart. Come to your father, Kit-

ten,'' he wheedled, reaching out to stroke her injured face, but
she coldly evaded his touch. ''Where's my son?'' he snapped
sharply.

''In the kitchen,'' she answered, loath even to speak to him.

''How is the *bairn*?''

''Hungry, cold, and grieving, like the rest of us. The doctor
wouldna come because there was no money and nothing left to
sell,'' she stated, taking a savage pleasure in the way her father
winced at her words. ''The only food in this house this past
week has been what I could beg, scavenge, or steal.''

''Royal offspring forced to survive by begging,'' he
mourned. ''We hae the blood of kings, Katrine. Think on our
clan motto. *'S rioghal mo dhream!* Royal is my race! And to
think a child of mine had to beg. Och, those sons of Diarmid
shall pay!'' he ranted.

''So, 'tis fine for a MacGregor to steal and cheat, but
shameful to beg?'' returned Kat. ''And it was no Campbell
that brought us to this, but *you*! You, who left us to starve
while you rutted with whores!''

For the second time that day, and the second time ever,
Gregor slapped his daughter's face.

''You'll nae speak to your father like that. You'll hae
respect!'' he shouted. ''Och, lassie, what are you driving me
to?'' he groaned, wanting to pull her into his arms but was intimidated by her disdainful stance. ''We should be comforting
each other at this sorrowful time, not tearing ourselves apart.
You're very young and you dinna understand. We are Mac-
Gregors, outlaws in our native land. Children of the mist. Not
able to use the name MacGregor unless we wish to die or be
transported as bonded servants to some hostile land. Mac-
Gregors, hunted like dogs for two hundred years, all because
of the Campbells. All the MacGregor lands—Glengrian, Glenlyon, Glenstrae, Glenorchy, Glengyle, and more—all appropriated by the Campbells. Well, I shall wrest my lands from
their grasping hands, and my son and his sons shall claim their
birthright. And you, my wee *bardach* lass, shall feast your
eyes on your namesake, the beautiful Loch Katrine in Mac-
Gregor country,'' he vowed. ''You hear that, Suibhan?'' he
shouted, turning to the shrouded shape of his dead wife,
unable to bear the scorn in his twelve-year-old daughter's eyes.
''I shall take our children home to Scotland.''

Kat stormed out of the room, not wanting to hear the empty

promises that could never come true, lest she be tempted to believe them, as her mother had done.

Two months later, Gregor MacGregor, with his three children and two servants, Agnes and Simon Fletcher, boarded a boat bound for the west coast of Scotland. It was mid-January of the year 1760, and the sea was turbulent, the waves crashing and echoing like cannon fire through the timbers, and the gale-force winds icing the drumming sails.

Kat huddled in the cramped cabin, deafened by the violent buffeting, sickened by the overturned chamberpots that rolled back and forth with the listing vessel, and suffocated by the thick, heavy darkness. She tried to daydream, numbly recalling the months since her mother's death. They had stood wrapped in ragged blankets, silently watching Sim and Gregor bury Suibhan MacNiall MacGregor. Macaree had fretted that it wasn't a real graveyard but just a forlorn place beside the river Seine.

"No wife of a MacGregor shall lie in a pauper's grave," her father had declared, and despite herself Kat had felt a grudging respect.

They had buried her mother in the eerie bluish time just before dawn, that uncanny suspended span before living things resumed their daily life. There had only been the sound of the water lapping against the muddy river bank and the whine of the wind through the bare branches of the trees that stood like stark, spectral hands against the lightening sky. A cat had screamed once, a bloodcurdling screech that had served as the eulogy and the coronach. There were no words. There was nothing left to say. It was just a gray, aching space of nothingness. Even little Rob had been respectfully silent, and all eyes, including Macaree's, had been dry, as though their tears were frozen like the cobweb-thin ice in the puddles by the shore.

A violent listing caused Kat's head to crack painfully against the rough wooden wall, bringing her back to the present. She couldn't believe that they were actually on their way home to Scotland. Maybe they weren't, she mused cynically, as the vessel bucked and keeled from side to side, causing agonized groans from Aggie and Macaree. The sour smells of vomit and urine and the smothering closeness were unbearable.

"Robbie's sleeping, Aggie, and he's tucked in tightly so he'll not roll off the bunk. I'm going out. I need air," Kat whispered, feeling her way through the thick blackness to the door.

"Nay, your father said to stay hidden," Aggie remonstrated weakly. "You maun stay hidden."

"We've not seen him since we first boarded. For all we know, he could've jumped ship and we're bound for slavery in the Colonies."

"Feels like we're bound for purgatory," groaned the old woman. "I've never wanted to die as I do now. Take care and remember your new name," she managed to say before she collapsed over a bucket, her empty stomach heaving painfully.

Kat opened the stiff cabin door and with difficulty wrested it closed behind her. The movement of the ship sent her careening against the wall, and she clawed blindly at the ridged wooden paneling. Seeing bars of gray light ahead, she staggered toward the iron-runged ladder that was dripping with water. She clambered topside, thankful for the freezing wind that scoured the staleness from her cheeks and drowned out the groans and wretchings of the seasick. Hanging on to the rail, she inched along the slippery, listing deck by the gunwhales, thrilled by the savage turbulence. The churning sea, of every conceivable shade of green and gray, seemed to rage forever. The foam-crested waves arced and bled into the threatening firmament.

The relief of being free of the stinking confines of the cabin made her heedless of the bitter cold. She exalted in the danger, standing like a valiant little figurehead at the prow, daring the very elements as the vessel laboriously dipped and rose through the battering waves. She laughed aloud with the screaming gale that twanged the frozen ropes and ballooned the iced canvas, but soon her numb fingers and sea-drenched clothes transmitted the chill. The wind was no longer a mischievous playmate but a taunting enemy that dug into her muscles and bones. Kat tucked herself under the protective curve of the gunwhale and wrapped her cloak tightly about herself, thankful for the serviceable boy's attire her father had insisted she wear. She sighed, remembering the very last time she had worn female clothing. It had been by the river when her mother had been buried. In the months since, she had become her father's constant companion, his partner in crime. He distracted the victims and she stole—from shops, pockets, carriages, and stalls. He gambled and she was his second pair of eyes. Between them they had managed to cheat and steal enough money for the passage to Scotland.

Every night for the past two months, Gregor MacGregor had spent more time with his children than he had ever done before. He sat with a bottle of whiskey, recounting the glorious and tragic history of their clan. They were the MacGregors, the children of the mist. He had them perched on the edges of their seats as he boasted of the feats of his father, the notorious Rob Roy MacGregor, for whom young Robbie was named. Despite her disillusionment, Kat was enchanted, carried away by the romantic pictures her father described of the majestic MacGregor countryside, and she was fired with anger against the Campbells and the English who had conspired to exterminate the MacGregor heirs, hunting them like vermin through many generations. Each night, Gregor had coached his children, impressing upon them the need to keep their identity secret. They were to take their mother's clan name of MacNiall, because to be known as MacGregor meant certain death.

The violence of the storm abated, and large fluffy snowflakes floated and danced above the frozen deck. Kat was mesmerized and reached out a cold hand to capture one, only to have her wrist caught in a steely vise.

"Get belowdecks, lad, before you freeze yer ballocks off," growled a seaman, and she was yanked to her feet and propelled toward the hatch. She was thankful for the man's rough strength, because her cramped, cold limbs hardly functioned and her worn boots slipped and skidded on the icy deck. He left her clinging to the metal ladder, when her numb fingers lost their grip and she plummeted down the sheer shaft.

Darach Campbell had the breath knocked out of him, and once more he gazed into the wild, startlingly green eyes. The boy had fallen into his arms, and he instinctively cradled the ragged imp against his broad chest. Kat's apology was swallowed as she stared at the chiseled, hawklike face above her. She frowned at its familiarity, and its silver eyes seared her.

"I'm sorry, sir," she finally managed to say as she struggled to be free. The strong arms didn't release her. She longed to

bow her head to avoid his sharp scrutiny, but her innate pride
caused her small nostrils to flare, and her green eyes glared defiantly.

"Who are you?" barked Darach, setting the child down but
keeping a firm hold. Kat wished she had spoken French and
that she had obeyed her father and kept hidden. She hung her
head and examined her scuffed boots as her sharp mind wrestled with possible replies. "Well?" he persisted impatiently.
Kat tried a tactic she had practiced from the cradle. She
sighed, shrugged, and gave him an engaging grin, her emerald
eyes wide and innocent, but there was no softening of his hard
expression.

"I am . . . just me, *monsieur* . . . *un pauvre garçon*," she finally answered, not knowing which language to speak. Darach
frowned, hearing the Scottish burr in the French and the
French lilt in the English. He swung the child back into his
arms, wanting to examine the hauntingly familiar face more
closely.

"And your name?"

"Whatever *monsieur* wishes to call me," returned Kat, trying to hide the terror that thundered through her veins. She
gasped when the intimidating, dark man gently traced the
faint scar that crossed her left cheekbone, the only visible rem-
nant of the hurts she had suffered the night her mother had
died. She watched the enigmatic play of emotions that crossed
his handsome face, and she refused to utter another word as
she tried to quell her rising panic. Darach's brain struggled to
understand what fascinated and bothered him about the waif's
face—the finely etched features, the unusual emerald eyes,
and the glossy ebony hair, all so like his own.

"Your family name?" he demanded. But there was no
answer, and he knew the child was afraid. He saw the rapid
pulse in the thin column of the boy's neck. Without warning,
the little mudlark twisted out of his arms, one moment lying
terrified and throbbing like an injured nestling and the next
becoming a snarling feral animal with teeth bared. . . . The
boy backed away, holding a lethal dagger in a clawed hand,
before whirling into the fetid darkness belowdecks.

Kat reached the safety of the cabin, rushed in, bolted the
door, and turned about. She leaned against it, fighting to control her terror, the *skean dhu* still clutched in her shaking fist.
A lantern emanating a reddish glow swung back and forth.

Macaree and Robbie slept curled together, but Aggie sat propped up against the wall of a top bunk and stared down at her, her face haggard and appearing unearthly in the arcing light.

" 'Tis snowing outside," Kat muttered defensively.

"Aye, and you always fight snowflakes wie your dagger," the old woman replied caustically. "Your father's tearing this vessel apart searching for you, and I've been praying for a quick, merciful death. He even offered to kill me hisself for allowing you out of here. Och, I am too sick to worry about you," she groaned, rolling onto her side and trying to get comfortable. Kat couldn't breathe. The hot stench crawled into her nostrils. She unbolted the door, but before she could escape, her father strode in and shook her like a rat.

"What did you tell him?" he hissed furiously, his strong fingers digging into her narrow shoulders. Sim entered behind him and hurriedly closed the cabin door.

"Tell who?" Kat gasped, her teeth chattering from her father's violence.

"That Campbell!"

"What Campbell?" she asked, her eyes widening as she thought of the hideous monsters she'd heard about. "There's a Campbell here? *Ici? Sur ce bâteau?*" she babbled, lapsing in and out of French.

"What did you tell him?"

"*Rien* . . . nothing."

"What name did you gie?" he demanded roughly.

"*Aucun.*" She wept. "Papa, I told him nothing . . . *rien. Je promis.*"

"Are you sure? It could mean the death of us all."

"I am sure, Papa. I said nothing. I told nothing."

"Why did you disobey me?" he asked gruffly, releasing her. She fell back on the nearest bunk, cracking her head on the top bed, where Sim curled up to sleep beside his protesting wife.

"It was so hot and everyone suffered from the mal de mer." To illustrate, she held her nose, and he laughed suddenly and wrinkled his in agreement.

"Aye, 'tis no rose garden."

"Papa, there is a Campbell near?" she asked. "On this boat?"

"Aye, and he had his foul hands on you, lass. That dark-haired de'il wie the bony cheeks.''

"But he doesna look like a savage. He's bonny—scary but bonny," she protested, feeling rather let down. After years of hearing about the bloodthirsty sons of Diarmid, she had expected a fire-breathing dragon, not a handsome human being.

"Tha's why they're so dangerous, lass. Now, no more disobedience. You'll stay here, stench or no stench, and you'll bundle yourself in skirts and shawls and tuck your hair into a bonnet, and keep your eyes on your feet until we reach your Aunt Ailsa's house," he commanded. "They'll be no card-playing on this voyage wie a Campbell so near." He sighed, regretfully.

"Tell me more of my Aunt Ailsa," begged Kat as she dutifully dressed herself in layers of ill-fitting skirts. "A fussy, broody hen, you said. Always clucking and pecking. Will she like us?"

"Doesna matter whether the *auld* biddy likes us or no. She's a MacGregor wie as much to hide as us."

Kat shivered as she recognized the frightening ruthless expression that suddenly distorted her father's face, revealing a strange fervor. One minute he could be gay and loving and the next a terrifying stranger. She curled away from him into the darkness of the hard bunk and closed her eyes, trying to block out the stench and her roiling fears, but her mind whirled with thoughts of the Campbell with the silver eyes and the excitement of going to her native land, a land that was totally alien to her. She lay hearing the medley of different breaths, sonorous snores, murmuring groans. None was steady. They were anxious sounds of her small family—all that existed between her and complete aloneness. Even Aggie and Sim were family, servants to her mother and father long before she had been born. Rob's sweet little-boy mutterings as he cuddled into Macaree's restless form caused a tenderness to well within Kat's breast. She had to be strong for all of them, she told herself—even for her untrustworthy, unpredictable father. She had promised this to her mother. What was it her mother called her? *Bardach,* the Gaelic word meaning "fearless." Terror clawed through her.

"Papa, what's our name?" Kat whispered, her sleepy mind panicking.

"The same as your puir sainted mother. You are now Kat

MacNiall, and when you're helping me by playing the lad, you'll be Kit.''

"What if I forget?" she asked worriedly.

"Then it'll mean the death of your father, sister, and brother,'' her father stated harshly. "No, my *braw, bardach* wildcat, you'll nae forget.''

"Nay, I'll not forget.''

"And remember that your sister is now Caree—never Macaree, for that's a MacGregor name—and Rob Roy is just Robbie or Robert.''

"And you are Rory MacNiall, and Aggie and Sim are still Aggie and Sim Fletcher, and our mother is still dead.'' Kat sighed, drifting off to sleep.

"Aye, and my sweet Suibhan is still dead,'' Gregor said broodingly, feeling more in love with his wife than he had when she was living. "And know it, my angel, that by tomorrow I shall have brought our children home to Scotland and have fulfilled part of the promise I made you.''

chapter 2

Not even her father's most whiskey-embellished description had prepared Kat for her first sighting of Scotland. She felt such an overwhelming emotion that she clutched little Robbie's hand so tightly that he shrieked, and her father's punishing elbow bruised her ribs. Nothing could douse her elation, not even the driving sleet that stung their cheeks and brought tears to her eyes. The unfettered wilderness stretched before her, and her heart soared with the majestic peaks, delighting in the dramatic vistas. Macaree whimpered and shrank, cowed by the savage splendor, finding no comfort in the looming mountains and endless moors. She wished for the gentle cultured gardens of France. She wanted soft greens, not the menacing purplish-grays that surrounded her as the ship sailed up Loch Linnhe toward Ballachulish. Tears coursed down the lined, weathered cheeks of Sim and Aggie Fletcher, and they clasped hands like a courting couple, unable to believe they were finally coming home after fourteen years of exile. Gregor MacGregor's face was lit with that strange, mad fervor that frightened Kat to the very core of her being. She turned her gaze back to the breathtaking scenery, and the stark magnificence reminded her of the Campbell's chiseled features and silver eyes. She furtively glanced about, secure that her drab black bonnet successfully shrouded her face, but there was no sign of the imposing man.

The first glimpses of Scotland remained etched in Kat's memory, and would nurture her through the next confusing and frightening years. Most of what happened later became an unreal blur, but that moment on the deck just before they docked was crystallized in her mind. A wonderful feeling of exhilaration shivered through her, and she knew beyond a doubt that she had come home, that she belonged to this land of the mist-mantled mountains and heathered moors.

They stayed in the port town of Ballachulish until the spring thaw, in lodgings every bit as squalid as the Paris attic. Then, with monies procured by crooked gambling and outright theft, they set off across Scotland, bound for their kinswoman Ailsa MacGregor, known as Ailsa Clarke, who lived in genteel seclusion in a large manse within a private park on the outskirts of Perth. Macaree sighed with relief when she saw the savage countryside give way to the softer lines of rolling hills with neat hedgerows and stone walls dividing fields, but Kat felt a tightening in her belly upon seeing nature harnessed within cottage gardens, and within straight plow lines and rows of symmetrically placed trees. She had gloried in the grueling trip across Scotland and was sad and apprehensive about its ending, fearfully sensing that it might be the beginning of much grief.

The Fletchers, Macaree, and Rob had traveled within the confines of a closed coach, but Kat and her father had served as outriders, galloping along with the Highland winds in their hair through the awesome majesty of Glencoe, with its romantic but tragic history—the Glen of Weeping, where in 1692 the loathsome Campbells of Breadalbane and Argyle had cold-bloodedly slaughtered their Catholic neighbors, the MacIans, part of the clan MacDonald, after accepting their hospitality for nearly two weeks. Macaree had refused even to peek out of the carriage window for fear of seeing barbaric Campbells about to pounce on them. She huddled against the leather seat, cuddling a squirming Robbie and singing a soothing French lullaby. Kat rode, hearing the imaginary clashes of ghostly swords, hungrily feeding her senses and storing up memories to sustain her through what she supposed would be some nightmarish times. They had ridden through the quaint villages of Tyndrum and Crianlarich, which were nestled in the rugged Grampians beside rushing crystal streams, when Gregor MacGregor reined in under the cover of the budding trees and glared furiously across the winking expanse of a serene lake. Kit frowned at her father's thunderous expression, hoping she hadn't inadvertently incurred his wrath.

"There it is!" he barked.

"What?"

"Balquhidder," he said with a snarl. "Those turrets over there belong to Balquhidder, where your grandfather, Rob Roy MacGregor, is buried."

Kat couldn't fathom why her father was so angry, nor could she equate the tranquil scene with the stories she had heard about her infamous kinsman. She sat on her horse, silently appreciating the idyllic beauty. Balquhidder seemed a fairy-tale castle set in a jewellike rolling glen beside the still waters of Loch Voil, with the pine slopes of the Trossachs looming in the background.

"He died in 1734, when I was but eighteen. He gave me no chance to prove my manhood. I was the youngest of five sons, the unfortunate runt born when my mother thought herself past the age of childbearing. I dinna ask to be born! I dinna ask to be the youngest! Nor the shortest! I dinna ask my mother to hold me so close to her breast and teach me the gentler arts instead of bloodletting and whoring. I couldna do anything right. If I pushed awa' from my mother's smothering arms, I was guilty of disrespect, and if I dinna, I was called a milksop or a molly-caudle. Well, *auld* mon, I'm the only son of five still living. The only son of five, mon enough to sire a male child. There's none of your precious heirs left except me to guarantee the immortality of your loins—no one but me to bring the Campbells to their knees and bring honor to the name MacGregor—a name outlawed and proscribed by the English since 1519. None but me, *auld* mon!" He laughed, an ugly raucous sound that echoed over the *loch*, bouncing off the gray turrets of Balquhidder and returning to mock him.

"What happened to your four brothers?" Kat ventured, looking back regretfully at the shimmering lake, set amid the various greens of pine, birch, and oak, as they resumed their journey. Gregor threw back his head and brayed gleefully.

"All stupid enough to be captured by the English after the Jacobite uprising of '45. I was the only one of Rob Roy Mac-

Gregor's sons who was *braw* and cunning enough to escape the gallows," he boasted.

"You had no affection at all for your very own brothers?" whispered Kat, appalled by her father's cruelty.

"Why should I have a shred of affection for them!" he spat. She shrank from his venomous attack. "They made my childhood miserable—telling lies to my father so he couldna look at me wie any favor. Affection? Nay, I despised the lot of them, especially my oldest brother, Donald."

"And your sister?"

"I had no sister. They called *me* the girl!"

"But, Aunt Ailsa?"

"She was my brother Donald's barren bitch of a wife."

"He was executed by the English for helping the bonny Prince?" asked Kat, trying to temper her father's harsh tone and lead him to glorious, exciting stories.

"Nay, the weak-livered bully escaped the gibbet by succumbing to jail fever. I wonder if my father, the great Rob Roy MacGregor, would've thought that a *braw*, manly way for a MacGregor to die," he jeered, and Kat asked no more questions, not wanting to have her fantasies and memories tarnished.

The rest of the journey was a bone-jarring vagueness. Kat was blind to the passing scenery, chilled by her father's malice, and filled with apprehension about the welcome they would receive from Donald MacGregor's widow. She had sustained Macaree, Robbie, and herself through the harsh winter in Ballachulish with the promise of the comforts of their aunt's home, weaving happy tales about a strong, loving woman who would take their mother Suibhan's place. Kat had even dared to hope that now they were in Scotland, her father would return to the romantic figure of her childhood, but if anything, his bitterness seemed to have intensified until there was almost a maniacal fervor about him. It was a rare day when she didn't receive a bruising blow from the back of his hand or even from his boot.

It was late afternoon when they finally reached the tall, forbidding fence and gates of Linnmanach, only to be emphatically denied entrance by a ferocious hound and a most ancient man who scuttled into the gatehouse and slammed the door when Gregor bellowed at him. Before Kat realized what her father meant to do, he coldbloodedly shot the dog, and she was hoisted up on his shoulders. In a daze, she shinned up the wrought-iron palings, shimmied through the sharp, crowning spikes, and dropped numbly to the other side. It took all her strength to draw back the massive, rusty bolts, and the gates swung open with an agonized screech that sent shivers down her spine. She kept her eyes averted from the still bundle of fur but made sure that she stood protectively close so her father wouldn't callously ride over the corpse. As Simmie guided the dusty carriage through the gates of Linnmanach, Kat glanced at the gatehouse and was shocked to see the ancient man staring at her with an expression of absolute terror, tears pouring down his lined face. She hoped he knew how very sorry she was, and she silently pleaded with him for forgiveness before receiving a sharp cuff about the head from her father, who bellowed at her to mount up. They rode silently up the overgrown driveway, and Kat turned back to see the old man seated on the ground, cradling and rocking the large hound. She looked at Macaree, who gazed out of the carriage, her beautiful eyes haunted and fearful. Kat tried to smile reassuringly at her sister, but Macaree covered her face with her hands, too terrified of the encroaching wilderness and the twittering swarms of bats that rose out of the shadowy undergrowth. They flickered against the striated sky as the horses trotted wearily up the rutted carriageway to the looming gray mansion.

Linnmanach appeared deserted, abandoned to the ravens and crows that roosted on the windowsills and chimneys, left to the vines that clung to the roughhewn stone walls and trailed across the mullioned panes. The forest was starting to reclaim the sloping, weedy lawn.

"Welcome to Linnmanach," Gregor declared expansively before dismounting and striding pompously up the wide steps to hammer at the fortresslike door. They could hear the sounds reverberating through the vast recesses of the house, diminishing to silence. Nothing stirred. The only noise was the harsh, squabbling sounds from the nesting rooks against the red sky. "I know you're in there, Ailsa MacGregor!" he roared, renewing his pounding with boot and fist.

"Papa said we maun never use that name or we will die," Robbie whispered, peering furtively about, expecting English soldiers and Campbells to spring out of the rhododendron bushes that towered menacingly on each side of the carriage way. Macaree held him tightly, wishing she were as brave as her younger sister, who sat in the saddle with her small chin courageously raised and her thin back straight and true.

Kat would never forget the moment that the massive, metal-studded door slowly creaked open to reveal four very ancient people armed with even older weapons.

"Go . . . awa'!" pronounced a trembling treble voice, and Kat once more saw abject terror, but this time it was etched on the face of a tiny, frail woman who held an enormous claymore in her shaking hands. The woman seemed like the most fragile cobweb.

"Well, if it isna Ailsa. Och, the years hae nae been kind to you, old girl. Near bald, you are, and that red hair of yours was your only pride and joy, wasna it?" Gregor guffawed, and Kat held her breath for fear the wizened little figure would be blown away by her father's blustering callousness.

"Wha' do you want?"

"And wha' sort of welcome is tha' for your prodigal kinsman?" chided Gregor, a cruel light in his eyes. "Why, dear sister Ailsa, I've brought my puir dead brother Donald's nephew and nieces to lighten your dark years."

"Traitor!" she hissed with such venom in her voice that Gregor took an involuntary step back. "How dare you show your face to me! You and your spawn are not welcome here at Linnmanach!"

"Dinna call me that, you *auld cailleach*, unless you desire your ain death," he stated, wrenching the claymore from her trembling hands with such force that she tottered backward, and her three ancient servants, an old man and two old maids, impotently brandished their weapons—a crossbow, a flintlock pistol, and a cudgel. "Dinna gie me an excuse for violence," he warned, and to her horror, Kat knew he was deriving a malicious pleasure from the exchange. "Whether welcome or no, we're here to stay! Any objections?" he added, waving the claymore. The only answer was the clatter of weapons on the flagstone floor as the ancient band clung together out of fear.

"Och, still the bullying coward, Gregor MacGregor," taunted Ailsa.

"The name is Rory MacNiall," was Gregor's terse reply. His rage flared, and he fought the overwhelming desire to batter the wraithlike, taunting figure of his sister-in-law. "And

from the looks of the decay and rot not only to Linnmanach
but to you, *auld* hag, 'twould seem I've arrived just in time.''
With that, he strode into the house, the claymore still in his
hand.

Kat and the Fletchers straggled in awkwardly behind him,
but Macaree ignored her father's order to follow. She held
Robbie tightly and sang a soothing carol about a shepherd,
refusing to leave the comparative safety of the carriage.

"Good day, Aunt Ailsa," Kat greeted, feeling great embarrassment and wanting somehow to make amends for the rude
intrusion. "My name is Kat."

" 'Tis a cat, a pussy cat! Meow! Meow!" screeched one of
the ancient maids, clawing her bony hands and scratching
wildly in the air. Kat recoiled hastily from the sudden display
of madness, and Ailsa cackled with mirth.

"Meow! Meow!" she imitated. Then she hissed venomously, her shriveled face distorted with hatred, before she and
her loyal band scuffled into the sinister shadows of the ominous, crumbling mansion.

Silently, Kat followed her father through Linnmanach,
through room after room of ghostly remains. She gazed obediently where he directed, staring wide-eyed at the tattered
banners of past glories and seeing the abandoned nests and
bird droppings that encrusted the ornate cornices of the great
hall, where in some bygone age enormous banquets had been
served and elegant balls had taken place. She felt a hollow
sadness when their feet echoed sharply down the long portrait
gallery, where empty squares edged with grime spoke of the
paintings that had hung there, proudly displaying ancestors.
The name of their ancestors had to be kept achingly hidden inside, never to be spoken aloud. Seeing the empty frames and
spaces caused this realization to dig into her more sharply than
ever before.

"We are the children of the mist," she whispered to herself.
"Maybe we deserve to be," she added, feeling a terrible guilt
claw at her when she looked at Macaree's beautiful sad face.

"Well, wee-ans of mine, what do you think of Linnmanach?" asked Gregor, throwing open the tall French doors
that led off a small salon and stepping onto a stone terrace,
overgrown with wild roses, that overlooked the lake. Kat
thankfully breathed the crisp evening air and leaned over the
balustrade, enchanted by the sight of a hind and fawn

silhouetted against the blood-red sky. "Och, isna that a bonny sight!" he exclaimed, following his youngest daughter's gaze. "The hunting's guid here. Both red and roe deer, grouse and pheasant . . . and tasty wood pigeon. Och, we'll never hae empty bellies again, my Wild Kat," he rejoiced. "And do you hear the music, Caree? Can you hear it drifting over the waters of the *loch*? Can you hear the rustle of your beautiful gown? You'll be the bonniest lass at the ball—in the whole length and breadth of Scotland," he declared. But his older daughter didn't speak. She stood clasping Robbie's hand, trying to quell the panic that pulsed through her as the flames from their candles snaked upward with the cobwebs, causing the shadows to grow into terrifying shapes that danced eerily through the vast interior. Gregor followed her eyes. "Och, lass, I know it is not as grand as it could be, but 'tis better than some of the places we've had to rest our heads these past sad years."

"Are there fish in the *loch*, Papa?" asked Robbie, pulling free of Macaree and scampering across the terrace to Kat.

"Aye, great big ones, bigger than any for miles, because the *loch* has no bottom. 'Tis true. It is as deep as Loch Ness, where the monster lies. Legend has it that a daft monk tried to find the bottom and drowned during the effort. That's why 'tis known as Linnmanach—monk's pool. Linn-nan-manach —pool of the monk. And we'll go fishing, Robbie, and riding, and I'll fill the stables wie the finest horseflesh," he said, fired with excitement.

"And I'll have my own pony again?" the boy asked eagerly.

"Nay, no puny pony, but a horse, a fine Arab stallion. You're nearly a mon, not a wee-an, and a mon rides a horse," he declared.

"I like ponies better," the little boy whispered apprehensively.

" 'Tis going to be a grand life, you'll see. I'll refurbish Linnmanach until 'tis a palace fit for my beautiful, gentle princess Caree. And we'll hae grand balls, and you'll hae rich, handsome young lords paying court," he vowed, sweeping his elder daughter into his arms and dancing her about the darkening terrace, oblivious of the way she shrank from his touch and the bleakness that hollowed her blue eyes. But within seconds, she hummed a minuet, and a dreamy smile lit her beautiful face.

There was one touching memento of that first horrendous introduction to Linnmanach, and that was Sian. The day after their arrival, Kat was exploring the woods, and she came across the old gatekeeper digging a grave. Silently, she helped him, and they laid the massive black bitch to rest beside the *loch* near the ruins of an ancient monastery. The old man wept, and Kat thought of her mother, buried under a towpath beside the Seine with no one to mourn her, with the workhorses trampling the earth above as they hauled the barges along the river. The old man had shown her a litter of pups, blind and squealing, wriggling on top of one another as they hungrily tried to find their dead dam. Only one survived, and Kat named him Sian, Gaelic for "storm," because his coat was as dark as a thundercloud. She was very careful to keep him hidden from her father for fear that his anger, so often wreaked up on her, would kill the rambunctious young dog as it had his dam.

So Linnmanach became their home, but Gregor never quite got around to restoring it to its past glory, and his children learned to become familiar with its decay. They learned to love their wraithlike Aunt Ailsa and her ancient band, who kept themselves hidden whenever Gregor was in residence. She and her cohorts would timidly tiptoe out of the shadows during his frequent long absences, drawn to the three beautiful children.

The first years went by happily while Gregor was away. Kat and Rob ran free, fishing and swimming, hunting and riding within the wilds of the rambling private park. Macaree was content to watch from the window of Ailsa's small cluttered parlor as she mended clothes and listened to the chatter of the ancient maids. Aggie unobtrusively took over the running of the house and the kitchen gardens, and Simmie allied himself with the two old menservants. During the long winter evenings, the children sprawled in front of the blazing hearth in either the well-stocked, albeit dusty, library, reading aloud to the delight of the old folks, or else in the kitchen, listening to reminiscences of Scotland's past glory.

Every three or four months, Gregor would remember the existence of his offspring and return to Linnmanach, and Ailsa and her ancient band would scurry back into the shadows until the decay and discomfort would chase him away. Gregor would return dressed in the richest, most elegant clothes with a spanking-new carriage and a superb team of matching horses. He would be laden with extravagant presents. There would be bolts of costly silks and laces to delight Macaree. Her nimble fingers fashioned gowns more suited for the ballrooms of Europe than for the crumbling gray fortress that nobody visited. There would be glittering gems: diamonds, emeralds, and rubies set in the finest silver and gold; tiaras, necklaces, bracelets, and rings to be admired with awe but never claimed, as within a few months they would disappear when Gregor was short of funds. Kat shuddered to think how he had acquired such jewelry, but she was relieved that he no longer relied on her to be his partner in crime. The stables had been filled several times with magnificent horses, but now both Kat and Robbie knew not to become attached to the animals because their father would soon reappropriate them.

Gregor would stay for a week or so, trying too hard to break through his children's reserve. With each trip home in those first two years, he hardly recognized them. They were growing too fast and leaving childhood behind, and he couldn't grasp the time. It slipped through his fingers, and he gazed into the faces of strangers who did not seem his offspring. He felt guilty and disgusted at the decay that surrounded Macaree's ethereal sixteen-year-old beauty, and he'd hear himself repeating the same old promises. Fury would well up inside Gregor upon seeing the sardonic gleam in fourteen-year-old Kat's green eyes, and he'd strike out to wipe it away. Even if his hand connected, she wouldn't flinch, and he withered at her contempt. Even his little Robbie had changed. He was no longer the trusting little boy who gazed at him with admiration. He was a seven-year-old youth who barely seemed to tolerate him, wishing him gone from their crumbling domain. Each time Gregor came home, he tried desperately to recapture the camaraderie he remembered sharing with his children for that brief dark time in the squalid attic after Suibhan died. He would drown his frustrations with whiskey and talk at his children, unnerved by their silence, and he would loudly fill in all the pauses when they didn't answer. He would glare at Kat's rebellious little face and blame her for the gap that existed.

"It won't be long now, I promise. I hae not forgotten. I swear to you upon your puir dead mother's grave that I'll bring the Campbells to their knees and you to your rightful inheritances!" he shouted, as if loudness could make it be so.

"Every day I am getting closer. My plan is working but I canna be rushed," he would add defensively, seeing the scornful skepticism on Kat's small face. "I hae to be sly and canny. I hae to slither like a serpent into their exalted circles. Och, you dinna ken those Campbells. They think themselves above mere men, think they're gods, they do. Och, the arrogant snobs—but soon, my wee-ans, soon."

Kat would relax with relief when their father rode away, often taking Simmie with him to act as coachman or valet. The perfumes that emanated from his satin and velvet clothes caused her stomach to heave; she knew it was the stenches of other women. She knew Gregor lived in Edinburgh with a rich widow and in Perth with an equally wealthy old maid. She'd even heard Sim telling Aggie about other loose females in Glasgow, Dunbarton, and Aberdeen. So her father sowed his wild seed far and wide, and when she spoke to Aggie about it, the old woman merely shrugged and said it was the way of men. Kat could not understand what women saw in her father. Once he had been handsome, with thick flaxen hair just like Macaree's and Rob's, but now his hair was thin and lank and his once golden skin was pasty and loose. She rarely saw the boyish mischievousness that used to dimple his cheeks and charm her mother into forgiving his many faults. Kat would fling the windows wide open, trying to dissipate the heavy, cloying smell of perfume that lingered after her father had left. She would swear for the thousandth time in her young life that she'd never allow a man to use and discard her.

Mindful of the promise she had made to her dying mother, Kat made it a point to find out all she could about her father's activities. She would wait until he had passed out with his whiskey bottle and been put to bed by Sim. Then she'd methodically search through his pockets and luggage, where she usually found pawn tickets, promissory notes, and money. She always helped herself to a good portion of the money, hiding some under a floorboard in her room in case of some unforeseen disaster, and giving the rest to Ailsa to use for household staples.

Life at Linnmanach was a hand-to-mouth existence. The work was too strenuous for the very young and the very old, and it was petite Kat they had to thank for their survival. In winter they huddled together in two or three rooms, unable to cut and stock enough wood to warm more of the vast drafty mansion. Macaree hardly ever went out. She hated to see the stark, gray fortress without the fragrant wild roses softening its harsh lines. The naked branches of the trees reminded her of her dead mother, alone in France, so she kept busy either in the kitchen helping Aggie or in Aunt Ailsa's room aiding the old maids, who grew frailer each day, while Kat and Rob assisted the two old men outside.

Kat loved the silence of the winter woods. She would trudge through the crisp snow to check her traps, with Sian bounding ahead, his giant paws spraying the rainbow-hued crystals. Their feet would mark the snow where no one had stepped before, and their breath would mist the frigid air. Late winter was a hungry time when the dried venison and preserved fruits would nearly be gone and the oatmeal barrel was empty except for weevils. In February, even the abundant wood pigeons deserted them, knowing somehow that the people at Linnmanach were hungry; the woods were almost ghostly in their stillness.

Somehow in those first two years, everyone at Linnmanach survived until spring, delighting in the first tender green that peeked through the bare brown vines that curled about the cold gray stones. But the third spring was different. There wasn't the usual brisk renewal of energy. Harsh winter coughs lingered, and Ailsa and the frail old maids sat nodding in the weak sunshine, bundled up against the capricious breezes. The old men moved more slowly, their gnarled joints stiff and sore. Kat's worried eyes assessed each person, and she was frightened by Robbie's pallor and thinness. His eyes were unnaturally bright, as their mother's had been when she fell ill. She met Aggie's anxious glance, and to her horror she noticed that her old nurse had aged terribly. Her shoulders were bent with weariness, and a tired resignation lined her face. Only Macaree seemed untouched by the long cruel season. At nearly eighteen she was breathtakingly beautiful. She was the magical princess their mother had always said she would be.

The two old maids and one of the old men died that autumn. It was as though they evaluated their lives, compared them to the long, cold winter that yawned ahead, and decided that they weren't worth the battle. Kat and the old gatekeeper dug the three graves, and Macaree sang as she picked Michaelmas daisies while Aggie tended to Ailsa, who clung tenaciously to life, and to Robbie, whose cough had worsened.

Gregor arrived the night after the burial. Kat was riding through the woods with Sian leaping into the piles of crackling leaves when the coach horn sounded imperiously. She had been lost in brooding thoughts. She, too, had evaluated the approaching winter, and she was afraid. Her hands were raw from cutting wood and there was barely enough for a month. Robbie's illness terrified her to her core, and there was nobody in whom she could confide. Aggie was too busy with Robbie and Aunt Ailsa, rushing every minute of the day as she tried to run the home and hearth. She was overburdened and undernourished, her once rotund body now brittle and thin, too fragile to shoulder any added weight. Kat felt more alone than ever before. Macaree was no comfort; she would only acknowledge sweet, gentle things. Several times in the nearly four years that they had been in Scotland, Kat had tried to converse with her older sister, attempting to talk about things more important than flowers, embroidery, and baking, but she had met the usual resistance. Macaree's beautiful face had somehow shuttered, becoming like a mask, a porcelain doll, devoid of any emotion. She had remained breathtakingly perfect, and she had hummed an irritating nursery tune. When it happened, Kat would feel an overwhelming guilt bordering on madness.

Gregor was too excited and pleased with himself to notice the air of mourning that shrouded everyone except his older daughter. He rang for food and drink, grumbled about the cold empty grate in the library, and finally exploded when Macaree waited on him as though she were a mere servant.

"Where's Aggie Fletcher?"

"Tending Aunt Ailsa and Robbie," explained Macaree softly, and Kat noticed the serene mask that had descended across her sister's face as soon as her father had raised his voice.

"Robbie's sick?" he shouted.

"He's just a little sleepy," Macaree murmured, carefully arranging a display of dried grasses and autumn leaves while humming to herself.

"I think he's dying of what Mother died of," stated Kat sharply, needing to share this heavy burden and also wanting to hurt her father, to cause him to do something to stop these deaths.

"No! You are wicked! Wicked!" screamed Macaree, covering her ears and rushing from the room. Gregor's hand shot out so fast that Kat had no time to duck, and she was knocked to the floor.

"Aye, you are wicked!" Gregor repeated. "I come home wie wonderful, glorious news, only to be greeted like this! I debase myself from dawn to dusk building a fit future for my children for this ungrateful display of cruelty? I deny myself a home and hearth for you to behave like this?" he ranted, further infuriated by his sixteen-year-old daughter, who slowly got to her feet, making no move to wipe the blood that streamed from her lip. Her flashing green eyes told him how very much she hated him. "Och, Katrine, what do you push me to?" he lamented. Unable to bear her silence, he turned away and reached for his whiskey bottle.

All that evening, Kat waited for him to start talking, to make his usual promises, but this time he just drank, occasionally throwing back his head and bellowing with gleeful mirth, slapping his thick thighs with delight.

Kat was shocked at the change in Sim. He looked as feeble as Aunt Ailsa, his lips and fingertips blue and bloodless, as if he were very cold. Everyone was crumbling and decaying before her eyes. Gregor saw his daughter's reaction to Sim's changed appearance, and he nodded musingly before demanding several packs of playing cards. Kat's stomach sank sickeningly when he curtly dealt her a hand. All night he coached her in the finer points of cheating, and even though her body ached with weariness, she refused to rest. Instead, she waited for him to drink himself to sleep so she could search through his pockets and find the reason for his gloating elation.

That night Kat lay awake while fear churned her belly. She had found a thick wad of promissory notes adding up to the enormous sum of five thousand crowns, all with the initials R.C., and after eavesdropping outside Aggie's and Sim's room, she knew that they belonged to one Riach Campbell, younger half brother of Darach, Lord Rannoch, the silver-eyed man she had bumped into four years before. Kat's eyes had filled with tears as she heard Sim's hoarse, breathless voice. The strong bass tones that had comforted her through childhood were now a sound of the past, stolen by age, and this increased her terror. Sim cursed her father, calling him the very devil for coldbloodedly ruining the young Campbell, who was no more than a lad.

"You're too harsh on the master," Aggie had chided. "No mon, be he the de'il hisself, can debauch another wie potions and whores unless the mon is weak and wants it. The master canna force the young Campbell to smoke tha' foul-smelling poppy weed nor gamble his money awa'."

"The lad is barely nineteen," Sim had protested.

"*Auld* enow to know better. Dinna blame a Campbell's weakness on a MacGregor, or you sound like them," hissed Aggie. "By nineteen I had laid four children beneath the turf and been married to you for nigh on five years. Now, 'stead of *fashin'* aboot a bastard Campbell, tell me why you are lookin' sae peaked and thin."

"You look no better yourself, you *auld cailleach,*" grumbled Sim.

" 'Tis *auld* age creepin' up on us."

" 'Taint creepin', 'tis galloping." The old man sighed.

After several minutes Kat tiptoed away, as their snores shuddered through the sleeping house. She lay wondering why Aggie's hatred for the Campbells was suddenly as intense as her father's. Unable to lie still, she leaped off her bed and studied herself in the mirror. Was she crumbling and decaying like the others? Moonlight flooded through the open window and she stared in awe at her shadowy reflection, enthralled by the mysterious dark woman who solemnly regarded her instead of the familiar urchin from the Paris streets. It was the very first time she had ever observed a change in herself. She pulled her sleeping shirt over her tousled head and stood naked, staring at herself, oblivious to the chill late-autumn wind that skirled through the bare branches of the trees and whined into the room. She prayed to the powers that were— whether they were the ancient gods of merriment with cloven hooves and pipes gamboling in some verdant glen, or the awesome pompous ones that hid behind ceremony in ornate churches—that she would awaken in the light of day and still appear so grown up and mysterious. The years had gone by, and she had watched Macaree grow from a fairylike golden princess into a tall, regal goddess with full, rounded breasts and graceful, curvaceous hips. She, Kat, had seemed to stay the same, suspended, growing no taller and remaining a ragged waif. Macaree was so radiantly beautiful that she constantly surprised Kat, though she saw her every day—she was so absolutely, stunningly perfect that Kat had felt grubby and insignificant in comparison. But now in the moonlight she saw an exquisite, petite woman gazing thoughtfully at her from the shadows.

Kat awakened in the harsh light of morning to the disappointment of the wild-haired waif in the mirror and to the relief of learning that her father had left taking Simmie with him instead of herself. Her relief quickly turned to guilt when she saw Aggie drawn and worried about her poor husband. The old woman was in no mood for Kat's queries as fear gnawed into her aching bones. She sensed that she'd never see her spouse again.

"I heard Simmie tell you about the young Campbell," Kat insisted stubbornly. "I heard how Father is using him as bait to catch a bigger fish, Darach Campbell of Rannoch."

"Then you'd best get busy preparing a bedchamber for our guest, as I hae my hands full wie everything else," snapped Aggie.

"Guest?"

"Aye. If'n you're going to listen to tha' which dinna concern you, 'twould be best if'n you listened to the whole, 'stead of part."

"Here," said Kat, holding out several coins. "I took it from his pocket."

"Stealing—listening at keyholes." Aggie sighed, tying the coins in a rag and hiding them in a crock.

"Are you a MacGregor, too, Aggie?" asked Kat after a long silence. "Is that why you hate the Campbells, too?" she probed, when the old woman didn't answer but kept bustling about the kitchen.

"Aye," was the terse reply.

"But you always told me it was a sin to hate, said that Father had enough hate for the whole wide world."

"There's a world of difference between wha' should be and wha' is. A wide, wide world between wha' a person should feel and wha' a person does feel. So many times over the years I'd tell myself to let the past rest in peace, but then it rears its ugly head," ranted Aggie. "And I wake up and see you puir motherless *bairns* in this comfortless ruin. I see you, growing old before your time doing a mon's work—hunting and chopping, worrying, and being the provider to us all—and you, a lass of not even seventeen. Then the hate grows hotter. I want more for you than this meager, miserable, scrounging life, and if it means that one debauched, overfed Campbell has to pay, then so be it. I say go to it, Gregor MacGregor, in any way tha' you can! Even if it means death and destruction to a Campbell!''

Kat was appalled by Aggie's vehemence, and she sat quietly, not knowing how to respond. The old woman panted for breath, exhausted by her unaccustomed tirade. Macaree glided gracefully into the room, singing sweetly to herself. She froze, sensing the charged atmosphere, her blue eyes shifting from her old nurse to her petite dark sister. She backed away apprehensively.

"Caree, my pet, would you arrange some pretty dried grasses and flowers in the small green bedchamber across from yours?" Aggie asked softly. "And air the linens tha' you embroidered so delicately wie forget-me-nots," she added soothingly.

"And should I sprinkle lavender and rose petals to chase away the moldy smells?" asked Macaree.

Autumn turned to winter, and there was no sign of Gregor or Sim. Each morning, Macaree dusted and scented the green chamber, never asking for whom it was intended, and Kat and the ancient gatekeeper trudged through the snow to scrounge for pieces of wood and scraps of food. Each morning, Aggie was relieved to see Robbie's pixie face grinning wanly at her, and she was surprised to find Aunt Ailsa still clinging tenaciously to life.

"I'll nae die before tha' traitorous MacGregor," the old woman swore. "He killed his ain brothers!"

"Dinna spout such gibberish stite!" snapped Aggie. "Pay no heed to your auntie, Miss Katrine. She's just a spiteful, addled *auld cailleach*," she added when she saw Kat's shrewd green eyes narrow with speculation.

"You're an addled *auld* hag yourself, Agnes Fletcher!" cackled Ailsa. "You canna see wha's at the end of your ain nose! Canna smell his stench neither! Gregor MacGregor is an evil mon. Sad, it is, tha' he's your sire, wee dark lass." Kat didn't need Aggie's urging to leave the room. She was uncomfortable with her aunt's mad ramblings, even though she knew

the woman was senile and should not be taken seriously.
"Dinna let the Campbell see the wee dark lass. He'll ken who
she is! You know who she looks like, don't you, Agnes
Fletcher?" chanted Aunt Ailsa warningly.

"Who do I look like, Aggie?" probed Kat.

"Och, dinna pay tha' batty *auld* woman no mind," Aggie
said dismissively.

"But Macaree and Robbie have golden hair like our father
and mother, and blue eyes, too," the girl persisted.

" 'Tis the black Scot you hae mixed up wie your blood from
some bygone time. 'Tis said the Spaniards invaded this land
hundreds of years ago, leaving their mark to appear throughout the generations, and you are just such a one."

In what Aggie called "the daft days" between Christmas
and the new year, Gregor returned, driving a sedate black carriage. Kat opened the gate for him, and Sian snarled, baring
his fangs to show his intense dislike of the man. Luckily, her
father didn't respond. He whipped his horses so that they
sprang forward, and Kat slowly closed the heavy gates, wondering why Simmie wasn't holding the reins.

As soon as Kat stepped into the crumbling ruin of a house,
she sensed that something was terribly wrong. Aggie stood
swaying, her face drained of all color, and a dark-haired youth
sprawled in a chair and stared about in a daze.

"No pauper's grave for my loyal Simon Fletcher. Och, Aggie, you should see the magnificent marble tombstone wie the
angel Gabriel atop blowing his horn so Saint Peter opens the
gates of heaven," Kat's father lied expansively.

Simmie was dead. Kat and Aggie stood as motionless and
pale as the marble tombstone that Gregor so colorfully described. They were unable to grasp this awful reality. Macaree
floated into the room with a swish of pink taffeta. She was
icily composed and hummed a lilting little tune while Gregor
bragged rapturously of the location of the graveyard on the
other side of Perth.

Simmie Fletcher was dead, and Kat's throat was painfully
constricted, with all the unsaid, inappropriate words forming
a meaningless knot. She was frozen with one small, callused
hand outstretched toward Aggie, desperately wanting to comfort and be comforted. But there was no comfort. "Go to it,

Gregor MacGregor, in any way tha' you can! Even if it means death and destruction . . . !'' Aggie's words echoed in her head.

"Even if it meant Simmie's death and Aggie's destruction," she whispered, turning bleak eyes to her father, unable to comprehend his lack of grief.

"It is Hogmanay, and you've brought the dark stranger, Papa!'' Macaree exclaimed with delight, her blue eyes widening with joy at the sight of the handsome but befuddled young man. "And your bedchamber is ready with prettily embroidered linens scented with lavender," she sang. Kat opened her mouth to protest her sister's denial of the shocking news, but instead she shook her head in sad defeat and followed Aggie out of the room.

"Och, Aggie," she sobbed, yearning to throw herself into the nurturing arms that had always been open to her from babyhood, but the old woman turned hard, dry eyes upon her.

"Make the Campbells pay. Your tears will nae bring my Simmie back, so just make sure tha' he dinna die for naught!''

Riach Campbell gaped at the angelic, golden vision. He had never seen such perfection. He rubbed his eyes, expecting the graceful young woman to be a figment of his imagination, conjured up by the opium he had been smoking, but the glorious maiden remained smiling sweetly at him. He rose to his feet and bowed; she curtsied.

Gregor watched the exchange and smirked greedily. Let the stupid Campbell cub fall in love with his beautiful Macaree. What better way to ensure that his prisoner remained securely locked within Linnmanach's crumbling walls, while he was in Edinburgh seated at a gaming table, ruining the arrogant Darach Campbell of Rannoch. He made his plans gleefully, clapping his hands together, unable to contain his mounting excitement. His ill humor, caused by what he perceived to be Simmie's treachery by dying, rapidly dissipated. It was all for the best—the old man had outlived his usefulness. Once more he would use his wildcat child as his partner in crime. She and her ferocious hound could make an awesome team.

chapter 3

Darach Campbell cursed his young half brother and the foul weather that made visibility nearly impossible and the roads nearly impassable. He rode alone, scorning outriders, reasoning that any highwayman with cunning enough to better him would have the sense to stay at home beside the comfort of a roaring hearth. Instead, he himself was riding from London to Edinburgh in a blizzard to extricate once again a spoiled young idiot from yet another tangle. He bent his dark head against the icy particles that whipped his lean cheeks, curbing his impatience as the poor horse slowly and laboriously plodded across Ancrum Moor toward Melrose. He knew the weary animal could go no faster. He contented himself by devising all manner of horrendous tortures to inflict upon his errant sibling, whose extravagance at the gaming tables and sybaritic way of life had already cost a small fortune and caused his expulsion from Oxford. He savagely blamed his equally pleasure-loving stepmother for her negligence and casual overindulgence of her only son, using the boy as a plaything and a tool to get Darach's attention. His flesh crawled at the thought of that conniving woman. She hadn't even waited to be out of mourning for his father before she had slithered into Darach's bed. She had had the reverence to wear black, albeit an extremely lacy wisp of black and he had

had the wisdom, despite his tender years, to hastily escape from her greedy hands, even though he had been achingly tempted by her exposed charms.

At the recollection of exposed female charms, Darach sighed. Although he mistrusted women—his own mother died at his birth, and most other ladies of his circle were unfaithful and unscrupulous—he was forced to acknowledge a basic need for them. He infinitely preferred the comfort of a large bed with a compliant woman between the sheets to the narrow celibate cots of the seedy posting inns that he had endured the past four nights.

"Och, Riach Campbell, you'll pay for this latest escapade," Darach vowed, thinking longingly of the voluptuous redhead he had just set up in a Chelsea town house for the sole purpose of warming his nights while he sojourned in the English capital for the Parliamentary sessions. It wasn't the sole purpose, he amended, for he had made it a point to appear very much attached to a different mistress each season, not only to provide himself with a safe outlet for his healthy male appetite, but, just as important, to stave off his stepmother, Felicity Campbell, and other clutching society females.

In the nine years since his father had died, leaving a twenty-five-year-old widow barely five years Darach's senior and a small son of ten, Darach had tried to be a responsible older brother and avoid the sexual advances of his stepmother, who fortunately preferred the social whirl of London to what she called "the barbarous north," where he spent most of the year. Somehow, he had failed in both areas, Darach concluded, thrusting the irritating memory of Felicity's naked breasts aside and turning his mind to the even more disturbing facts of his half brother's latest tangle.

Riach Campbell had disappeared somewhere during the height of the Christmas festivities. At first, it had been assumed that he was making the usual rounds of parties and was probably tucked away in a drunken stupor with some winsome wench, but his drinking partners had all emerged to groggily face the new year of 1764. Riach was not among them. January drew to a close and there was no trace of the youth. A thorough search of his lodgings brought to light a wad of promissory notes that amounted to more than twenty thousand crowns. They were all owed to one Rory MacNiall, and from the meticulously dated chits, it was apparent that the relationship between the two had gone on for more than a year. Yet no attempt had been made to collect on the enormous debt. Hospitals, jails, and mortuaries also turned up no sign of Riach, and numerous inquiries turned up no knowledge of a Rory MacNiall. For a while, Darach feared his young half brother had cast himself into the river, despondent over his gigantic debt, but his mind had been set to rest on that score by the delivery of a letter the previous week.

Darach dug his heels into his wretched animal's heaving girth as he remembered the insipid pastel paper scented with lavender and covered with a flowery script. It was more suited for a love note from an adolescent virgin than for the ominous invitation demanding the presence of Darach Campbell, Lord Rannoch, at a game of chance. The place, date, and time were explicitly stated, as were the stakes: his family estates of Strathrannoch and Glengrian against his nineteen-year-old brother's life. It was signed with a confident flourish by Rory MacNiall.

Darach Campbell arrived in Edinburgh with less than a day to spare before his meeting with Rory MacNiall. The grueling trip from London had taken seven days instead of the usual three, and he had spent more than seventy precious hours pacing the greasy floors of a vermin-infested tavern in Glendearg, imprisoned by a treacherous March storm. Cold, tired, and in a thunderous temper, he had stormed into his town house, imperiously demanding a bath, a meal, and the immediate presence of at least a dozen people, all of whom lived in various districts of the sprawling city. He was too worried and fatigued to observe any niceties, and his deep voice echoed authoritatively throughout the elegantly appointed house, reducing several downstairs maids to tears and the upstairs maids to fluttering distractedly in all directions like frightened chickens. His housekeeper, Missie MacKissock, clucked with disapproval and was about to remonstrate when she recognized the steely glint in his silver eyes and the granite set of his chiseled face and thought better of it.

"Do as you are told and dinna open your mouths," she warned the trembling upstairs maids, who were too afraid to enter the master suite with fresh linens and towels.

"I canna go in there—he looks like the very de'il hisself, and he's taking his clothes off," chattered a timid girl.

"Och, you silly goose! A mon has to take his clothes off if'n

he's to hae a bath. You've nothing to fear from the laird except his temper. He doesna foul his nest. He'd nae lay a hand
on any lass in his employ, except maybe if she doesna jump
when he says to jump, and then maybe he takes a whip to her
backside," she snapped, losing her patience and shoving the
timorous maid into the room with great force. The maid
nearly fell into the large bath while a chain of servants filled
it with buckets of steaming water.

"Have you sent for all the men I demanded? I want to know
who lives at number fourteen Comyn Square! I want to know
all there is to know about a man named Rory MacNiall, and I
want to know *now*!" roared Darach, wrenching his travel-
soiled shirt over his ebony head and taking a long, punishing
swallow of brandy. "And I want discretion!" he added, stripping off his tight riding britches. He was oblivious to the
high-pitched squeal of the embarrassed maid and deaf to the
resounding smack as she collided with the door before staggering into the corridor.

Missie MacKissock smiled and ran her fond eyes over the
tall young man's virile body. She had first lovingly examined
him twenty-nine years ago, when he'd been tiny and soft from
his mother's womb, and there had been nothing about the
vulnerable pink babe to presage the magnificence of the naked
male who now prowled impatiently back and forth, growling
his orders. He had a broad-shouldered brown body that
tapered to lean, hard buttocks and long, strong legs. There
was nothing soft or pink remaining of the wee boy *bairn* now,
she mused, her eyes alighting with admiration upon the core of
him.

Unaware of his old nurse's perusal, Darach stepped into his
bath with the brandy snifter still in his hand.

"Where's Calum?" he demanded roughly, asking after his
personal manservant, who had attended to his needs for as
long as he could remember.

"My brother is out doing your bidding," Missie replied
curtly, rolling up her sleeves and briskly lathering his back
after noting the tensed, bunched muscles. "Och, I dinna think
to see the day when I'd be bathing you again like I did in the
nursery," she chuckled, expertly massaging his strong neck
and shoulders. Darach groaned and leaned forward, content
for a few moments to allow her competent fingers to knead
away some of the aching fatigue. "Storming in here wie your

dark brow furrowed, putting the fear of the de'il into my puir lassies. Maun be master Riach and tha' scandalous mother of his tha's put you in such a pucker,'' she probed shrewdly.

"Aye," Darach answered noncommittally.

"Och, the lad'll turn up like a bad penny. He always lands on his feet. Och, he's a guid lad. It's that terrible mother! I've said it before, and I'll say it again, and maybe 'tis time you listen to your *auld nurreych*—gie yourself a wife and stop that Lady Felicity once and for all. Dinna get a namby-pamby English female but a *braw* Scottish lass who'll fill the nursery and put tha' stepmother of yours in her place. Then maybe master Riach'll mend his ways. 'Tis disgusting how his ain mother behaves! Like a bitch in heat, rubbing her behind wherever she can." She jabbered on, and Darach let her words wash over him.

Despite his resolve to stay awake and utilize every precious minute of time, Darach fell asleep in his chair, lulled by the hot bath and the brandy. Missie MacKissock, determined that he should not be disturbed until it was absolutely necessary, shooed away the maids and tiptoed in herself to remove the tray of uneaten food. She covered him tenderly with a quilt, and resisting the temptation to smooth back the rebellious lock of hair that fell over his forehead and gave him a rakish air, she quietly left the room.

Darach was awakened several hours later by Calum Mac-Kissock's large hand gently shaking his shoulder. He fought free of the thick layers of sleep and groaned, his stiff muscles complaining from the awkward position in the chair. He stared with confusion into the glowing embers of his bedroom hearth, trying to orient himself, and then with a loud curse he leaped up as he remembered where he was.

"What the hell is the time?" he roared, seeing that the heavy velvet curtains were drawn and yanking them back to glare at the dark sky.

"Early evening. No more 'n seven," replied Calum. "The men you sent for are downstairs in the library."

"What has been learned of Rory NacNiall?" demanded Darach, throwing off his robe and proceeding to dress himself in the fresh clothes that had been laid out across the enormous bed.

"Nae much, and nae very savory," the manservant answered, his ruddy face creased with concern. "The mon first arrived in Edinburgh aboot four years ago and no one kens frae where. He doesna stay aboot along at any one time—a month or two, and then disappears for a month or two. 'Tis said he preys upon old rich women, and there's talk tha' he trades wie Chinese powders, selling the stuff to certain gaming clubs and bawdy houses.''

"Gaming clubs," Darach repeated musingly.

"There's talk of crooked card games."

"And fourteen Comyn Square?" probed Darach, stamping his feet into his gleaming, newly polished boots.

" 'Tis owned by an eccentric widow who hasna set foot outside for several years. She has but two servants, and they are as strange as their mistress. Wouldna talk or open the door."

"And the neighbors?"

"Canna see over the untrimmed privet hedge tha' hides the house. The windows are always shuttered, nae allowing any light in nor sight of any person within. The house is set back from the road and there's nae much comings or goings except on a rare late night, and then nothing much but a plain, black, unmarked carriage," recounted Calum. "Is there still no word of master Riach?" he asked quietly.

"Read this," Darach said roughly, thrusting the scented notepaper at the stocky, sandy-haired man, then shrugging into his well-cut unadorned jacket. Calum read haltingly, stumbling over several words. Then he whistled softly beneath his breath. He sniffed the paper and wrinkled his nose.

"Smells like a female. Could it be one of your stepmother's nasty tricks?"

"Not this time," sighed Darach. "She's not so accomplished an actress," he added savagely, remembering the nearly naked, distraught woman of less than a fortnight ago who had thrown herself into his arms. The soft womanly parts of her had shaken seductively against the hard length of him as she had sobbed out her terror for her son's safety. He had found himself drowning in her silky curves, his loins aching, stimulated by the rhythmic brushings of her hiccoughing cries. "Her motherly concern might not be as profound as some of her other emotions, but . . ." Darach's voice trailed off, and he snorted with disgust, recalling how quickly Felicity's anguished weeping had turned to hungry moans as she had sensuously rubbed against his aroused body. He had firmly thrust her aside.

"Are you sure tha' Lady Felicity hasna got her busy fingers mixed up wie all this?" Calum repeated later, after Darach had spent a frustrating hour talking to more than a dozen men. None of them could shed much light on Rory MacNiall except to substantiate what Calum had already recounted. They added a vague description of a sandy-haired, paunchy man between forty and fifty years of age who was always expensively dressed, albeit in a rather a flamboyant style.

"For what purpose?" Darach snapped impatiently.

"For tha' same purpose she's had in her mind ever since she first set her greedy eyes on you, a nine-year-old virgin lad—and she your ain father's betrothed. Och, she might hae been nae more 'n fourteen years old herself, but she was already a proven woman."

Darach's mind flew back through the years to the nearly forgotten time when he had first met Felicity. It was a memory that he had almost purposefully locked away in the recesses of his mind. He had gone to Strathrannoch Castle for the summer, unaware of his father's engagement to the young English girl. All his life a succession of beautiful, worldly women had warmed his father's bed, and so it hadn't occurred to him that his father would remarry—especially to a female young enough to be Darach's sister. At nine years of age, Darach had been an innocent, too busy with horses, hawks, frogs, and dogs to pay attention to the opposite sex. Felicity had destroyed that innocence. Her exploring hand had made a thrilling descent down his trembling body and between his legs. Her soft, hot mouth had fed greedily on the very essence of him, and he had felt a mixture of ecstasy and terror. The shock of learning that she was to become his new mother chased away the last vestiges of childhood and caused an aching gulf between him and his father. Instead of the relaxed enjoyment they had shared in each other's company, there was a painfully awkward reserve that was to remain between them for the ten years before his father's death.

"For God's sake, Calum! If the stupid female's purpose is to crawl into my bed, she'd hardly send me several hundred miles in the opposite direction!" Darach hissed with irritation, trying to thrust aside the painful memories.

"Och, she wants more 'n your bed, Lord Rannoch! She wants your title! She's nae content being a dowager! She wants to be your wife."

"And for that purpose she would abduct her own son to use in a game of chance wie the Campbell lands at stake? Nay, Calum, she has not the brains. Felicity is not part of this, unless you take into account her negligent mothering, which made Riach such an ideal pawn." He sighed wearily.

"Well, Darach Campbell, whoever it is tha's causing all this doesna bode well, and I dinna care wha' you say—you're nae going alone to fourteen Comyn Square," Calum stated belligerently. "I am going wie you!"

"Aye, Calum MacKissock, you're coming wie me," the tall dark man agreed, much to his servant's surprise.

"Do you think we'll be finding master Riach there?" Darach shook his head.

"I think this Rory MacNiall is too canny for that. He's too sure of himself. Why would the man give me the address within plenty of time to have the runners there?" He set about cleaning and priming a number of small firearms that could be concealed upon their persons. "And it would seem that Rory MacNiall, whoever he is, has been carefully planning tonight's diversion for some time. Why else would he make no attempt to collect on Riach's debt of over twenty thousand crowns?"

"Twenty thousand crowns?" gasped Calum.

"Aye, twenty thousand crowns accumulated over the last eighteen months," Darach answered grimly.

"And in all tha' time the mon dinna dun you for payment like all master Riach's other creditors?" Darach shook his dark head. "Well, wha' do you think of tha'?" queried Calum after a long pause. "Wha' sort of mad man doesna care about claiming twenty thousand crowns?"

"A madman who maybe wants even more," Darach surmised. "A madman who is using my careless young brother to get to me?"

"But, why?" Once again Darach shook his head and splayed his large, well-shaped fingers. "You dinna even ken the mon," chattered Calum, unable to keep still and quiet. Fear curled through his gut, and he was amazed that his young master could appear so relaxed. The only sign of tension was the tightening of the chiseled features. "Well, we'll be making Rory MacNiall's acquaintance tonight at his little card party," Calum stated with mock joviality as he watched Darrach's steady hands expertly prime the lethal little weapons.

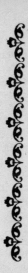

chapter 4

"Comyn Square, my good man," ordered Gregor pompously, opening the door of the rickety hackney he had just hailed and shoving Kat inside. He glared with fury at the huge hound, which growled menacingly, disturbed by the rough treatment of his young mistress. "Get tha' ugly beast to obey me, or I shall shoot it on the spot," he threatened, backing away from the large fangs that gleamed eerily in the yellow lamplight of the Edinburgh back street. Kat whistled hastily, and the dog bounded into the stale interior and cuddled close to her. "I'll ride wie you," Gregor decided, heaving his paunchy flabbiness up to sit beside the coachman. He wanted to clear his head of the cheap spirits he had imbibed in the sordid tavern where they had spent the past hours.

Kat entwined her small cold fingers in Sian's shaggy coat, relieved to be free of her father's terrifying presence for a while. He had been gripped with a maniacal, mounting excitement ever since leaving Linnmanach three days before, and she had been forced to sit by him within the enclosed curricle and listen to him fervently hissing, swearing and laughing. He spat saliva, which stung her face, all the way from Perth to Edinburgh. Her head and eyes hurt from lack of sleep, but her pulses raced, making it impossible to relax and take advantage of her brief respite from his frenetic company. None of the feculent posting inns where her father had chosen to spend the

past three nights had allowed dogs into their questionable
establishments, so Kat had decided to sleep with her pet in
the stables. She preferred the relative cleanliness of the straw,
but each night she had been kept awake by rats, insects, and
drunken men who staggered in to urinate, vomit, or ineptly rut
with equally intoxicated women. She had been sickened by the
sight and sounds of the crudely fumbling couples, and she
determined never to be a party to such disgusting debasement.

Kat's mind churned with the wheels that rumbled through
the slushy roads, bringing them nearer to their destination.
She stared out at the misty darkness, feeling caught in the
midst of a nightmare. Everything had an ominous unreality to
it. Even the clop of the horses' hooves seemed shrouded, ally-
ing with the numb beat of her heart.

It was the Ides of March. Her father had exultantly proclaimed it as the date he would destroy the Campbell—the
same date that Julius Caesar had been murdered by his
friends. Kat wished she could roll back the years and return to
the library hearth, where she read Shakespeare's plays aloud
to her Aunt Ailsa and the ancient band. She stared down at
her severe black clothes, more suited to a pious curate than to
the seventeen-year-old daughter of an outlaw Scot. She
absently brushed the lint and straw from the tight black knee
britches and fitted frock coat. She was thankful for the warm
wool but wished her father had had the foresight to include
new boots. Hers were worn through, and her feet were wet and
freezing.

"Oh, Sian, I wish it were all over. I wish it were tomorrow
and we were on our way home to Linnmanach." She shivered,
fondling the warm velvet ears of her hound, who sensed her
terror and whined his unease. "What if I do something wrong,
and it means the death of everyone?" she worried, trying to
remember her father's oft-repeated instructions. Her hands
nervously checked the *skean dhu* in her boot and the two dirks
hidden at her waist and heart.

The hackney shuddered to a halt, and for several seconds
there was no sound. Kat sat petrified in the darkness, too
afraid to look out to see where they were. Then there was a
hoarse whisper, the clink of coins, shuddering creaks of old
leather, and gasps of exertion as Gregor heaved his weight to
the ground. The door was wrenched open, and a chill breeze
blew in like a premonition of doom. Sian tensed, ready to attack.

"Curb that miserable cur," snarled her father, and she numbly clutched the hound's shaggy coat. She stiffly climbed out of the carriage. The horses moved forward with a weary groan and slowly clopped into the black, still night.

Gregor listened intently, one hand grasping the nape of his daughter's neck in a painful warning vise. Kat was certain that the only audible sounds were her rapidly thumping heart and her father's rasping breath. Confident that nothing stirred, Gregor steered Kat up a narrow, paved pathway that threaded between high, dense hedges. She didn't look to either side but concentrated on putting one frozen foot in front of the other. Gregor stopped behind a sinister-looking shuttered house where once again he listened intently, his eyes probing the dense shadows. Kat stifled a scream when he pushed her into an icy yew, the heavy, spiked branches whipping her face. She gasped when he wound his hand through her thick hair and jerked her head, demanding total silence. The sharp sound of his key cut through the suspended silence, and she felt all his muscles tense. Nothing stirred. The door swung open noiselessly on well-oiled hinges, and she was propelled into a narrow scullery that smelled unpleasantly of boiled cabbage and sour wetness.

"Follow me," hissed Gregor, releasing his painful grip on her hair. She obediently followed him through the deserted kitchen, trying to muffle her tread on the stone floor. Every few steps, her father stopped, straining his ears, alert to the hound's keener sense. Cautiously, he pushed open the tall swinging doors that led to the main entrance hall. He grinned victoriously in the dim light, which caught the bubbles of spittle on his teeth so that he appeared like a demonic apparition to Kat's fearful eyes.

"It won't be long now," he rejoiced with a self-satisfied sigh of relief. Kat watched him confidently turning up the wicks of the lanterns. She was unable to stop her knees from shaking. It felt as though the house was crouching, ready to pounce, its unnatural stillness like a mighty breath before something horrible happened. Kat was grateful to her hound, who leaned his warm, comforting strength against her.

"Take the beast outside and chain him," ordered Gregor, rubbing his chubby hands together in greedy anticipation. Kat gaped at him, astonished by what he was telling her to do. "Chain him at the bottom of the steps so he'll warn us when the Campbell approaches."

"But he'll warn from here. His ears are very keen. He can hear a wee mouse from . . ." she began to protest.

"Do as you're told," snarled Gregor. "Use that door, you idiot!" he added impatiently, when his daughter, with great resignation, started to retrace her steps through the servant's quarters.

Kat opened the narrow front door and stared out at the tranquil night. She wished she could take her dog and run away, but she would be deserting not only her father, but also Macaree and Robbie. She took a deep breath of the sharp cold air and looked about. Patches of snow gleamed, and the wet, dark foliage shone in the misty moonlight. Carefully, she tried to tiptoe down the steps, but her worn boots skidded on the icy wood, and the clatter of her rapid descent rattled loudly through the stillness.

"Sian, I'll not chain you, but you maun stay here and gie warning," she whispered, kneeling on the cold earth and hugging her pet. She could not bear to tie him up, knowing how she would feel so confined.

"Get back in here!" her father growled furiously, and she slipped again on the treacherous steps, causing a clatter. He slapped her viciously across the face, first making sure that he had closed the front door. He did not want her protective hound to defend his young mistress from his assault. "Your carelessness will be the death of us all," he snarled, pushing her into a small study that led off the central hall. "This is where it will take place," he whispered, and Kat nodded, unable to talk as her mouth filled with blood from a cut lip. She glanced about, noting the gaming table and two chairs. "I will sit here," he continued hoarsely, and Kat wondered why he was still whispering when the house seemed deserted. "And there are the mirrors. Stand over there, just as we practiced," he directed. "Now, can you see?" he asked, holding cards in his hand.

"The light's not right. It's making a glare in the mirror," Kat answered huskily. "Now the mirror is too high."

"Then lower it," he snapped. "And dinna drop it or I'll kill you."

Kat's heart was in her throat, and her hands trembled as she held the heavy mirror, certain that it would slip through her fingers. Luckily, her father was of the same mind. He helped her, and she stared at her reflection, seeing his handprint vividly raised on her cheek. Even the imprint from his rings was etched in her flesh.

For the next hour they rehearsed, moving lanterns and adjusting mirrors, until Gregor was satisfied that Kat could see the reflection of the cards in one mirror, and that he could see her reflection giving him silent signals in another. He had devised a subtle movement for every possible combination of cards. Kat concentrated, trying to calm her mounting terror, but a lingering cloying scent that clung to the velvet draperies made her skin crawl. She remembered the glassy-eyed, painted people from the nightmarish parties of her childhood, and Macaree's beautiful masked face screamed in her mind.

Sian's wild barking caused them both to gasp, and an imperious knocking reverberated through the house.

" 'Tis the Campbell," Gregor said breathlessly after a stunned pause. "Let him in," he ordered, drinking a long swallow of spirits and leaning back confidently in his chair. Kat looked imploringly at her father, but he didn't see her. His face was lit with frightening maniacal fervor, and his eyes were fastened beyond her to the entrance of the room, eagerly watching for his guest.

Kat's throat was dry, and her heart pounded painfully when she saw the silhouette of a tall man against the frosted pane of the front door.

"Rory? Rory? Is tha' you?" came a ghostly voice, and Kat, whose trembling hand was already fumbling with the door latch, stared wide-eyed up the dark, twisting stairs. The thunderous knocking was repeated. It reverberated through her outstretched hand, an eerie contrast to the faint, ghostly cry.

"Rory? Rory?" The quavery voice caused shivers to snake up and down Kat's spine.

"Open the door," Gregor ordered, and she pushed down on the stiff latch.

Darach Campbell was not prepared for her small figure. He looked down the steps to the enormous hound, whose menacing growl still rumbled, then back to the slight, dark youth who stood before him with head bowed.

"Welcome, Lord Rannoch. I hae so much looked forward to this night," purred Gregor. Darach gazed over Kat's ebony head to the man who lolled confidently in the brightly lit room across the dark hall. There was something obscene about the sight, he mused, making no effort to move from the front doorway toward his host. From descriptions of Rory Mac-Niall, he recognized his flamboyant, foppish dress and debauched paunchiness. MacNiall's sprawling, thick thighs were encased in yellow satin, which molded unattractively about rolls of flabby flesh. Short, stubby fingers were intertwined across an ornate waistcoat that stretched over a portly belly. Even at a distance of several yards, Darach could see the paint, powder, and patches that decorated the sagging features of the smirking man. A rancid staleness hung about the cold house, and the faint sickly smell of opium drifted down the stairs.

Kat sank into the shadow behind the open front door, awed by the male whose very presence exuded an inexplicable power. She saw her father's foot start to jiggle, the lamplight catching on the bejeweled buckle of his shoe, and knew that the Campbell's silent scrutiny was unnerving him.

"Close the door, Kit, and bring my guest to me," demanded Gregor.

As she moved to obey, she was stopped by the ghostly voice that spiraled from the stairs.

"Rory? Rory? I need you, Rory." The voice wept, and a flicker of irritation crossed Gregor's face. He lost more of his composure.

Darach noticed the youth's fearful reaction; he gazed thoughtfully from the colorfully dressed man to the black-garbed boy. One exuded a gleeful confidence, and the other a bewildered terror.

"I said close the door, Kit," repeated Gregor. She hurriedly pushed against the door, expecting the Campbell to move out of the way. Suddenly, a second man stepped out of the shadows to stand by his side. "If you desire to see your rash half brother alive, I suggest you leave your servant outside with my dog . . . and any damage to my animal will incur the same to your unfortunate sibling," Gregor informed smoothly, regaining his former composure.

Darach Campbell nodded reassuringly at Calum Mac-Kissock, who stepped back outside. Then he closed the front door, making sure that the latch did not click into place.

"Rory? Rory?" the treble voice screeched, and instinctively Kat looked up the stairs. She gasped, seeing strange reflections of flames flickering through the darkness. She stifled a scream as a strong, warm hand roughly grasped her chin, and her face was forced upward. Remembering her father's admonishments to keep her eyes averted, she closed them quickly, but not before Darach Campbell had seen their startling green color. Kat's heart was beating so rapidly she thought it would burst. She kept her eyes squeezed shut, and yet she could feel his searing scrutiny. The brutal fingers that dug into her neck and jaw sent strange sensations to the very core of her being.

Darach Campbell could feel the youth's frantic pulse, and he almost smelled the child's fear. He frowned at the nightmarish familiarity of the delicate features and noted the crescent scar on the high cheekbone. The trembling mouth was cut and swollen; a hand other than his own had left a harsh mark on the smooth, hairless cheek.

"Unhand my servant or your brother shall die," snarled Gregor, but the Campbell kept the same painful grasp on Kat's small face. He willed the green eyes to open, but she kept them tightly shut, even though her feet were off the ground and her head twisted at an agonizing angle.

"Rory? Rory? I need you! I need you!" screamed the treble voice, losing its wraithlike quality and sharpening to strident tones. Kat's eyes flew open. With a shock, they met hard silver eyes that seemed to pierce straight through her, leaving her defenseless. There was a still, shocked moment as silver and emerald met, and then she saw the reflection of flames mirrored in his eyes and smelled an acrid burning.

"Papa?" she cried, and Darach wrenched his gaze away and looked to the flamboyantly dressed man. Gregor abandoned his indolent pose and lumbered to his feet.

"Papa?" Darach repeated wonderingly, shifting his grip and catching the back of Kat's slim neck. "Well, now, Mr. MacNiall, it would seem I have something precious of yours to exchange for my brother. A son, no less," he said softly, moving slowly toward Gregor MacGregor.

"I'm sorry, Father." Kat sobbed as she fumbled for the dirk at her waist. But the icy muzzle of a gun was pressed into her pounding temple, and her limp hands fell to her sides in defeat, the dagger clattering onto the wooden floor.

"I'm sorry, Father. I'm sorry, Father," imitated Gregor with impotent rage. His many rings caught on the embroidery of his coat and frustrated his attempt to find his own firearm.

"I suggest you also rid yourself of your weapon, Mac-Niall," Darach said almost casually. "Unless your own child is dispensable?"

To Kat's increased horror, her father was transformed

before her. The madness that had flickered behind his eyes suddenly flared up and consumed him, distorting his face and body until he was unrecognizable.

"Aye, the filthy unnatural spawn is dispensable!" he screeched. "Turning my own sweet wife against me! Causing the despoilment of your own sister! And now the destruction of us all." Despite the gun held to his daughter's head, he flew at her, viciously pulling her hair and punching her face.

Darach was appalled by the man's brutal insanity. He swung the child away from Gregor's flailing fists as the door burst open, and Calum rushed in with the enormous hound.

"The house is afire!" shouted Calum. For Kat, stunned by one of her father's blows, everything became a vortex of confusion. Sian leaped to protect her, the Campbell's gun exploded with a sharp report, and a spine-chilling cackle swept down the stairs with a great rush of bright heat. Darach loosened his grip, and Kat collapsed to the floor. She crouched there, trying to collect her addled wits, not knowing whether this scene was a figment of her overwrought mind.

Down the stairs floated a woman enveloped in flames. Even her hair appeared like a halo of fire. Her gown flared and her face was bright with hideous triumph. Then she screamed with pure animal pain and flew toward Gregor, who had staggered back to his chair. He lolled there, staring with stupefaction at the hole that marred his expensive waistcoat and the bloodstain that seeped onto its bright colors. Calum wrenched one of the thick velvet drapes from the window and flung it over the screaming woman, but she fought him. It took all his energy to wrestle her to the ground.

"Is my brother upstairs in that inferno!" demanded Darach, gripping Gregor's shoulders and shaking him. "Is Riach upstairs?" he roared, trying to make himself heard over the hysterical screams and the hungry crackle of the fire. Gregor suddenly realized that he was dying. He experienced neither pain nor fear, but felt utterly relaxed. He was in control for the first time in his life. Sneering at the desperate young Campbell, he felt elated that the positions were reversed, that he now held the winning hand. "Is my brother upstairs?" shouted Darach, lifting him from the chair and shaking him ruthlessly. Gregor smiled and a thunderous crash reverberated.

"We'd best get out of here, your lordship, afore this ceiling caves in," Calum urged.

"Get the woman and child out," answered Darach, not taking his eyes from the victorious expression on the dying man's face.

"I've won, you stinking Campbell! There's nothing you can threaten me wie. Do you see me, Father? Och, I'm a *braw, bardach* mon. I'm looking at death straight in the eye and I'm not afraid," rejoiced Gregor. Her father's exultant words penetrated Kat's stunned mind. She scrambled to her feet, and through smoke-stung eyes she saw the blood that oozed through his embroidered waistcoat.

"You shot him?" she cried, pushing against the Campbell's immovable arm. Darach's hand still grasped her father's slumped shoulders.

"Is my brother upstairs?" demanded Darach, ignoring the small fists that pummeled his back. He furiously shook the jubilant man.

"Let him be! Your precious brother isna upstairs!" she screamed, and Gregor's triumphant mirth turned to vitriolic hatred for the slight youth. Darach's hands fell away with disgust, allowing Kat access. "Och, Papa, you canna die and leave us all alone." She sobbed not knowing why she wept—except that to be an orphan seemed a terrifying thing. All the wretched years fell away, and once again, he was the handsome, strong father who had placed her before him on his stallion. Riding like the wind, he had been her knight protecting her from all evil.

" 'Twas not the Campbell who delivered my death blow, but you, my own seed!" he snarled. His face was distorted with rage, and she backed away from him. "Dinna tell the Campbell more, or it'll mean the deaths of . . ." A horrible rattle drowned the rest of Gregor's words. His eyes bulged, and he sagged limply in the chair.

"Papa? Father?" Kat whimpered, reaching tentatively out to him. When she did not receive the usual cuff, she entwined her hands in his lapels. "I'm sorry, Papa," she continued. She waited for him to forgive her, but he said nothing. Fearfully, she looked at his face and shuddered. All the rage and hatred he had felt in his life was imprinted there, seemingly directed at her.

"Let's get out of here," muttered Darach beneath his breath. He pried the small hands from the rich brocade of the dead man's coat, while Kat fought him with every ounce of strength in her exhausted body. Her enormous wolfhound whined with fear as he padded back and forth from the open front door to his young mistress. He pulled at her clothes. "All right, you great beast, we'll get your young master out of here," soothed the Campbell, swinging her into his arms and striding out of the inferno into the cold night.

Kat stopped resisting and stared with shock at the house. It collapsed with a low rumbling roar, entombing her father. Unconsciously, she wound her hand in the Campbell's dark cape and felt the steady beating of his heart beneath her ear. She lay motionless in his arms, cradled like a small *bairn*, watching the hungry flames stabbing the darkness and expecting to see some sign of her father being consumed by them. She waited breathlessly for his accusing face to appear in the flaming tongues that licked the velvet blackness.

"The woman's dead," murmured Calum, getting stiffly to his feet and staring down at the rolled bundle. "How's the lad?" he added, absentmindedly patting Sian's shaggy head.

"Unharmed, save for a few bruises," Darach answered shortly.

"Well, we'd best hand him over to the authorities and get some answers as to master Riach's whereabouts." Calum sighed.

"I'm leaving you to deal wie the authorities. Answer as little as possible, and for now dinna mention this boy. Refer them to me, preferably late tomorrow." The Campbell strode down the path toward the tethered horses, followed by the large dog.

Kat debated with herself whether to resume her fight. She quickly decided that being the prisoner of one man, even if he was a Campbell, was preferable to being imprisoned by the "authorities." She remained docile, her agile mind planning her escape. Part of her brain felt detached, not fully comprehending the swift chain of events. She gazed up at the strong jaw and the resolute features of the man who carried her, feeling an eerie remembrance of another time and another death.

Darach tossed the slight youth up into the saddle of his patient horse. He did not notice the nimble movement of the small hand disappearing into the scuffed riding boot. He untied the reins and swung himself up behind the boy, swearing aloud as a sharp *skean dhu* flashed in the moonlight and slashed his forearm. The horse whinnied and reared, frightened by the struggle atop his back, as Kat fought to keep her weapon. But the Campbell's steely grip on her wrist soon forced the lethal little dagger to drop from her grasp.

"Have you any other wee toys about you?" sighed Darach, ignoring the blood that dripped thickly down his arm from the deep gash. It splattered onto the youth, whom he pinned roughly across his hard thighs. He glared down at the rebellious face as he searched thoroughly for other hidden weapons.

Kat tried to steady her ragged breathing as she looked up at the dark forbidding features of the Campbell. He ran his large hands down her legs and across her flat belly, his long probing fingers moving upward toward the dirk over her heart. She knew she was no match for his strength, so she hid her rising panic with a mocking expression, carefully watching his face. She noted the satanic way his thick black eyebrows scowled as his large hand encountered her breast. He seemed to recoil, as though burned, but then he touched her again, cupping her rounded firmness as if he didn't believe his discovery.

"You're female!" he cried, as though her gender was the lowest form of vermin. But his hand remained on her quivering flesh. Terror—and another unnamed emotion she had never experienced before—stabbed through her at his intimate touch. Kat frantically tried to twist out of his arms, but he tightened his hold to a bone-crushing grasp, kicking his mount into a brisk gallop down the icy road. Kat felt the punishing jolts shock her aching body, and her breathing was restricted by the iron arm that flattened her tender young breasts, as if he somehow were trying to eradicate their very existence.

A strange lamenting howl joined with the sound of racing hooves, penetrating Darach's furious thoughts. He glanced back down the frosty moonlit road to the exhausted hound who had tried desperately to keep pace. He reluctantly tempered his speed, allowing the loyal beast to catch up. Kat stilled her frantic struggles and stared up with surprise, but there was no softening of the tyrannical features. Darach glared down, hardening his resolve, refusing to be swayed by the battered little face. He steeled himself against the pathetic sight of sooty cheeks where tears for a dead father were imprinted.

"Dinna be misled by my compassion for that puir misguided animal," he stated curtly. He laughed mirthlessly, seeing how quickly her piteous demeanor changed to defiance.

chapter 5

Kat fought to stay awake, to clear her confused mind, but the
steady rhythm of the horse's hooves and the warmth of the
Campbell's body lulled her. Darach's punishing hold upon her
body had eased. Feeling a shiver convulse her slight frame, he
had wrapped his voluminous cape about her. He did not act
from compassion. He simply wanted to ensure her survival
long enough to locate his brother. He knew of her grim battle
to stay awake, and he was in awe of her stubbornness. He
would feel her slowly relax, sagging and settling against him.
Then she would tense, jolting herself to awareness, her sharp
elbows digging into his ribs. Several times, in the few seconds
she had slipped into sleep, he had looked down at the gleaming
ebony head that was nestled against his chest and felt a strange
yearning. She had appeared so tiny and defenseless, seeming
to belong within his protective arms. Her body was soft, and it
cuddled compliantly, fitting perfectly against his hard torso.
Her lithe legs dangled intimately between his muscular thighs.
But then she would jerk herself awake and there would be
nothing defenseless about her. He would gaze down into a
snarling, feral face.

"If Kit is your name, you are aptly labeled." He laughed
harshly. "Kit—a spitting wildcat, a young vixen."

Kat welcomed his derisive tone; it kept her awake and on

guard. It banished the traitorous yearnings that had crept
through her desperately tired body at the feel of the Campbell's warm strength. He was the enemy. He had killed her
father. She was his prisoner, she reminded herself, angrily trying to push his cape away. She did not want to accept any
comfort or protection, but he swaddled her more tightly, pinning her arms to her sides and once more increasing the
pressure of his grip.

"Be still or I'll tie you and make you run beside wie your
hound." He was furious with his own fanciful thoughts and
too weary to deal with any more of her wild struggles. At the
mention of Sian, Kat listened intently, trying to hear him, but
all that existed was her labored breathing and the clop of the
horse's hooves. Darach watched her eyes widen with panic and
her small nostrils flare, not understanding the sudden distress.
A piercing whistle from her cut, swollen lips soon enlightened
him. "Your unfortunate beast is padding along aside us. He's
near dead on his feet. I wonder how you warrant such devo-
tion." He tried to see through the defiant expression, haunted
by the familiarity of the unusual green flashing eyes.

Kat's addled mind seethed with nightmarish thoughts of
Macaree and Rob at Linnmanach, with no one to protect them
but the frail, senile Aunt Ailsa and Aggie. They both seemed
to be crumbling with the stones and mortar of the old manse.
What did the Campbell mean to do with her? Her father's last
words had been a warning for her not to tell the Campbell
anything. Otherwise, it would mean more deaths. But she
couldn't leave the man's brother at Linnmanach. Somehow
she had to escape and free Riach Campbell, but then he would
know where he had been and would bring the authorities upon
them. What would happen to the remains of her family? At
the thought of the authorities, she glanced up at the stern
features that were silhouetted against the night sky. There was
no mercy in the chiseled lines of the Campbell's face, and she
realized she had only one recourse. She somehow had to
escape, but with enough money to buy weapons, horses, and
provisions. She wanted to take her family back to France, or
to a safer part of Scotland where they would never be found.
Her Aunt Ailsa's mad ramblings galloped into her mind, and
stark terror pounded through her. What if the Campbell
found out who they were? It would mean death or deportment
to the Colonies as slaves. The old lady had warned that the

Campbell mustn't ever see her, or he'd know who she was.

Darach reined his horse in the courtyard of his town house, and Kat's frantic thoughts were interrupted when he dismounted. He carried her with him as though she were no more than a piece of excess baggage.

"Take care of the hound, too," he ordered a sleepy ostler, who nodded and led the tired mount into the warmth of the stables.

"No!" shouted Kat, resuming her struggles, but Darach tightened his hold and strode into the house, slamming the door behind him. "Let me go!" she yelled. When his large hand covered her mouth, muffling her screams so that the whole household would not be disturbed, she bit down savagely and he swore, grinding his hard palm against her sore lips, reopening the cut caused by her father's rings.

Kat was more terrified than she had ever been before. Awful realizations tore through her—both her mother and father were now dead; Macaree and Robbie were defenseless and alone; she had promised to protect them; the dreaded Campbell had her in his clutches; she was separated from her only comfort, Sian. She fought for her life, no longer rational enough to comprehend the futility of pitting her exhausted strength against the strong man.

Missie MacKissock awoke with a start and lay with her heart thumping, listening to the sounds that shook the rafters. She was convinced that the full moon had raised the *Nuckelavee* who now bayed outside, rattling the windowpanes, exciting the bogles and ghosties to do mischief in the house.

"The milk'll be curdled, and no mistake," she muttered. " 'Tis one of those nasty nights. First Calum and the master gallivanting off, and then that shameless, English hussy pushing her way in, giving orders as if she owned the place, when she has her own dower house to sleep in. And now all this noise and howling enough to wake the dead." She pulled her nightcap about her ears to hide the rags that curled up her hair and struggled into her robe. Lamp in hand, she furtively crept through the house, followed by several half-dressed servants armed with a motley assortment of mops, warming pans, and chamberpots. They all skidded to a halt on the highly polished floor and then silently backed away. Their infuriated master strode up the stairs with a wildly fighting, raven-haired figure in his arms. They gasped, seeing the snarling face streaked with blood and soot. They shivered, hearing the eerie keening that spiraled through the stillness outside.

"Is there anything . . . er . . . your lordship . . . er . . . needs?" the housekeeper ventured after a stunned pause. She trotted behind at a safe distance, her sleepy eyes pinned on the kicking legs that were encased in tight black britches and worn riding boots.

"Aye, your keys and a length of stout rope. I mean to lock this small savage in one of the attic rooms," he snapped harshly. Kat's weakening struggles were renewed with fresh vigor, but Darach stopped in his tracks and suspiciously sniffed the air. "The devil take it!" he swore. "What the hell is my stepmother doing here?" He recognized the nauseating scent of hothouse orchids.

"If you dinna ken tha' by now, there's a lot wrong wie your gray matter," Missie MacKissock murmured under her breath.

"When did she arrive?" he snapped, ignoring her impertinence.

"At some ungodly hour when all decent women are safely in their own beds," retorted the housekeeper. "And if I hadna barred the doors, she'd be rolling in yours this very minute."

"Darach? Is that you?" Felicity's voice trilled.

"She's in the blue suite," whispered Missie. "I'll get my keys," she added, seeing fury contort Darach's features and watching the large hand clamp over the struggling child's mouth. Kat's green eyes flashed eloquently with impotent rage.

"Forget the rope and keys and bring a bath and female night attire," he ordered, after a long thoughtful look at the rebellious little face.

"Female attire?" squeaked Missie.

"As you can see, my wife has obviously met with an unfortunate accident," he stated softly, kicking open the door to his master suite of rooms.

"Your wife?!!" the housekeeper squealed, convinced she was in the throes of a vivid dream.

"I dinna need an echo, Miss MacKissock. I need a bath and nightgown for my wife," he repeated impatiently, turning Kat onto his wide bed and pinning her down with his tired body.

Kat lay back on the comfortable mattress, panting for

breath, gathering her energy to renew her desperate battle for freedom. She gazed up at the ceiling, tracing the elegant curves of the classic molding and avoiding the handsome, brooding man above her. She was oblivious to the apple-cheeked woman who stared curiously at her, and the happy grin of approval that finally beamed, nearly splitting the good-natured face in two.

"You'll be needing this, your lordship," chuckled Missie MacKissock ten minutes later, bustling in behind the footmen with their pails of steaming water. Darach frowned at the gold ring that his old nurse offered. "Slip it on the lassie's finger," she prompted, nodding her capped head toward Kat, who was curled asleep in the middle of the large bed. "Och, the puir wee-an. She looks no more 'n a mucky wee *bairn*," she crooned.

"Looks can be very deceptive," retorted Darach, removing his coat and rolling up his shirtsleeve to show the ugly gash across his forearm. "That mucky wee *bairn* can wield a ruthless knife, and her teeth are used quite competently." He examined the teeth marks on his hand.

"Guid, any wife of yours'll need knowledge of all weapons to deal wie that stepmother of yours," approved the shrewd woman. "Och, and you'd best be getting a move on, for Lady Felicity kens you're home and is most likely sharpening her conniving claws this minute—waiting for the servants to go to their rooms so she can steal along the corridor and slide between your sheets. You'd best hurry and get your wife into your bed and put the hussy's nose out of joint. Good night, your lordship. Happy I am that you've taken my advice and got yourself a rare, spirited lass at last."

"Just a minute, Missie. Where are you off to?"

"My bed, of course. I need my sleep. Now, wash your puir wee bride carefully. She looks a mite battered and bruised, and I dinna want my bed linens soiled wie all tha' soot and gore," she quipped mischievously before trotting out of the room. Darach scowled at the closed door for a few moments and then purposefully turned the key in the lock and removed it.

Kat flailed, protesting the strong hands that disturbed her sound sleep. Her eyelids were too heavy to open, so she blindly pushed and kicked, tucking her body into a ball and wrapping her arms about her knees. She gasped as she was picked up.

Her green eyes flew open, and she squinted groggily at the strong neck and jutting jaw of the Campbell. Her fatigued mind, too long deprived of sleep and thoroughly traumatized by the events of the past night, couldn't cope. She closed her eyes and snuggled against the hard warmth of the broad chest, lulled by Darach's safe masculine scent and the steady beat of his heart.

Darach was astounded by her sudden passiveness. He sat down in his favorite chair. He faced the hearth, staring bemusedly at the bath that steamed before them, waiting for a resumption of her wild fight for freedom. He leaned back and closed his eyes, his arms unconsciously tightening about the cradled girl as the hectic chain of the night's events churned through his head. He had no time for sentiment, he decided harshly, remembering his missing brother. He roughly shook the slender shoulders, but Kat grumbled sleepily and snuggled closer like a disgruntled puppy. Firmly, Darach lifted her from his lap and stood her up between his legs, but her knees kept buckling.

"Wake up, you mucky nuisance. Stand up," he ordered roughly, and she sleepily obeyed. "Get undressed and into that bath," he continued, but she made no move to comply. Instead, she swayed from side to side, bumping against his parted thighs. He propped her between his knees and peered into her small face. Recognizing the extent of her exhaustion, he snorted with exasperation and started to unbutton her jacket and shirt.

There was something infinitely touching about her childlike docility in comparison with the spitting wildcat of a scant fifteen minutes before. Her manner broke through his hard cynicism, and he found himself marveling at each inch of skin he uncovered. Undressing females was by no means a new experience for Darach Campbell, but disrobing the raven-haired, green-eyed rebel who now stood so quietly was more disturbing then he could possibly fathom. The haunting pain that shimmered across her delicate features caused his brain to play tricks on him, and it seemed he had searched the little face before and seen those silent screams. Where?

Despite her thinness and the scratches and bruises that marked her body, she was perfect. He had never seen such gracefully formed limbs. From the top of her aristocratically held head to the tips of her arched, blistered feet, she was exquisite. She stood naked between his outstretched legs; he leaned back, appreciating the sight of her much as he would a priceless work of art. He was outraged by the abuse that careless handling had caused, wanting to erase the swelling and discoloration from the creamy skin of her finely etched face. Very gently, he traced the sensuous, impudent curve of her lips, remembering the fat, ringed hand that had repeatedly struck her. She didn't react but kept her haunted green eyes fixed to a spot beyond Darach's shoulder. Her proud, high breasts trembled with her heartbeat, and he saw the bruises made by his own brutality. He was ashamed and reached forward, taking her small hands in his. He frowned, feeling the harsh, abrasive calluses. He was appalled to see evidence of hard manual labor marring the palms. Suddenly, he realized that he preferred these strong, little hands to the limp-wristed, well-manicured ones of Felicity and her ilk.

At the thought of his stepmother, Darach shuddered and scooped Kat into his arms. He lowered her into the bath, where, despite her exhausted detachment, she gasped as the hot water stung her blistered feet.

"Och, you certainly are a battle-scarred wee warrior," he said with unaccustomed tenderness. He flung her offending boots—boots that had caused her feet such pain—across the room, determined that they would burn on the gardener's bonfire the following morning. He added the rest of her appalling attire to the untidy pile and knelt beside the bath.

He washed her objectively, almost dispassionately, soaping every inch of her lingeringly and yet feeling no desire. He marveled at her perfection much as he would a superb piece of horseflesh. His tired mind grappled with his jumble of uncharacteristic emotions. Deep in thought, he absently lifted her from the water and swaddled her in a towel, using another one to dry her dripping hair. He had declared her to be his wife in front of witnesses, albeit his own servants, and she had not denied the claim. This made it a fact according to Scottish law. She was really his wife, and he felt a surge of fulfillment at the realization. He briskly rubbed her tousled mop of hair, ignoring the wetness that seeped through his clothing as she sat passively in his lap. She was his wife, he repeated to himself, waiting for the feeling of proud gratification to change to stark horror, but instead he found himself grinning with delight.

"You, my green-eyed mud lark, are my wife." He laughed, cupping her chin and gazing at her poignant sleepy face, knowing she was infinitely preferable to the simpering, painted females who paraded before him as prospective brides. "You, my battered rebel, are now Lady Rannoch!" he proclaimed.

Kat had no notion of Darach's thoughts and was deaf to his elated words. She was suspended in limbo, feeling nothing except nurturing hands that returned her to dependent infancy before she was burdened with the care of her siblings. She docilely submitted to being stripped, bathed, toweled, and dressed in a large flannel nightgown more suited to Missie MacKissock's middle-aged girth than to her own elfin beauty. Darach wrenched off the offending article and added it to the pile of discarded clothes, as he planned a more appropriate wardrobe for his new bride.

Kat sighed with contentment when he finally tucked her between the fragrant sheets of the large bed. Her long sigh was like music, floating through the silence and twisting about his heart, softening his expression.

Darach swiftly stripped off his own clothes and lowered his rangy body into the rapidly cooling water, taking pleasure in the idle thought of the intermingling of the night's blood and tears. A furtive rapping cut sharply into his sleepy, muddled musings, and his stepmother's voice caused his flesh to prickle. His relaxed features once more hardened into forbidding lines. Ignoring her, he hurriedly soaped and rinsed.

"I know you're there, Darach, darling. I can hear you. It's me, Felicity, and I'm lonely and afraid. Please let me in," she begged. "I'm positively distraught with worry about my son, and I dare not sleep because of horrid dreams in which I see him lying dead with his throat cut in some foul robber's den." She began to sob.

Darach stepped out of the bath and toweled himself roughly, trying to drown out the whining tones.

"And there's a wolf howling in the courtyard outside my window," she continued, and the door handle was carefully tried.

Darach heard her whimper of frustration upon finding the door locked, and he looked thoughtfully toward the connecting dressing room, debating whether to secure that door against Felicity's intrusion. Soon enough, his stepmother would meet the new Lady Rannoch and have one of her famous tantrums. But not now. He was too tired, he decided, turning the key in the lock and hiding it above the mantel. He looked pensively at the dark girl, who lay sleeping soundly in his bed, her lithe arms cuddling a pillow, much like a small child with a stuffed animal. She looked deceptively angelic, he noted with a rueful grin, recalling her savage battle less than a hour before.

Darach opened the closed curtains, allowing the moonlight to ripple across the room. The hound had ceased his mournful baying and was probably curled up in the stables. He turned down the lamp wicks.

"Persistent bitch," he muttered, hearing Felicity rattle the handle of the dressing room door as she tried to gain admittance. He climbed into his bed and lay on his back, staring at the ceiling where the warm reflections of the hearth mingled with the cold shimmer of the moon. He silently willed his stepmother to abandon her quest as his weary mind ached with a host of unanswered questions.

Darach rolled onto his side and gazed at Kat's face, awed by its poignant perfection despite the cuts and bruises. He was looking at his wife, and he had no clue as to her real identity. He rejected the surname NacNiall, reasoning that a man intent on extortion would hardly use his own name. Tomorrow, he thought, after a healing sleep, all his questions would be answered. Kit would tell him everything. It was obvious that her father had been a cruel, brutal man, guilty of many crimes, including the abduction of Riach. And the unfortunate daughter had been forced to cooperate. But now, with the death of the so-called Rory MacNiall, the girl would lead him to his brother with no fear of reprisal. He traced the small crescent-shaped scar on one of her high cheekbones and scowled, recalling the ragged little waif of the Paris streets five years before. The sorrow-filled face flashed sharply into his brain, and clearly he saw blood mingling with tears that streamed from the unusual emerald eyes.

"I've a lot to learn about you, my wee savage," he murmured huskily, pulling her unresisting body into his arms, where she curled naturally and contentedly against his nakedness. "I dinna even know your name." He sighed, burying his face in her freshly washed hair and wrapping a muscular leg possessively about her warm softness.

chapter 6

Darach felt he had only just closed his eyes when a frantic scratching and a persistent howling assaulted his senses.

"Go away, Felicity!" he roared, wrapping his arms more tightly around the soft silkiness curled about his body. He tried to resume his sensual dreaming, but bright sunlight pried at his eyelids and a loud, mournful howling pierced his ears.

" 'Tis me, your lordship," his housekeeper called, a tinge of hysteria ruffling her usually calm voice. "And 'tis ever so important, or I'd not be disturbing you 'fore noon."

"Come in, Missie." He yawned, staring blearily down at the dark head that nestled possessively on his bare chest. The latch was urgently agitated, and the frenzied howling and scratching continued with fervor. "What the hell is going on?" he muttered sleepily, struggling to comprehend the small hand that rested on his cheek. A plain gold band on one of the fingers winked sharply in the clear morning light. "Use your key!" he bellowed, as realization cracked through his befuddled senses. He was surprised when the sleeping girl didn't stir. He frowned and was about to check her breathing when the door suddenly burst open. Missie MacKissock was propelled in by the enormous hound who surged forward before she could remove her key from the lock. Her arm was nearly wrenched from its socket.

"Och, I'm so sorry about this, your lordship, but this great *baistie* got into the house and has been leading everyone on a fine chase. And there was none who'd brave the fiercesome teeth." She panted. "Och, would you look at tha'?" she remarked reverently, gaping at the dog, who had bounded onto the bed and was gently nuzzling the dark girl. "Shoo, you *meikle* brute! Off the furniture wie you!" she remonstrated, remembering her position in the house. To her astonishment, the huge beast obeyed. He gave his young mistress one slobbering lick, his saliva dripping onto Darach's arm. Then he jumped off. "Och, would you look at tha'?" the frazzled woman repeated, watching the animal circle and then lie down on the rug beside the bed. He thumped his heavy tail and, resting his massive head on his front paws, regarded them dolefully. "Would you look at tha'?" she marveled again, trying to smother her fond grin. She tactfully pretended not to notice the naked female cradled against her master's strong bared length.

"What is so important?" growled Darach, rolling Kat's inert body off his chest and stifling a stark feeling of regret. Kat muttered fitfully and tried to curl back to his warmth, but he steeled himself and modestly covered her lithe nakedness, tucking the covers to her chin.

"The authorities are downstairs wie Calum," Missie whispered. "They arrived together about fifteen minutes ago, and Calum said to fetch you and tell you tha' he's said nothing about the . . . lad."

Darach swung his long legs from the bed and shrugged into the robe Missie MacKissock held out for him. Her anxious eyes were pinned to the peacefully sleeping girl.

"Calum said something about a fire," she added, her good-natured face creased with worry. She remembered the smoky smell of their soiled clothes and the blood and soot that had streaked the screaming little face. "Calum also said something about bodies, dead bodies in the fire," she continued, following him across the room and wringing her hands in her apron.

"Unlock the dressing room," Darach ordered tersely after feeling about on the mantel. He was unable to locate the key he had hidden the night before.

"The dead bodies? In the fire?" she asked fearfully, unlocking the door and tottering on the threshold. "None was master Riach?"

"No, Missie, none was Riach," replied Darach, rummaging through drawers and wrenching clothes from his armoire. Miss MacKissock was too upset to help him dress. She wound the long chain that dangled from her waist around her worrying hands. There was the sound of keys jingling. "I want all these doors to stay locked, do you ken? I dinna want . . . the girl disturbed, and I dinna want her escaping, do you ken?" he asked harshly, not seeing the woman's nods because he was too intent on his hurried efforts to dress. "She is to remain in here!" he emphasized.

"Aye, I ken. But wha' about the great *baistie?*"

"Let him stay. 'Twill keep her company and keep Felicity at bay. And take those wretched clothes and see that they are burned—discreetly," he added, nodding his dark head toward the untidy pile.

"Tha's my guid nightie," Missie spluttered indignantly, retrieving the article. "And wha's the wee mistress to do wie no clothes?" she added angrily.

"She'll need no clothes in here, for there'll be no one to see," he retorted, ignoring her reference to the mistress.

"And wha' about feeding your puir wee wife? She's nothing but skin and bones now!" the housekeeper challenged. "And wha' about those wet towels and the dirty water? 'Tis nae proper for Lady Rannoch to awaken to such an unsightly mess! I'll send some footmen in . . ."

"You'll do no such thing! I said I dinna want her disturbed. You'll leave everything save those rags, which I want burned immediately, do you ken?"

"Aye, I ken," Missie answered sulkily. "You mean to leave the puir *bairn* naked as the day she was born . . . so she canna escape."

"Aye!"

"You mean to starve her, too?"

"If I have to," was the blunt answer.

"She's truly your wife, you ken. By declaration in front of witnesses and all tha's binding, you ken," she insisted.

"Aye, I ken. Which means she belongs to me to do wie as I so chose, do you ken?" he stated. Missie MacKissock nodded unhappily. "Now, pick up those rags, lock all the doors, and follow me."

Kat slept soundly, her depleted body shielding her from

Felicity's raging tantrum when she heard about the new Lady Rannoch. The sturdy town house shuddered with the crashes of screens, chairs, and shoes, and the windows rattled with her strident screams. Missie MacKissock, although worried about the petite new mistress, derived enormous satisfaction from the Englishwoman's uncontrolled outburst.

"I demand to see her!" screeched Felicity.

"She went riding wie his lordship," Missie lied glibly, knowing the woman could not have observed Darach's departure. He had gone with the authorities to examine 14 Comyn Square by daylight.

"He's married? My Darach is married?" ranted the overwrought woman.

"Aye, your *step-son* is married," repeated the housekeeper. "And the whole staff is very happy for the master."

"Who is she?" demanded Felicity. "Not that red-haired harlot from the London stage?"

"She's Lady Rannoch, and her hair is as black as jet."

"But what's her maiden name?"

"Doesna matter now tha' she's not a maiden. It did my *auld* heart guid to see her nestled in the master's strong arms this morning, the flush of loving on both their bonny faces." Missie sighed, turning the knife wickedly and watching the ugly blush of fury mottle Felicity's pale skin. "Now, if you hae finished, shall I send some footmen in to clean up this mess?" she asked innocently, turning her mischievous eyes to the shocking disarray of broken vases, pictures, ornaments, chairs, and perfume bottles.

A low snarl of impotent rage gurgled in Felicity's throat. It built to an enraged howl, and Missie MacKissock barely managed to trot out of the blue suite before the tantrum resumed with renewed fervor.

Darach returned in the late afternoon. He frowned at the glass that littered the cobbled courtyard and scowled up at the broken windows of his house.

"What the hell has been happening?" he roared. "And why hasna this been swept up?" he added with irritation when his horse's hooves cracked painfully through the sharp shards. "Why are you all standing about with your mouths gaping open?" he demanded of his servants, who cowered with brooms in the doorways. He managed to maneuver his frightened mount to one side, avoiding a lethal shower as another pane shattered, pointedly answering his question.

"It is the Lady Felicity," a stableboy informed Darach. "She's bin at it ever since Missie MacKissock told her of our new mistress. Och, congratulations on your marriage, your lordship. I hope you and your new bride will be very happy."

Darach curtly strode away from the enthused ostler without bothering to acknowledge his good wishes. His head pounded. He had spent more hours talking to the incompetent authorities than he had resting the previous two nights. It had been a wasted day. The plodding officials had not listened to each other but had constantly reiterated what they surmised had occurred. They concluded that the widow Baxter had inadvertently set fire to her own house, causing the deaths of her two servants, who were asleep on the top floor. It was also generally supposed that the widow Baxter had been under the influence of opium supplied by the man known as Rory MacNiall. Darach had wearily and repeatedly admitted to the accidental shooting of the man, and more than a dozen times had explained his presence at 14 Comyn Square. He had offered the pastel, scented invitation with its explicit terms of extortion as evidence to support his claim. It was not news to the Edinburgh magistrates that his brother, Riach Campbell, had been missing for more than four months, nor were they ignorant of MacNiall's unsavory reputation and questionable activities. Yet they continued to waffle and cluck.

"Why would I deliberately kill the only person who could lead me to my brother?" he had finally exploded. In the dim recesses of his aching brain, he wondered why he was bothering to protect the green-eyed chit. To aggravate his disgust, the droning officials closed the books on the case, exhibiting no interest in the true identity of Rory MacNiall.

Darach stormed into his house, determined to wrest the answers from the small guest who was locked up naked with her enormous pet in his suite of rooms. He was equally determined to ignore his tiresome stepmother, but he was met with a veritable fusillade of shoes, pictures, books, and pillows—anything Felicity could throw. She had exhausted most of the ornaments on the mantels and sideboards. Darach stopped abruptly and stared about at the destruction of his orderly, elegant house. His already furious expression darkened, and an ominous calm hardened his craggy features.

Felicity squealed with alarm and backed away from the

piercing silver eyes that cut through her hysteria. She was
sharply sobered. What had she done? She had gone too far.
She frantically avoided his steady gaze and looked about,
shocked by the incredible devastation she had wrought. Had
her frail, pink little hands caused such impressive plundering?
She looked at them with amazed admiration.

"Don't kill me," she whispered hoarsely, licking her suddenly dry lips and pressing her back against the carved newel-
post on the second-floor landing. She was mesmerized by his
thigh muscles, which rippled beneath his tight riding britches
as he slowly took the stairs three at a time. His boots were
molded to his well-shaped calves. "Don't kill me, Darach,
darling," she repeated, excitement flaring through her. She
was fired by his deliberate, menacing approach.

Darach had never felt so close to killing anyone with his
bare hands as he did now—striding through the destruction of
his house toward the cringing Englishwoman. He stopped
several paces in front of her, trying to curb his murderous
rage. She reminded him of a bitch he had found abandoned as
a boy. The poor animal had been abused so much that she
cowered, her belly and teats dragging on the floor, while her
tail wagged fawningly. The debasement had sickened him
then, and it sickened him now, helping to temper his killing instinct. He could not bear to touch her with any part of his person, not even his hands.

Felicity sagged limply under his look of withering disdain.
Her mouth flapped soundlessly, and she waved an uncertain
hand in circles, not knowing what she was trying to com-
municate. But in a second he had gone, walking past her
without saying a thing—not even a word about her precious
Riach, she realized.

"Where's my son?" she screamed. "I want my son!"

Darach and Missie MacKissock stared silently down at the
peacefully sleeping girl. The huge dog lazily thumped a heavy
tail in greeting. Felicity's strident screams reverberated
through the house.

"She slept through it all, and 'tis a blessed wonder! You saw
the door—all my years of polishing," lamented Missie. "I
locked myself in here wie the wee mistress, and the rest of the
servants barricaded theirselves in the kitchens. I think Lady
Felicity's brain has snapped and would be best to get a doctor
before she does harm to herself or another. Och, if I had

known I wouldna hae told her." The housekeeper sighed, then blew her nose loudly. "Och, I am sorry, your lordship, but sometimes I am a wicked *auld* woman, and it did my heart guid to put your stepmother in her place. But I dinna mean for all this to happen."

"She didn't wake at all?" he asked sharply, and the woman shook her gray head. "Not even for a few minutes?"

"Lady Felicity was pounding at the door wie anything she could set her hand to, and that great *baistie* was howling enough to wake the dead. But the lass dinna stir—not a hair."

"Send Calum to fetch Dr. MacFarlane," Darach decided, sitting on the bed and placing a hand each side of Kat. "Lock the door after you; I canna cope wie the Lady Felicity right now."

Missie stood watching him for a moment. He looked so dark and forbidding, glowering down at the quietly sleeping figure. She opened her mouth to remonstrate but decided better of it. She sighed and obediently left the room.

Darach heard the decisive sound of the key turn in the lock, and he continued leaning on his stiff arms. He stared down at the motionless Kat, and he silently willed her to wake. His hands were clenched into fists, his knuckles pressing painfully into the mattress.

"Time to wake up," he stated aloud, his breath ruffling her hair. "Time to wake up and answer some questions." But she didn't respond and his barely suppressed rage simmered. How dare she sleep so serenely when his house was in virtual ruins! Why should she have the luxury of blissful repose when his peace of mind was being destroyed? He seethed, throwing caution aside, and roughly gripped her thin shoulders. "Wake up!" he ordered, to no avail. Kat remained peacefully sleeping, but her huge protector tensed to attack, a deep warning growl vibrating in his thick throat.

Darach snarled back at the dog and dropped the inert girl back against the pillows. He stalked across the room and poured himself a generous portion of brandy. He did not trust the violent feelings that made his pulses pound. He breathed deeply, calming himself, and gazed through the amber liquid at the merrily blazing hearth. He wondered what he had done to cause this chaos.

A sharp rapping at the door disturbed him, and he sat up with a start, surprised that Felicity's screams had diminished to a stark silence. He must have drifted off to sleep, he reasoned, frowning at the hound, who sat companionably by his side, its large head resting on his knee.

"Come in," he answered, absently scratching the dog behind a floppy ear.

"Dr. MacFarlane is here to see your wee wife," Missie informed him, ushering a gaunt, middle-aged man into the room.

Darach and Sian remained where they were, silently watching the doctor examine the inert girl.

"Well?" Darach asked impatiently. Missie retucked the covers about Kat's shoulders and the doctor closed his medical bag.

"Your wife is asleep," replied the dour man.

"My wife is asleep?" Darach repeated after a long pause. He had been waiting for the taciturn man to elaborate.

"Aye. Och, to be sure, 'tis a very deep sleep, but 'twould seem her young body is in need of it. There's a lot of wicked bruises about her, and the dark smudges 'neath her eyes indicate total exhaustion. She's sorely weakened. Too thin, too. Seems life hasna been too kind to your bride, Sir Darach, so 'tis guid she'll now have a soft, comfortable time."

"How ever long will she sleep?" inquired Miss MacKissock, smothering a giggle at the incredulous expression on the young man's face.

"Until she wakes," was the terse reply.

"And when might I hope that to be?" probed Darach, his voice laced with sarcasm.

"Now, young sir, you mustna be so impatient wie your bride. You hae a long life ahead of you both," chided the doctor. "But, about your puir stepmother—I'm afraid she's quite overwrought wie worry about her son. I've given her a draft, but I advise you to seriously consider sending her to spend time at Lochland Sanitarium again."

"Lochland Sanitarium again?" echoed Darach.

"Again?" repeated Missie.

"Aye," replied the patient doctor.

"Please explain," snapped Darach.

"Surely you were aware that your stepmother has a delicate condition of the nerves?"

"It always seemed to me tha' she gave everyone else a delicate condition of the nerves," Missie muttered to herself, sitting on the bed and smoothing the shining black curls back from the sleeping face.

"I was aware of her petulance when she's thwarted, but not of . . . Do you mean to tell me that this destructive, unbridled display has happened before?" Darach ejaculated angrily, removing the stopper from a crystal decanter.

"Several times. Och, I dinna ken if she had the opportunity to wreak quite the havoc tha' I see about here. But, then again, your late father kept her on a very tight rein," answered the doctor, accepting a snifter of brandy and standing before the fireplace. "I'm surprised that neither you, Mistress MacKissock, nor your brother had knowledge of Lady Felicity's sad affliction."

"Missie and Calum became part of my household when my father remarried," Darach informed him, a fleeting sadness crossing his face at the memory of how completely he had lost his father twenty years before. He had felt abandoned to the servants, while his father started a new life with a young wife. And within a year, his father had a new son.

"The puir woman first spent time in Lochland Sanitarium the day after her marriage and then again right after the birth of her son, Riach. There were several other times, but you were most probably off at school or at Strathrannoch," the doctor said. "Your father was a proud mon; maybe he dinna want you to ken tha' he had a problem controlling his young wife."

A low, shuddering snarl caused them to look toward the door, which Missie had neglected to lock after the doctor's entrance. It creaked open very slowly until they saw Lady Felicity swaying on the threshold. Darach swore harshly beneath his breath. He sounded as menacing as the dog and would have forcibly ejected his stepmother, but Dr. MacFarlane put out a warning hand, sagely shaking his head.

"Dinna touch her," he hissed. "She's sedated, and it could be dangerous to her brain to rudely awaken her."

Felicity weaved from side to side, putting one foot in front of the other, as though she were unsure of the stability of the floor. Carefully following the intricate pattern of the thick carpet, she hesitantly circled the bed. Sian's teeth were bared, but his warning growl did not deter the woman, who giggled softly and pretended to study the pictures on the walls.

"Control the hound," the doctor whispered frantically,

when the dog bounded onto the bed. Sian planted his large feet on either side of his vulnerable mistress, with his hackles bristling.

"She's got a dirk!" gasped Missie, seeing the wicked little blade catch the reflection from the fire. Both men rushed forward, but the insane woman had raised her hand, intent on stabbing the sleeping girl. The enormous hound leaped up at her.

A terrible scream tore into Kat's sleeping mind, and she opened her eyes. Warm wetness dripped thickly onto her face and between her breasts. Above her, Sian reared on his hind legs, his massive front paws pushing against the shoulders of a hideous, shrieking woman. Her ripped cheek flapped, and blood poured from it. Her wild eyes bulged and flashed venom. The horrendous apparition exuded pure hatred at the girl—accusing, poisonous hatred that she had also seen in her father's dying face. Kat closed her eyes and whimpered, trying to block out the ghastly spectacle, but the screams still tore into her ears.

Darach and the doctor wrestled the frenzied woman away from the bed, and the loyal dog curled beside his small mistress, licking the deep stab wound in his left foreleg.

"Stay wie her, Missie," Darach ordered tersely, managing to carry the hysterical Felicity from the room. The housekeeper nodded. She stood panting, trying to calm her painfully racing heart, staring down at the sight of the naked blood-spattered girl and the ferocious animal. She reached out to comfort her, but Sian snarled and tensed to attack, not trusting anyone. Missie recoiled and tottered backward in a daze. She sat, keeping her eyes pinned to the bed and hearing the Lady Felicity's crazed laughs. Felicity's cries became fainter. Finally, Missie heard carriage wheels, and then there was silence. A log settled noisily in the hearth, the wood cracking and spitting, but Missie MacKissock sat, too drained and appalled by the day's events to react. She was deaf to the brisk clip of booted feet approaching, and she did not feel Darach Campbell's strong presence.

"Missie?" he called, but she made no motion. "Missie?" He shook her plump shoulders, and she turned startled eyes, then promptly burst into tears.

"I dinna ken tha' she was a lunatic! Och, I knew she wasna right in the head, but I dinna ken she was lunatic, or I'd never

hae told her aboot the wee mistress! I dinna ken and I nearly
caused a murder to happen. And there the puir wee-an lies
covered in tha' mad woman's blood, and 'tis all my fault. And
tha' great *baistie* willna let me near to . . ." She sobbed.

"One hysterical female is more than enough, Miss Mac-
Kissock," Darach snapped roughly. "Now, pull yourself together and let's set this house to order."

"Aye, sir. Och, I'm so sorry, sir." Missie wept, scrambling
in her apron pockets for a handkerchief and trying to stop her
torrent of tears. She blew her nose loudly and stood up. "But I
canna tend the wee mistress 'cause tha' great brute willna let
me near," she wailed.

"I'll tend to your mistress, and you tend to the house. I
have not had a decent meal for well over a week, and that
doesna help my disposition one whit. You assured me that
Lady Felicity left the kitchens intact, so I'm hoping to dine
within the hour."

At the mention of his stepmother's name, Missie burst into
a fresh flood of tears.

"Och, I dinna ken she was lunatic or I'd hae never rubbed
her nose in it," she wept, as Darach firmly ushered her out of
the room.

"Send Calum to me wie a length of stout rope!"

"Nay, you canna tie up the wee lass in the attic," protested
Missie, remembering his order the night before.

" 'Tis for the dog!" he roared impatiently, slamming the
door and leaving her fretting in the littered corridor. "I want
this house set to rights by morning." With those orders, he
turned wearily to the bed and watched the huge hound worry
at his shaggy leg for a few moments. Darach quickly realized
that the animal had sustained an injury. "Let me see, you big
beast," he coaxed resignedly, but Sian bared his sharp teeth.
Undeterred, Darach patted the large head, crooning reas-
surances as he examined the ugly wound. "Och, that's a nasty
one," he observed. His eyes narrowed with concern, seeing the
silvery sinew that was exposed in the long gash. "It appears
that Felicity's knife severed one of your tendons so you'll be
lame the rest of your days, you puir beast. I hope your rebellious mistress is deserving of your sacrifice." He sighed,
genuinely disturbed by the maiming of this magnificent animal. Reasoning that there was nothing to be done, as the cut
was well cleansed by the constantly licking tongue, he turned

his attention to the girl, not knowing how much of the blood, if any, belonged to her. She was liberally splattered, but he had supposed that to have been caused by Felicity's badly mauled cheek. He poured water from a pitcher into the wash-bowl and dampened a towel, intent on washing the serenely sleeping face and the gently rising breasts. Once more the huge hound snarled and tensed to attack.

"I mean your mistress no harm. Now, get down," Darach ordered sternly. "Down!" he repeated, his tone brooking no disobedience. The dog slowly submitted, growling softly and favoring his maimed foreleg. "How can one such small female cause so much trouble and be oblivious to it all?" snorted Darach, resisting the desire to shake her awake.

Kat remained blissfully asleep for the following night and day. The clatter of the carpenters setting the town house to rights, the frantic bustle of the servants, and the Campbell's loud temper at having to wait for information about his half brother did not penetrate her healing slumber.

"Och, tha' wee bonny lass is the very first person ever to be leaving our bossy master dangling, whether she means to or not." Missie giggled as she sat knitting beside the hearth in the master bedroom. "Och, tha' lad is too used to having his own way tha' 'tis guid for him to be thwarted."

" 'Tis no funny matter, you silly slummock. While tha' small felon sleeps, who's to tell what danger's happening to master Riach," snapped Calum, poking angrily at the blazing logs.

"Och, you canna think our wee mistress was party to the kidnapping? Och, dinna prate such *stite!* She's no criminal! Just take a peek at tha' angelic face, and you'll ken she'd not be guilty of any such thing," she scolded, staring fondly across the room to the large bed where Kat lay. "Shame on you, Calum MacKissock, for even thinking such terrible things. Lord Rannoch canna think such things hisself, or he'd not hold her so lovingly in his arms each night. Nay, he'd not hold her pretty nakedness to his own if he believed her a criminal!"

"Tha's not loving, you romantic *auld* maid!" Calum remarked derisively. "He holds the skinny chit close to stop her escape and to be privy to any words she might mumble in her sleep that'd gie clue to young Riach's whereabouts."

"Why on earth would he marry such a wicked female, then? And dinna tell me it was just to keep Lady Felicity away!" she challenged triumphantly.

"Och, you ken as well as I tha' the master thinks all females are immoral and unprincipled. Well, it so happens tha' the one lying over there in his bed canna pretend to be anything else. We caught her embroiled in the whole stinking *schlorich* right up to her wee ears. He married her knowing fu' well her wickedness—said it was the lesser of the evils," Calum recounted with relish, recalling Darach's brooding words the previous evening.

"Well, I'll no believe evil of tha' dark lass. Very soon she'll open those green eyes and you'll be proved wrong. Just you wait and see if you don't." Missie hissed, her knitting needles clicking furiously.

"She should be in jail wie the other *futrets*, not pampered between the scented sheets of a marriage bed," stated Calum bitterly.

The low-pitched disturbing conversation and the ominous crackle of the fire slowly seeped into Kat's awakening senses. She lay quietly with her eyes still tightly shut, trying to calm her rising panic. Her small nostrils flared as she smelled the unfamiliar perfumes of cedar and beeswax mixing with the nightmarishly familiar fragrance of the Campbell.

chapter 7

"Between the scented sheets of a marriage bed." These words, uttered so scornfully by the unseen man, resounded hollowly in Kat's head. She instinctively kept her eyes shut and her body still. Was she between the scented sheets of a marriage bed? Her fingertips felt the fine linen, and her cheek rested on a fluffy pillow. She sniffed, and waves of painful nostalgia swept through at the subtle scent of lily-of-the-valley. *Muguet*, she recalled, unable to remember the English name for the delicate spring flower that had been her mother's favorite. *Muguet*, reminding her achingly of the sloping lawns and fragrant woods of the château near Chartres. *Muguet*, reminding her sadly of Easter in Paris, the sprays of tiny white bells pinned to her and her siblings' ragged clothes as the rich tones of the cathedral bells pealed. They would breathe the heady redolence of the pure flowers, following their mother's eyes to the clear blue sky, gazing above the wretched, stinking poverty around them.

So she was between fine linens scented with *muguet*, but was it a marriage bed? And, if so, whose? The disquieting masculine musk of the Campbell elusively teased her, and Kat thrust the terrifying confusion aside. Who were the two people who disagreed so vehemently? The woman's voice had been warm and soft, seeming to defend her, while the man's harsh tones condemned her to jail with the other *futrets*. Who was he to call her vermin? Kat concentrated on summoning up fury, preferring the safety of that emotion to the vulnerability of abject terror. The cedar logs in the hearth crackled, and she smelled the acrid smoke of Comyn Square. She saw her father's accusatory eyes bulging grotesquely in death. The sight of his ornately embroidered waistcoat ripped into her mind, its colors garish, the bloodstain widening along its intricate silken threads. She saw his mouth foaming as he blamed her for his death. He was dead. Her father was dead. Kat made the statement in her mind and waited for the grief, but she felt nothing except a gnawing guilt. The unknown man's words about her being evil, unprincipled, and deserving of a jail melded with her frightened confusion. A good, moral daughter would mourn the violent death of a parent.

The elusive fragrance of the Campbell made her think of the long, punishing ride as she was held against his hard body and her frantic battle when he had carried her into his house. She had tasted the salt of his blood in her mouth when she had bitten deeply into his hand. Fire and fighting, death and terror, hoofbeats and screams blazed red and black in her brain and then softened to a languid surrender. Her skin tingled at the recollection of gentle nurturing. Had that been merely a restful dream that nature had sent to soothe her mind after the flaming violence? Had the Campbell really bathed her and cradled her as though she had been a small child in need of comfort? She pictured his stern, chiseled face, searching for warmth, unable to reconcile the memory of such gentleness with those uncompromising features.

The sharp sounds of booted feet reverberated through the quiet house. Kat tensed, knowing that the Campbell approached. The door was thrust open, and his strong presence overwhelmed her. She kept her eyes tightly shut, hoping that her rapidly beating heart could not be heard.

"How's the wee mistress's puir *baistie?*" inquired the kindly woman, and stark dread settled in Kat's gut.

" 'Tis as I thought, the hound is maimed." The brutal answer tore into her, and Kat bit down on the soft flesh inside her cheeks, trying to control herself. There had been no tears for her father, but now a scalding, aching torrent was ready to erupt.

"You put the wretched creature out of his misery, I hope," growled the unknown man. "Sinfu' waste of a fine beast."

"How's the chit?" The Campbell's deep voice broke through her waves of misery.

"Hasna stirred."

Kat couldn't believe her only friend was dead. Through layers of whirling pain, she heard the rustle of starched skirts and labored breathing, as though the kindly woman was of heavy girth and having trouble regaining her feet.

"Could be she's faking. There's many a sneaky *futret* canny enow to play dead as they bide their time awaiting to stab an unsuspecting man in the back," the gruff voice remarked.

"Dinna be a fool, Calum," chided the woman, and Kat stiffened, hearing the voice so near. She held her breath when warm fingers gently stroked her cheeks, wiping away the hot tears that streamed. "Puir wee-an, even in her sleep she weeps. Is there anything more you'll be needing tonight, your lordship?"

"Nay." The Campbell seemed to sigh after a long pause.

"Then I'll be saying good-night and getting to my bed."

Kat listened to the woman's trotting gait diminish into the recesses of the house.

"I dinna shoot the hound, Calum," the Campbell confessed wearily.

"You're nae your usual self, Darach Campbell," Calum observed gruffly. "Seems you're growing soft and sentimental now you're nearing your thirtieth year. First not turning tha' scruffy female over to the constabulary, and even marrying her to boot. And now tha' scruffy cur!" He snorted derisively.

"I assure you that it's not sentimentality."

"Wha' do you call it, then?"

"I dinna ken," admitted Darach.

"Well, whatever it is, you'll live to regret it," Calum proclaimed sagely. "And 'twill be another night wie no sleep. Tha' great *baistie* will be howling and putting the fear of the de'il in the scullery maids."

The door closed behind the surly man, and Kat clamped her lips together to stifle the sobs of joy knowing Sian was alive. What was the Campbell doing? she worried, not able to hear a movement in the room. She strained her ears but could only detect the hiss and crackle of the fire and the beating of her own heart. Her muscles were cramped with tension, and it felt as though her skin were alive with picking stinging ants. But she lay motionless with her eyes firmly shut, wishing that the Campbell would make a sound so that she could locate his position in the room. The long seconds ticked by with agonizing slowness, and she willed her body to relax, resisting the temptation to sit up and look about. Her nerves stretched to their limits—she did not know whether he was within arm's reach, staring down at her with those disconcerting silver eyes. Kat forced her mind into the past. Where had she seen that piercing gaze before? She remembered falling into his hard arms on the boat from France to Scotland five years ago, but even then—despite her terror—she knew it had happened before. She had been held against that firm body before. She had felt his steely grip on her shoulders before. She had stared up at the ruthless, hawklike face and felt the same conflicting emotions—fear, shyness, safety, and a compelling magnetism. Was it *déjà vu*? she pondered.

Maybe the Campbell had left the room and gone to his own bed. But she would have heard the door open and shut. Maybe he had left with the unpleasant, surly man. But she had heard only a heavy, shuffling tread, not the distinctive stride of the Campbell. No, Kat knew without a doubt that the tall, dark man was still in the room. She could feel his disturbing presence through every pore of her body. Would the insufferable man ever go to his own bed? she wondered, longing to rub her nose, which tickled unbearably.

Darach sat staring into the embers until his eyes were hot and dry, mulling over Calum's censorious words. His steward was right. His actions of late had been unpredictable and inconsistent with his usual behavior. Why had he felt such a surge of compassion for the dark-haired chit? He had acted without sensible thought, reacting like an unthinking animal. Why? What was it about that ebony hair and those bright green eyes that robbed him of the ability to make rational decisions? He should have turned the brat over to the authorities. She was the daughter of a known felon, apprehended in the middle of the execution of a crime—a crime, he might add, that was punishable by death. And what had he, Sir Darach Campbell of Strathrannoch, done? The very same Sir Darach, who was feared for his unbiased inflexibility as a magistrate; noted for his uncompromising ruthlessness in his business transactions; respected for his rational logic in the House of Lords; and celebrated for his sardonic lack of sentimentality toward the opposite sex. Why, he had actually married the little vixen!

What was it about the rebellious chit that had softened his

resolve? He saw a heart-rending sorrow behind her spitting defiance, sorrow that echoed intangibly through his memory. He stared into the fire, seeing those delicate, poignant features at other stages of life, from a small, grubby child barely reaching his elbow to the emerging young woman who now slept so peacefully in his bed. Darach frowned, realizing that there there was also another age—older and more sophisticated—a mature, sensual matron with a mischievous hint of merriment twinkling in the emerald eyes that belied her formal pose.

Darach wrenched his burning gaze from the glowing hearth and swiveled about to look at his bed. A mournful howl wafted on the night breeze, and a derisive sneer curled his lips as he remembered Calum's cryptic remark about a sleepless night. Why hadn't he shot the pitiful hound? he asked himself. He had taken the suffering animal to a secluded spot, but at the last possible moment, he had been unable to pull the trigger. He had tried to avoid the soft woebegone eyes, but the hollow sorrow that had emanated from the proudly held head reminded him of the wolfhound's young mistress; his fingers had frozen. Was the black-haired wench a witch who had slowly and inexorably seeped through his pores to ensnare his very soul? Since the tender age of five or six, he had been taught to put a suffering animal mercifully out of its misery, and in the years since, he had sensibly disposed of several faithful hunting dogs that had been struck down by age or disease, gored by rutting stags, or mauled by hidden traps. It had not been pleasant, but he had fostered no guilt at being the swift instrument of death. The haunting memory of a horse's agonized scream shattered his brooding thoughts, and he was taken back to the stark magnificence of Rannoch moor, where he had been forced to shoot the first stallion he had ever owned. He had been eight years old, and had been watched silently by his father and uncles. The sharp report had reverberated off the peaks and corries of the surrounding mountains, but Iolair's frenzied screams had ceased. Since that day long ago, all his favorite stallions had been called Iolair, the Gaelic name for "eagle."

Darach snorted, impatient with his nostalgic reminiscences. He poured himself a dram of whiskey and threw it down his throat, appreciating the sharp burn and the ensuing warmth that radiated in his gut.

Kat listened to the sounds of the Campbell and tried to picture what he was doing. She heard him pouring a drink and pacing for several moments. Then she heard a clumping sound of boots being discarded. She realized that he was disrobing. She lay still trying to curb her impatience, hoping that soon he would be asleep in his own bed and she could find Sian and escape. A door was firmly closed, and a key turned in the lock. She could tell that it wasn't the door leading to the corridor, as it was positioned to the other side of the crackling fireplace. She joyfully concluded that it had to be a connecting bed-chamber and that at last she was alone. She sighed and was just about to indulge in a much-needed stretch, when to her consternation she heard a floorboard creak, and her keen ears detected the stealthy tread of bare feet approaching on the thick carpet. To her horror, the mattress sagged under his weight, bouncing her rigid body. The male scent of him para-lyzed her senses. The full import of the phrase "between the scented sheets of a marriage bed" burst into her brain as strong hands pulled her against his hard body.

Darach knew instantly that she was no longer blissfully unconscious. Instead of the pliable silkiness that curled so naturally and trustingly, he held a tense quivering body. He could feel her frantic pulse reverberating through him, and once again he swore that he could almost smell her fear. A sharp image of a tossing ship flashed into his mind, and he saw snowflakes sticking to the thick black eyelashes of the green-eyed boy. The child had lain in his arms like a harmless nes-tling and then had swiftly transformed into an avenging hawk. He was glad of the foresight that had made him sleep in his britches, not wanting to be embarrassingly vulnerable if his mysterious wife decided to attack. Soon, all his questions would be answered. Excitement tingled at the knowledge, but he made no sign that he knew she was awake. He waited to see what she would do.

Kat's befuddled brain was incapable of thought. The Camp-bell's large hands were splayed over her naked flesh, his thumbs touching the peaks of her breasts, eliciting an aching hunger. Part of her pulsed with excitement, and part of her thumped with terror. She yearned to turn and burrow into the safety of his strength, pressing closer until she fused with him—no longer existing, no longer cold and alone and respon-sible for so many other people.

Darach's eyebrows raised sardonically as he felt the gradual change loosen and heat her lithe body. Her frenzied pulses

calmed and altered to the unmistakable rhythm of mounting
desire. He pushed her back against the pillow, curious to see
the expression on her exquisite face. He had seen sadness,
anger, fear, and defiance. Now he would witness passion in
the emerald depths of her eyes.

Kat's trepidation returned when she was turned onto her
back and she gazed up at the chiseled face that loomed above,
silhouetted against the frost moonlight. She felt desolate,
wanting to feel his warm embrace, but his hands were on each
side of her shivering body, not touching her. She shuddered at
the intensity that emanated from his shadowed eyes. The painfully nostalgic aroma of *muguet* intermingled with his musky
fragrance, and she remembered that she was between the
scented sheets of a marriage bed. She was his wife, his chattel,
his possession to do with as he wished. Fear clawed through
her as she recalled her mother's long-suffering debasement
—having to follow her husband into exile, from château to
slum and eventually to an anonymous grave beneath a towpath. Would the Campbell try to claim her as a husband did a
wife? Would he stagger home, stinking of cheap whores?
Would he then force himself between her legs, gracelessly
thrusting until he collapsed heavily upon her breasts? And
would she have to lie docilely, submitting to him and stifling
her sobs of revulsion so that her children wouldn't wake and
watch? Various sights of copulations ground into her mind—
furtive and ugly, fumbling and grunting, murky and shadowy.
And then bright rainbow colors exploded, and she saw Macaree's perfect doll-like face screaming, screaming, her child's
body jerking and red blood spurting over pristine white lace.
What was it her father had screamed in the fiery chaos before
he died? "Filthy unnatural spawn." And he had blamed her
for her sister's despoilment.

"What's your name?" the Campbell's deep voice softly
probed.

"Kat," she whispered spontaneously, then stiffened with
panic. She must tell him nothing, or it would mean more than
her sister's despoilment. It would mean death.

"Kat?" questioned the Campbell, wondering what had
summoned such abject dread to hollow her eyes, successfully
cool her passion, and to douse his own ardor. "Diminutive for
Katriona?" And Kat nodded. "And your surname?"

"MacNiall."

"Truthfully," he demanded gently.

"MacNiall," she repeated, her voice sounding hoarse.

"I dinna believe you."

Kat stared steadily up at him, trying to hide her terror. She felt naked and exposed, and he was masked in shadow. Maybe it was as well, she thought, recalling the merciless silver eyes.

"My name is Katriona MacNiall."

"You're lying!"

"Aye." She sighed, after a very lengthy pause during which her agile mind had swiftly assessed her predicament. It was obvious the Campbell would keep probing unless she soothed his vanity by seeming to capitulate. "I'm lying," she admitted.

"Who are you?"

"Katherine Clark," she improvised, knowing the surname was so common that it would take nearly a lifetime to contact everyone so named. Her mother's name of MacNiall could very well lead the shrewd man to trace Suibhan's marriage to a MacGregor, putting Robbie and Macaree in danger. Kat frowned, realizing her father's shortsightedness. She had not much respect for her sire's morals, but she had never questioned his intelligence until that moment. "My name is Katherine Clark," she repeated, not knowing if she was believed. The man didn't acknowledge her words but turned up the wick of a lantern. Kat backed away from the revealing circle of light, uncomfortable with the Campbell's silent scrutiny.

"And Rory MacNiall?"

"My stepfather . . . Rory Clark," she lied, loath to admit direct parentage. Another lengthy pause ensued, and Kat felt the Campbell's anger prickling the air.

"I'm waiting." He seethed. His voice was low and threatening.

"Waiting?" She played for time, wishing she knew what he already knew.

"Aye." His terse reply didn't help her at all.

"My name is Katherine Clark, and I am seventeen years old, and my mother is dead. And I dinna ken my natural sire, and I dinna ken my stepfather very well. He married my mother and then ran off, returning when he needed gin money or the like," she recounted. "Might I hae a drink of water? I'm very dry." Her nervousness made it very difficult to swallow.

"What are you doing at Comyn Square?" he snapped.

"The woman was one of his mistresses," Kat confessed, shrewdly reasoning that she should use elements of the truth whenever possible, to make her story more convincing.

"Why were you there?"

"He meant to cheat you at the gaming table." She was positive that such an honest admission would soften his steely stare.

"Why were *you* there?" he repeated.

"I dared nae disobey him. With my mother dead, I had no one else between me and the streets, or the workhouse, or a brothel," she said sadly, playing for sympathy.

The Campbell gave her a hard, assessing look. Then he stalked across the room to the water pitcher that resided on a sideboard, surrounded by crystal decanters. Kat took the opportunity to sit up and glance about the large chamber, unaware of her nakedness as she frantically sought a means of escape. Several doors were in evidence, and she wondered where they all led. The furnishings were luxurious but sparse. Beside the enormous bed and the sideboard, there were two imposing chairs on each side of the wide hearth and a low table. Her eyes scanned the broad mantel, scrutinizing the visible objects.

Darach watched her thoughtfully. She was a glorious vision. Her glossy ebony hair rioted about her vivacious little face, and one long tress snaked down her graceful swan's neck to curl sensually under one impudent breast. Though appreciative and more than slightly enamored of her perfect beauty, he was astute enough to observe her curiosity as her green eyes lighted speculatively upon a matched pair of dueling pistols that had belonged to his great-grandfather. They were useless as weapons and were of historic ornamental interest only. Their barrels had been artistically engraved with scenes from the battles of Killiecrankie and Dunkeld, and their firing pins had long since been removed.

Kat hurriedly averted her eyes from the mantel and followed the Campbell's searing silver gaze to her naked breasts. Her pulses raced tumultuously, and she hurriedly yanked the sheets up about her chin.

"Where are my clothes?" she demanded imperiously, attempting to hide her shocked fear. She suddenly realized that she was bare from the tips of her toes to the top of her head, and she glared at the Campbell furiously, resisting the temptation to shrink away as he strode toward the bed.

"Burned!" he snapped curtly, offering her a crystal tum-

bler. Unable to think of an adequate response, Kat wordlessly
took the glass and drank. Silently, she handed him the empty
tumbler. All the terrible tales about the ruthless Campbells
were true, she thought with panic. He meant to keep her naked
in his bed until she told him everything. How on earth could
she escape back to Linnmanach without a stitch to put on her
back? How would Macaree and Rob survive until spring
without her? The long silence lengthened. Kat was more than
conscious of his unwavering appraisal, but she kept her chin
raised haughtily and her eyes averted, trying to calm herself
and plot logically her actions.

"Katherine Clark?" He laughed harshly. "Nay, my wee
Wild Kat, you'll not beguile me wie your saucy breasts and
those seductive feline eyes." He stated this derisively, more
for his own benefit as he tried to quell the ache of desire that
spread from his loins. He felt confusion and then a creeping
shame at the embarrassed blush that stole upon her soft
cheeks. She anchored the concealing covers beneath her arms
so tightly that she flattened her graceful curves. To his further
bewilderment, he watched her proudly fight back tears and he
stifled a groan as one salty drop escaped and trickled slowly
down, more effective alone than amid a torrent.

Kat tried to smother the hiccoughing sobs that choked her
throat. Inadvertently, the Campbell had called her "wee Wild
Kat," conjuring up in her bruised mind memories of her
mother. She battled the rising storm of tears, refusing to allow
them to consume her, and when his large brown hands reached
out to touch her, she welcomed the diversion to fight him. She
would be strong and fearless, not weak and weepy. For her
mother, Suibhan, she would be *braw*, *bardach* Kat, protecting
her siblings with her very life if need be, foregoing modesty by
dropping the sheet and balling her small hands into fists to
pummel the enemy of her clan.

Darach was incredibly moved by her valiant struggle, not
just against himself, but against her own grief and fear.
Despite her petite size, weakened by at least two days without
food, it took all his strength to contain her without doing her
injury. Finally, as a punishing blow bruised his cheekbone, he
reasoned that she was less fragile than she appeared. He swore
aloud and rolled her up in the discarded sheet, pinning her
arms and legs. He pulled her against him and attempted to
soothe her, but she tried savagely to sink her teeth into his

chest. Still swearing, he managed to manipulate her into a position in which all she could do was futilely toss her head and make impotent squeals and grunts. He glowered down at her, marveling at her strength and discipline. She was nearly out of her mind with grief and terror, yet she kept a rein on her tongue. He had expected—even hoped for—a furious stream of words that would betray her identity.

Darach's own stream of furious curses tempered to a few gruff words of comfort. She lay across his knees, panting for breath. He gazed down at her flushed little face and very slowly and deliberately lowered his head and kissed her petulant mouth, tasting the salt of her angry tears. Her lips were tremulous and docile beneath his gentle pressure.

Kat couldn't believe what was happening. One moment she had been blindly battling in a spinning vortex of panic, and now incredible sensations whirled her into a different pool of emotions. For several shocked minutes, she lay across his lap, feeling the hard muscles of his firm thighs, wondering about the turbulence that roiled and intensified until she tentatively opened her mouth to the teasing urging of his tongue. The Campbell groaned between her lips, and she felt a tenderness spring from the sound to join with her hungry aching. She was being kissed. She was being held against his heart like a precious child. But she wasn't his precious child! He wasn't kissing her like a precious child, she realized through the culminating waves of passion. He was kissing her like a woman—a wife—and at that thought she struggled to break free from the inexorable tide. She bit down viciously on his lower lip.

Darach's swearing resumed when Kat's sharp teeth met with his tender flesh. She hung on like a vicious little kitten, and he slapped her cheek, forcing her to release her excruciating hold. He raised his head and glowered furiously at the scowling face. His blood was smeared on her kiss-bruised lips, and her eyes flashed triumphantly.

"Och, you need taming, vixen!" he snarled. To his slight satisfaction, he detected a fleeting quiver of fear before she bravely covered it with challenging scorn. "You, my Wild Kat wife, shall submit to your husband even if it means muzzling your snapping jaws!" he growled, goaded by his own stupidity in relaxing his guard.

"You'll hae to do more than muzzle me!"

"Dinna tempt me!"

"I'll never be bedded by a bastard Campbell!"

Darach's eyes narrowed with speculation. The bright silver honed to an icy steel. The bitterness in the chit's tone when she said the name Campbell denoted a deep resentment, a vengefulness that had been nurtured for a long time.

"And what have the Campbells done to you and yours?" he asked, his mild tone belied by the intensity of his expression. Kat stiffened, realizing her rash words had been picked up by the astute man. She sneered derisively up at him.

"What has a Campbell done to me?" she repeated, subtly changing his question. "How can you ask me that when you have me bound in this winding sheet ready for the grave, unable to move hand and foot? Kept me naked in your bed, locked wie-in your chamber, a prisoner! And you ask me what a Campbell has done to me?" she blustered, hoping he was unaware of the stark terror that cut through her. She must be more careful and restrain her unruly mouth, not only from hungering for his kisses, but from recklessly betraying her true identity.

"Och, I wouldna complain, my lady," Darach snapped. "I can name less desirable prisons."

"There canna be a less desirable prison than your bed!" hissed Kat, battling the traitorous emotions that surged through her nubile young body from his touch.

" 'Tis an unnaturally cold March to be chained naked in a rat-infested cellar," he snarled, goaded by the sparks of contempt that flashed in her green eyes.

"One *futret* is much like another!"

"Aye, you're right. Maybe it would be better for you to share company wie your fellow felons in an Edinburgh jail!"

Panic clutched Kat's gut, but she didn't blink. She kept her gaze fixed on his cruel mouth, trying to deafen her ears to his threatening words. She concentrated on his swollen lower lip, counting her teeth marks and watching the blood well up in the little holes and slowly trickle down his stubborn chin.

"You were captured in the process of committing a crime—a crime punishable by death or deportment as a bonded servant for the rest of your natural days. Maybe you should be turned over to the authorities. Perhaps that is how I shall obtain some truthful answers," he continued. "So, what's it to be, lady wife?" he demanded harshly, giving her a rough shake when she didn't respond.

"What is it to be?" repeated Kat, turning the question back

to him as her frantic mind scrambled desperately for a solution. If she was jailed, there would be no hope of escape, and then what would happen to everyone at Linnmanach who depended on her?

" 'Tis your decision."

"Naked in your bed, or naked in an Edinburgh jail?"

"Dinna try my patience more," he warned, his deep voice soft and deadly, reverberating through her rigid body.

"Naked . . . in . . . your . . . bed," she eventually spat through gritted teeth, nearly choking on the words.

"And you'll submit to me?" he demanded brusquely, quelling the guilty feeling that arose when he glared into her pale, trembling face.

"Aye, my lord husband, I shall submit to you," she whispered piteously, feigning fear and obedience, while inside she seethed with fury. Aye, she would submit, deriving as much pleasure from his body as he would steal from hers. Aye, she'd appear to be his compliant wife, lulling him into a false sense of security, then making good her escape. She licked her dry lips nervously, staring anxiously at his stern mouth, remembering the delight of his kisses.

Darach felt curiously deflated. He sensed sarcasm in her tone, and yet she lay across his lap the very picture of malleability. Kat gasped when she was suddenly thrown onto the bed like a bundle of laundry. She was afraid and braced herself to be brutally taken, her eyes wide and her teeth bared like those of a cornered animal.

"Sheathe your claws, Wild Kat!" the Campbell laughed mockingly. He was relieved to see the battle lights sparkle in her eyes again. "I dinna rape skinny, unfledged chits," he added insultingly, before leaving the room and locking the door after himself.

Kat sat up and stared about the empty room, feeling a curious mixture of emotions. Why was she feeling rejected when she ought to have been relieved?

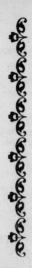

chapter 8

A long week had crept by, each agonizing second painfully felt by Kat, who paced the floor and clawed at the walls. Never had she been so inactive, never had she been so restricted. Her movements were confined to two rooms, the Campbell's bed-chamber and an adjacent dressing room, which in itself was an irony, considering that she had only a flimsy nightrail to wear—probably borrowed from a kitchen maid. Maybe she should be thankful for small mercies, she mused bitterly. At least the skimpy shift and bare dressing room afforded her a little privacy. It had been a long seven days fraught with anxiety for her brother and sister. She moodily stared out the window at the snow that swirled and settled, covering the sill and mounding halfway up the panes. Who was cutting the wood and stoking the fires at Linnmanach? When she had left nearly two weeks ago, the larder and pantry had been almost bare. Who was setting the traps and hunting for meat for the table?

"Looks like we'll be having a white Easter this year," remarked the housekeeper, who sat by the hearth patiently knitting. She gazed fondly at the dark girl. "In all my born days I've never seen such weather in March. The poor farmers'll be late sowing their crops this year." The kindly woman's idle chatter grated on Kat's nerves and increased her concern for her family's welfare. Robbie's hacking cough needed warm sunshine and plenty of fresh food. What did Aggie and Mac-aree think? She and Gregor had been expected back days ago. How would she tell Robbie about their father's death? How would she get home? Sian's mournful howling from the stables increased Kat's distress.

"Missie, could you not smuggle my hound to me? Just for a wee while?" she wheedled. "The Campbell isna here. Neither is that surly brother of yours. What harm would it do?" She saw the indecision on the round, homely face.

"Och, little mistress. I darsent," lamented the kindly woman.

"Then let me go to him. I'll not escape, I promise. And how could I dressed like this, wie no shoes wie the blizzard and all?" pressed Kat, curling her bare toes into the carpet.

"You'd catch your death of cold," argued Missie, her knitting needles clicking furiously. "And then that'll set off his temper, and you've yet to hae a good taste of tha', my lass."

"Och, I've tasted the Campbell's foul temper—"

"Nay, you've not," the woman interrupted. "You've seen a wee bit of ill humor, but not his terrible temper—or you'd hae no skin left on your wee backside."

"I'm not afeared of him," lied Kat.

"Why dinna you tell him wha' he wants to know?" Missie asked softly, laying down her knitting and gazing beseechingly at the girl.

"I dinna ken what to tell him. He doesna believe a word from my mouth."

" 'Tis no wonder, you've told the puir mon at least a dozen names. What's he to believe? You canna be Clark, Smith, MacNiall, Carr, and Wilson, just to name a few," she chided sadly. "Trust his lordship, he's a just mon. Whatever pickle you've got yourself in, he'll help."

"But I dinna ken where his precious brother is—so what am I supposed to do?"

"I dinna ken." The housekeeper replied unhappily, picking up her needles and knitting furiously again.

"Even you said that Riach Campbell was a spoilt, wild youth—reckless and always up to his neck in trouble. Maybe he's wenching and drinking somewhere and doesna want to come home. And who's to blame him if the Campbell treats his brother like he treats his own wife?" she ranted.

"Oh, dearie me." Missie sighed, not knowing what to say.

She stared with consternation at Darach, who leaned idly against the doorjamb, listening with amused interest.

"Och, you say tha' my husband is a just mon," sneered Kat. "But would a just mon keep his own wife near naked, a prisoner? Would a just mon deny her comfort from her only friend in the whole world—her faithful hound? Would a just mon deny her all diversions? Books, games, playing cards? Anything to help pass this heavy time? Would a just mon do that?" she demanded hotly, remembering how he had cruelly removed each object that interested her, until even the walls were devoid of paintings. She had been most careful to keep her eyes averted from the dueling pistols on the mantel. "If he could, he'd probably board up these very windows and consign me to darkness!"

"Admirable idea," the Campbell murmured in a deep voice, and she spun about to see him lounging comfortably by the door. Why wasn't he ugly and loathsome to look at? she fumed, furious with the excitement that darted through her at the sight of him. "Thank you, Missie," he dismissed, holding open the door for the heavy woman and locking it decisively behind her. "And how was your day, my lady?" he asked mockingly.

Kat longed to spit in his face, but did not quite have the courage. She rudely turned her back to stare at the snow that swirled against the darkening sky. Even the view from the window imprisoned her—the confining rows of uniform roofs stretched like a wall, blocking the sight of anything soft and natural. There was no green, only gray and brick-red beneath the white snow.

"I take your truculence to mean that you still refuse to cooperate?"

"How can I tell you what I don't know?" she shouted, still turned away from him, her breath misting the cold windowpane. Sian's mournful baying filled the tense silence. Kat's pride made it impossible for her to beg the Campbell for anything, but the brimming green eyes she turned to him were very eloquent.

"What a pretty liar you are," he murmured caressingly, his deep tones sending shivers down her spine.

"I should dearly like to kill you." Kat's voice shook with rage, and she balled her hands into fists. She wanted to strike his dark sardonic face and wipe the mocking grin from his

handsome features. How could such a demonic, cruel man be
so compelling?

"Come here," he ordered softly, and she hesitated. Her
treacherous emotions were safer when there was some distance
between them. "Afraid?" he taunted. Kat's nostrils flared,
and she shook her glossy jet hair. It whirled about her snarling
face. She was unable to speak because of the wild racing of her
pulses. "Then obey me!" She took an involuntary step
backward when he took a sudden step forward. "I'll meet you
halfway," he conceded, offering a large brown hand.

Kat was confused by his unexpected kindness. Her eyes narrowed with suspicion. One minute he was coldly dictatorial,
and the next warmly flexible. Was he setting a new trap for
her? Well, she'd not be caught, she decided, and she defiantly
turned her back to him. She gasped aloud when he grasped her
shoulders and spun her about to face him. The Campbell
hadn't so much as laid a finger on her person since she had
promised to submit to him, and now the hard pressure of his
hands caused tremors to ripple through her. Every night, they
had slept together in the same large bed, but he had made no
move to bridge the cold space between them; she had found
relaxation impossible. The long minutes of the night ticked by,
each second painfully measured. She would curl as far away as
she could, but every inch of her skin was burningly conscious
of his presence. The space between them seemed to crackle
and hiss like the logs in the hearth, but the Campbell gave no
indication that he was aware of her nearness. For seven long
nights she had lain awake, listening to his even breathing, as
he slept oblivious of her discomfort.

Kat stared straight ahead, keeping her gaze pinned to a pearl
stud that fastened his snowy-white shirt, but one blunt finger
under her chin relentlessly forced her stormy face to look up.
She glared, expecting to see smoldering anger, but something
else smoldered in the depths of his eyes. Their keen silver, a
startling contrast to his golden skin, was muted to a misty
gray, subtle and softly dangerous. Their seductiveness mesmerized her, and she unconsciously offered her parted lips.
His hard hands gentled their grip and splayed possessively
down her back, molding her to him. She surged closer, standing on the tips of her bare feet wanting to merge with his
strength and for a while forget everything.

Darach groaned and lifted her against him, cupping her

firm buttocks and grinding her to the hard ridge of his man-hood, which strained the fabric of his tight riding britches. The nights since he had captured his provocative bride had been the most agonizing he had ever known, and he wondered at his sanity for putting himself through such torture. He was determined that she should break before him. He had been more than aware of her restlessness; the thought of her lithe body being within arm's reach had persecuted him throughout the long dark hours.

Kat reveled at the feel of his masterful mouth, rebelliously warring with his probing tongue for dominance, and battling against his confining hands, which molded her to him. She yearned for the freedom to move at her own rhythm and pace.

"Och, my wee Wild Kat, maybe there is a way to school you to obedience," he murmured huskily, rolling her onto the bed. Pinning her beneath him, he tore off her flimsy shift and reared back to look into her passion-glazed eyes. She whimpered a protest and tried to connect back to him, but she subsided into gasps of ecstasy when he captured a rose-tipped breast in his mouth, nipping and flicking it tantalizingly with his tongue.

Kat couldn't believe such rapture could exist. The aching hunger that had pulsed through her each night, making sleep elusive, had been the mere whispered promise of what she was now experiencing. She arched toward him, wishing she could press against his naked flesh instead of the clothes that withheld from her the sensuous heat of his hard body.

"Please?" she begged huskily, plucking at the studs that fastened his shirt.

"Where's my brother?" he demanded hoarsely. His words didn't penetrate Kat's fevered brain. She thrust toward him, instinctively parting her lithe legs, but he removed himself from temptation and ground his aching loins into the mat-tress, cursing his stubborn martyrdom. "Where is my brother, Riach?" he repeated, longing to sheathe himself in her heat.

"What?" she mumbled, offering her lips, her hips, her breasts—anything so that he would resume his delicious assault on her newly awakening woman's body.

"Where's my brother, sweetheart?" he repeated softly, brushing his lips against her own.

"Your mother?" Kat queried innocently, her keen mind struggling through the swirling fog of passion. "I dinna ken your mother, my love,'' she added wickedly, mischievously poking her tongue between his stern lips and pretending to be aroused, despite the icy panic that streaked through her, replacing the burning ecstasy of a scant second before.

The fury that blazed from the Campbell's silver eyes cut Kat to the quick. She tried to mask her fear but was unable to stifle an instinctive wince, recognizing the violence that threatened. Her tiny movement seemed to infuriate the dark man even more, and she closed her eyes, expecting brutal blows. There was a taut moment, and then her body jerked when his weight abruptly left the bed. The sound of the door slamming shuddered through the quiet house.

Even in the middle of a nearly ungovernable rage, he still remembered to lock the door, Kat noted dully, too disgusted with herself to do anything but lie where she had been abandoned. Outside she heard the crunch of hoofbeats in the snow and surmised that the Campbell was riding out his fury. She sighed, wishing she had the same option. How could he suddenly rein in his passion and continue his relentless inquisition? Maybe he had no passion for her, she thought reluctantly, and she saw Macaree's perfect features framed by flaxen hair. In her mind's eye, she traced her sister's regal stature and majestic curves, comparing herself unfavorably. She concluded that lack of passion for her enabled him to sleep beside her each night and not attempt to possess her. That she had so nearly submitted to his contrived seduction caused her anger to mount. She had been no better than a bitch in heat! No better than one of those overperfumed, painted courtesans! No better than a ragged slut in a back alley in Paris, spreading her skinny legs for the thrusts of faceless men. She miserably decided that she was worse than all of them put together, because their crudely offered favors were never rejected as hers had been. How could she debase herself so utterly? She seethed, and her mother's sad, patient face flashed into her mind.

"I'll not be like you. I'll not." Kat wept as Suibhan's words wafted back through the circles of time.

"One day, my wee Wild Kitten, you'll fall in love, and you'll follow your man to the ends of the earth if need be."

"Never!" spat Kat, tossing her glossy hair from side to side, trying vehemently to deny the love she felt for the Campbell. " 'Tis not love I feel, but a sickness, a terrible sickness of the blood that can destroy me, just like my father destroyed you, Mother!''

"One day you'll fall in love and do and accept many things you could never before," the sorrowful voice persisted.

"Never, Mother, never," muttered Kat. Making no attempt to cover her nakedness, she fell into an exhausted sleep and dreamed she was back in the squalid attic in Paris, hearing the heavy steps approaching up the rickety stairs.

Kat's eyes flew open, and she lay rigid in the darkness, the terrifying stench of cheap perfume and stale spirits flooding her senses. She was bitterly cold and could hear the whine of the wind between the broken panes; it blustered around the rag-stuffed cracks in the eaves. He was home and drunk, and she must be very still and quiet.

Darach had imbibed, but to his disgust he was still sober. He wished fervently to be blissfully inebriated, to be released from the painful confusion of emotions that battered every part of him. He had foolishly risked the life of his stallion, Iolair, by rashly riding into the treacherous blizzard, hoping to cool his flaming desire for the unprincipled witch who slept contentedly in his bed. But the rhythm of the horse between his thighs had been a torturous reminder of the way she had thrust against him, and he had decided to slake his consuming hunger on an uncomplicated whore. He reasoned that one female was as good as another in accommodating lust. But there had been no accommodation. He had been repelled by the artifice and bawdiness, and the painted women's brittle laughter grated on his stretched nerves. Their hard enameled nails had gracelessly clawed the air, while inferior brandy had slopped out of their greedy mouths to mingle with the sickly sweet scents that failed to disguise their unwashed bodies.

Darach swore loudly, consigning all women to purgatory, furious that Kat slept peacefully while he was awake and in turmoil. He tore off his cape and jacket, repulsed by the cloying stink of the brothel that clung to the wet wool. He flung them across the room. Muttering savagely, he sat heavily on the bed, keeping his eyes averted from Kat's prone body for fear that the dull ache in his groin would sear through him again. He wrenched his boots off and kicked them noisily away, trying to ignore the convulsive shudders that shook the bed at each violent sound. He pulled his shirt over his tousled

head, not bothering to remove the studs. They popped free
and showered melted snow over the bed, over the naked,
trembling girl. He fiercely toweled his black hair before lying
back against the pillows. He kept his eyes averted, but the
agitated tremors continued. With a snort of impatience, he
reluctantly turned to look at his bedmate.

Darach scowled, realizing that she lay exactly where he had
left her more than four hours before. The ripped night-shift
was still partly pinned beneath her, the only difference being
the position of her legs. An image of her lying totally open
and vulnerable to him ripped through his mind. Her lithe
limbs were now clamped together, her ankles locked, her arms
held stiffly to her sides, and her small hands clenched, the
knuckles gleaming white.

"Kat?"

"Oui, papa," she whispered, and the fear in her childlike
voice chilled his blood. He tugged the coverlet over her
nakedness and tucked it about her, trying to still the tremors
that shook her. He smoothed her tangled tresses back from
her face and was about to waken her gently from her nightmare when he stopped himself.

"Comment t'appelle toi?" he ventured, using the familiar
form of address, hoping that in her dream she would think
him a friend.

"Je m'appelle Kat."

"Mademoiselle Kat . . . quoi?"

"Non! Non! C'est seulement Kat," she protested earnestly.

"Pourquoi?"

"Parce que mon nom veut dire le mort."

"Because your name means death!" he exclaimed. In his
astonishment he forgot his French, but the sleeping girl didn't
react.

"Oui, mon nom veut dire le mort," she repeated.

Darach didn't know how to respond to such a statement. He
stared at her silently for a few moments, trying to devise an
approach. *"Mais je suis un ami, ma petite. Dis moi ton nom,"*
he cajoled her, as he would a tiny child.

"Non! Mon nom veut dire le mort!" she insisted, and he
sighed with defeat.

"Où est Riach Campbell?" he asked, trying another tack.

*"Tous les Campbell sont malfaiteurs! Tous les Campbell
sont dangereux! Tous les Campbell veulent dire le mort a*

moi!'' she recited like a well-rehearsed litany.

"All the Campbells are evildoers. All the Campbells are dangerous. All Campbells mean death to me." Kat's words pounded through Darach's aching skull. Who could she possibly be that even in sleep she was afraid to state her own name?

"Toute la lignée de Diarmid est vénimeuse!'' she snarled anxiously. *"C'est vrai, papa?''* she asked. Darach shook his head with consternation. She was even informed enough to call his clan by its ancient name "the race of Diarmid."

"C'est vrai, papa?'' she urged.

"Non, ce n'est pas vrai,'' he disagreed, unable to malign his clan by admitting that they were poisonous. Had her father filled her with such dread and hatred for clan Campbell? And if so, for what purpose? Despite her constant denial of the fact, it was obvious that the green-eyed little witch was a key to his brother's disappearance.

"Menteur!'' Kat suddenly shouted, springing up and pummeling him with small, sharp fists. *"Menteur!* Liar! How dare you come to my mother's deathbed stinking of whores! How dare you leave us to starve and come home stinking of cognac! How dare you let my mother die in rags, while you strut in silks like a rutting cock!'' she screamed. Eager to hear all her words, Darach raised himself so that she battered harmlessly against his broad chest.

Darach stared down, remembering the bedraggled urchin on the dark street in Paris. Instinctively, he knew what had occurred that night. The same hopeless sorrow hollowed the emerald eyes.

"Your mother died in Paris on that stormy night," he murmured, and the furious little fists stopped pounding. She froze, squinting up at him through angry tears.

"Maman is dying, you maun come home," Kat said in a daze, trying to focus on her father's sagging features. But the light was dim. "You maun come home," she repeated, staring about the bedchamber. "This isna Paris!'' she cried disjointedly. Then she awoke fully. "You are the Campbell!''

Kat gaped with horror at the shadowed hawklike face that loomed above her. She had been dreaming. What had she said? What had she revealed? It had been so very real. She had thought her father had been near, but he was dead. Yet she could still smell his presence. Kat's small nose wrinkled with revulsion, and she reared back from the Campbell.

"You stink of a whorehouse!" she cried, brushing his hands off her forearms as though he were filth. She scrambled under the covers as far away from him as she could without falling off the bed. She curled in the darkness, hugging her knees, not knowing which made her feel worse: his preferring a whore, or her unknown statements to him while she slept.

Darach was stung by her scornful rejection. She made him feel like a grubby schoolboy, and he cursed the impetuousness that had sent him to an establishment he hadn't visited since his callow youth. He resisted the urge to ring for service and demand hot water for a bath, savagely reasoning that he would smell any way he damned please. He unfairly blamed her stubbornness for the discomfort that drove him to seek such solace. He scowled at the provocative round shape beneath the covers, recalling the words from her dream and trying to form a credible resolution to the mystery of her identity and his brother's disappearance.

The sky was lightening to a dismal gray. It mirrored the same morose color of the cold hearth. Still, Darach sat braced against the headboard of the bed, naked to the waist, struggling to understand the elusive information he had heard from his mysterious bride. At some time during the dark night, she had turned and stretched like a sleepy kitten. Now she lay nestled against his flank, one lithe arm and several long tresses curled about his upper thigh. She was probably one of hundreds of Scottish children born in exile, offspring of outlawed Jacobites who had followed the young pretender to France after the Stuart cause was finally defeated on Culloden Moor. That would be reason enough for a father to warn a child against revealing a family name, especially if they had returned to Scotland without a pardon. But why would a man warn his daughter against the Campbells? And why would the same man abduct Darach Campbell's brother?

Darach idly played with a ringlet of ebony hair, delighting in its silken texture and recalling Kat's furious demand of her father. "How dare you let my mother die in rags, while you strut in silks like a rutting cock!" she had screamed. Into his weary mind flashed the obscene image of the plump man flamboyantly arrayed in satins and brocades, blood staining his embroidered waistcoat, and his vicious mouth accusing . . . accusing her of what? Darach wrestled to remember the dying man's tirade, but it had been such chaos. The insane woman, the frantic hound, the smoke, the fire. He closed his eyes and concentrated, seeing furious foam-specked lips, but the words evaded him. All he could recall was vitriolic spite directed at the petite dark girl.

Darach's back ached with fatigue and his head pounded with frustration. He eased his cold, stiff body into the bed until he lay with Kat cuddled to his chest. She was so relaxed and trusting in her sleep, he mused, and so willful and stubborn while awake, that nothing he had attempted so far had penetrated her defenses. Maybe it was time for a different strategy. As soon as the weather was less treacherous, he would appear to allow her freedom, to let her seem to escape. Then he would follow her and hope to find his brother, ending the mysteries that plagued him. He tugged the blankets from her greedy grasp. Ignoring her disgruntled murmurs, he covered them both and fell into a sound sleep.

chapter 9

Kat was free! Exhilaration pounded with the horse's hooves when they finally broke free of the city's bustle and galloped down the Stirling road toward Linlithgow, ignoring the shouts of irate stragglers whose plodding animals shied with fright at her furious pace.

It was the first week in April, but a cold Marchlike wind still blustered and a watery sun lighted treacherous ice slicks, slowly shrinking the patches of crisp snow. No tender green or delicate blossom softened the starkness of the silvered trees, whose branches creaked against the frigid sky. But to Kat, it was spring. She was going home to Linnmanach after nearly a month of imprisonment. What would she find when she got there? Panic stabbed at her, cutting through her elation, and she suddenly became aware of the biting wind that whipped her cheeks and tore at her clothes. She hunched down, attempting to bury her frostbitten ears below the raised collar of her shabby cape. She tried to calm herself as her thoughts wandered back through the preceding weeks to the night when she had been so humiliated—rejected for a common whore.

The Campbell had grown careless since, she gloated, her fury fired at the memory of her rude awakening the following morning. For some demented reason, Kat had dreamed that she had slept curled against his warm flesh, within his possessive embrace. Why on earth would her traitorous mind conjure up such an image when his contempt was so evident? The question haunted her. Was she destined to be just like her mother? Devoid of every vestige of pride? Totally debased by the love she felt for a man who abused her so utterly?

"Cover your nakedness!" His curt words had sliced through her sleep-muddled mind, and he had flung an armful of clothes onto the bed before slamming out of the room. She had felt shame burn and stiffen her cheeks, knowing her exposed breasts were abhorrent to him. She had numbly examined the scattered garments, insulted and hurt by his choice. There were no soft lace underclothes, no silken gowns or kid slippers that would befit the wife of a Campbell lord. There were not even any plain homespun frocks, cotton shifts, or sensible brogues. There was just the humbling attire of a stable gillie—coarse trews, smock, jerkin, and boots.

"Well, all to the guid!" she had hissed aloud, trying to stifle the simpering image of herself dressed in a graceful flowing gown, looking tantalizingly beautiful just for him. "I couldna escape the Campbell's clutches wie skirts to trip and snarl my movements."

Kat dug her heels into the mare's firm girth, remembering the boots. They had been new, the leather soft and supple, a jarring contrast to the clean but obviously well-worn clothes. She had shrugged, supposing that a stableboy had either died or outgrown them before wearing them. But the knowledge that a stableboy would not warrant such expensive boots had nagged at her. Then she had berated herself for being weak by trying to read kindness into the Campbell's grudging accommodations.

Many things had changed that morning, Kat recalled, slowing the mare's brisk pace when her hooves skittered on an icy patch in the road. One of the ornate doors had been unlocked, and she had been relegated to the adjacent mistress's suite, which consisted of a bedchamber and salon. These elegant rooms contained many diversions to help while away the long idle hours of her imprisonment. She knew she should have been relieved to be away from the Campbell's bed, but instead she felt discarded, banished from his sight like a repulsive object. Despite her firm resolve to the contrary, she would catch herself listening for his movements, her eyes pinned breathlessly to the door. She had been too restless to concentrate on reading books, and there had been no worthy adversary to battle across the ivory-and-ebony chessboard, except the placid housekeeper who only played whist. Kat had spent her time gazing out the window at the wintry city vista, ignoring the beckoning spinet that reminded her nostalgically of the golden part of her childhood when her mother had been radiant. She had patiently taught her daughters how to play lilting Scottish reels and soothing lullabies.

Each morning, Calum MacKissock silently took her down to the stables to visit Sian, who limped to greet her, hampered by his maimed front leg and the cruel short rope.

" 'Tis for the wretched beast's ain guid," the surly man had growled, but Kat had turned scornfully away, refusing to hear his lies. Instead, she would feed her consuming hatred for the merciless Campbell. Each morning she would kneel, hugging her faithful hound, her shrewd eyes scanning the roomy stable for anything that could aid her escape. She was impressed by the golden stallion, Iolair, and would have dearly loved to have stolen the magnificent animal from under the Campbell's arrogant nose. But she had ruefully conceded that it would have looked too suspicious for a ragged stable urchin to be mounted on such superb horseflesh. She had finally selected a roan mare that seemed fleet but inconspicuous and whose stall was conveniently located by the door. She had also discovered a row of hooks where several roomy saddlebags and dusty capes hung forgotten. At the thought of Sian, Kat's eyes filled with tears. It had nearly broken her heart to leave him behind, abandoning him to the Campbell's cruelty. But she had no recourse—her wounded hound could not keep pace with the fleetfooted mare.

"I promise I shall find a way to return for you," she had wept hours before dawn, as she had put her plan into action. She had bound Sian's jaws securely shut so that his grieving howls would not awaken the sleeping household. Then, without a backward glance, she had ridden the mare slowly into the cobbled courtyard, feeling the blanket-wrapped hooves jar her senses. Each step was leaden, a deadly thump that joined with her pulse. She had slowly edged the horse along the shadows, avoiding the bluish patches of icy moonlight, expecting at any second to hear a warning cry. Her knees ached, and her hands were tightly wound in the stringy mane. She rode bareback, for fear that leather would creak in the still silence and alert the household.

She was free and must look ahead, she firmly told herself, trying to expel her misery and urge the mare into a brisk canter. She had plenty of money, which she had methodically stolen a little at a time from the Campbell's discarded clothes each night when he lay blissfully sleeping. She was also well armed, and she felt the dueling pistols at her waist. She had nothing with which to load and prime them, but she comforted herself with the thought that there weren't many people stupid enough to question a cocked pistol.

Terrible visions of what she would find at Linnmanach tortured her. She imagined everyone dead; she recalled her first glimpse of the crumbling gray manse: its dark, hollow windows and the ravens roosting in the dusty rooms, the scrape of rodents' feet on the marble floors, and the graves in the ruins of the monastery beside the somber waters of the loch that reflected the dolorous clouds.

At a bone-wearying gait, she rode without stopping past Linlithgow until she reached the outskirts of Falkirk. The sun was low in the sky, and a drizzle misted down, inexorably soaking through her woollen cape and homespun clothes until she was chilled to the bone. Beside her walked women and children, their thin faces soiled from the darkness of the coal and iron mines, their bodies stunted from long hours crawling through the cramped shafts. There was an eeriness about the sound of feet dragging through the wet sucking mud. Kat felt a melancholy harmony with the fatigued masses. Unable to ride above those bowed heads, she slid off the mare's back and walked beside the miners. Cold rain furrowed their masklike faces, streaking the hollow cheeks with melted coal dust. Kat was appalled to see terrible burns on the frail limbs of tiny children no older than five or six. She wanted to reach down and set them upon her horse's back, but she was deterred by their grim stoicism. They trudged past long rows of anonymous houses, their rhythmic plodding broken by the sharp slamming of doors. The dull wet dusk was pierced by brief glimpses of warm kitchens, and then Kat left the town and walked alone, looking for an isolated barn.

Kat rode through the pitch-black night, her head bowed against the driving rain, knowing the horse was in need of rest. The poor animal shuddered beneath her, echoing her own violent shivers. There was no sign of shelter, and she wished

she had sought cover in one of the miner's cottages in the war-
renlike back streets of Falkirk. The raucous sounds of
drunken voices rang through the drumming rain, and bars of
golden lamplight splintered the shining darkness. She edged
the mare furtively toward the roadhouse, keeping close to the
stone wall that surrounded the adjacent farmyard. The odors
of pigs and stale spirits replaced the sweet scent of wet earth,
and she reined in the exhausted animal. She stared with
dismay at one of the unsavory posting inns where she and her
father had spent the night on their way to Comyn Square.

Summoning her courage, Kat dismounted and boldly led the
trembling mare into the shelter of the stables.

"Och, laddie, thee look as *drookèd* as a drowned rat,"
chortled a wizened little man, leaping spryly from the shadows
with a lantern in hand. Kat recoiled from his rank stench.
"Och, if'n it isna the green-eyed sprout from several weeks
past!" he exclaimed, lifting the flickering light to see her better. "Where's the fat fancy mon, boy? I ken more'n seven
guid, hard-working *gillies* who'd sell their sainted grand-
mithers just to lay hands on the *swicky mucker* who cheated
them of their coin."

Kat looked at the open door and saw the rain lashing
through the inhospitable darkness. She was debating what to
do when a gnarled hand shot out and grasped the mane of the
shuddering mare.

"Och, this puir *sholtie*'ll nae last twenty paces. She's
spent," the man cackled gleefully. "Try it, laddie. There's a
howff fu' of drinking men who'd catch thee afore thee cleared
the yard."

"I dinna cheat anyone," stated Kat, standing with her feet
astride and feigning a bravado she didn't feel.

"Aye, but a mon is known by the company he keeps." The
ostler chortled, thoroughly enjoying himself. "Now, where is
the fat *mucker?*"

"Dead," spat Kat.

"Och, now, tha's a pity. Who's going to gie the puir *billies*
back their coin?"

"I dinna ken, but I'm willing to pay you for sheltering me
and my horse."

"Och, thee hae thy pockets well lined, hae thee?"

"I hae a few pence," lied Kat, relieved that she had had the foresight to separate her money, hiding most of it in the hose beneath her high boots.

"Show thy coin?" he challenged with disbelief. Kat dug deeply into her pocket, withdrawing several pennies. She deliberately dropped several more; they rolled into the straw. The wizened man's eyes widened greedily. It was more money than he earned in a month. "Gie it to me!"

"But 'tis all I hae," whined Kat, holding her hand out and allowing him to scrape the coins from her palm. She watched him scramble about on the floor for the rest. "Leave me a penny?" she whimpered piteously. Instead, the grasping man slapped her pockets, feeling for more.

"Six pence, two hae' pennies, and three farthings," he rejoiced, carefully tying his precious hoard in a grubby handkerchief.

"A hae' penny?" Kat pleaded.

"Here, rub tha' puir shivering lump of horsemeat doon wie this," answered the groom, shoving several hemp sacks at her. "And take her way doon yonder behind the hay bales so the publican doesna find her when he makes his rounds, for if'n thee is found I'll claim no knowledge," he gurgled, pulling a battered flask from his ragged coat and taking a long swallow. "Here, laddie, tak' a healthy swig, 'twill warm thy bluid a wee bit."

Kat reluctantly accepted the offered flask, hoping the cheap spirits would afford some warmth. The groom's slack mouth leered; his teeth were broken and black, and she carefully wiped the rim before throwing her head back and recklessly pouring the amber liquid down her throat.

"Whoa! Laddie, tha' has to last me the night," he protested, snatching his flask back. "Prissy wee thing, ent you?" he added, mocking her by wiping the rim in exaggerated imitation before taking another swallow.

Kat led the exhausted mare deep into the comparative warmth of the drafty stable. The chortling old groom followed and agilely hauled himself up onto the piled bales of hay. He sat there, one thin bandy leg swinging along with the lantern, which he had hung on a rusty nail. Kat longed to remove her heavy sodden cape. She was afraid of what she would expose to the wily groom's eyes. She energetically scrubbed the shivering horse with the coarse dry sacking, hoping that this strenuous exercise would also warm her own frozen limbs.

"How did the fat, *swicky mucker* die?"

"He was shot," Kat answered shortly, loath to discuss her father's death with this man. But she knew that she should make an attempt at civility, lest he throw out her and her horse before they could regain their strength.

"By a mon he was trying to cheat?"

"Aye." She sighed wearily. Her arms ached, but she continued to scour the poor horse until steam rose from the damp hide. Then she covered her with dry sacks. "Is there water and feed?" she asked hesitantly.

"Where's your coin?" he chuckled, opening and shutting his gnarled hand.

"But I gave you all I had," she pleaded. After a long moment while the groom sucked pensively through his broken teeth, he gestured toward a trough and some bins. Kat gaped with disgust at the slimy green water and the dry chaff that was liberally mixed with rat droppings.

"Dinna turn yer snout up, this ent Holyroodhoose, so ye can take it or leave it," snarled the man. "And keep yer mouth shut and the nag well hidden," he hissed, hearing the sharp clop of hooves and a low rumble of voices approaching. He unhooked his light and agilely leaped off the bales. "I'll be right with thee, sirs," he called loudly, prancing toward the door. The lantern swinging in his hand caused ghostly shadows to snake through the dusty recesses of the cobwebbed rafters before it left Kat in welcome darkness.

Relieved to be free of the man's rank presence, Kat thankfully removed the saturated cape and blindly felt about until she located a plow handle. She hung it up to shed a little of its moisture, knowing that there was no way it would be dry by the morning. Then she wrapped the remaining dry sack about herself and burrowed into the prickly hay, determined to ignore the hungry rumbles of her aching stomach. Although exhausted, sleep eluded her, and she lay listening to the voices drunkenly singing and laughing in the taproom. They mingled with the driving rain that drummed against the roof and the sodden earth. Several leaks plinked into full buckets and against various surfaces, causing a discordant rhythm.

For some inexplicable reason, she was reminded of the graceful spinet in the Campbell's house that she had so pointedly disregarded for several days. Kat had finally seated herself on its bench, but it had taken several minutes to summon up courage to lift the lid. It had been nearly an hour before she dared to touch the keys. To her surprise, the instrument had been in perfect tune. She had felt the tears that flooded her face as she played one of her mother's favorite pieces, a Bach fugue, but she had been unaware of her silent audience until he had seated himself beside her, his large brown hands looking incongruous on the delicate keyboard.

Kat thrust the disturbing recollection from her mind and turned restlessly in the straw. She didn't want to recall anything gentle about the dark, domineering Campbell. She hated him. He was cruel and barbaric. In fact, he was everything she had been taught about the race of Diarmid. It was just a cynical twist of fate that had given such a monster a magically tender touch. She coiled into a tight ball, trying to get warm and comfortable, but the haunting Bach fugue played in her head. Its moving melody had been created by the caressing fingertips of the Campbell . . . caressing fingertips that had played her as expertly as he had played the spinet. Kat fell asleep with angry tears on her cheeks.

A foul smell enveloped her, and prying hands painfully pinched her. Kat struggled through layers of sleep and finally opened her eyes to the horror of a leering face and fingers cruelly squeezing her breasts.

"Why, thee ent a lad at all," cackled the groom, his fetid breath causing her stomach to heave. She kept her knees protectively drawn up to her waist as she furtively felt for a pistol that she had hidden in the hay beside her.

"Halloo? Is there an ostler here?" Calum MacKissock's distinctive gruff tones echoed through the stable, and Kat's groggy brain wasn't sure if she was in the middle of a horrible nightmare. The groom's greedy hands slid reluctantly off her breasts. A wave of revulsion flooded through her as the wet slack lips grazed the side of her mouth.

"I'll nae be long, my sweetie, and then we'll hae ourselves a lusty tumble." He giggled, scrambling out of the hay and patting the front of his britches lewdly. "I'll be right wie you, sirs!" he shouted, taking up his lantern and prancing away.

"Nae too many travelers about tonight," remarked Calum, looking at the empty stalls and the three sorry-looking wet nags.

"T'ent a guid night," the ostler agreed impatiently, eager to return to the warm, sleepy girl.

"I want these animals well rubbed down, watered, and fed—and ready for the road within the hour."

"Within the hour?" the old groom echoed with dismay.

"Aye."

"But it ent a fit night for mon nor beast."

"Within the hour, or my master will hae something to say," threatened Calum, striding out of the stable, desiring a warming dram and a hearty dinner.

"Within the hour or my maister'll hae something to say," the old man imitated derisively.

Kat listened to this exchange as she hastily tucked the pistols back into the waistband of her trews and slung the heavy, sodden cape about her thin shoulders. She stealthily crept around the hay bales and watched the bandy-legged little man leading Calum's horse and the Campbell's majestic Iolair into adjacent stalls. She frantically debated what to do. If only the repulsive groom hadn't discovered her sex; then the decision would have been simple. She would have let the Campbell ride on, and she and the mare would have benefited from a night's rest. But now that was out of the question. Even if she evaded the Campbell's clutches, she still had the lecherous groom to contend with—and a mare that was too spent to be useful.

Kat gazed speculatively at Iolair's lustrous golden coat. Despite the heavy rain, it shone richly in the dim lantern light. The spirited stallion seemed hardly winded. He pawed the packed-dirt floor impatiently, tossing his large head at the rancid-smelling groom, who muttered all manner of foul curses. If Kat acted swiftly, she would have nearly an hour's start, she planned. She held one of the pistols by its engraved barrel and edged around the bales. She was about to hit the man on the back of the head when she nearly lost her nerve, but the memory of his pinching fingers and putrid, rotting teeth gave her courage. She knocked him senseless, and he sprawled in the filthy muck on the floor. The terrible sound of the blow caused her to drop the weapon and stand for several moments in appalled shock while she fought off nausea. With great effort, she pulled her ragged thoughts together; while her heart hammered wildly, she untethered the horses. Her hands shook with fear and cold, but she managed to undo all the wet knots and release the stiff latches on the stalls. She saved Iolair for last. Quickly, she uncinched the wet saddle, knowing she had no time to readjust the stirrups that were fitted for the Campbell's long legs. She led the huge horse to a mounting block. She clambered upon Iolair's high back and, holding a whip that she found, rode the magnificent stallion out of the stable, herding the rest of the horses before her.

Kat was certain that the clattering of hooves on the slick cobblestones and the protesting whinnies of the horses, which preferred the shelter of the dirty stables, would bring a rush of roaring men from the posting inn. To her surprise, the raucous voices continued to laugh and sing without pause. She ushered her small herd through the darkness, until the rowdy tavern sounds were muffled by distance and the relentless rain. Then she cracked her whip and screamed to disperse the other steeds. Iolair pranced and reared, unaccustomed to the strange lightness of his small rider, but Kat hung on, trying to soothe him through her chattering teeth. Soon he accepted her and settled into a rhythmic gallop, easily overtaking the other four horses.

Darach stretched out his long legs before the roaring hearth, idly watching the steam rising from the wet capes draped around it. He breathed in the bouquet of the brandy, holding the snifter between his fingers.

"This *howff* is filthier than a pigsty," complained Calum. "A mon could draw a picture in the muck and grease upon this table," he grumbled. He scrubbed his elbows as though he was permanently soiled. "I couldna eat a morsel for fear of catching some foul disease," he continued, peering suspiciously into his whiskey glass.

"Plain bread and cheese washed down wie spirits canna harm you," Darach remarked, irritated by his steward's gripes. These had been as constant as the rain throughout the grueling, drizzling day. He sorely wished he had left the carping man back in Edinburgh.

"Bread and cheese willna warm my innards after thirty miles wie nary a stop. She couldna hae come this far on tha' wee mare in this coarse weather. I think we maun hae lost her about Falkirk."

"She was seen," Darach snapped savagely. He did not want

to consider that possibility. However, anxiety gnawed at him.
He had not entertained the remote prospect of the small female eluding him.

"Aye, at least five miles back in Falkirk!"

"Aye, but this side of Falkirk on the Stirling road," he
stressed, trying to convince himself that he was right. He stood
up. "Are you certain that the roan mare wasna in the
stables?"

"Aye, as I've said before many times, there wasna but
aboot four other nags. And none in the taproom had seen hide
nor hair of any green-eyed lad—and, for tha' matter, no lads
at all," repeated Calum. "And I'll no ask more or they'll be
supposing me *gowkèd*, and will cart me off to the nearest
asylum!"

A sudden furious bellow interrupted the drunken revelry,
and the house shook with violence, rattling the dusty tankards
and the pictures that cluttered the walls, dislodging greasy
cobwebs and sooty grit. Darach silently motioned for Calum
to investigate, glad of the excuse to rid himself of his irksome
presence. With an exasperated snort, the burly man sullenly
obeyed, knowing not to argue with his master whenever a certain expression hardened those handsome chiseled features.

Darach paced back and forth before the crackling hearth,
trying to rid himself of the terror that ate into his gut. Everywhere he looked, he saw a small poignant face, the eyes filled
with pain and confusion. The image tore into his very soul.

"Somebody has stolen all the horses and nearly kilt the
groom," gasped Calum, hardly waiting to get into the room
before imparting the news. "And the worst of it is this," he
added, hastily closing the door. He showed Darach the distinctive dueling pistol with the battle scenes of Killiecrankie and
Dunkeld engraved upon the barrel and butt.

Darach silently took the weapon, noting the blood that
still stuck to the handle. "Was there a struggle?" he asked
hoarsely. He imagined Kat cornered and finding the weapon
useless.

"Nay, 'twould seem she coldbloodedly attacked the puir
auld mon from behind. 'Tis doubtfu' he'll live. Puir little
mon's skull is near crushed—like an eggshell," Calum exaggerated. "I dinna ken why I troubled to conceal the pistol
from the crowd—except to protect yourself."

"Silence!" snapped Darach. His rage and fear flowered.

"Iolair is stolen, too," Calum dared to say, deriving great satisfaction in stating this news. For it proved without a doubt how very right he had been about the mysterious ragged urchin.

"I am warning you, MacKissock!" thundered the Campbell, thrusting his gloating steward out of the way and striding into the public saloon. Here, infuriated men clustered, drunkenly vying with one another over the most horrendous punishment for the horse thief.

"Five hundred crowns for a horse within a quarter of an hour!" the Campbell offered in ringing tones. He didn't have to weaken his position by repeating the offer; his commanding voice and magnetic presence silenced the rowdy throng.

"Five hundred crowns for a horse?"

"Just any old horse?"

"What about my horse?"

"The *best* horse," Calum corrected, pompously taking over, knowing his young master would not repeat himself. Suddenly, there was a burst of energy as everyone tried to be first through the door. Each was determined to earn the fortune of a lifetime on that miserable night.

Within twenty minutes, at least a dozen horses invaded the cold air, their hooves rattling on the slippery cobblestones, their warm coats steaming in the frigid rain. Darach's experienced eye traveled down the line of sway-backed nags and spavined cobs, finally alighting on a gleaming black stallion whose proudly held head reminded him of Kat's innate dignity. The gracefully arched neck and ebony mane were the equine epitome of the defiant, jet-haired girl. The thought of those distrustful but intelligent eyes seared through him, causing him inexplicable pain. The vital young animal pranced sideways, and Darach knew without a doubt that his ownership of the untamed beast was destined—just like his marriage to the wild green-eyed female.

Darach cursed the bucking horse, who was trying to dislodge the strange, heavy weight. It was apparent that the stallion hadn't even been broken to a saddle, let alone the burden of a full-grown man. He laughed ironically, realizing the similarities between this beast and his spirited wife, as he fought to dominate the animal. Their progress along the Stirling road was questionable as the skittish young horse refused to be guided. It reared and screamed in the dark, wet silence of the lonely countryside, rashly endangering its own life by bucking near hedgerows and ditches, trying to unseat the indomitable Campbell.

Calum sighed and shook his head, watching his young master disappear into the inhospitable darkness on the devilish black stallion.

"Clavan," the happy peasant chortled, stowing the heavy leather bag of gold coins next to his heart. He grasped his staff firmly, for fear that someone would try to rob him.

"Clavan?" Calum echoed with dismay. He was met with a great roar of merriment. "Clavan?"

"Aye, Clavan Dubh." The publican chuckled, pretending to clean a tankard with a greasy, stained rag. "Black Buzzard," he cheerfully translated. "Chakie Hendricks, he bin trying to sell tha' de'il horse for two years now."

"Aye, 'tis the Nuckelavee—the fairy horse of the sea from the Orkneys wie his fiery eye and poisonous breath."

"Aye, or 'tis Each Uisge, the Highland water demon who'll wash your master's liver to shore in the morn," another man wheezed.

"Aye, now the Unseelie Court will catch him. The host of the Unblessed Court will descend as thick as crows and pluck your young master off the back of the Nuckelavee and take him to their wicked queen. They'll suck his seed to sire the changeling babes."

"Enough of this ignorant *stite!*" roared Calum, unnerved by the long shadows of the isolated tavern and the dire warnings of the superstitious country folk.

"Aye, 'twas not a mere mortal," groaned the bandy-legged groom, cradling his aching head, and unable to admit being bested by a small girl. "One minute it was a wee laddie, and the next a beguiling woman. And then a terrible, *meikle* monster wie fire snorting from his snout," he embellished. "And eyes as green as evil."

"Black Annis," gasped a quaking little man. "Did she have a blue face?"

"Aye," the groom lied. The clustered men dolefully shook their heads and pressed closer to one another. "Bright blue," he stressed.

"Who's Black Annis?" Calum asked with a sneer, determined not to be frightened.

"An English witch from Leicestershire who eats people. She

can change from a beautiful, innocent maiden to an ugly hag within the twinkling of an eye.''

"Och, and wha's an English witch doing so far from home? Dinna you think she has enough mischief to do wie the *sassanach muckers* in her own country?'' scoffed Calum.

"Well, maybe her face wasna blue,'' amended the groom. "But green was aboot. Bright, evil, fairy-green, and she changed shapes from a sweet, pretty thing into an ugly *cailleach*, nearly splitting my skull wie her little finger,'' he lied, trying to sway the suspicious men, who stared with disbelief. "Well, look at my head, will thee?'' he offered. "And did any of thee find a weapon?'' he challenged.

"Nay,'' the men muttered, looking from one to another and then to the man's bald pate.

"There be something writ on thy head!'' exclaimed one of the men, and the awed mob jostled each other to see the groom's battered skull.

"Aye, but 'tis pictures!''

"Kilted men and horses!''

"Och, 'tis the de'il's work and no mistake.''

Calum rolled his eyes heavenward, giving thanks that his master had taken the incriminating weapon with him. The farm laborers clustered about the groom, quaking with trepidation at the battle scene of Killiecrankie that was imprinted on the shining bald head. Calum sighed and tried to get comfortable on the hard settle by the hearth, happy that he wasn't the Campbell on that wild steed, galloping behind the green-eyed little witch who could quite possibly turn out to be a glaistig, *urisk,* or other evil host of the Unseelie Court. He drifted off to sleep, lulled by the intense, low rumble of voices, but he awoke less than an hour later, as a furious pounding painfully jarred his head. He sat up and stared blearily about at men who were frantically hammering. They were fashioning rude crosses to protect them on their way home across the fields in the pitch-blackness.

chapter 10

The rain had mercifully stopped, and long rays streaked the eastern horizon. Crystal drops sparkled, trembling precariously on the tips of dead grasses and stark boughs. Kat reined the weary stallion on the crest of a steep hill by a stand of pines, their lush branches sagging low with the weight of moisture. Breathing the heady resinous fragrance, Kat stared behind her at the gray ribbon of road that wended through the fallow fields below. She frowned, observing a fleeting, almost imperceptible, movement under the mist that hung over the valley. She strained her tired eyes, wondering if her fatigued mind was playing tricks. All through the interminable night, as the stallion had carefully picked his way, she had sensed that someone—or something—was relentlessly dogging their heels. But each time she had listened, she could only hear the pounding of the rain and her heart, in the impenetrable blackness. Kat sighed and gazed down regretfully at the tempting barns. She imagined the mounds of warm, dry hay and reluctantly turned away, satisfied that she and the birds were the only creatures around. But, again, something caught her eye. A bright spark of gleaming jet flashed through the film of low-hanging clouds, and Kat tried not to blink as she waited for it to reappear. But the haze thickened, blanketing the lowland, leaving a suspended stillness.

"It must have been a solitary raven or crow," she remarked aloud, kneeing Iolair forward. "Soon we'll rest," she comforted him. She felt guilty about the patient animal who had carried her all night without rest while she had dozed, soothed by the steady gait. "But where can we rest?" she fretted, knowing it would be dangerous for her to be seen riding the spectacular stallion. Visions of being roughly hauled off the magnificent animal and accused of horse stealing tortured her fevered mind. She had to hide by day and travel to Linn-manach under the cover of night. Kat felt dizzy, not having eaten since leaving Edinburgh more than two nights and a day before. She had hoped to find a few morsels along the way, but the dormant winter fields were barren. Not even a nibble of grass for the hungry stallion peeked through the soil by the thorny hedgerows. "I'm so sorry, Iolair," she whispered, stretching forward along the animal's arched neck and burying her small nose in the cool dampness of the mane. She was so cold, yet her head seemed on fire. She closed her burning eyes, trying to calm her swirling thoughts, reminding herself that she only had another twenty miles to go. "We can last until then," she stated. She took a deep breath and straightened herself; she sat proud and tall on the high bare back of the noble horse. Her hands looked blue, and she wound them through the stallion's golden mane, unable to flex her numb fingers. She wished the cruel icy wind would stop. It plastered her drenched clothes to her shivering, aching body.

Darach stared up the steep hill and saw the telltale glint of the morning sun on Iolair's lustrous hide. He had followed Kat all night through the driving rain, awed by her stubborn resiliency. Yet he had wished she would stop and take cover for all their sakes. They had ridden past Stirling and Bannock-burn, through the Windy Pass, and past the Burn of Sorrow and the Burn of Care. They had been unable to see the historic scenery in the thick, wet darkness, unable to see the desolate charred stones of the ruined Castle Campbell that had been razed by Cromwell's troops a century before. Darach had snorted with irony, knowing his rebellious wife would have derived great satisfaction at seeing the burned shell of one of his clan's great houses.

Reckoning that Kat was too fatigued to speed away, Darach decided he could afford to feed and water himself and the young stallion. He dismounted at one of the inviting barns that the girl had so stoically resisted and entered its dim interior, glad to be out of the wind. Half an hour later, warm and comfortable in dry clothes, the edge of his hunger dulled by bread and cheese thoughtfully packed by Calum, he remounted the refreshed horse and rode up the steep hill. At the crest, he scanned the road that stretched before him. He was able to see several miles, now that the sun had risen high enough to burn off much of the morning mist. Seeing no sign of his quarry, he urged his mount into a canter. He scowled at the density of the woods on either side, hoping that Kat hadn't taken shelter. He leaned out of his saddle, sharply scrutinizing the wet earth, seeking a sign of Iolair's large hooves before the busy traffic between Stirling and Perth obliterated all clues.

Kat rode through the forest, hunched against the icy drops that fell methodically from the trees and sizzled sharply on her prickly, hot skin. There seemed to be a strange red film veiling her vision, hampering her search for a dry sheltered place to spend the daylight hours. Everywhere she looked was dark and dank—or flaring with icy blades.

Kat's head ached unbearably. She struggled to cling to her sanity and stay balanced on the animal's vast back. Her legs were heavy and leaden, unable to bend, and her numb fingers clutched at the air, unable to find a hold. Iolair sensed his young rider's weakness and slowly reduced his pace until he came to a standstill in a small glen. Kat fought to focus her burning eyes, but everything spun into whooshing mass, sucking her in until she sagged and toppled to the ground, cracking her head against a jagged rock. The golden stallion stood protectively over the small inert body, shielding her from the piercing wind that savagely whipped the trees, spraying sheets of frigid water across her seemingly lifeless form.

Once Darach located the distinct track in the muddy bank leading into the forest, he had no trouble following the trail through the thick carpet of disturbed wet leaves. Taking his time, he weaved in and out of the trees, enjoying the serene stillness and clean fragrance. A shrill, terrified whinny split the tranquillity, and a frightened flock of rooks burst clamorously against the pale sky, forsaking their clutter of nests in the bare tips of the swaying trees.

Darach reined in the skittish black stallion, who sidestepped nervously, spooked by the cawing birds and high-pitched neigh. Darach fought furiously to control the lunging animal, whose unshod hooves slithered in the decaying leaves. He tried to locate the direction of the sound. He recognized Iolair's warning cry, but it reverberated teasingly off the surrounding tree trunks, spiraling into a muted mocking around them. Hearing a frantic thrashing in the distance, he urged his mount forward. Loud guttural snarls and sharp yelps of pain rent the dripping pall of the sodden forest, and Darach dug his heels into the sweating girth and galloped toward the violent clamor.

In a small clearing, the golden stallion reared, his top lip displaying menacing teeth, his blood-chilling screams threatening a pack of skulking curs that were torn between near starvation and cringing cowardice. The wretched creatures' bones were clearly visible through their mangy fur, as they tried to slink past the slashing hooves to snap at the limp figure of the girl. A sharp report shattered the wet woods and echoed off the encircling mountains, as Darach shot the largest of the pack. Before the unfortunate dog had stopped twitching, it was being devoured by its ravenous companions.

Kat battled the groom's pinching hands, and she tossed her aching head from side to side to avoid his slack, fetid mouth, which threatened to suck her life's breath. Every inch of her body was being attacked by the man's sharp nails, her skin painfully raked as he searched for money. She kicked and punched, defending herself against the invading fingers that pried her legs apart and wrenched the boots off her aching limbs. She heard the splatter of heavy coins, and she screamed every insulting, foul word she knew in French, Gaelic, and English.

"Och, tha' wee-an certainly has an awesome command of languages," a white-haired man remarked dryly.

"Uncle Angus, I would appreciate it if you'd save your observations for later," hissed Darach, through gritted teeth, as he struggled to remove the sodden clothes from the cursing, writhing figure. "Where's the hot bath and dry blankets I asked for?" he roared impatiently, as a sharp fist hit his nose and a foot savagely struck his stomach.

"Dinna *fash*, young Campbell. Your wee page'll be well attended by my servants."

" 'Tis not my page, but my wife!''

All traces of benign amusement were wiped off Angus Campbell's face.

"Did I hear correctly?" he barked after a stunned pause, his eyes pinned to the thrashing girl, who now was bared to the waist.

"Aye, so I'd also appreciate it if you'd avert your gaze from my wife's breasts." A wave of possessive jealousy flooded through Darach. "Where the hell are those servants?" he bellowed, peeling tight britches down the wildly kicking legs and then rolling the naked girl into the only available blanket. "Did you send for the doctor, as I asked?" he ranted, frowning at the blood that stained the white pillow from the wound on Kat's head and worried by the heat that pulsed through her dry, flushed skin.

"Aye, the doctor's been sent for, but from tha' amount of energy tha' sma' filly is exhibiting, I dinna think she's in danger of expiring," Angus answered wryly. Undeterred by his nephew's curt manner, he strode to the bed, intent on satisfying himself about his newly acquired niece. He stilled the wildly tossing mane of ebony hair by firmly cupping the hot little face and scrutinizing its delicate features. The aristocratic, small nose flared with panic, and pearly teeth were bared in a feral snarl. But it was the thickly lashed, bright green eyes, glazed and ferociously glaring, that caused him to catch his breath.

"Filthy *sassanach!* Stinking pig!" spat Kat, fighting the lecherous groom who'd magically grown another pair of hands. *"Scunnering muc! Nathair!"* she continued in Gaelic. *"Bâtard! Puant salaud!"* she finished weakly in French.

"Who is this fluent linguist?" probed the tall white-haired man. He kept his hold on the spitting face of the girl, who was pinned across Darach's muscular thighs.

"My wife."

"You ken my meaning, lad."

"Aye." Darach sighed. "But the truth is, Uncle Angus, I dinna ken save the name Kat or Katriona," he admitted wearily.

"Or Katrine," muttered the older man, and he nodded sagely, noting the panic that froze the delirious movements.

"Katrine?" puzzled Darach, feeling the tension tremble

through the burning body that he cradled in his arms.

"It would seem there's much to discuss, but now isna the time," Angus murmured, releasing the soft, hot cheek and making himself comfortable in an easy chair. A stream of servants bustled into the room laden with buckets, basins, towels, and blankets. He was intrigued by the uncharacteristic behavior of his usually cynical, harsh nephew. The young man's stern features were set on their usual ruthless lines, but the large brown hands unconsciously caressed the curves of the captive female.

"Do you honestly propose to sit over there swilling your spirits and watching me tend the lass wie that smug smirk on your face?" Darach challenged when the last of the servants had left.

"Aye," Angus replied, after taking a savoring sip of rare old whiskey. " 'Tis not every day that a mon has the wondrous opportunity to witness Sir Darach Dugald Campbell, Lord of Strathrannoch and Glengrian, playing nursemaid to a ragged chit. Are you quite sure you'll not leave such mundane ministrations to the housekeeper and maids?" he mocked. "Are you in love wie tha' naked wench?" he asked sharply, after his brooding nephew refused to answer.

"Dinna be ridiculous!" scoffed Darach.

"Ridiculous?"

"This naked wench is the only key to Riach's whereabouts," Darach said harshly. He was grimly satisfied to see the amusement drain from his uncle's face.

"Are you sure the puir lad is still alive?" probed Angus after a long silence. He had taken another punishing swallow of the burning spirits and shrewdly noted how the brooding man absently twirled a glossy tress about his finger.

"Nay!" snapped Darach, turning his attention to Kat, who was shaking with violent tremors. "I dinna ken whether to put her in a hot bath or a cold one," he added anxiously, as her teeth chattered with cold while her skin burned with a crackling dry heat.

"Set her 'neath the covers in the bed, pour yourself a few drams, and wait for the doctor," Angus suggested. "Or, better still, let's retire to more comfortable surroundings where you can inform me just what the hell is happening."

"I'll not leave her unattended," Darach stated curtly.

"She's not going anywhere."

"She's unpredictable and could be gone before you know it."

"Nae in tha' condition, she won't."

"Uncle Angus, you dinna ken this untamed wildcat," sighed Darach. "But pour me a few drams."

Kat struggled desperately to comprehend the voices through the painful pounding of her head. She sensed danger—no longer from the black-toothed groom, but from the silver-haired man he had magically become. A tall unknown figure who smelled of heather and whiskey, who had held her cheeks in strong, cool fingers, who had pronounced the forbidden name "Katrine." The Campbell's deep voice reverberated through her shaking body, and she smelled the safety of his masculine fragrance. Urgently, she tried to curl into the protective hardness of his chest, but suddenly she was cast aside, cruelly rejected and shoved between icy sheets that stung her throbbing skin. She moaned as pain knifed through her joints. Then she screamed and battled the demons who twisted pointed instruments through her eyes.

Angus and Darach dropped their drinks and leaped forward to the thrashing, screaming girl, who arched in agony, clawing at her head, reopening her deep wound. Blood poured between her fingers and streamed down her arms.

"Maman, je fais mal!" she cried. "I hurt too much!"

Darach opened and closed his mouth, unable to speak a comforting word, as aching emotion dammed his throat. He had never felt so helpless in all his life.

"Where in blazes is the doctor?" he roared impotent, trying to gather Kat into his arms. But it seemed that his very touch caused unbearable agony.

"Papa, je regrette! Absous-moi, papa?" she asked, sobbing. "I promise I will obey you in all ways. Please forgive me!" she continued, backing away from the terrible sight of Macaree's broken, bleeding body. "I'll never, never disobey again! *Jamais, papa, jamais!"*

"Hush, *ma petite,"* Darach crooned, and his uncle's thick white eyebrows rose quizzically at the uncharacteristic tenderness.

"Absous-moi?" begged Kat before lapsing into merciful unconsciousness.

"Absolve me?" queried Angus. "And just what sins is tha'

wee de'il guilty of tha' she pleads so passionately for absolution? And what sort of father inspires such fearful fervency?"

"Not a very loving one, it would seem," muttered Darach, sharply recalling Rory MacNiall's spiteful dying words. "Where the hell is the doctor?"

"Would seem he has arrived," Angus remarked, hearing the clatter of feet in the stone corridor outside.

Angus Campbell lounged comfortably in a chair by the roaring hearth, calmly sipping his whiskey and idly watching his tall, dark nephew. Darach observed the doctor intently.

"Nay, no leeches or cuppings!" Darach protested violently.

"She needs to be bled."

"Och, you're no doctor but a blood-sucking parasite!"

"Sir Angus?" whined the offended man.

"Dinna address me. 'Tis Lord Rannoch's wife, nae mine." Angus laughed.

"Get out of here!" roared Darach, and the terrified man hastily scrambled to collect his paraphernalia together and then scurried away. "Uncle Angus, I canna believe that you of all people would countenance such practices," he ranted.

"Wait a minute! It wasna me but you, Darach Campbell, who demanded a doctor. I myself hae no use whatever for the miserable profession. I use the *auld* ways and hae sent word to Cailleach Cuilleann, who lives in the forest on the eastern slope of Ben Vorlich," returned the elderly man. "Stop pacing aboot like a silly goose. Seat yourself. The lass is free of pain for the moment and canna appreciate your fretting."

"Cailleach Cuilleann?" mused Darach, ignoring his mischievous uncle's goading and pouring himself a dram. "Hag Holly. I have not thought of her for years. I maun have been no more than seven or eight. There was a mishap wie a falcon and my eye was gouged by a talon."

"And many including myself thought you'd been blinded, and here you are not even squinty-eyed." Angus chuckled fondly.

"I remember being blind for a very long time."

"At seven years old, a week can seem an eternity. Hag Holly conjured a powerful spell of natural herbs and sealed your lids shut. Your father and I, and your uncles Colin and John, were forced to stretch our brains devising ways to occupy your impatient hands so you wouldna tear the bandages before time," the white-haired man recalled. He was an older, more weathered version of the rangy Darach Campbell, who sipped his drink and gazed reflectively at the motionless girl dwarfed by the enormous bed. "Darach, dinna *fash*. Tha' wee wife of yours will be healed by Cailleach Cuilleann," he comforted hoarsely, secretly rejoicing that finally a woman had broken through his ruthless nephew's cynicism. Yet he was suspicious as to the girl's identity, but he decided to keep his suspicions to himself for now.

"Aye, she'd better be healed if we're ever to find my brother, Riach," the dark Scot stated harshly. "Now, what were you saying about Katrine?" he queried.

"Loch Katrine?" repeated Angus, pretending bewilderment. "I dinna recall mentioning one word aboot Loch Katrine, nor the hairy *urisks* tha' hide in the corries aboot the shore."

"I wasna speaking of hairy fairies or kelpies, and well you ken," snapped Darach. "You mentioned Katrine in reference to my wife."

"Och, did I, now?"

"Aye, you ken you did."

"I maun be getting *auld* and muddled in the gray matter," Angus sighed. "When did you last see your Uncle Colin, lad?" he asked innocently, trying to change the subject. Darach glowered at him, refusing to answer, but Angus wasn't fazed. He just raised his glass mockingly to his irate nephew and chuckled. "Och, you remind me of myself, boy. Except I was never so caught, but, then again, being the younger son, I dinna have the awesome duty tha' you have to produce an heir."

Darach was about to respond with a sarcastic remark when there was a cursory knock and a spry old woman was ushered into the room.

"Cailleach Cuilleann," Angus greeted, rising to his feet to welcome the strange little creature, who was draped in layers of gaily colored material, with bright ribbons and beads festooning her head, neck, and wrists.

"Och, Sir Angus, you grow bonnier each year, but 'tis no longer Black Angus, as your ebony hair has turned to silver. Aye, Angus-*dubh* maun gie way to Angus-*argent*," she chortled. "Och, but here's another *braw*, bonny mon wie hair to rival the raven's wing," she added, staring appreciatively at Darach.

"And you dinna ken this wee lad?" teased Angus.

"Why, 'tis the acorn grown into the fine oak. Strong and straight of limb. 'Tis the oak, Darach Campbell. Och, it has been many a year since I looked on you, and I am thrilled at the change," she gurgled, running her eyes approvingly over his tall, strong frame, ignoring the impatient gestures he made toward the bed. "Sad, I was, Sir Darach, to learn of your sire's passing, and also tha' of your puir Uncle John." She sighed sorrowfully. " 'Tis a crime agin nature and woman when such handsome, lusty men die so young."

"It is good to see—"

"Now, why am I here?" she interrupted, busily divesting herself of several layers of rainbow shawls. Darach pointed silently to the bed. "Who is she?" the hag demanded sharply, after a long look at Kat's fevered face. "Hair of the black Campbell. Fine bones of a Scottish *banrigh*," she murmured, tracing the high cheekbones and straight nose. "Is this your *nighean,* Sir Angus?"

"I have no daughters, as well you ken, Hag Holly," Angus retorted tersely.

"Can you be sure?" spat Darach, gazing with horror at his uncle.

"Aye, I can be very sure," the white-haired man stated bitterly. "Dinna *fash,* your wife isna your first cousin. I can never sire daughters or sons. Due to a childhood malady, there's no living seed in my loins."

"I dinna ken. I'm sorry," the younger man apologized.

"I'm nae impotent, so I dinna need your pity," Angus retorted angrily. "I'm as lusty a mon as I was a youth," he boasted.

"Go do your bragging in another room and leave me wie the lass," the hag ordered imperiously. "Both of you," she added when Darach stubbornly resisted.

"Come on, lad," coaxed Angus, but Darach was adamant.

"Then you set yourself over there and dinna make a peek!" spat Cailleach Cuilleann. "Not one peek, do ye ken?"

Darach sat quietly by the fire, watching and listening to the old woman, who scrambled about the room muttering long strings of curses as she threw handfuls of dried leaves, mosses,

and powders into a pot of boiling water. She hung it on a hook
over the flames in the hearth until the air was thick and steamy
with a sharp redolence that teared the eyes and stung the
nostrils.

"Soon, wee-an, soon . . . let the mullein, rue, and balsam
seep deep into your lungs to mix wie the saps of chrysanthe-
mum and hound's-tongue, while I brew valerian and jasmine
to calm your tortured dreams." She crooned this soothingly to
the restless girl, who whimpered and turned from side to side,
trying to dislodge the heavy blankets. "Let go your cares, wee
columan dubh," she chanted. "Let go your cares, little black
dove." But Kat shook her aching head furiously in an attempt
to rid it of the thick, aromatic mist that choked her nose and
mouth.

"No, I maun . . . I maun . . ." she muttered anxiously,
unable to think of what she had to do, then panicking at the
knowledge.

"Let go your cares, wee *columan dubh,* let go," intoned the
hag, and Kat thrashed more wildly, trying to break the hypnotic rhythm that lulled her fevered senses. "Och, my wee-an,
who has burdened you so wickedly?" she questioned, staring
accusingly at the stern face of the young man. "Come here,
Darach Campbell," she ordered sharply.

"Non! Tous les Campbell veulent dire mort a moi!"
screamed Kat, renewing her struggles.

"Wha' is she saying?" demanded Cailleach Cuilleann.
"Wha' tongue is tha'?"

"French," Darach snapped curtly, staring down at the
writhing figure under the mounds of covers.

"Dinna be so timid wie your wife! Lay agin her, sharing
your body's heat. Pin her doon wie your lusty thighs while I
brew an elixir to calm tha' puir hurting mind. And make sure
tha' moss poultice of comfrey, flax, and yarrow stays tight
aboot her head. 'T'will stem the bleeding and aid the healing
of tha' cruel wound," she chattered. Darach stretched himself
upon the bed and took the tossing girl into his strong arms.
"Aye, tha's the way. Maybe you're the remedy the wee black
dove needs, Darach . . . 'Tis said tha' bark of the *darach* is the
most powerful killer of pain. Aye, maybe I'll infuse some bark
of oak wie the jasmine and valerian—'twill gie the puir wee
lass some sorely needed tranquillity."

Angus Campbell cautiously popped his head around the

door and tried to stifle his coughs as he breathed the thick, spicy steam.

"Hag Holly?" he called chokingly, unable to see through the vapor.

"Close the door after you. I dinna want any of the spell to escape," she scolded impatiently. Angus sidled in and stood waving his arms, trying to part the mist and see the old woman. "Come close to the bed," she directed and he carefully felt his way. "Look at tha'!" she proclaimed reverently. He wiped his streaming eyes and tried to focus. "Like two innocent wee *bairns*," she crowed, gazing fondly at the sleeping couple.

Angus peered closely, flapping his large hands and holding his breath, unable to abide the noxious fumes.

"Are you sure they've nae been suffocated?" he gasped.

"Dinna blaspheme," the hag chided. Then she dragged him to the door.

"How is the lass?"

"Take me awa' from this smothering heat and pour me a few drams and I'll tell thee," she chortled, scurrying into the relative cool of the corridor and sagging against the stone wall. "Your nephew and his wee bride will nae be waking for hours," she informed him, answering the question that furrowed his brow. "Take me to your library. I always was partial to tha' fine chamber of learning wie all those words I canna read."

"Now, Cailleach Cuilleann, tell me of the dark lass," said Angus when he had poured them both generous portions of his finest old whiskey. The woman didn't answer for several minutes. She took a mouthful of the amber liquid and rolled it about her mouth before swallowing it with relish.

"Och, *usquebaugh.*" She sighed appreciatively. "The water of life."

"The dark lass?" probed Angus. The old woman ran her gnarled fingers longingly down the embossed spines of a neat row of books.

"And to think you can read all the knowledge contained within these covers," she marveled.

"I can, but I have nae," he snapped impatiently.

"Och, if I could've, I surely would've."

"Tell me of the lass."

"You tell me of the lass," the crone retorted.

"I canna," answered Angus. "My nephew arrived wie her just this very afternoon. All I ken is tha' they're mon and wife."

"Nay, you ken more," the woman accused shrewdly, after a long pause.

"I have nae had a moment alone wie Darach." He thought for a minute. "Well, will she live?" he added sarcastically.

"Aye, if she doesna snap in two wie the forces tha' tug her in separate ways!"

"I dinna ken."

"Och, you Campbells can be an overbearing, tyrannical lot, and tha' tiny lass is too young to be so burdened."

"I assure you, Cuilleann, I've had no dealings wie the girl. The lad arrived wie her this afternoon, and when I saw her sickness I sent straightaway for you."

"Hah! And tha' *swicky* doctor from Perth," derided the hag.

"That was Darach and his educated ways, but as soon as the mon talked of bleeding, the boy kicked him oot!"

"Gie me another dram," she ordered imperiously. " 'Tis as though the wee woman carried the weight of the world on her frail shoulders. And though weakened by the fever and tha' great blow to her head, she fights wie a determination unequaled by an army of Highland warriors. And what puzzles me is the great terror she has of the name Campbell, yet like a wild animal she sniffs the scent of her mate and curls submissively to him." Angus listened to the crone as he refilled their glasses. "Sir Angus, you maun trust me. I canna heal just half a body. You maun tell me wha' you ken," she wheedled.

Angus shook his shaggy mane of silver hair. "I dinna ken what to tell you." He sighed and took a long swallow of whiskey. "Do you ken Darach's half brother, Riach?" he finally asked gruffly.

"Spawn of the English *saidhe?*"

"I'd not liken Felicity to such a noble creature. Aye, Riach is that wretched woman's spawn, puir lad. He isna a bad lad, just a weak one, preferring to waste his time gaming, wenching, and causing all manner of petty mischief."

"What has Riach Campbell to do wie the dark lass?"

"The boy has been missing since last Christmas, and Darach claims his wife is the link to his disappearance," recounted Angus. "Dinna gie me that look, Hag Holly, tha's all I can tell you, and I am as eager to learn more as you are."

"But you hae some suspicions," the crone accused. "Och, you might be able to read all these wise books, Sir Angus, but I can read your face, you canny mon," she cackled.

"What do you think of her . . . looks?"

"You think she's a black Campbell wie tha' polished ebony hair?"

"Did you mark the color of her eyes?"

"Nay, the puir wee *bagrel* has them tight shut," replied the hag, before slurping her drink and leaning forward in her chair. "Are they as silver as yours and the lad's?"

"Nay, her eyes are as green . . . as green can possibly be," Angus growled, unable to find an adjective to describe the vivid color.

"Magical, fairy eyes," the old woman intoned.

"And Darach said her name was Kat, and when I mentioned the name Katrine, she became agitated."

"Och, you think her one of the host of the Unseelie Court!" exclaimed Cuilleann. "Why, tha' the most ridiculous *stite* I've ever heard! Tha' wee-an has nae a drop of evil within her!"

"Nay, tha's nae wha' am . . ."

"Tha' bonny lass is no *urisk* or *glaistig*! Aye, she might be as beautiful and as seductive as a *glaistig*, but there's no sign of the goat about her. And I saw her from the top of her head to the tips of her toes!" ranted the incensed crone.

"I'm nae implying the wench is a blood-sucking fairy or a Jenny Greenteeth, Kelpie, Bean-Nighe, or any other of the evil green hosts of the Unseelie Court," roared Angus.

"Wha' are you saying, then? For I'll hear no evil said of tha' wee *banrigh*."

"What is it aboot that skinny, wee scrap of woman that inspires such championing?" Angus probed after a long shocked pause. "You've barely met the ragged wench, and yet you call her 'wee *banrigh*'—little queen. Why?"

"I dinna ken wha' inspires me," the hag pondered. "Except she is so very brave—and alone."

"Solitary, like a Highland fairy," he teased, trying to lighten the atmosphere. "A solitary undine washing her blood-stained clothes in a mountain stream."

"Nay, solitary like a lost, frightened child. Solitary like a young doe in her first winter who maun protect her wee faun from the hungry snapping teeth of the world and from the spiteful, kicking hooves of her ain herd,'' she stated sorrowfully, refusing to be cajoled.

"Aye, that would mesh wie my suspicions."

"Which are . . . ?"

"I think she's a MacGregor," whispered Angus, looking about him to see that the door was tightly shut. "But dinna say a word to my nephew."

"A MacGregor? Tha' doesna make a peck of sense. Wha' hae green eyes and black hair to do wie being a MacGregor? Why, I've known them wie red hair and flaxen, wie blue eyes and brown, but never wie . . ." Hag Holly scoffed.

"There was but one, and somewhere there is a portrait. I dinna remember where, but I can see it in my mind's eye as clear as day."

"Black MacGregor?"

"Hush yourself. You ken the MacGregors are still proscribed," warned Angus.

"Och, just maybe I hae the sight, after all," the hag marveled gleefully. "You ken I called the wee lass *banrigh?*"

"You called her queen—so what, *auld cailleach?*"

"You dinna ken the motto of clan MacGrioghair?"

"Nay."

" 'S rioghal mo dhream,' " she quoted triumphantly.

"Royal is my race?" Angus chuckled derisively. "Ha! The MacGregors hae been nothing but common thieves and border raiders for the past hundred years or more!"

"Och, beware, you arrogant Campbell, persecution can make scavengers of us all," spat Cailleach Cuilleann. "Now I maun return to my wee charge. I'll send the lad to you. And you and he maun keep your distance, do you ken? I'll brook no interference until I hae healed and gained her trust."

"I dinna think my nephew'll take kindly to your bossiness, *auld* hag, and I canna speak for him. But, as for myself, I shall obey your orders." He jokingly bowed to her as he opened the door.

"If he wants a living wife, he'd better obey!" she snarled, whirling out in a swirl of rainbow shawls, ribbons, and clinking beads.

chapter 11

Angus attempted to ignore the tense ticking in the lean cheek of the stony profile, knowing very well at what the young man scowled so ferociously. It was the same every morn. Unable to relax and enjoy his hearty breakfast, Angus regretfully pushed his full trencher away and sheathed his dirk. He strode across the dining hall and stood beside his brooding nephew, staring out the window at the graceful maiden who sat serenely on a terrace listening to the chorus of busy birds. The gaily garbed *cailleach* soothingly brushed the thick ebony hair so that it gleamed in the crisp sunlight. The lacy, silver haze of the surrounding forest was imperceptibly tinged with the tenderest of new green, and a shimmering of dusky pink veiled the budding maples. Daffodils splashed spots of yellow in the rich lushness of the rolling lawns, and the air was redolent with that undefinable sweetness that caused his sluggish blood to pump with renewed vigor.

"Och, the long cruel winter is over!" Angus shouted happily, his jubilation somewhat forced as he strove to lighten Darach's moroseness. "Lad, why dinna you ride to Strathrannoch? Your wee wife'll be safe wie Cailleach Cuilleann and me here at Duncreag. I'll send word if there's any change." There was no acknowledgment. "Och, laddie, I ken that you're impatient to find Riach, but it does no guid to *fash* and pace."

"It is too bloody convenient!" hissed Darach, not taking his eyes from the pastoral tranquillity of Hag Holly and Kat. "I sense those two conniving females are making fools of us. It has been more than two weeks now since the fever broke, and nearly three since we arrived at Duncreag. And still the old hag willna let me near."

"Aye, and you ken why."

"A malady of the brain that has, oh, so conveniently stolen the puir innocent lamb's memory?" Darach scoffed derisively. "And do you honestly believe that? Och, Uncle Angus, you're more touched by age than you know!"

"We maun hae patience," soothed the older man, feeling very uncomfortable with his complicity.

"I have been too damned patient!"

"Och, where's the cool, level-headed Campbell who's renowned for his circumspect, unruffled sagacity?"

"Gone! Destroyed by that unprincipled chit!"

"We maun respect Cailleach Cuilleann's judgment and be patient," Angus repeated lamely.

"To hell wie that!"

"Hush, lad!" the elderly man snapped, attempting to pull his raging nephew away from the open window. He observed how the old woman glowered in their direction and how the proud, slender back stiffened under the luxuriant mantle of glossy ebony.

"Nay, I'll not be shut up like a recalcitrant child! I was a fool to bring the wench to Duncreag, even though it was easier to bring her here than to the authorities in Perth. And I was an even greater fool for agreeing to that old hag's demands. But I'll not keep my distance any longer, do you ken? The wild brat is my wife, whether I wish it or not, and 'tis time she accepted that fact!" he ranted.

"This isna like you, Darach," Angus lamented in defeat, as the irate young man stormed from the room, slamming the door with such ferocity that the goblets on the table clanged together. He listened to the firm steps ringing on the hard stone floor for a few moments, then ran hurriedly back to the window. He whistled frantically and gestured to Cailleach Cuilleann, warning her that his furious nephew was on his way, when, to his consternation, he espied Darach's cynical features regarding him with knowing interest from an adjacent window. He groaned and futilely attempted to cover his incriminating behavior by pretending to do rigorous exercises.

" 'Twould seem that our brief peace is ending. We've held the dark Campbell at bay long enow and he's on his way in a fearsome *stamash*," whispered the hag. "Shall I gie you a draft to cause a faint, or can you manage?"

"I can manage," Kat returned with more courage than she felt. She smoothed the billowing velvet of her burgundy robe, taking comfort from the soft warm fabric.

"You look a treat, my *dawtie*," the crone said fondly, and Kat smiled tremulously. It had been a healing two weeks. She had been cosseted by the dignified, white-haired Angus and the comical little old woman. For the first time in years she had been loved and admired, gently stroked and proudly dressed.

"Thank you," whispered Kat, knowing the short respite was over. The scant few days of being cherished like a precious child were erased by the sharp, distinctive clip of the Campbell's boots.

"Och, now look who's come to visit thee this wondrous, spring morning, my lady," the old woman sang out with exaggerated surprise. "Why, 'tis none other than your *braw*, handsome husband, Sir Darach," she continued, clapping her gnarled hands together happily, yet giving the stern man a warning glare.

Darach glowered back at the crone and the hesitantly smiling girl. He then stared suspiciously up at the window where his uncle hovered apprehensively.

"Good morning, my lord," Kat greeted brightly, hoping he couldn't see her nervousness. She lowered her eyes demurely toward her lap, unable to bear the lacerating contempt that flashed from his icy eyes.

"Come," he snapped peremptorially, after a long searching glare, holding his hand out autocratically to her. There was a long tense minute. Then Kat placed her small trembling fingers in his wide palm and stood up. He regarded her reflectively, noting the way the velvet dressing gown molded to her small firm breasts and tiny waist. He felt robbed of the shape of her long, lithe limbs and craved to tear off the concealing folds. Silently, he tucked her hand in the crook of his arm and led her away from the terrace to the privacy of the topiary garden, where he knew they could not be observed from the house.

Kat concentrated on her feet, placing one delicately shod foot in front of the other, pretending an overwhelming fascination with the inlaid stonework of the path and the intricate stitching of her new kid slippers. Sir Angus had been most generous with his hospitality and gifts, she mused, preferring to think of the older man instead of the intimidating young one who stalked by her side. She had awakened from the tormenting delirium of her illness to the nurturing kindness of the colorful crone and the white-haired man, to gentle hands and voices and to a wardrobe filled with wonderful clothes fit for a cherished daughter—all purchased by her elderly host.

Kat self-consciously stroked the velvet pile of her dressing gown, wishing the Campbell would break the oppressive silence and not scrutinize her so threateningly.

"Your new robe becomes you," he stated harshly, unaccountably infuriated by his uncle's presumption in supplying such an intimate article for the dark radiant beauty. Kat felt as though he had slapped her. She raised her head and stared with what she hoped seemed like startled bewilderment. She frowned at the sardonic twist of his well-formed mouth and remembered the meaning of the name Campbell. Her father had told her it came from the Gaelic for crooked mouth, *cam beul.*

"Is this a new gown?" she answered innocently, hoping that none of her thoughts was visible on her face. "You mean I dinna have this robe before?"

"Och, you are a cunning vixen." He laughed harshly.

"I dinna ken your meaning, my lord," she stammered. "I hope I havena done anything to offend you."

"Och, now what would put such an idea in your scheming wee head, my love?" he returned jeeringly.

"Well, you appear to be a wee bit cross," she understated.

"And is there a reason why I would be a 'wee bit cross' wie my dear wife?"

"I dinna ken. Maybe a small infraction that dinna meet wie your approval? Something I inadvertently did before I lost my memory?" she dared.

"Maybe," he parried, a wicked gleam darkening his silver

eyes. "But 'tis more likely I'm impatient to reclaim my husbandly prerogative."

"Husbandly prerogative?" Kat repeated guardedly.

"Aye, it has been several weeks since I have availed myself of your body, and my base hunger tends to sour my disposition."

"Base hunger?"

"Aye," he purred roguishly. "Och, sad, it is, that you canna recall the rapture we shared, but now we shall have to make up for lost memories," he continued mercilessly, grinning triumphantly at the blush that stained her cheeks.

"My lord, you are embarrassing me," Kat protested. She decided that she should be offended by his blatant talk, whether or not she had really lost her memory.

"Embarrassed? You?" Darach reared back with mock surprise. "That is not possible, my lusty wench! You have not a shy bone in your luscious, sensuous body! You are more natural and at ease naked than you are clothed. And I am overjoyed that I can now relieve you of the restrictions of that confining gown so that we might once again resume our wedded bliss."

"Wedded bliss?" Kat repeated ingenuously.

"At last it is spring and all around us in this verdant paradise you can observe the randy, rutting antics of the birds," he expounded, thoroughly enjoying her discomfiture.

"Aye, I can see the puffed-out pomposity of the arrogant cocks as they strut about making comical spectacles of themselves!" she snapped.

"And the demure pretense of the devious, promiscuous hens as they coyly feign disinterest," he returned. "Enough of your demure pretense. 'Tis time you resumed your wifely duties."

"Wifely duties?" Kat squeaked. "Och, I sadly fear that I've forgotten them, my lord."

"Och, dinna fret," Darach replied cheerfully. "I shall derive the greatest possible pleasure in reinstructing you in the arts of submission, obedience, compliance, docility, servility, and all the other admirable traits you possessed before you were unfortunately robbed of your memory."

"You are very kind, but I wouldna want to take up too much of your time. I ken you're a very busy mon wie other 'duties' in London, Edinburgh, and the west of Scotland. And

I am aware that a wife maun defer to her husband—defer and revere him, esteem, and honor him, worship and respect him above all other men—and I will do my utmost to make that attempt no matter how hard and near impossible it appears to be," she promised earnestly, her green eyes flashing dangerously as she was goaded to battle.

"Respect goes two ways, minx," he remarked mildly, trying to hide his grudging admiration and amusement at her quick wit.

"We were speaking of wifely duties," she hastened to reply, afraid that her fury had given her away. She instantly regretted her rash tongue when he lifted a roguish dark eyebrow.

"Och, so you are as eager as I to resume our conjugal relations." He stared at her heaving bosom.

"Conjugal relations?"

"And what better place than beneath the newly budding trees," he planned, his piercing silver eyes pinned to her dry lips. She bit them nervously, and an impudent finger lazily circled the points of her tremulous breasts.

"It would appear that my husband is a poet," she observed dryly, trying to conceal the tumult of emotions that exploded at his touch, knowing he was cruelly toying with her as he had done before. She stepped back and closed her eyes, refusing to be seduced by his tormenting game. One such humiliation was all she needed, she seethed inwardly, remembering her previous debasement.

Darach saw the frantic pulse in her long graceful neck. He had noted the flash of terror that had flickered through the green depths of her eyes before she had quickly closed them. He had also observed the darkening veil of passion and felt a corresponding ache tighten in his groin.

"Come here," he ordered, but she rebelliously backed farther away. "Och, aye, you've forgotten dutifulness, and I maun teach you," he said huskily, reaching out and drawing her to him. He ran his large hands through her cool silky hair and down her taut back, pressing her against him. She remained stiff and unpliant. "It would seem there's a lot to teach you," he murmured, undeterred by her rigidity. He rubbed his lips against her stubborn mouth, teasing it with the tip of his tongue. When she refused to yield to his gentle seduction, he pressed her lips firmly until she parted them, allowing him entrance. But he was alert to her sharp teeth, keeping his kisses elusive and light as he adeptly undid the buttons on her bodice and released her breasts.

Kat stood stiffly, trying to deny the traitorous feelings that weakened her legs, turning her limbs to liquid. She yearned to thrust against his hardness, easing the unbearable ache that radiated from her core. She did everything she could to detach her mind, as his hands and mouth played havoc with her ears, neck, and breasts, slowly and tantalizingly descending to the fluttering, tender flesh of her belly. Then he went lower, to the burning center of sweet agony.

Darach knew Kat was as aroused as he was, despite her efforts to appear unmoved by his ministrations. He ran his hands possessively over her naked body, reveling in the satiny perfection of her skin. He gazed at her exquisite face, noting the flaring nostrils and the languorous drooping of her lids as they veiled her smoldering green eyes. Her parted lips were curled seductively, and small, sweet breaths spurted. Her firm breasts moved tantalizingly in time with her building excitement. Mutely, she shook her glossy head, trying to deny the tumultuous desire that threatened to sweep her away. She pressed back against the rasping bark of a tree, her velvet robe in a discarded pool at her feet.

"I'll not be bedded by a Campbell!" she shouted, desperately trying to salvage herself.

"There's no bed here," he replied huskily, reaching for her hips and pulling her against the hard ridge of his manhood.

"I hate you!" she cried passionately, clawing at the wool of his coat, trying to connect with the firm muscles of his back while she writhed against him. She craved more, but her fury and fear erupted; she resisted, not knowing if she fought for freedom or greater bondage.

"Aye, I ken you do, my wee Wild Kat," he whispered, releasing himself from the painful confines of his tight britches and guiding himself beneath the damp, black curls. He cupped her firm buttocks and thrust.

Kat gasped as a sharp pain tore through her white-hot ecstasy. She whimpered as his movements froze. The brutal Campbell was going to do it again—bring her to the gates of bliss and then leave her open and vulnerable, panting like a bitch in heat.

"You'll nae reject me again and return to degrade me with the stink of whores clinging to your clothes!" she screamed, trying to push him away. But they were securely coupled, and she was afraid. She had never felt so closely linked with anyone before. "I reject you, Campbell!" she hissed savagely, but his large hands kept a possessive hold on her small bottom while his pulsating part remained deeply embedded in her aching heat.

"Come on, wee Campbell wife, show me thy hate," Darach challenged, once the shock and miracle of her virginity had receded, restoring his equilibrium. "Show me how much you hate the Campbells, my Wild Kat!" he taunted, daring to loosen his grip. He laughed as she set the pace, attacking him earnestly, grinding her lithe hips, and warring with his tongue for dominance. Every part of them battled, and then they surrendered to the swirling rhythm that built, until they fell onto the crackling leaves, beneath the nesting birds on that brisk April morning.

Darach breathed appreciatively of the fresh, clean earth and Kat's fragrant hair. Nothing existed for him in those precious moments except the woman in his arms and the encompassing golden feeling of harmony that suspended him in tranquillity. He regretfully felt himself slip from her warmth, and his anger flared when she pushed herself sharply away from him. He arranged himself and sat up, brushing the leaves from his clothes. He glowered at the naked curve of her graceful back, so insultingly presented. She shivered, and he scanned about for her warm velvet robe.

"I dinna want you ailing again," he said roughly, feeling as awkward and callow as a green youth. "Get dressed," he ordered, handing her the bundle of burgundy material. He frowned, seeing tears streaking her flushed face.

"I feel like a whore," she sniffed, angrily scrubbing the wet weakness from her cheeks.

"You're my wife," he stated.

"Whether you want me or not!" she derided, flinging his words back at him.

"Gie me a few minutes and I'll show you how much I want you," he retorted, piqued by her moroseness. He had been elated, thrilled by her uninhibited passion and the unexpected gift of her maidenhood.

"I feel naked, exposed," she struggled to explain, sitting in the leaves and cradling her robe in her bare arms.

"That is because you are," he observed sagely, trying to lighten her dark mood.

"And you are not," she attacked, resisting thoughts of her own unbridled behavior. She had rutted with a Campbell! Joyfully rolled about under the trees, coupling like a bitch in heat wie a dog of a Campbell, her chiding mind berated her.

"And I am not," agreed Darach. He scowled when she continued to sit, shivering with cold and muttering furiously to herself as her small hands mangled the rich velvet.

"I am no better than a . . . than a . . . a filthy Campbell!" she ranted not able to find a more appropriate adjective. "How could I have done such a thing?" she lamented, ferociously digging her hands into the leaves and shredding them into tiny pieces. She gasped when she was unceremoniously hauled to her feet. She started to fight but was swiftly stopped by a sharp slap across her bare buttocks, which quickly changed to a sensuous caress.

"Och, I'm looking forward to teaching you submission," Darach growled provokingly, pulling the robe over her tousled jet mane as she stood shaking with barely suppressed ire. He very slowly buttoned up the bodice, mischievously tickling the points of her breasts with an idle finger and grinning roguishly as they hardened. "Aye, you're a comely wench, and I'm a most fortunate groom," he teased, lowering his dark head and brushing his firm lips across her rebellious mouth. He laughed harshly, avoiding her sharp teeth as she snarled and tried to nip him. "To bed, my little bride. 'Tis time we truly celebrate our marriage in proper Scottish custom by remaining secluded in the privacy of our own chamber for several days and nights—"

"Days and nights?" she interrupted, horrified.

"Or several weeks," he added cheerfully, swinging her into his arms.

"Weeks?"

"Or even months, depending on how soon I tire of you or you supply me wie an heir," he gibed.

"Dinna flatter yourself, Campbell. I'm already world-weary of you," she snapped, fighting against the tantalizing scent of him as he carried her toward Sir Angus's imposing domicile.

*   *   *

Cailleach Cuilleann shook her long snakelike gray locks at the tall young man with the petite dark girl acquisitively clasped in his arms.

"I dinna like it," she muttered.

"Whether you like it or no, I dinna think there is a damned thing you can do aboot it, *auld* hag." Angus sighed.

"We'll see about tha'," she retorted, keeping her rheumy eyes pinned to the dark couple.

"We've interfered enow. 'Tis time to let nature take her course—and would seem she already has," the white-haired man remarked wickedly, noting the disarray of both dark heads and the leaves that clung to the mussed clothing.

" 'Tis nae the time for loving of tha' nature," the crone fretted, and Sir Angus scrutinized her shrewdly.

"Wha' is thee keeping from me, Cailleach Cuilleann?" he asked harshly. "We agreed to share all knowledge wie each other."

"So we did, and I'm keeping naught from thee."

"Then why your long face, *auld* woman? 'Tis springtime and those two young'uns are fairly bursting wie love and lust."

"Aye, they're bursting wie lust, and 'tis nae the time for it!"

"But 'tis spring!" he shouted.

"Aye, and tha' lust can flower into hatred!" protested the hag.

"Tell me why?" Angus begged after a long pause, recognizing the anguish in the *cailleach's* eyes.

"I dinna ken, except I sense the wee-an has a promise to fulfill and naught maun stand in the way. And any tha' does will be chosen second. Och, I wish I had more time for our wee lass to confide and trust us, but life hasna been easy for the lass. She's used to standing alone. She's used to abusive hands and spitting mouths. We needed more time to gentle her," she grieved.

"My nephew Darach is too proud ever to be chosen second," the man remarked, feeling weighted by his years despite the pulsating sap of spring.

"Aye, I ken."

"He's already embittered agin females, wha' wie that *saidhe sassanach,* Felicity, and his ain puir mother renouncing this life at his birth. And the sadness is that I sense that our wee dark lass is destined to be his mate. It feels so right, like it should be written in the stars, and in the waves of the infinite oceans," chaffed Angus.

"Aye, I ken," repeated Cailleach Cuilleann.

Darach stared into Kat's spitting green eyes. He towered above her, keeping her pinned firmly to his claiming hips. She tried to buck against him in an attempt to dislodge his arresting weight, so that she might thrust at her own building pace. Small furious whimpers burst from her pouting lips, and her breasts strained to connect to his muscular chest as he reared above her, his smoldering eyes seeming to pierce to her very soul.

Kat stilled her movements and concentrated on the sensations that radiated from the proprietary shaft that pulsed deeply inside her. She'd not beg or plead. She'd not demean herself by showing her aching urgency. She'd feign total boredom, she plotted, and executed her decision by loudly pretending to yawn. She was unprepared for the deep laughter that shook the Campbell and the strong hands that cupped her buttocks so that his unbridled mirth did not uncouple them by shaking him free of her yearning depths.

"Och, Lady Campbell." Darach chuckled, wiping his streaming eyes against her lush hair, unable to say what was in his heart. If there ever was a mate created solely for him, she was the mischievous, unpredictable female who lay beneath him—rebellious, spirited, and exciting, and in her own very unique feral way so very precious. She was as destined to be his as the moon was destined to circle the earth and the earth to circle the sun—his and no one else's, he ruthlessly determined. And he staked his claim by inexorably plunging into her welcoming depths and glorying in the way she rose to meet him.

All coherent thoughts were erased from Kat's mind as the battle resumed and she lunged to meet him, her hipbones crashing and grinding against his powerful muscles. She tossed her pride aside and allowed herself to drown in the ecstatic sensations that culminated, and she arched with all her strength toward the instrument that could so easily change her stubborn resolve into pulsating jelly.

Exhausted, Kat lay against the Campbell's strong chest, feeling their combined heartbeats slow to an evenly measured thump, echoing those exquisite spasms that regretfully diminished. She sagged drowsily, thoroughly sated and sighing dreamily upon his nakedness.

Nakedness. His nakedness, she silently mouthed as his peaceful, stentorian breaths steadily lulled her. She cautiously flicked back the sheets and objectively surveyed their clinging nude bodies, reluctantly admitting to the aesthetic meshing of his hard, brown limbs and her delicate, vulnerable frame. Kat leaned on her elbow, watching him peacefully sleep, wondering what she really felt about the intimate joining of their separate selves. She always smothered a mournful lament when he slipped out of her, making them very much apart. She was filled with an aching tenderness at the sight of his coiled vulnerability. The throbbing, imperious staff that had so thrillingly dominated her a scant few moments before now nestled tamely upon his relaxed thigh, and she saw the slick of her own moistness shine.

A tremendous feeling enveloped Kat. She felt like choking when she admitted to herself how she loved the dark male who slept so trustingly against her trembling breast. He was exposed to her, open and defenseless. Very tenderly, she traced the distinct line of his stern lips, delighting in the way he unconsciously nuzzled toward her. She softly ran her fingertips down the hard cords of his neck, reveling in the constancy of the steady pulse that imperceptibly moved the warm velvet hollow beneath his ear. She wonderingly examined his strong arms and broad chest, experimentally tickling the flat nipples with her tongue and tasting the salty fragrance of him. She splayed her small curious hands across the firm expanse of his flat stomach and down to the springy jet curls so much like her own. She gasped in awe of her own power as she watched his curled manhood stiffen and grow, rearing excitedly toward her, and at a deep chuckle she stared up with startled passion into his amused, smoldering eyes.

For several days and several nights, they furiously battled upon the marriage bed. It was a confusion of twining and warring mouths and limbs, an assault of fervent young bodies struggling against and toward all that they most feared and desired. It was a muddle of conflicting emotions that stormed and distracted them, soaring them to exploding heights and to the lonely, secretive pits of despair as each withheld, refusing to admit what was in their hearts.

Five or six times a day a cursory knock or an impatient pounding on the locked door of their bedchamber would herald either the inquisitive Sir Angus or the fretting *cailleach*. They each came with various lame excuses or trays of sustaining victuals and mysterious, impertinent brews to strengthen and invigorate. It was as though no servants resided in the myriad rooms of the imposing castle of Duncreag, except the dignified white-haired laird and the bent rainbow-clad hag. For a little while, Kat gave herself to the prodigious, new sensations, biding her time and summoning her energy and resolve for the moment when she had to break away and return to her responsibilities at Linnmanach.

part two

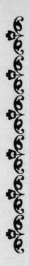

chapter 12

Macaree gazed lovingly at the sleeping male who was tied securely to the bedpost. He belonged to her, she mused dreamily, and only to her, because she knew him as she knew no other person. She had withstood all his emotions, from the awesome violence of an enraged man to the pathetic, graceless sobs of a penitent youth and the heartbreaking, silent tears of a lost little boy.

"Yes, you belong to me," she whispered, gently brushing his hair and delighting in the way the light gleamed in the thick dark curls. She wet a rag and softly traced the familiar lines of his face, tenderly cleaning him as she would a tiny baby. "How could I have ever been afeared of you, my darling?"

Macaree had been cowed by the savage roars and obscene curses that had spewed from his foaming mouth in the first days of his imprisonment. But when she had realized that no matter how he struggled, he couldn't escape his bonds, she had found the courage to step closer to his wild, tormented writhings, until she finally stood so near that his saliva sprayed her clothes. He hissed and spat on the exposed skin of her clasped hands. She had sung softly to herself, avoiding his crazed, rolling eyes, remembering how dashing and handsome he had been through the Christmas festivities before her father and sister had gone away. It had been a Christmas reminiscent of happy yesteryears, with sugared fruits and cakes and prettily wrapped gifts. He had been her beau—gallant and amusing, revering her as though she were a precious princess and he a charming prince from the wonderful stories of early childhood. But then he had magically transformed into a wicked ogre from the same fairy tales, and his graceful, fluid movements had become frenetic and jarring and his melodious voice loud and abusive.

Macaree shuddered, recalling how he had raged like a frenzied, possessed animal, tearing up the already disintegrating mansion, desperately searching for something he had accused her of stealing from him.

"Give it to me, you witch!" he had screamed. Macaree wrapped her arms about herself and stroked her thin forearms. She could still feel his hard fingers painfully digging as he furiously shook her until she was afraid her slender neck would snap. She had tried to sing and drown out her terror and his ugly words. She had tried to sing to change the dark, horrendous scene into the pastoral serenity of the sloping lawns where she had skipped on little-girl legs. She had tried to sing, but his violence stopped her throat and chattered her teeth; the only sounds were unharmonious clicks and grunts.

Macaree had desperately tried to sing when she saw Aggie's arms raised, clutching a heavy cudgel. But a discordant, strident scream had torn out as the blow landed with a sickening thud. The young Campbell had clutched her as he sagged to his knees, ripping her clothes. His blood had flowed, beading on the thick dust of the floor like quivering red dew drops. She had screamed again when Aggie hit him again and again, until he collapsed on the carpet. He had lain motionless among the tattered pages and broken spines of the books he had destroyed on his rampage.

He had been so very, very heavy, Macaree remembered, stroking his still cheek and feeling the prickle of his youthful stubble. She had wept aloud, believing he was dead, as she and Aggie had laboriously dragged him from the library along the cold, stone corridors, his wonderful clothes ripping and soiling, his handsome head sharply bumping over the uneven flags, leaving traces of bright blood in the powdery dirt. Together they had heaved him onto the bed and securely tied him in a spreadeagle position to the carved wooden posts. They had sat on the sagging mattress on each side of his inert body, each panting for breath and scrutinizing to see if he still breathed.

"Caree, this mon is yours," Aggie had firmly stated when she had ascertained that the young Campbell lived. "I've only two hands and they are as full as can be wie wee Robbie and *auld* Ailsa. He is yours, do you ken?"

At the thought of Robbie, panic pounded, and Macaree walked to the window, singing one of her mother's lullabies from a time when everything had been golden—a wonderful time when she had worn little white dresses and swans had glided on the gentle river and nothing bad had ever happened. She soothed herself, watching the snowflakes. Then she sat down and picked up her sewing.

Riach Campbell struggled through the aching, stuporous layers. A sweet voice sang quietly, yet pain shot sharply through him with each movement. He opened his eyes and blinked at the floating dust motes dancing on bars of crystal light that pierced the thick gloom.

"Am I alive?" he asked himself hoarsely, remembering a terrible time when a million stinging insects had seemed to crawl beneath his skin, devouring his flesh, digging under his eyelids, prying them open. He had heard himself scream and plead for death. In unbearable nightmarish sequences, he had become disembodied; he had stared down upon himself—a wretched, puking, sweating man who lay in his own soil, while a flaxen-haired, exquisite beauty sat by him serenely singing. "Am I alive?" he croaked again, and the singing stopped.

"Aye, and tis more'n you deserve," snapped a caustic voice. He swiveled his neck to see an ugly old woman who glared balefully.

"Were you singing?" He gasped. He lifted his aching head and followed the cronie's gaze to the beautiful girl who sat calmly sewing by the window. He struggled futilely against the cutting cords that bound his wrists and ankles.

"Hopefully all tha' heathen poison has seeped out of your pores," Aggie rasped. Riach looked from the wrinkled woman to the ethereal beauty, marveling at the incredible contrast between the two as he remembered who he was and where he was.

"You are Aggie, housekeeper of Linnmanach."

"Aye, I am Aggie," she replied shortly.

"Then release me, dear Aggie. Feed me? Shave me? Draw me a bath? Och, I smell foul," he cajoled with a charming, boyish grin, hoping to soften her disapproving expression.

"Aye, I'm well aware of your stench, but I dinna think

I should untie you—well, nae yet awhile," Aggie said worriedly, her breath frosting the air of the room.

"Why?"

"I dinna trust tha' you'll nae hurt my gentle Caree again."

"I hurt Caree?" he whispered, straining his neck and looking toward the girl, appalled that he would hurt this beauty who had so captured his heart. "Nay, I'd nae hurt Caree for the world," he protested.

"Maybe, and maybe nae, but tha' evil poison of the poppy tha' you hunger for wouldna think twice aboot murdering the lot of us."

Riach closed his aching eyes as his head spun painfully. He shivered, remembering his terrifying delirium. He was aware of the biting cold.

"I'm sorry if I hurt anyone," he ventured to apologize.

"Sorry never mended any gates."

"My head hurts. It feels like it's broken," he complained, hoping for sympathy. He sensed Caree stiffen with concern, but the old woman laughed cruelly.

" 'Tis no more'n you deserve. Och, you Campbells hae thick skulls. It took four mighty blows to fell you," she snapped.

"I am truly sorry, but, as you said, it wasna me but the opium acting. And now there's none, so please release me," he coaxed.

"I dinna ken," she wavered.

"You canna leave me tied here to freeze and starve," he pleaded.

"If the rest of us have to freeze and starve, a debauched Campbell whelp might as well, too!"

"I dinna ken."

"There's no food and it has been more'n a fortnight since Rory MacNiall and our Wild Kat should've returned," Aggie fretted. "There's no wood for the hearths, and I'll nae steal wha' little sustenance is left from the mouth of my *bairns* to feed a Campbell!"

"But there was plenty of food and a great yule log," said Riach. "Or was that a dream?" he added, closing his eyes and trying to distinguish between reality and hallucination. He remembered a carriage filled with Christmas presents and every type of delicacy. He and his friend Rory had had a veritable spree in the shops in Edinburgh and Perth.

"The Yuletide is long gone, and so is the food—gluttonously devoured and vomited so that even more could be crammed down greedy craws,'' Aggie attacked bitterly, recalling the orgy of eating and drinking in which Gregor and the Campbell youth had indulged. "And the capon and goose carcasses have been thrice boiled, and the bleached ham-bone is all that is left for us to exist on."

"If you willna untie me, then at least light a fire, give me more coverlets, and send a valet to bathe and shave me," wheedled Riach.

"You spoilt, pampered young pup!" Aggie blustered. "Och, you make me so cross I could pull your fingernails oot wie pilliwinks! If'n it's a bath you need, my smelly Campbell, then go jump in the icy waters of the *loch!* But how you can lie there demanding your comforts while wee-ans are dying . . ."

"I have no choice but to lie here, my good woman!" shouted Riach. "I'm bound hand and foot," he added in a more moderate tone when his pounding head thumpingly complained.

"Aye, I ken."

"What wee-ans are dying?" he asked, pretending interest when he saw the stubbornness on the old woman's face; he knew he had to change his tack if he was to be untied. Aggie Fletcher sighed and looked at Macaree. Riach twisted his neck painfully, trying to scrutinize the girl who sat dreamily watching the snowflakes. He frowned, noting the pallor and thinness of her face and the bulky layers of clothes that distorted her graceful, majestic curves. He remembered those curves from the halcyon time before the opium and spirits had run out. He turned back to the old woman. She had been buxom and sturdy when he had first arrived, but now she was aged and bowed, her bones prominent under the sagging skin of her weary face and callused hands. "There is a boy?" he asked suddenly.

"For now there is—but barely." Aggie sniffed, trying to stem the tears that streamed down her parchmentlike cheeks. Against her better judgment, her gnarled, aching fingers busied themselves with the tight knots that bound his wrists.

Macaree sang louder, uncomfortable with the disturbing talk about her little brother. She sang louder, trying to pretend that she didn't know what was happening behind her. How dare Aggie undo the Campbell's bonds! He belonged to her, not Aggie. It was up to her to decide what was to be done with him. She wanted to scream at the old woman, but she couldn't express anger because she was her mother's gentle daughter. She wished Kat would return.

"There, now you can undo your ain legs, and if'n you mean to run off and leave us all to die, there's none to stop you. I hae my hands full wie Robbie and the *auld* Ailsa." Aggie sighed. "Come along, Miss Caree, we should leave the Campbell so he can learn how to wash hisself. There's a spot of water under the ice in the pitcher," she added, bustling out of the chamber. "I said come along now, Miss Caree." Her voice echoed along the cold stone corridors with her shuffling feet.

Riach remained prone, waiting for the girl to leave as he rubbed his chafed wrists and flexed his stiff arms. He stared at the ripples of white light on the ceiling, reflections of the winter sun shining from the virgin snow. He listened to the hauntingly familiar tune that Caree sweetly sang. He awkwardly pulled himself to a sitting position, stifling the groans that arose when his muscles agonizingly protested. How long had he been tied in that humbling position? he angrily wondered, stretching his arms and trying to reach his ankles. He grunted with the effort. Swearing, he collapsed back on the foul mattress, his fingers cramping in their futile attempt.

"Miss Caree, will you untie these damnable cords?" he barked. He was further infuriated when she simply sang louder. "Miss Caree, I am truly sorry if I harmed you in any way." He lowered his voice, but she continued to sing. "I am deeply shamed," he tried, suddenly terribly aware of how exposed he was. His legs were pulled wide apart and bound in different directions. He struggled wildly to sit up, needing to protect the vulnerable parts of himself; once more, he tried to undo the cutting cord. "Goddammit! Do you derive pleasure in my humiliation?" he bellowed with frustration. "Help me!" he roared. Her sweet song stopped abruptly, and she stood poised like a startled deer before silently collecting her sewing and calmly leaving the room, gliding out like a shadow. "Come back here and untie me, you bitch!" he screamed. He collapsed back on the bed and listened to the rustle of her long skirts receding through the cold, stone corridors.

An hour later, with angry tear stains dried upon his face and his once beautifully manicured nails broken and bleeding, he tore the loosened strands from his left ankle and rolled toward his other outstretched leg, crying aloud with the agony of cramped muscles. He stared about with disgust at the shabby room and the filthy mattress where he lay, recoiling from his own base odor and the wretched state of his soiled clothes. Then he tackled the bonds on his right ankle with fervor.

Riach stared with horror into a tarnished, broken mirror, its shattered splinters fragmenting his disreputable image. Gone was the debonair, handsome youth who made females young and old forgive his many sins. Here instead was an old, hairy vagrant with sunken, dark-rimmed eyes and hollow cheeks. How long had he been incarcerated at Linnmanach? he wondered. He stood and swayed, clinging to the carved bed-post. He felt the grease of accumulated polish mixed with years of dust embed beneath his broken nails as the room spun alarmingly. He staggered to the window, his feet feeling heavy and his legs unstable. He clutched the wide sill and stared out at the shimmering *loch,* seeing the sparkles of ice in the shallows by the shore and the gleaming vista of white snow. It was still winter. No sign of spring warmed the starkness. Which winter? he thought, panicking, remembering his old face in the mirror. Why did he look and feel so very ancient? Was there a dreaded spell or disease that not only crumbled the gray stones of this accursed place, but also the virile bodies of its inhabitants?

Riach struggled to remember the time he had spent in the rambling manse. He had arrived to spend the Christmas festivities as a guest of Rory MacNiall and his family, and in the rosy haze of poppy and spirits everything had appeared wondrous, especially the exquisite Macaree. It hadn't been until he had been denied the intoxicating substances that he had become distressingly aware of the rotting, filthy decay that surrounded him. Everything was sharp-edged and cor-roded, splintered and choked—everything except Caree. She remained enchanting and bewitching.

"How long have I been here?" he yelled, but his voice jeer-ingly reverberated down the dark, dusty hallways. Christmas and Hogmanay had passed, as had other carefree magical days. He had spent them with Caree, walking through the si-lent forest where no feet had ever trod before. They had curled beside a roaring fire in the library, reading poetry or playing charades. When had Rory and the dark-haired impish girl left? Riach shook his head, unable to recall any milestone that could aid him. All the days after Christmas had whirled into one until the nightmares came. "The Ides of March," he mut-

tered musingly. "Rory mentioned he had to be somewhere for
the Ides of March. But it canna be March," he added, staring
out at the cold winter scene.

Determined to find out all he could, Riach looked about for
a bellpull to summon a servant. He would bathe, have a shave
and a manicure, and dress himself in clean clothes. Then he
would have a breakfast of ham, eggs, and steak and kidney
pie, all washed down with sturdy ale. He would be ready to
face anything. But the tattered bell rope tore off in his hand,
leaving him in a cloud of dust. At the sight of the cold empty
grate, reality finally dawned on him. Aggie Fletcher's sarcastic
words mockingly rang in his head: "Come along, Miss Caree,
we should leave the Campbell so he can learn how to wash
hisself."

Macaree put her needlework aside and walked to the window, hearing the lusty splashes and shocked cries. She pulled
her shawl tighter about her slender shoulders and walked out
on the terrace to stare over the waters of the *loch*. Small ripples ruffed the still surface, sending shards of ice bobbing and
scudding in widening rings. Pensively, she trod down the wide,
stone steps and made her way across the crunching snow to the
shore, following the prints that led to the water. The bright
sunlight played on Riach Campbell's bare skin, defining the
contours of his long, lean muscles. He stood in the shallows
with his back turned to her, and she marveled at his beauty.
He was hers, and he was as magnificent as any Greek statue.
He belonged to her, every glorious inch of him, she reveled.

The girl was sweetly smiling when Riach turned around. He
frowned quizzically and then was shocked that such an angelic, ethereal woman would stare so blatantly at his naked
body. Only whores and other promiscuous females would
have the effrontery not to deflect their eyes, he thought. To his
absolute horror he recalled her cool, slender fingers intimately
touching him, taking care of his most basic needs. He stepped
backward and sat sharply in the icy water, unable to understand her madonnalike expression. Then she laughed—a genuine, earthy giggle that shocked him even more.

Macaree could not remember having laughed so deliciously
before. She felt free and open—not bound by gentleness and
sweet harmony. She seemed to expand and grow to rich
heights. She threw her blond head back, and her laughter bubbled loudly. Aggie heard the unaccustomed sound and scur-

ried through the snow, unsure whether the girl was being
attacked by the wild Campbell again.

"Macaree? Macaree? Wha's the matter?" she shouted. In
her haste, she forgot herself and called the girl by her Mac-
Gregor name. "Macaree?" she screamed, but there was no
answer, just the ribald laughter ringing off the still, white
countryside.

Riach squatted shivering in the water, condemning both
females to the depths of purgatory as they stood on the sloping
bank. They sagged against each other, overcome by the loud
mirth that steamed the frigid air.

"Och, lassie, it does my heart guid to hear your sweet voice
raised with laughter like it used to be," Aggie gasped when she
caught her breath. She wiped her streaming eyes with the back
of her work-roughened hand. "Well; I maun get back to them
who need me most. I wouldna set too long in tha' cold water,
Campbell, for you dinna ken wha' you might freeze off! Och,
and there's talk of a monster wie *meikle* great teeth. Linnmanach is as bottomless as Loch Ness, you ken . . . and we
wouldna want you bottomless, too," she added wickedly.
Chuckling merrily, she trotted back to the house, leaving Macaree convulsed in fresh whoops of laughter.

"When you've quite finished wie your amusement, I'd appreciate a blanket. Not so much for modesty, as you dinna
seem to care, but for warmth," Riach snarled, trying to control his chattering teeth. "Unless, of course, you wish me
dead!" he shouted. He was rewarded when she spun about
and ran up the steep bank, small bursts of hilarity still puffing
from her mouth. She returned a few moments later and stared
with bewilderment at the empty *loch*. Then she caught sight of
his head bouncing from behind a straggly gorse bush as he
leaped about, trying to restore his circulation. "Throw it to
me," he ordered. She smiled fondly and made no move to
comply. Instead, she invitingly held the blanket out to him.
"You might have the appearance of the Blessed Virgin, but
you're no better than a common trull!" he shouted angrily.
He was unaccountably enraged by her behavior, not because
he was painfully cold, but because she was doing her utmost to
destroy the angelic image he so revered. At her reaction to his
furious words, he forgot all modesty. One moment she had
been a glorious, seductive vision, her cheeks delicately tinged
by the crisp breeze, and the next she became a petrified, frigid
statue, her face devoid of all color. He stepped out from the

thorny branches of the shrub and grabbed the blanket from her lifeless hand. His already shivering body was further chilled as he saw fear receding from her perfect features to be replaced by a horrifying mask. She had the smiling molded face of a porcelain doll, and she began to sing a French nursery rhyme, her voice high and clear, like that of a very young child.

Riach watched Macaree skip happily back to the house. Still singing, she danced up the cracked steps that led to the terrace and disappeared through the broken doors, deaf to his imperious shouts for her to stop. The sooner he quit the loathsome ruin and its odd occupants, the better, he resolved, wrapping the thin coarse blanket about his trembling nakedness and racing after the girl on numb, bare feet. He left distinct wet prints in the thick dust, and he cringed with disgust at the rodent and bird droppings that stuck to the soles of his feet. Long, sticky cobwebs dangled from crumbling cornices, where clumps of bats hung sleeping and ravens roosted, their sinister feathers plumped against the aching cold. Tattered banners and filmy drapes waved eerily in the chill drafts, causing ghostly shadows to prance over the vast empty walls.

"What a horrible hellhole!" he hissed, making his way cautiously through the decaying rooms and along the echoing corridors, hearing Caree's lilting voice dwindling into the dim recesses. He couldn't wait to get back to his comfortable, civilized lodgings in London. Even his brother's austere castle at Strathrannoch was preferable to this place. He would even welcome Darach's censuring silences—or his mother's hysterical, cloying demands. He finally reached the green chamber and glared with repugnance at the filth, unconscious of his own responsibility for it. Oh, what he would give for a hot scented bath and the efficient ministrations of his valet. He wrenched open the wardrobe and was somewhat mollified to find some of his clothes, wrinkled and slightly soiled, but certainly preferable to the foul rags he had discarded by the *loch*. He swore aloud with frustration when his numb fingers fumbled ineptly with his buttons. His broken nails caught on the silken foulard. With a bark of ironic mirth, he threw the cravat aside, realizing the absurdity of trying to appear elegantly attired amid such tawdry surroundings.

"Where the hell are my boots?" he roared, scanning the despicable room, which evoked such embarrassing memories. He was loath to dirty his britches by groveling under the bed.

In stocking feet, he stalked through the labyrinth of dark corridors, searching for a sign of life other than the rats that scurried out of the dank shadows or the bats that shrilly swooped about his head. Through the great banquet hall and the empty portrait gallery he padded, bellowing for Caree and Aggie, and smothering sharp squeals of fright when a lumbering raven launched itself into flight. Its heavy wings nearly brushed his cheek, and a flock of noisy starlings suddenly burst from a dark corner.

"Aggie? Caree?" he called, peering apprehensively about a large carved door and staring with dismay at the litter of broken books. An image of his own hands brutally ripping the pages tore into his mind. "Aggie Fletcher!" he shouted, slamming the library door and hearing the sharp sound reverberate. "Caree?" There was no answer, save the protesting caws and twitters of Linnmanach's natural occupants. Had he been abandoned, left to die of hunger and cold? He frantically raced back through the chilly mausoleum. Finally, he opened the door to the basement kitchen and was welcomed by a blast of hot air.

Riach felt incredible relief. He could only sway on the threshold and breathe appreciatively the warmth and fragrance that bubbled from the hearth.

"Shut that door, Campbell!" screeched Aggie.

"Where are my boots, woman?" Riach demanded, remembering their very different stations in life and chiding himself for feeling so unreasonably happy to see her.

"Shut tha' door! I'll nae hae you stealing the heat from those tha' need it!" she raged. He obeyed and stepped into the room, staring curiously at the two bundled figures that lay on mattresses each side of the fireplace.

"Something smells delicious," he remarked, saliva pouring into his mouth and his stomach contracting with hunger.

" 'Tis mostly water wie shriveled onions and a handful of herbs, but 'tis all there is, and you're nae having any," she snapped.

"Is tha' the Campbell?" asked a weak, treble voice.

"Is that the boy?" he whispered to Aggie.

"Aye, tha's young master Robbie, and you be gentle wie him," she hissed. "And maybe, just maybe, you'll get a taste of *brose.*"

"*Brose?*" Riach repeated with disgust, hating the idea of watery oatmeal.

"A beggar canna be a chooser," she cackled.

"Is it the Campbell, Aggie?" persisted the boy.

"Aye, laddie, it is the Campbell all spruced up like a new coin," she reassured, giving Riach a push in Robbie's direction.

Riach hated illness of any kind. Reluctantly, he sat down beside the boy, repelled and uncomfortable at the sight of the transparent cheeks and wide, burning eyes.

"Will you still take me fishing?" the boy asked eagerly.

"Fishing?"

"Aye, you said in the spring we'd go fishing for the *auld righ bradan,*" Robbie reminded him. "And *breac.*"

"Auld righ bradan?" he puzzled.

"He's a Campbell, Robbie. He doesna ken his Gaelic," Aggie said insultingly. "They're more friends wie the English than their fellow Scots!"

"Auld righ bradan is the old king salmon," explained the boy. "And *breac* is trout."

"Wha' I wouldna give for a plump trout rolled in oats and fried crisp in the skillet." Aggie sighed, staring into the thin, watery broth that steamed over the hearth.

"Or a fine *bawd,*" chimed Aunt Ailsa in a weak, quavery voice from the other pallet. "Aye, a fine, fat *bawd* jugged in earthy claret."

"Or even a modest rabbit stewed wie onions," continued Aggie.

"A fat *bawd* jugged in claret?" Riach questioned, imagining a voluptuous painted woman of the evening stewing in wine while Aggie Fletcher pranced about the cauldron.

"The Campbell dinna ken a *bawd, auld* lady." Aggie giggled.

"He looks lusty enow to ken many a *bawd,* e'en the furry kind," Ailsa said with a wheeze. "*Bawd* is a hare, young Campbell."

"You're not really a Campbell, are you, Riach?" asked Robbie, competing with his aunt for the visitor's attention.

"Why would you ask that?"

"Well, Campbells are mean buggers, bullying and murdering, and you're nae like that," the boy replied, propping himself up on a painfully thin elbow and staring worshipfully at the tall dark youth.

"Now, hush yourself, master Robbie, and lie doon and save your energy," chided Aggie.

"Who says that about the Campbells?" Riach queried. He saw the boy's blue eyes flicker nervously at the hovering woman.

"No one," lied Robbie.

"Where's Caree?" Aggie asked loudly, trying to change the subject.

"Who's filled your head with such lies about my clan?" Riach repeated as he towered over the trembling boy. "Was it you, *auld cailleach?*" he asked roughly.

"Dinna call me a hag, you spoiled *bagrel!*" Aggie spat, indignantly.

"Come over here, Campbell," Ailsa said quaveringly. Riach reluctantly crossed the room, staring down with horror at the shriveled crone, who was swaddled in blankets. He gaped into the tiny, birdlike face, amazed that anyone who appeared so ancient could still talk. Her sparkling, beady eyes moved back and forth, and a clawlike hand waved at him uncertainly, the distorted fingers trembling like aspen leaves. "Prove the wee lad wrong, Campbell," she rasped. "Show him tha' a Campbell needna be a monster."

"I haven't done anything!" protested Riach, and then he blushed, awkwardly meeting Aggie's accusing eyes.

"Maybe you havena, but your clan certainly has," Ailsa stated. "Doon through the ages they've done all manner of foul deeds."

"I'm not to blame for the sins of my ancestors."

"Aye, but the sins of the fathers be revisited upon innocent wee *bairns* like our sma' Robbie and gentle Macaree. Save their lives, Campbell. Prove to a wee MacGregor lad that the Campbells who murdered their line of chieftains and appropriated their lands hae compassion enow to nurture a ten-year-old outlaw," the old woman pleaded weakly, ignoring the shocked gasps.

"Ailsa, for pity's sake!" screeched Aggie, appalled at what the crone was admitting. "You'll cause our deaths!"

"We're dying anyway. You and I have had our lives, but our young Rob Roy and gentle Macaree maun be allowed to live."

"MacGregors?" Riach queried dazedly.

"He's the only chance that our wee-ans have, Aggie. Gregor MacGregor, that unholy bastard, will nae be returning, and I sorely grieve for our Wild Kat." Ailsa wept. "I have nae long, young Campbell. You maun promise to help our wee-ans," she begged hoarsely, clutching at his clothes.

"MacGregors?" he repeated again, an expression of repulsion marring his handsome features.

"Nay, you mustna say our name aloud or it'll mean our death," Robbie cried fearfully.

"Och, hush, sweet wee-an, dinna *fash*," Aggie crooned soothingly as the boy tossed and turned with fear. "Och, what have you done, *auld* woman? Now the Campbell will run off and bring the authorities so our loved ones'll rot in some filthy jail."

"You'll nae do that, will you, Campbell?" begged Ailsa, pulling on his trousers' legs. "You're nae just a fancy, useless fop, but a *braw* young Scot wie a use for being on this earth. You're nae a spineless, simpering wastrel who canna do a mon's fine job by keeping a pretty maid and a wee lad alive until spring, are you?" she challenged.

Riach stared down with horror, seeing her face distort grotesquely as she was overcome by great, railing gasps. Her skeletal hands clutched his clothes, as she tried to drag him down to her. "Promise, Campbell, or I'll curse you from the grave!" she hissed vehemently.

"I promise!" he spat hurriedly, hoping she'd release her clawing grasp. But she held tighter, arching toward him and then subsiding with a long, low sigh. She stared mockingly at him, her bony hands firmly entangled in the sagging hose on his bootless ankles. "Oh, my God," he intoned, tearing his fascinated but sickened eyes from the hideous, smirking dead face and looking into Macaree's startling beauty as she stood poised at the kitchen door.

"Is Aunt Ailsa dead?" Robbie's high voice broke the heavy silence. "Aggie, is she dead?"

"Aye, my pet, your puir *auld* auntie has at last found peace, unless the Campbell breaks the sacred deathbed vow. Then she'll return to gie him a living hell on this earth."

chapter 13

Riach had to stoop to get through the door without cracking his head. He stared with absolute horror at the tiny dark cupboard of a room. It was nothing more than a storage hole.

"You cannot expect me to sleep in here," he said in disbelief.

"Suit yourself, Campbell. " 'Tis warmer than any of the chambers upstairs, seeing as how it's behind the kitchen flue. But if it's beneath your dignity to rest in a scullery maid's nook, go freeze your proud ballocks off in any room of your choice. 'Tis no skin off my nose. There's more'n fifteen bedchambers, and all are unoccupied, 'cept by birds, bats, and rats, but they dinna take up much room." She dumped an armload of clothes onto the narrow cot. "Here's some things you'll find useful," she added before trotting into the adjacent kitchen, where Robbie leaned on his thin elbow, straining to hear her words. Macaree sat nearby gazing dreamily into the embers of the fire.

Riach gaped in disbelief at the cracked hobnail boots, still caked with mud and straw. He then looked to his own pitiful stocking feet. His silken hose was soiled and torn and his toes peeked out, looking pink and vulnerable. They were delicate, pedigreed feet—not bred for such rude, common shoes. Between his finger and thumb, he gingerly picked up a leather jerkin. Repelled by the dark sweat rings around its armholes, he immediately dropped it for fear of contamination. A coarse peasant's smock, much-darned woollen hose, and shapeless trousers completed the ensemble.

"You cannot expect me to don these *gillie*'s rags!" he protested, as Aggie watched from the open doorway, a bright grin of amusement twinkling in her eyes and lifting her weary wrinkles.

"You canna expect to do a mon's work in them dandy, prissy frills," she retorted.

"Where are my boots?" he demanded petulantly.

"I dinna ken where your silly tasseled boots be, and the more time you waste asking the same question, the longer it'll be 'fore you eat!" she snapped. "The *auld* lady Ailsa needs to be buried."

"And you expect me to bury her?" Riach gasped in outraged astonishment.

"Who else?"

"But I don't know how," he lamented, after looking hopelessly at the frail Robbie and the ethereal Macaree. "I've never buried anyone before."

"Well, well, aren't you the lucky one! Seems here at Linnmanach we're always burying one puir soul or another."

"My *maman* is buried in France, but I dinna remember her *funéralilles* too well," piped Robbie. "But there was a river —and it was very gray and quiet. Was it in the wintertime, Aggie?"

"Aye."

"Everyone at Linnmanach died in the autumn when the red and yellow leaves were falling," the boy mused. "All except Auntie Ailsa. She died in the spring—but it isna spring, is it, Aggie? I dinna think spring is ever going to come this year."

"It'll come, master Robbie," whispered the old woman.

"Nobody dies in the summer. Maybe I shall die then, when the sky is that special blue that goes on forever, and the lark rises and rises, singing until she seems to reach the sun. And bees buzz in the hollyhocks and everything is golden. Then the earth is warm and mellow. I'd nae like to die in the winter. My grave would be too cold."

"Och, master Robbie, dinna babble such morbid *stite*," chided Aggie, trying to stem the tears that streamed down her deep wrinkles. "Och, now, see wha' you've gone and done?

You've set your sister off again." She sniffed as Macaree started to sing. "And you, Campbell, I dinna care a hoot wha' you wear! Go barefoot wie a feather behind your ear! Ruin your popinjay silks and satins, but get digging!" she ordered furiously, blowing her nose and slamming the door to the scullery alcove.

Riach folded his arms mutinously and sat on the hard cot. He listened to Aggie's furious mutters and clatters mingling with Macaree's sweet singing. His aristocratic nose twitched, smelling the savory fragrance of the broth, and his stomach rumbled hollowly. Realizing the childish stupidity of his sulk, he decided to don the abhorrent attire. At least shod, he had a chance of escape, he mused, ruefully acknowledging the futility of trudging barefoot through the snow. And where in the world was he? That frightening question tormented him. He racked his brain, trying to recall the journey to Linnmanach, but everything was a blur of taverns, bawdy houses, and shops from Edinburg to Perth. For all he knew, he was isolated in the uninhabited Highlands, miles away from civilized life. With shoes, no matter how old and filthy they were, he could explore the outbuildings, locate the stables, steal a horse, and ride away from the loathsome ruin where everybody seemed to crumble and die. He apprehensively lowered his cringing feet into the foul darkness of the hobnail boots. He recoiled when his bare flesh touched their cold, sticky interiors. He hurriedly took off his torn stockings, replacing them with woollen hose.

Riach opened the door to the kitchen and sullenly presented himself, expecting great gales of derision, but he was virtually ignored. Piqued, he stood bowed on the threshold, unable to stand erect, holding the greasy jerkin in front of him as if it were a dead rat. He cringed at the thought of touching its sweat-stiffened holes.

"Look long and hard at it, Campbell. Tha's an honest mon's sweat, in case you've nae seen it before," Aggie snapped tartly, snatching the jerkin from his disdainful clasp and holding it out for him to put on. "I hae enough sickness, you overindulged *bagrel*, so put it on!" To her complete surprise, the youth sullenly obeyed. He was a mere boy, she reminded herself. "Now, lad, I've dragged the puir *auld* lady outside near the wine cellar, as I dinna want her to turn putrid in the kitchen warmth and foul the air. Macaree'll show you, and she'll fetch the spades," she continued briskly, pointedly opening the door. "Dinna be a sissy, Campbell! Show the gentle Macaree wha' a *braw, bardach* mon you can be if'n you put your mind to it."

Riach pretended not to hear Aggie Fletcher's goading words. He followed Macaree out of the cozy kitchen and into the freezing stone passageway. He tried to stride manfully in the enormous boots, but instead, they forced him to shuffle demeaningly. He held his arms away from his body and kept his elbows bent, so the soiled leather jerkin would not touch his armpits. He also pretended not to hear the little chuckles that sputtered from Macaree's pursed lips.

"I am quite well aware of how ridiculous I must appear!" he finally spat, incensed by her lack of maidenly diplomacy.

"You appear very handsome, Riach, but . . . 'tis because you're strutting like . . . a *hubbley-jock*." She giggled, demonstrating by bending her arms like wings, puffing her chest, turning her feet out, and striding with high, exaggerated steps. Despite himself, Riach laughed, and soon they collapsed together, overcome with amusement. He wrapped his arms about her, and they strained against each other, helpless with merriment. Their young voices echoed happily through the oppressive, dank passages.

"What's a *hubbley-jock*?" he asked when he was able to speak.

"A turkey cock," she explained with a chuckle, but her mirth ceased abruptly at his silence. His arms dropped from her, and they resumed their way with a chill space between them.

"Well, I suppose you could've called me worse," he stated grudgingly, after a reflective pause, knowing he should be grossly insulted. Young women of his acquaintance did not try to gain his attention by comparing him to a bird—unless, of course, it was one that denoted masculine beauty, such as a peacock, eagle, or peregrine falcon.

Macaree stopped walking and stared solemnly at a shrouded bundle in the shadows.

"What is that?" he demanded anxiously.

"Aunt Ailsa," was the brief answer. "You carry her and I'll fetch the shovels," Macaree added, wanting desperately to block out the macabre sadness with a soothing tune. But she sensed that she had to be strong for her young Campbell, who suddenly looked extremely wan.

"I carry her?"

"I dinna think I am strong enough, but you are, Riach. I know you are," she urged softly, instinctively feeding his male vanity.

"Don't leave me!" he cried sharply, his voice cracking like an adolescent's when she turned away.

"I maun fetch the shovels. I'll be right back," she reassured.

"We shall fetch them together," he stated autocratically, struggling to bring his voice back to deep, sure tones. "You'll not go alone!" Macaree nodded and bit her lips, trying to stop the singing that ached to come out.

Riach took a deep breath, summoning every ounce of his courage. He then bent down and hooked his arms beneath the inert bundle, hoping no spiders or mice were hiding under the shrouded shape. He became paralyzed with revulsion at the hard, brittle weight. He had expected a soft, yielding body and was unprepared for the very feel of death—that heavy, dreadful finality. He closed his eyes, praying that Aggie Fletcher had had the foresight to securely wrap the corpse. He straightened his legs, lifting the gruesome burden, but his fervent pleas were unanswered, and the blanket flapped open. Ailsa's grotesque, bloodless face lolled onto his shoulder, and one clawed hand waved obscenely. A shrill scream burst from Riach's throat, and he sagged against the wall, fighting waves of nausea, still clutching the poor dead woman.

Macaree struggled against her own terror. She longed to sing and skip away to happier times, but one look at Riach gave her strength. She swiftly pulled the blanket about Ailsa's leering features and tucked the cold hand out of sight.

" 'Tis all right now," she whispered gently, daring to stand on tiptoes and press a comforting kiss on Riach's pale cheek. " 'Tis all right now, my Riach," she soothed, as she had done in the nightmare days and nights when he had been bound by cords and terror. " 'Tis all right, my mon," she crooned, disregarding the corpse between them and brushing her soft lips against his own.

Riach's hands were blistered and bleeding, yet he had barely made an impression in the frozen earth. He was determined not to give up.

"You'll not dig!" he had proclaimed. So Macaree perched

on a gravestone, watching his slow progress. For some unknown reason, he was determined to fulfill this one obligation before turning his back on Linnmanach. He would inter the old lady in the frigid soil and show the MacGregors that a Campbell was a man to reckon with, so he continued to attack the unyielding ground. He stamped upon the shovel, feeling a concussion stab painfully through his ill-fitting boots. He heard the sharp metal of the tool ringing through the chilly air. It seemed he was the only sound left on earth, and he was glad of Macaree's serene presence—of the knowledge that someone else lived and breathed in the snowy waste. He had never been so isolated, yet, to his surprise, he didn't feel as lonely as usual.

"There," he gasped wearily, wiping the stinging sweat from his eyes and staring with great satisfaction at the two-foot-deep hole. He did not see Aggie Fletcher approaching.

"Och, 'tis a guid thing puir *auld* Ailsa wasna very big," she remarked disparagingly. "But I guess it'll hae to do, 'specially if we scrunch her a wee bit wie her legs tucked up like a sleeping *bairn*."

Riach glowered at her and then frowned at the darkening sky. He had been slaving like a madman, toiling steadily beyond pain, until his muscles had worked of their own accord.

"I'll dig deeper if you wish."

"Nay, there's no wolves left to scavenge our puir *auld* Ailsa. You've done a fine job, young Campbell. I dinna think you had it in you, but you've done a fine mon's job of work." Riach grinned sheepishly, feeling a joyful sparkle in his blood. "Och, look at those puir hands." The old woman fretted. wincing at the sight of the dirty wounds on the youth's tender palms. "Set yourself doon, lad. Macaree and I shall finish up."

"You'll not. 'Tis my job, and I'll finish what I start," Riach snapped roughly, hearing his brother's cutting words accusing him of never completing his projects.

Aggie sat beside Macaree on a gravestone. They huddled together, sharing their body heat and watching the youth's measured movements in the dim light as he shoveled the earth over the shrouded corpse.

"Can you shoot a gun?" asked Aggie.

"Anybody can shoot a gun," he replied, not losing his steady rhythm.

"Aye, but can you hit wha' you're aiming at?"

"Depends on the target."

"There's a brood of wood pigeons in the elms back of the stables. They'd make a toothsome supper stewed wie onions, garlic, and a pot posy, and I just might be able to scratch up a crust wie oatmeal siftings if'n the birds are plump enow and put out some fat." Riach's saliva flowed at the thought. "Pigeon pie." The old woman tempted.

"I've never been much of a shot," he admitted ruefully. "Now, my brother, Darach, can hit just about anything—a buzzard that the eye can barely see, a swift hare. Unfortunately, I didn't inherit the family trait."

"Dinna inherit—or dinna try?" asked the shrewd woman. Macaree seethed inside, wishing that Aggie would stop teasing the young man. Riach didn't answer, but put more energy into his work.

Riach furiously spaded the dirt. There had never been any point in trying to excel—whatever he did, he was always compared to his matchless older brother. Even his own mother seemed to prefer her peerless stepson to her very own flesh and blood. It had always been the same. He recalled his uncompromising father and was firmly convinced that he had died of disappointment with his younger son.

"Dinna inherit—or dinna try?" Aggie repeated. Macaree was so angry that she pushed herself away from the woman's sheltering warmth and stood at a distance.

"There was no use in trying. Whatever I attempted had been done before, and far better than I could ever hope to attain," he stated bluntly, flinging soil into the hole and refilling the shovel. "I could never be first in anything—or to anyone. Not in the doing, completing, or being!" he added, without breaking his pace. Darach had ridden his first horse at the tender age of three—not a pony, their father had pointedly stressed, but a full-grown horse of fifteen hands. And he, Riach, at the ripe old age of five, was still mortally afraid of his small pony.

"Tha's the way of the world, lad. There's always someone bigger, better, bonnier, and cannier," Aggie commiserated softly.

"I'm not speaking of the whole world, but just one man, my only brother. He's not even a full brother, but a measly half. Och, what I would give for just half of that damned perfection!" He hissed, forcing his numb arms to lift the leaden spade.

"Cain and Abel—'tis an old story." The old woman sighed.

"My sister is everything I wish I was," Macaree stated bravely. "And she's younger." There was no answer, just the gritty rasp of the spade, and she didn't know if he had heard her.

"What about those juicy pigeons? Tha' incomparable big brother of yours, Riach, and the matchless little sister of yours, Macaree, are nae here at Linnmanach. They canna keep us alive. It's up to you two unchosen *bagrels* to put your heads together and keep wee Robbie and *auld* me from dying of cold and starvation," challenged Aggie, when Riach had exhausted the mounds of earth. He leaned on the spade, panting for breath. "And, speaking of wee Robbie, I should get myself back so he doesna *fash* hisself to death."

"But, wait. Shouldn't you say something? A prayer? A few words? Something?" asked Riach, waving a hand at the muddy mound in the snow.

"I've said my piece to the *auld* lass. 'Tis up to you now to reaffirm your deathbed vow so she'll nae rise from the grave tha' you created and haunt the rest of your days!" Aggie spat, as she pulled her layers of woollen shawls about her head. She trudged back through the crisp whiteness to the hulking shadow of the hollow-eyed house, her arms filled with kindling.

Riach and Macaree stood apart, the grave separating them. They silently watched the bowed woman until she disappeared into the dusk. Then they looked quietly at each other. Riach held out his hands to her, and she swiftly ran to his side.

"What shall I say, Macaree?" he whispered, feeling her soothing fingers rest softly on his hot, stinging palms.

"That you'll take care of us? That you'll keep us safe? Even though we're MacGregors?" she responded hesitantly, expecting him to withdraw his hands and turn away, leaving her alone in the wintry twilight.

"But what if I cannot?" he asked hoarsely.

"Because we're MacGregors?"

"No, because . . . because I just can't. Because I'm not able to. Because I'm not . . . man enough!" he stated.

"Oh, Riach, you're mon enow to do anything."

"Och, you don't know me, Macaree MacGregor. I'm a whimpering coward afeared of my own shadow," he scoffed derisively, tears spurting from his eyes. "See, I even weep like a puling babe!"

"I know you, Riach Campbell, and I saw you fight the demons—Terrible demons that would make most men die of fright. But you battled them and conquered them all. Do you not remember them? They ate of your flesh. They pried open your lids and fed on your eyeballs, and you survived them. You destroyed them!" she shouted earnestly.

"And you helped me. You were there through all of that horror. I recall your cool, soft touch and your gentle voice. I was never alone," he said wonderingly.

"And because of you I was never alone. It was the first time in my whole life I was not alone, because I had you," Macaree admitted, gazing up at his face. She gloried in the hot wet tears that splashed from his eyes onto her cheeks and mingled with her own.

Riach tried to focus on her beautiful face, but everything was a rainbow blur. He pulled her close and stared over her head to the grave.

"I promise you, Ailsa . . ." he began, then stopped. "I buried her, carried her dead body and buried her in the earth . . . such an important, somehow personal thing to do, and I don't even know her name. I've never done anything so important before."

"Her name is Ailsa MacGregor."

"I promise you, Ailsa MacGregor, that I shall try my utmost to nurture and cherish all the people at Linnmanach. So rest in peace," he said solemnly. "Please, rest in peace," he begged, and Macaree giggled tearfully in the comforting folds of the leather jerkin.

Aggie kept a fond eye on the young couple as Macaree tended the youth's lacerated hands. She soaked them in warm water and gently coaxed the grit from the painful abrasions. She tried not to chuckle at the young Campbell's masculine pride as he attempted to grin and disprove the pain, only to grimace comically.

"Doesna it hurt terribly?" Robbie asked, in awe of the tall

Campbell's courage. He had inspected the raw, bleeding hands, wanting to be part of the new camaraderie that existed.

"Just a touch," Riach dismissed bravely. "Have you nearly finished, Macaree?"

"Am I hurting you?" she asked anxiously.

"No," he denied hastily.

"When do we get pigeon for supper?" probed Aggie, shaking her gray head at the hands that Macaree lovingly bandaged. She was unable to envision those hands handling a gun or chopping firewood with any accuracy.

"My gentle Macaree will have to turn savage and bag the first few," Riach pronounced. "But rest assured, my sweet, I shall teach you to be cruel and merciless," he teased, but his engaging expression sobered when he met her startled gaze. "Your eyes are like Robbie's summer sky . . . they're that very special blue that goes for ever and ever," he murmured.

"Soup!" Aggie shouted as she saw the Campbell's mouth descending to claim Macaree's trembling, parted lips. "Soup!" she repeated awkwardly when two bewildered young faces regarded her. "I thought you were very hungry," she added defensively.

"Have you known many wenches?" inquired Robbie, causing everyone to gasp. "Have I said something amiss?" he added, noting the shocked expressions.

"That is a very impertinent question! Why would you ask such a thing?" Riach demanded roughly.

"I'm sorry. It was just how you looked at my sister and what you said to her before Aggie shouted 'soup!' " the boy explained miserably.

"And what about it? That did not give you the right to ask such an improper question!"

"I dinna ken," the boy mumbled unhappily, unable to deal with the older youth's fury. "I'm very sorry," he repeated, then burrowed down into his blankets. Riach looked at the small, trembling shape. His anger melted away and guilt took its place. He turned apologetically to Macaree, but she gazed sorrowfully toward her brother.

"I dinna think the *bairn* was speaking biblically," Aggie said in defense of Robbie. "He doesn't know of such things."

"Robbie, I shouldn't have shouted at you, but you shouldn't have called your sister a wench." He tried to make amends and return the cozy kitchen to its former warm gaiety.

There was no answer from the boy, and, aware of Aggie's accusing glare, Riach got up and sheepishly crossed to the pallet, conscious of his clumsy gait. "Robbie?" he said, seating himself and patting the small mound with one bandaged hand. "Come up for air?" he urged, wanting to play the kindly big brother. It was important to him. He had never been regarded with such awed reverence before. It was the way he used to look at Darach, he realized.

Robbie threw the covers from his flushed face and stared up at Riach, tears brimming and brightening the already too bright eyes.

"I'm sorry, Riach, truly I am. I dinna mean to make you angry wie me. I dinna mean disrespect to you and Macaree," he wailed. He hurled himself against Riach's chest and sobbed. Riach held him close, his own eyes streaming.

"Nay, wee Rob Roy MacGregor, I'm the one who's sorry," he answered huskily, his face against the flaxen hair that was so much like Macaree's. The boy was about ten, the age Riach had been when his father had died. Ten, the same number of years that separated him and his older brother. "It was my fault. I don't know why I was so cross, except . . . at the risk of losing my prestigious reputation with the fairer sex, I'll admit to its being a lie. The truth is, I have never been very adept with wenches. Och, I tried, but they scared the very dickens out of me. Now, old ladies and wee lassies, I can charm them from the trees, but those wenches put the fear of the de'il in me," he confessed jokingly.

"Another example of your big brother's awesome infamy?" Aggie taunted dryly, incensed that the youth should have bullied the sick boy. "Intimidated by his randy reputation wie the wenches?"

"How little you know my brother, Mistress Fletcher. The incomparable Lord Rannoch doesna trifle with mere wenches. 'Tis only mature, worldly, voluptuous women for him." Riach laughed sardonically.

"Why did you get so loud and uppity wie the lad?" the old crone probed. Riach shrugged and smiled down at Robbie, who lay exhausted against his pillows.

"I'm tired and it has been a long day," he lied, unwilling to admit that he was angry with the boy for reducing his very magical moment with Macaree into something cheap and tawdry. "Do you forgive me?" he asked Robbie, wondering why on earth he cared. What was it about these three raggedy outlaws that was so important to him?

"If you forgive me," replied Robbie with a watery grin.

"There's nothing to forgive. Can we be brothers?" Riach offered his hand.

"Is it all right, Aggie?" Robbie asked anxiously.

"Why wouldna it be?"

"He's a Campbell and I'm a MacGregor."

"Do you want to be his brother?"

"More than anything," whispered the boy.

"Then it has to be right," decided Aggie. "Now shake your big brother's hand and hae a wee nap," she fussed, then blew her nose and bustled busily about the hearth. "Well, young Campbell, if'n you can teach our gentle Macaree how to kill a bird or two, maybe we'll be eating a mite more substantially on the morrow," she snapped acidly, after watching him stare broodingly into his watery broth for several long minutes. She thought him judgmental of the frugal fare.

"You had better pray that I'm more of a teacher than a doer." Riach sighed. "I honestly cannot recall doing anything right in my whole life," he admitted, cupping the mug between his swaddled hands and breathing deeply of the savory steam. He felt no hunger, just pangs of grim foreboding gnawing into his gut. He stared at Aggie's concerned wrinkled face, seeing the uncomplaining, loyal lines and understanding the eloquent plea in her old, tired eyes. And then he looked at Macaree's exquisite little face. She smiled tenderly, and he knew without a doubt that she trusted him completely. And so did the little boy who stared up at him with such worship in his eyes, blind to any weaknesses or faults.

Riach was utterly appalled at the realization that he was responsible for their very lives, and he silently acknowledged that he had never acted responsibly, even for his own life. He had never had to—there had always been his big brother, Darach, to pick up the pieces. He abruptly excused himself and sought refuge in his squalid scullery nook, unable to meet Macaree's eyes.

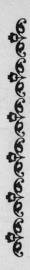

chapter 14

Riach stared pensively out at the rain that pounded relentlessly against the snow, changing the stark white vista into a dreary mottling of browns and grays.

"Och, there'll be no dry wood for the hearth," lamented Aggie, shaking her head at the pitiful pile stacked to one side of the fireplace.

"There's plenty of dry wood—enough to keep us warm for a year," Riach declared expansively.

"Where?"

"There's about thirty rooms full of furniture up there," he explained, twirling a finger at the ceiling.

"You canna burn tha' guid furniture—tha's a criminal waste!" protested Aggie. "Besides, it doesna belong to us."

"Who does it belong to?"

"I dinna ken, but nae us. I suppose it did belong to Lady Ailsa, so now 'tis her next-of-kin's, and tha's Gregor Mac-Gregor—if he's still walking this earth," she muttered.

"Gregor MacGregor. Rory MacNiall," mused Riach. "Where did he go?"

"I dinna ken," she lied.

" 'Tis very strange that he'd leave and not return. 'Tis very strange that in the year I knew him he never mentioned Linnmanach or his children."

"Why is tha' so strange? Seems to me tha' the two of you

were too busy playing to discuss things serious," Aggie snapped tartly.

" 'Tis strange because in all that time I don't think he ever came here."

"Wha's so unco' aboot tha'?" she retorted. "Och, there's many a mon who isna domestic, who'll leave his family to fend for theirselves while he's off in his fancy clothes, kicking up his heels wie strong spirits, bawdy women, and games of chance!"

"You think he went back to Edinburgh?"

"I said I dinna ken where the master went!"

"Do you know where your father went, Macaree?"

Macaree didn't acknowledge his words. She kept staring out the window watching the rain. She didn't know where her father had gone, and she didn't want to know. Just the mention of Gregor made her feel uncomfortable and frightened, changing the soothing, hypnotic rhythm of the rain into a portentous pounding. She concentrated on the harmony of the drops falling into the shimmering puddles. She traced their rippling, widening circles, drowning out the disturbing presences of Riach and Aggie. Spring was coming. The snow was melting, and soon there would be a sweet, tingling fragrance as new life thrust through the awakening earth to burst into glorious blossoms. Ducks and swans would land on the *loch* to build nests among the reeds. She and Riach would walk hand in hand, barefoot on the soft green grass, watching the yellow ducklings scud and the gray cygnets glide across the blue water that reflected the graceful willows and majestic oaks. Wild roses would cover the cold, gray stones of Linnmanach.

"She doesna ken where her father is," Aggie answered protectively, shrewdly noting the girl's preoccupation and hearing the soft humming.

"Macaree? Do you know where your father and sister went?" Riach repeated, gently touching her shoulder, but she shrugged off his hand and sang louder. He stepped back with a frown, recognizing the emotionless mask. "Why would your father take your sister, Kat, with him?" he demanded, trying to break through her invisible barrier, but Macaree kept singing a nursery ditty and drew childish pictures in the steam on the windowpane.

"He dinna say where he was going or why. He just said tha' he'd be back afore the week was oot," stated Aggie.

"And when was that?" he asked sharply, staring with concern at Macaree.

"Beginning of March, and now 'tis April, as I've told you more'n a dozen times. It isna going to change wie the saying!" the old woman spat crossly. "Why dinna you make yourself useful and check the traps you and Macaree set? Or take the gun and try to pop a few more pigeons. They should be easy targets in this drear drizzle. They be huddled in bunches trying to stay dry."

Macaree broke free of her panic, closing her lips tightly and stopping the song. She turned to Riach, but his expression was remote.

"Where are you going?" she asked, as he draped several dry sacks over himself and took down the rifle.

"There's an oilskin on the hook," said Aggie, marveling at how he didn't recoil from the burlap, which sprayed a choking cloud of powdered mud. The lad had come a long way in the cold days since digging Ailsa's grave.

"No, there's no use in two of us getting soaked to the skin," Riach snapped curtly when Macaree eagerly tied a shawl around her fair head.

"But I want to." She laughed. "I love to get wet."

"No!" he shouted savagely, snatching the tattered oilskin off the peg and storming out of the kitchen. He did not look backward, but left Macaree frozen in shock, her eyes filling with tears.

"What's happening?" muttered Robbie groggily, startled awake when the door slammed shut.

"Nothing, my pet. Snuggle yourself down and go back to your dreams," Aggie said soothingly. The boy grinned sleepily and closed his eyes with a contented sigh. "Sometimes a mon needs his solitude, lass," she whispered, patting Macaree's arm comfortingly. "Look at him," she urged, staring out the window. "You'd nae believe him to be the same prissy weakling of barely a fortnight ago," she mused fondly. She watched the youth stride manfully outdoors, not fazed a bit by the thick mud and the clumsy hobnail boots. He strode with his dark head held high, looking the very epitome of a confident, virile male animal despite his humbling attire of sacking and oilskin. "Och, if'n I were only a quarter of a century younger."

Macaree sniffed and dashed the blinding tears from her eyes. She stood beside Aggie and watched Riach disappear into the tangle of evergreen and leafless oak, wishing she was slipping in the cloying mud beside him, feeling his warm callused hand securely holding hers. The past two weeks had consisted of one delirious joy after the other—one triumph after the other. She had never known that such joy and happiness existed. At first they had tried too hard to be perfect hunters and woodchoppers, but instead of being depressed by their dismal failures, they had laughed at themselves and at each other. And they hadn't expected to succeed. So they had played, collapsing into the crisp banked snow and rolling in each other's arms, their merriment frosting the crystal air. Macaree pensively licked her lips, remembering a kiss, one that had lasted until they were breathless, their cheeks flushed and rosy and their eyes sparkling. She had relived that kiss countless times, from the first tentative touching of their trembling mouths to the long, sweet quenching of strange, inexplicable sensations. They had held each other tightly, their arms hugging their bulky layers of clothing, but along with the delicious mounting excitement had been an ominous pulse that had threatened to drag her down into a terrifying dark memory.

Macaree threw the terror aside and forced a brittle smile as she recalled Riach's first success—a very old, skinny rabbit. He had shot it at such close range that there had not been much to retrieve—just a splatter of blood, bone, and fur in the snow. But how victorious they had felt scrambling around to gather all the pieces together and rushing back to show Aggie. Macaree hadn't even felt sick.

"Remember the first rabbit?" She giggled, turning to the old woman, the tears from Riach's curt rejection still glistening on her cheeks.

"Puir *auld baistie*. I dinna think I ever saw such an ancient creature," Aggie chortled. "Och, but there's three fine fat *bawds* hanging in the larder, and pigeons in the pot. Who'd hae thought the young dandy would turn oot to be such a fine provider?" she marveled happily.

"And I havena been able to kill anything," Macaree stated sadly. "Even when his hands were too sore to hold the gun, and there wasna a thing to eat, I couldna provide for the pot. Maybe that's why Riach didna want me wie him."

"Och, dinna spout such *stite!*" chided Aggie. "You've done very well. Why, I can remember not too long ago when you couldna even look at anything dead nor bloody wie-oot turning green aboot the gills and fainting dead away wie a screech! But whose wee hands hae skinned the rabbits and hares? Whose wee hands plucked the picky feathers and drew the entrails? They werena my *auld* rheumatic fingers," she stated, displaying her painfully deformed hands. "It was you, my gentle Macaree."

"What would *maman* say?" the girl whispered fearfully.

"She'd understand," comforted the old woman.

"I dinna think she would," Macaree answered quietly, turning away from Aggie and staring out at the driving rain. She tried to still the clawing panic that tore into her belly as a sharp memory of a bloodied white dress ripped into her mind.

Riach enjoyed the aroma of the wet woods. He felt more alive and complete than he ever had before, yet many things bothered him. Where was the master of Linnmanach, and what was he, Riach, doing in the rambling, crumbling mansion? This question kept him awake at night, rousing him from deep slumber and causing anxious dreams. Night after night he tossed, trying to get comfortable on the hard, narrow cot in the dark alcove off the kitchen, painstakingly trying to recall the previous months and his relationship to Rory Mac-Niall, also known as Gregor MacGregor. He had met the affable, magnanimous man more than a year before at a party in Edinburgh. He had found himself out of pocket, somewhat bosky, and in the hands of some decidedly unpleasant ruffians intent on doing considerable harm to him in lieu of the monies owed. It had been Rory MacNiall who had come to his aid, dispersing the bullies and even offering hospitality and a generous loan. That had been the beginning of a friendship that had whirled madly from all-night gambling clubs to exotic opium dens—and finally to Christmas at Linnmanach, when he had become enamored of the beautiful Macaree.

Riach dug his boots into the rotting leaves and leaned back against a tree, lifting his head and letting the rain stream down his cheeks. He remembered the enormous amount of money that he owed. His recollections of that time were vague and distorted by excess spirits and drugs, but he knew his debt was more than a hundred crowns. Fragments of nightmarish remembrances caused his pulses to throb, weighing him down with guilt, and he stared through the stark, leafless limbs of the forest to the hulking ruin, thinking of Robbie and Macaree sleeping on mattresses on the kitchen floor. He had, in effect,

robbed those starving MacGregors of a vast amount of money
and had used it on foul substances to make him forget that he
was a cowardly, miserable failure.

A movement caught his attention, and he remained motionless, his eyes scanning, his hand tightening on the rifle. He
nearly gasped aloud at the sight of three deer. He held his
breath for fear that they'd catch his scent and swiftly disappear. They were three yearling does separated from their herd,
Riach thought. Or maybe this was all that was left of the herd.
The ravages of the long merciless winter were apparent by
their emaciated frames and listless coats as they slowly and
wearily picked their way through the dripping forest. Carefully, Riach lifted the gun, excitement making his hands tremble. He aimed. The smallest doe stood motionless, her delicate
nose quivering, her graceful neck raised. She presented a perfect target, but he was unable to pull the trigger. He lowered
the gun, remembering the three hares that were hanging to
season and the pigeons that were simmering in the pot on the
hob, and he enjoyed the shy animal's fluid movements. Winter was very nearly over, and it seemed brutal to wantonly kill
the winsome creature that had tenaciously managed to survive
the worst part of the season. He'd leave her to enjoy the spring
and summer, he decided, but the thought of his older brother,
who was never swayed by sentiment, flashed into his mind. He
imagined the admiring applause and thought of the esteem
that would shine in Macaree's and Robbie's worshipful eyes if
he were to stride across the lawn with a whole deer carried
proudly across his shoulders. The image of himself as the
victorious hunter nearly caused him to take aim again, but instead he misfired into the air. Flocks of pigeons, rooks, and
crows noisily burst from their huddled roosts into the wetness
above the trees, and the deer were sent crashing through the
brittle underbrush. Then there was silence again, except for
the continuous patter of the rain.

Riach trudged pensively through the woods, circling the
loch. He did not wish to be observed from the house. He
wanted to be alone with his turbulent thoughts and emotions.
He was inextricably bound to Macaree, Robbie, and even the
cantankerous Aggie Fletcher—bound not just by the overwhelming love he felt for the beautiful girl, or by his brotherly
promises to the sick child, or even by his guilt for owing them
so much money, but because it was his only salvation. Linnmanach was the only place he had ever felt needed, the only

place he had felt and acted like a responsible man.

Riach ran into the tumbledown stables seeking shelter when the rain intensified. Sheets of water poured straight from the heavens to the earth with such slashing savagery that it was impossible to see his hand in front of his face. He allowed his eyes to become accustomed to the gloom, and then he explored the large building, noting the many stalls that could comfortably stable more than three dozen animals. He imagined what Linnmanach must have been like when beautifully groomed horses nodded their elegant heads over the half doors, when the crystal candelabras in the grand ballroom and dining hall were lit, when each bedchamber was occupied, when the nursery wing was filled with children's laughter, when the lawns were manicured. His mind whirled with whens —when Gregor MacGregor returned, what, then?

Riach walked around the neglected stables, stopping to stare at the rusting plows and the saddles of different sizes, their leather gnawed by hungry rodents. There were sleighs with faded paintings of reindeers and tarnished bells, outmoded carriages, broken tools from earlier eras. He gazed upon the refuse and relics of several generations.

"For this generation, this present time, there is nothing," he stated aloud. Only two stalls showed any evidence of use, and those had been for the superb, matched grays that Gregor MacGregor had driven away more than a month before. Had the man left him at Linnmanach purposefully to tend to his family? What sort of man—a man who was obviously wealthy, from the way he dressed and lived—would leave his family in such dire straits? Riach puzzled, noting the absence of feed and just one meager bale of straw. He shinned up the splintery ladder to the loft, which was empty of hay but thickly coated with bird and rodent droppings. Chaff, dust, and cobwebs coated the exposed rafters and the planked floor. He stood at the opened loading door, staring over the sprawling estate from the ruffled surface of the *loch* to the surrounding woodland and sloping pastures. He saw the rhododendron-lined, formal carriageway that circled from the crumbling ruin and the spiked wrought-iron palings that he had glimpsed on his walks with Macaree. It was a little patch of Eden, he thought poetically, feeling soothed by the consistent drumming of the rain on the roof. Suddenly he was excited by the prospect of exploring every inch of the place.

"This is my domain," he proclaimed proudly, thrusting out

his chest and swinging his arm in a confident arc. "I can plant,
I can farm, I can restore," he planned. "I can make Linn-
manach more beautiful, more gracious, more everything than
Strathrannoch and Glengrian."

The rain lessened, and he strode happily toward the carriageway, taking care to encircle the house. The shining-wet
rhododendron leaves grew so rampant that there was scarcely
room for a two-horse vehicle to pass, and he made a mental
note to chop back the encroaching bushes as he walked along
the winding half-mile approach. He gazed in awe at the soaring, majestic, somewhat corroded gates, noting the remnants
of gilt still adhering to their crowning spikes. Then he looked
at the quaint house that adjoined.

"Why the hell are we living in the cellar of that unholy
monument when there's this little treasure here?" he demanded of the surrounding dripping trees and quiet road.
Realizing that he stared upon a genuine road that linked
civilizations, Riach peered between the blackened bars,
searching for hoofprints, footprints, and wheel ruts. Nothing
seemed to have disturbed the muddy route except the rain.

"Riach?" Macaree's frightened voice spiraled through the
pitter-patter of the rain and up the narrow stairs to the cozy
bedchamber, where Riach stared at the charming patchwork
order of the little room. He strode to the window, painfully
aware of the muddy tracks his spiked boots left on the lovingly
worked rag rugs. He watched her from the window for a few
minutes, filling his eyes with her dripping, flaxen hair and
glowing cheeks before rapping on the panes to call her attention.

"What are you doing in here?" Macaree whispered. She
seemed to fall into the little house as soon as he unlatched the
door. "We shall be seen," she warned.

"By whom?" he asked, noticing how her cornflower-blue
eyes flickered fearfully toward the road before she thrust
herself into the tiny hallway.

"Just be seen."

Macaree had never given much thought to whom they were
trying to avoid.

"By whom?" he pressed.

"Everyone," she answered finally. "Everyone in the whole
world." She leaned against the wall, trying to calm her wildly
thudding heart. She had thought Riach had gone and she

would never see him again. She had waited for him to appear, after hearing the one sharp shot tear through the drizzle and seeing the flocks of birds explode into the gray sky above the west forest. When he hadn't appeared, all manner of horrendous suppositions had crowded her mind. Suppose he was lying wounded, his life's blood draining away, the torrential rain beating down upon his helpless body? She had raced through the woods, heedless of the clawing brown brambles that impeded her progress, snagging on her long skirts, and whipping about her bare legs, heedless of the dank, heavy moisture that weighed down her cumbersome clothes and seeped through the cracked leather of her broken shoes, chilling her blistered feet. Her shawl had been torn from her head by a low branch that had also bruised her wide, pale brow as she had run through the dripping forest screaming for Riach. When she did not find him, she had supposed that he had managed to escape Linnmanach, never to return. She had dared to step onto the carriageway. She had forced herself to walk between the tall dark bushes, following the distinct pattern of his hobnail boots, keeping her eyes pinned straight ahead, expecting bats to protest her intrusion by flying into her hair. At first she had walked slowly. Then, as panic started to pound, she increased her pace until she reached the gates.

"Riach?" she had screamed in despair, believing he had abandoned her and returned to the outside world. "Och, Riach!" she had lamented, until the brittle rapping on the glass had penetrated her sorrow, and she had looked up to see him framed in the second-story window of the little gatehouse.

"Haven't you ever set foot in here before?" Riach asked, remarking on her wide-eyed interest as her terror receded, and she inquisitively peered about. She silently shook her wet head, spraying them both, and Riach helped her out of her sodden cloak. "It hasn't been empty very long. Who lived here?"

"*Auld* Sebastian, the gatekeeper. He died last autumn."

"He certainly kept a cozy nest. We should all be living here instead of in the basement kitchens. The roof doesn't leak and it's easy to heat. The furnishings are modest, but they're clean and comfortable. And I have seen no evidence of rats, mice, bats, or squirrels," he said, taking her hand and leading her through the little rooms.

"But we canna live here." Macaree sighed wistfully, after

they had explored the quaint brick kitchen with its frilly gay
curtains, the pretty little sitting room, and the three tiny
bedrooms upstairs.

"Why not?"

"Too near the road," she answered. " 'Tis not safe."

"Where does the road lead?"

"I dinna ken."

"What is the nearest town?"

"I dinna ken."

"Don't you ever leave Linnmanach?" he probed, and she
shook her head. "Never?" he gasped.

"Not since we first came here," she answered, ashamed.

"From France?" he asked after a long pause, remembering
Robbie's reference to their mother being buried in that
country.

"From France," she conceded, shivering as she recalled the
bitterly cold, hungry winter in Ballachulish.

"How long ago was that?"

"I was fourteen, and now I'm nineteen."

"You are nineteen years old!" Riach exclaimed. He had
thought her much younger. "Nineteen?" he repeated.

"I'm sorry. I'm an old maid, I know. My mother was married at fourteen, and Aggie at thirteen, and here I am an old
spinster of nineteen," chattered Macaree, feeling awkward
and frightened. She was losing him. She felt him slipping away
from her, and a heavy dread settled in the pit of her stomach.
"I am very sorry," she whispered.

"I'm nineteen, too, but I shall soon be twenty—in May,"
he stated forcefully. "When is your birthday?" he demanded
tersely.

"October," she answered fearfully. Suddenly it seemed that
everything was precariously balanced. Riach sighed loudly
with relief and then laughed.

"I am older than you," he crowed.

"What if I had been older than you?" she asked quietly.

"I cannot believe that you've not set a foot outside Linnmanach in all these years," Riach pronounced, purposefully
avoiding her questions.

"Katrine hadna either until Father took her away in
March," Macaree said defensively. "I am truly sorry that I am
so old." She shivered, wrapping her arms about her sodden
layers, feeling chilled and uneasy. She was suddenly terribly
aware of her vulnerability. What if Riach Campbell went out

of the gates and her father and sister never came back? She, Aggie, and Robbie would all die. She had to do something to make him stay.

"You're soaked through, and so am I," Riach stated, seeing her bloodless fingers and the blue tinge about her lips. "*Auld* Sebastian left a tidy pile of logs. So you run upstairs and get out of those wet skirts, while I kindle a healthy blaze."

"No! You mustna light a fire! The smoke'll be seen from the road," protested Macaree.

"And it wasn't when Sebastian lived here?"

"But you're not Sebastian," worried the frantic girl, trying to stem the song that ached in her throat.

"I am the new gatekeeper of Linnmanach, and I have a perfect right to keep myself, and my pretty wife, warm and dry on this dreary, gray day," he soothed huskily, stroking her pale cheek and gazing hungrily at her trembling mouth. He bent his dark head and softly kissed her before pushing her toward the stairs. "Go take off those wet clothes, pretty wife," he coaxed, feeling a tightening in his groin. He pulled her back against him and nuzzled her neck. "This is our secret cottage, and there is just you and me, my love," he whispered into her soft ear. Color charmingly rose, flushing her cheeks, and a fearful excitement tingled through her chilled body, making her blue eyes sparkle with a bittersweet anticipation.

Riach grinned at the sound of her feet skittering up the narrow wooden stairs, supposing her haste was due to impatience. Soon they would lie together, he resolved. Soon it would be his turn to touch all her forbidden places, as she had done when he had been too helpless to respond. His passion achingly flared as he recalled the intimate touch of her cool, silky fingers. He had tossed and turned every night, knowing she was just on the other side of the door, lying on her pallet beside the kitchen hearth with the glow of the embers illuminating her beautiful sleeping face. He had wanted her, ached for her, imagined her lying stretched beside him—their naked flesh touching from lips to toes. She belonged to him and nobody else, he vowed firmly, and he grinned with happiness at the knowledge that he was the only mate in her life. As shocking as it was to know she had been incarcerated at Linnmanach for five long years, it had ensured her purity. He could be confident and masterful, and he did not have to worry about being unfavorably compared. Finally, he would be first.

"Hurry up, pretty wife," he called joyously, hunkering on his haunches and staring proudly at the blaze in the hearth that mirrored the fire in his loins. It had taken several attempts; the room was full of choking black smoke, and his face was streaked with soot. But he had opened the damper, and now the wood crackled hotly. He whistled cheerfully, satisfied with his accomplishment as he stripped off his sodden upper clothes. He stood bare-chested before the blaze, feeling very much the virile male. "Macaree?" he shouted, staring about the quaint sitting room. For the first time in his life, he wasn't envious of his brother's more than six-foot stature. Darach Campbell couldn't stand up straight in *auld* Sebastian's parlor —the ceiling wasn't high enough, he mused happily. The untidy pile of discarded clothes bothered him, and he picked them up and hung them with Macaree's cape in the hallway. He chuckled to himself and wondered what his valet or Missie MacKissock would say about his domesticity.

Macaree snapped out of her strange reverie at the sound of his voice and stood trembling with cold and trepidation. She had slowly loosened her clothes and let them sag damply to the floor. She dreamily watched her shadowy reflection in a dusty mirror that hung on the sloping wall of the little bedroom under the eaves. It was as though she was a voyeur observing another woman through an elusive haze, another woman who had no fear and reveled in the sensuousness of her body. She cupped her breasts, rubbing the points until they hardened, but Riach's voice shattered the image and she saw a frightened naked girl in the mirror. She stood motionless with the saturated skirts and petticoats puddled about her bare feet. Her long wet hair dripped and made her spine tingle. The deep male voice vibrated through her quaking limbs. She opened her mouth to answer him, but there was no sound. A terrible terror pulsed, and she heard his heavy step on the wooden stairs coming closer.

Riach stood in the doorway and marveled at her perfection. She was half turned away from him, her silhouette framed against the window. He saw a long slender neck and firm thrusting breasts. Her limber flanks and the soft womanly curve of her belly fluttered like a quivering butterfly. She was even more magnificent than he had envisioned in his most exciting dreams.

"Macaree?" he said softly and hoarsely, but she didn't turn to him. She didn't acknowledge his presence. He suddenly realized how very cold she must be, as their breath frosted the icy air. "Macaree?" He wrenched the quilt from the neat bed and draped it over her trembling shoulders, turning her around to face him. Her eyes were glassy and blank. Her mouth curved in a frozen brittle smile. "Macaree?" he shouted, and he shook her roughly, trying to dislodge the petrified mask.

"*Elle était une bergère qui ron ron ron petite pattapon,*" she sang sweetly, curdling his blood so that his hands fell from her. "*Elle était une bergère qui garde les moutons, ron ron . . . qui garde les moutons,*" she continued. Then she giggled like a tiny girl and curtsied. "Do you like my little song, *monsieur?*" she asked coyly. "I am *maman's* gentle Macaree, *maman's* china doll, *maman's* little princess, *maman's* perfect gentle daughter," she recited.

"Go downstairs and sit by the fire," he ordered harshly, not knowing what to do. Like a small child, she docilely obeyed. Riach stood at the top of the narrow flight of steps, watching her descend until she disappeared into the parlor. Her voice spiraled up to him. Once more she was singing a familiar nursery tune. Why did he find the song so haunting? he wondered. He sat on the bed frowning, not knowing what to make of Macaree's bizarre behavior. He remembered the long terror-filled days and nights when he'd been tied to the bed, and he thought of her soothing voice and comforting hands. She had sung that lullaby to chase away the insects that devoured him, and now she sang it to console herself. He found himself staring at a wooden chest, and absently he lifted the lid to find neatly folded smocks, waistcoats, and trousers. The smell of camphor was overwhelming, but the dryness and cleanliness of the garments were irresistible.

Riach dressed himself in *auld* Sebastian's homespun clothes, which were a better fit than the ones Aggie had supplied. He took his time, not knowing how to deal with Macaree. Her childish singing had ceased, and he wondered what she was doing now. He selected an assortment of clothes for her to wear. He hesitated at the top of the stairs, hearing a busy clatter from the kitchen.

Macaree explored Sebastian's cupboards and giggled with delight at the treasures she unearthed: several pots of bramble and wild strawberry jam, a plum pudding, a stone jug of whiskey, two bottles of sloe gin, a tin of shortbread, and another one full of tea leaves.

"Riach?" she called excitedly, wrapping the cumbersome quilt more securely about herself and then balancing the goodies. "Riach? Come and see what I've found!"

"And see what I have found," he answered from the kitchen door. She squealed with surprise at his closeness and spun about to face him, nearly dropping the tins and jars. She grinned with delight at his new wardrobe and noted the thick, knitted hose that enabled him to make his stealthy approach.

"Camphor?" She laughed, comically wrinkling up her nose with distaste at the strong odor. "Look, there is strawberry jam . . . even a jug of whiskey, and a—"

"Get dressed!" he interrupted curtly, distracted by the seductive curve of her exposed breasts as the quilt slipped lower. Macaree's happiness swiftly fled at his brusque tone. He thrust a bundle of clothes onto the table and snatched up the whiskey jug before striding into the parlor, leaving her to her privacy.

Macaree stood staring at the firmly closed door and then turned to look at the male garments. Her mother's dying words seeped into her mind.

"I know I should wear silks and satins," she whispered, pushing her small cold feet into the coarse warmth of the knitted hose and pulling the homespun smock over her damp head. "But silks and satins won't keep me warm, *maman*. And Kat is dead, so there's only me to take care of Robbie," she explained, daring for the first time to express her fears about her sister. Tears rolled slowly down her cheeks, as she stepped into Sebastian's large trousers and yanked them up around her slender waist. "I'm sorry, *maman,* I canna be your gentle princess anymore."

Riach took a long punishing swallow of whiskey and stared broodingly into the fire, taking a perverse pleasure in the sharp burning pain that dug into his empty stomach. He heard a faint sob and turned about. Macaree stood in the doorway, looking pathetic in the outsized clothes, tears streaming down her wan face.

"What's the matter?" he asked lamely. Macaree desperately wanted to sing, but she bravely fought against that means of escape. She reached out to him for comfort.

"I . . . I canna . . . keep the trews up, and my sister Katrine is dead," she finally sobbed. "And I don't want you to ever leave me," she added with a wail.

chapter 15

Although Aggie grumbled, she soon settled into the little gatehouse and grudgingly admitted that the move might help Robbie, who became more alert and less inclined to sleep all day. A permanent bed had been made for him in the parlor. He could see and hear Aggie in the kitchen, and he could look out of the window and watch Riach and Macaree dig in the vegetable garden.

It was mid-May, and the young Campbell toiled bare-chested in the bright sunshine.

"If I grow to be a man, I wish to be just like that," the boy declared, admiring the muscles that rippled beneath Riach's brown glistening skin.

"Aye, 'tis certainly a change from tha' weak, prissy sot who came for Christmas," marveled Aggie, opening the window to allow the sweet, balmy warmth to stream over the child's bed.

"Aye, and 'tis certainly a change in our gentle princess Macaree." Robbie giggled. "She's wearing *auld* breeks and she's barefoot! If it wasna for her golden hair, she'd be just like our Kat." The boy slumped dejectedly back onto his pillows. "Do you think our Kat is . . . dead, Aggie?" he whispered after a long silence.

"Och, let's nae hae any dark clouds dousing this wondrous spring day," the old woman begged huskily. "It has been a long, cold winter. 'Tis now time to rejoice.''

"I canna rejoice thinking of my sister being dead."

"She's nae dead!"

"Then why has she nae come home to Linnmanach? I dinna expect our father to come home, but Kat belongs here wie us. And I miss her very, very much." The boy sobbed.

"Aye, I ken. So do I," murmured Aggie, stroking his fair hair. "And she'll be back. Och, she's just like her namesake—has nine lives and always lands on her nimble wee feet."

"Then she maun be in some awful trouble, or she'd be here. I think she's dead, and we'll never see her again," Robbie stated bitterly, pushing the old lady's fussing hands away. He sat up and glared out the window, angered by the merrily chirping birds that busily nested in the eaves. "Do they ever stop kissing?" he spat furiously. "Every minute of every day their mouths are stuck together—kiss, kiss, kiss! 'Tis disgusting!" he hissed, glowering at Riach and Macaree.

" 'Tis nature. 'Tis springtime," chuckled Aggie. "Och, and one day, my fine wee rooster, you'll be feeling the same stirrings in your blood," she promised, hobbling to the kitchen.

"Do you still feel stirrings in the springtime?" the boy asked curiously, eyeing Riach's hands which splayed across Macaree's pert bottom. "Or are you too old?"

"I dinna think a person is ever too *auld*, unless they're dead. The stirrings just get a mite fainter wie each passing year," she admitted regretfully, as she clattered about the kitchen.

Robbie kneeled on his bed and hung out of the window. He saw the couple passionately embracing.

"Do you think they'll hae babies?" he asked.

"Och, there's going to be lots of wee babies, ducklings and gray swanlets, speckled fawns and impish buns, all stealing the kale," chattered Aggie.

"But do you think Macaree and Riach'll hae babies?"

The boy's shrill voice penetrated Riach's ears, and he stared down speculatively into Macaree's upturned face. Her eyes were closed, and her thick golden lashes fanned on her blushing cheeks. Her mouth was moist and open, trembling, and wanting more. Her body arched toward him, her tightly budded breasts straining against her loose smock as he leaned away. But he held her hips possessively to the aching core of him. He yearned to claim her totally, and many times he had been brought to that tortuous edge, only to have his blood chilled and his passion doused by the childlike singing voice and the frozen mask.

"Let's go for a walk away from prying little boys," he whispered huskily against her parted lips. She nodded wordlessly, seeing the smoldering fire in his amber eyes. Maybe this time she would be able to give him what he wanted, and then she became afraid. Each time it was the same—the glorious golden excitement consumed her until a certain moment when he knelt between her open legs. Then a mindless terror tore into her mind.

Macaree and Riach walked hand in hand over the straggly lawn toward the tranquil *loch*. All nature was alive and busy. Bees, birds, and butterflies flew hither and thither, and even the hulking, hollow-eyed ruin was softened by rambling wild roses whose fragrance was pungent and intoxicating. They ambled leisurely, stopping to pick spring blossoms. They tucked cowslips, violets, and buttercups into buttonholes and behind ears, their hands brushing softly and intimately against each other. They stopped to kiss gently and then hungrily, arching their hips as they tried to unite.

"Macaree?" asked Riach, pinning her against the trunk of a willow tree. Its tender green branches arced down like a waterfall about them. He longed to thrust himself into the hot core of her, but instead he ground himself in frustration against her boyish clothes.

Macaree rhythmically moved against him, listening to the spring noises. She tried to ignore the ominous pulse that intruded and to stem the song that ached for release in her throat.

"Riach?" she cried when he suddenly pulled away, throwing himself down onto the sloping bank. He didn't answer but savagely tore at some long grass. He chewed it, keeping his eyes averted from her. "Riach?" she repeated, lying beside him and offering her lips. He rolled farther away and stared at the sky. He did not know what he would do if he was once again brought to the edge, just to be rejected again. It was too humiliating having to sneak away to relieve himself. A rage beat within him, and he didn't trust himself not to take her by force.

"We should go back to work in the garden," he muttered.

"Riach?" she whispered, leaning over his prone figure. He closed his eyes, not wishing to be tempted. "Riach, look at me," she murmured seductively against his firmly closed mouth. She unbuttoned her smock, letting her naked breasts brush tantalizingly over his quivering body. Macaree was bewildered by his passivity, but her excitement flared when she saw evidence of his arousal. Full of wonder at her own power, she softly traced the hard ridge of his manroot, and he groaned and bucked to meet her hand.

"For God's sake, Macaree! If you'll not let me possess you, at least touch me and put me out of this misery," he begged. There was a long, still moment, and then he felt her trembling hand slide down his taut belly beneath the waistband of his britches.

Macaree waited for terror to tear in as her excitement built. Her fingers inched down into the hot darkness to tentatively caress and then to firmly grasp his awesome hardness. They lay entwined, their hands beneath each other's clothes intimately touching, but suddenly Macaree recoiled.

"I'll race you into the water!" Riach challenged, sensing her panic. There was a flurry of undressing and then a joyous splashing to which the nesting ducks, swans, and geese loudly objected. Later, they again lay side by side on the soft velvet grass, their trembling hands curiously exploring each other's nakedness. Once again, they brought each other to ecstatic heights. But when Riach dared to touch himself to her springy golden hairs, hoping to thrust into her hot moistness, he saw terror petrify her exquisite features, and a chilling nursery song warbled from her kiss-bruised mouth.

The golden days of May passed happily, and the little gatehouse was filled with flowers and laughter. The vegetable garden thrived, and Macaree and Riach lived each day to the fullest. They worked hard and then stole away to play sensuously in the *loch* and the pastures.

Robbie withdrew himself, getting neither weaker nor stronger. He would lie listlessly, making no effort to join in conversations or be a part of his sister's glowing happiness. Aggie's joints ached fiercely, and she had sharp pains in her chest. She sensed that she was dying, but she didn't know how to broach the subject to Macaree and Riach. She hated to mar the young couple's glorious joy, but one June day a bird flew into the house.

Riach and Macaree heard the terrible scream and rushed into the gatehouse, not knowing what to expect. Aggie sat at the kitchen table with her apron thrown over her gray head, rocking and lamenting.

"What is it?" the young Campbell demanded after checking Robbie and seeing that the boy was unchanged.

"There's a bird in the house," Robbie explained dully. "It means death is near."

"That's just silly superstition," blustered Riach. "I'll chase the poor wretched thing out."

"No. 'Tis Simmie come for me, and each night I've told him tha' I'm nae ready yet. I canna leave you puir *bagrels* to fend for yourselves," Aggie wailed.

" 'Tis just a wee jenny wren," Macaree said comfortingly.

"I tell you 'tis *auld* Simmie. Three times he pecked at the window this past week, and now he's in the house e'en though I've kept the windows latched, barring him entrance," explained the old woman. "But one canna keep death frae the door. He flew in wie me when I entered after hanging out the wash."

"You canna die, Aggie," whispered Macaree.

"I dinna want to, my sweet lass, but I dinna think I hae much say aboot it. But you two maun listen up to wha' I hae to say. You canna play like grasshoppers anymore. You maun be like the industrious ant and hoard for the long, cruel winter. You maun hunt for the future and smoke and salt the meats. You maun search out the wild barley and oats for flour, and you maun harvest and preserve the herbs for medicines. Rhubarb and elder, honeysuckle and chamomile, thistle and coltsfoot. Remember all tha' I've taught you, Macaree?" she prattled agitatedly.

"Aye, I remember, Aggie," Macaree reassured, staring fearfully at the frantic little bird that flew about the house, chirping wildly. Riach opened all the windows and tried to shoo the twittering creature out.

"Dinna harm my puir Simmie!" screeched the crone, flying at Riach and hanging on his arms. " 'Tis all right, my husband, my Simmie, my heart," she soothed. "I'll be wie you soon, but first I hae to prepare our wee-ans." The tiny quivering bird perched on the mantel. There was a trembling pause, and then the wren flew out of an open window.

"Aggie, it was but a poor lost frightened bird. It didn't mean anything except tha' the creature hadn't a very good sense of direction and lost its way," Riach scoffed after a long silence.

" 'Twill do no guid to avoid the obvious, lad.'' The old woman sighed. "Whether you believe or no, I am going to die. Maybe today or maybe nae, but the question still remains. Wha' will you do?''

"What will I do?'' echoed Riach.

"Aye.''

"What will I do?'' he pondered. Dread was like a weight in his gut. "I shall take care of my family. My wee brother, Robbie, and my sweet wife, Macaree,'' he stated, gripping Macaree's hand in a painful grasp.

"How?'' Aggie barked sharply.

"To the best of my ability,'' he answered hoarsely, his mouth dry.

"And if you canna?'' she asked tartly. "What if you canna provide? What if you canna fill the cellars and cupboards so there's no hungry bellies in the winter? Will you be able to swallow tha' stubborn pride and go begging? Wha' if your clan will nae accept your MacGregor wife, Macaree?''

"They'll have to!'' he shouted.

"And if they dinna?'' she continued relentlessly.

"Macaree is my wife!''

"Before God?'' she demanded.

"Before God!''

"And you'll die for her if need be?''

"Aye,'' he whispered softly, staring into Macaree's blue eyes. Aggie sighed and nodded silently before laboriously heaving herself up from the kitchen chair. "But you'd not be thinking of dying, Agatha Fletcher.'' He laughed, gazing with affection at the tired old woman.

" 'Tis nae just thinking, you impudent pup. 'Tis a selfish longing. I miss my *auld* Simmie. I long to lie wie him again. To lie peaceful and cozy in his knotty *auld* arms,'' she stated, her rheumy eyes filling with tears and her voice catching.

"You'd leave me for Simmie?'' Robbie tried to joke.

"Och, 'tis a hard choice, my wee rooster.'' The old woman chuckled huskily. "But one day they'll be a bonny lass to stir your sluggish blood and you'll ken. But for now, close those droopy lids and hae sweet dreams while the rest of us go back to work,'' she ordered briskly, crashing her pots and pans together loudly.

A week later, Riach was lying with Macaree, watching the moon's reflection turn her straining breasts silver. She had gently coaxed his body to quivering tautness, when he heard a soft chirping and a flutter of wings. He lay open to her hungrily nipping mouth and urgent hands, listening curiously, but then Macaree's warm lips encompassed his. He gave himself to those consuming sensations, imagining that at last he was thrusting into the mysterious heat of her.

In the morning, they had discovered Aggie dead, and they buried her beside *auld* Ailsa in the graveyard of the ruined monastery beside the *loch*. Robbie lay listlessly waiting for a small bird to fly through the window and release him from the interminable earthbound days.

"I can carry you," coaxed Riach, sensing it was important for the boy to be present for Aggie's burial.

"I hae my pride," the ten-year-old snapped. "If I canna walk on my ain two feet, I dinna want your charity!" He had waited to be alone in the gatehouse before giving in to the torrent of aching sorrow for his foster mother, Agnes Fletcher. "Aggie, Aggie, send a bird for me?" he had begged, but by the time his sister and Riach had returned from their sad task, he was composed.

Each night Robbie dutifully bade Riach and Macaree goodnight and then listened to their feet mounting the wooden stairs and entering the bedroom under the eaves. He knew they slept in each other's arms, and he imagined what they did to comfort each other. He wondered if he would ever grow to be a man.

"*Maman?* Aggie? Kat? Please send a bird for me." He sobbed desperately in the long, lonely nights. "Please send a bird for me."

The balmy June days passed into a sultry July, and the bees and wasps droned lazily in the hollyhocks. Macaree struggled to fulfill Aggie's tasks, tending to her sullen, unresponsive little brother, who refused to lift a hand to aid himself. One day when she was gently bathing him, she sensed his intense stare. Looking into his wide blue eyes, so like her own, she was startled to recognize a male lust smoldering there. She glanced down at his hairless groin and was shocked to see his arousal. She recoiled as though burned and pretended not to notice, avoiding what she felt was a mocking smile. She hummed to herself and scurried to the safety of the kitchen, leaving him to his own ablutions. Robbie felt even more solitary after that incident. His sister avoided him. There were no more stories, and she would thrust his food at him and dart away. She would put clean linens on his bed and never look at him, but would hum a familiar tune from long ago. He waited breathlessly for something terrible to happen, waited for Riach's rage until the anticipation was unbearable.

"Katrine, Katrine, send a bird for me," he pleaded. "I want to die."

"What are you saying?" Riach demanded furiously, overhearing the boy's fervent plea. "How could you ask for such a terrible thing? And what has happened between you and Macaree?" he added when no answer was forthcoming.

"She dinna tell you?" Robbie sighed, glad that things were finally out in the open."

"Tell me what?"

"Ask her yourself," the boy returned wearily, seeing his sister hovering in the kitchen doorway.

"What happened?" asked Riach, but Macaree's face became a frozen, smiling mask. She started singing.

"I rose to her!" the boy spat bluntly. "It wasna purposeful. I dinna mean to be so wicked, but it just happened," he stated challengingly, trying to quell the childish tears that ached his eyes.

"I don't understand," Riach stated helplessly, looking from the weeping brother to the sweetly singing sister.

"My man . . . part . . . rose!" Robbie yelled angrily, furious at the tears that poured down his hairless cheeks. "I tried to stop it, but it wouldna be still, and my mind wouldna stop thinking. I have too much time to think. I canna stop my mind from imagining all the things I shall miss when I am dead! I mourn that I shall never be a man such as you!" He wept savagely. "But I dinna mean to offend Macaree."

"Leave us, Macaree," Riach snapped harshly. "Go to bed. I shall be there soon." He tried to temper his tone when he saw the bleakness in her blue eyes. To his relief, she quietly left.

"I'm so sorry," the boy sniffed, breaking a long silence in which the young Campbell searched for the right words.

"What happened to you, Robbie, has happened many times to me," he confessed candidly. "I dinna ken if it's a droll part of nature or just an affliction shared by you and me, because I was never as brave as you in owning up to it. But it has happened many, many times to me."

"But you're a mon and I havena a whisker, and I dinna hae to relieve myself," the boy admitted ruefully.

"Robbie, you're growing up to manhood, so maybe 'tis best

you take care of your own needs. Or ask me, so as not to put your sister to the blush," Riach suggested gently.

"You are nae cross wie me?" marveled Rob.

"I'm tremendously angry wie you for wanting to die! That's a coward's way!"

"But I dinna think I shall ever get better, and if I was dead and at peace like Aggie and Ailsa, you and Macaree would be free."

"You dinna ken how very important you are to me, do you?" Riach shouted gruffly, trying to stem the flood of emotion. Robbie shook his flaxen head. "I canna explain, but 'tis like you are a part of me . . . the good part, the part that makes me a man, that makes me aware of my own worth," he struggled to say.

"I'm not a burden?"

"Nay, you're my brother."

Macaree sat at the bedroom window rhythmically brushing her hair and staring blindly out at the crescent moon. She heard the irritating whine of the midges and mosquitoes. She was waiting for anger to erupt, waiting to be blamed for some terrible, unnameable sin. Every nerve and muscle was tensed, coiled as tight as a watch spring. Ears strained, she listened for his steady tread on the stair—waiting, waiting, unbearably waiting for the screams.

Her hand froze mid-stroke as she heard his steps. Into her mind flashed a bloodied white frock . . . and her father's furiously hissed words, his spit pitting her cheeks.

"You tempted him, you little whore, and if your mother finds out it'll be the worse for you. I'll nae hae her hurt by a filthy little slut who canna keep her legs together!" Macaree's terrified heart pounded, echoing those ancient words and the approaching footsteps. Nearer and nearer they came, and to her combined relief and pain they went right by the door. She sagged back onto the pillows as dread seeped achingly into her bones at the cold rejection. She listened to the rustle on the other side of the wall, knowing he would undress and slip into Aggie's old bed, preferring aloneness to her wicked company.

chapter 16

It was a hot, humid July afternoon. Not a whisper of a breeze stirred the heavy air. Kat rode the black stallion, and Darach was mounted on his golden Iolair. The pace was slow and languorous, the horses sweating and sluggish. Kat reined in and gazed over a shimmering stretch of water, recognizing the shape of the mountains before her. They were near Linnmanach. They couldn't be more than a mile or two away as the crow flew because she could see Fionnfail, the white cliff, gleaming through the thick pines. She thought of all those months at Duncreag; she had been no more than a few leagues from her own family.

"Can you swim?" Darach's deep voice broke into her brooding thoughts. He assumed that her pensiveness was merely a sign of her longing to cool off in the crystal waters of the mountain tarn. Kat nodded quietly and slid off her horse as her mind busily plotted. She led him to the shore to drink, and she gazed once more at Fionnfail, unable to believe her eyes. How could she not have noticed it before? Maybe it was the different direction they had taken that day, approaching from the east, or perhaps it was the time of day when the afternoon rays smote the sheer chalk escarpment. Whatever the reason, she was convinced that she stared upon the same white cliff that she could see from Linnmanach. She was so near, yet how could she escape? Her tall dark husband never let her out of his sight. His piercing silver eyes followed her distrustfully in the daylight hours, and his hard, claiming arms held her possessively at night.

Darach kicked off his boots and pulled his shirt over his ebony head, noting her preoccupation. He saw her green gaze rest speculatively on the distinctive mountain ridge across the lake and wondered what captured her interest. Suddenly she spun about on the balls of her bare feet, sensing his intense scrutiny. She snarled, her hackles raised like a wildcat's, and he shrewdly noted the fear that flickered across her poignant features.

"There was a *clavan,*" she lied glibly, pointing and pretending to track a buzzard across the hazy summer sky. She felt the color rise and stiffen her cheeks, and she covered her guilty awkwardness by seductively unbuttoning her shirt, hoping to distract him. Sometimes she felt he could read her mind. She looked up coyly into his handsome face, but her heart sank. She saw his sardonic, mocking grimace and knew she was not believed.

Darach was angry, impatient with the constant deception. They were miles apart, despite their closeness when they lay in each other's arms. Each night when he claimed her, he didn't know who she was or where his brother was. Even her sensuous, exquisite lovemaking was somehow a battle for supremacy, a battle to remain free of him, a battle to prove she stood apart. She was like a phantom—elusive, never to be grasped. She glowered back at him, looking glorious in her fury. Her thick mane of black hair curled about her naked breasts, which rose and fell with her passionate rage. The tension crackled between them, mirroring the dangerous stillness before a mighty thunderstorm, and each waited for the other to fling the first insult.

Darach longed to plunge into the water to cool his temper, but he didn't trust her not to leap upon the black stallion and ride away, never to be found again. He decided to keep on his tight riding britches, reasoning that he would be at a disadvantage having to chase her stark-naked through the populated countryside. Knowing Iolair could outpace the younger horse, he dove into the refreshing depths, leaving Kat in her warlike stance upon the bank.

Kat sagged with relief. His silent fury frightened her and

made her feel lonely. She had to fight against her instinct to throw herself into his arms, demanding comfort and protection. Yet she loved to do battle with him. She hated that cold, sardonic, mocking silence that curled his thin lips, causing him to be a Campbell, a *cam beal*—a cruel, crooked mouth. When he sneered down at her, he made her squirm and feel like a common felon. She wanted his active rage—the challenge of lovemaking that made them both equal.

Kat clambered onto a rock that overhung the tarn and stood watching her husband stroke through the water as she tried desperately to plan her escape from Duncreag. Angus's home was well named, she thought wryly. Duncreag meant rock fortress. It was strategically placed, commanding views on all sides so those coming and going were always in plain sight. She sighed in defeat, thinking of Calum MacKissock, whose disapproving glare was always apparent. Sometimes she felt he even lurked outside their bedroom door, distrusting her with his precious master. The Campbell's steward made her know just how much he despised her, and she admitted that she despised herself for her duality. But what could she do? She was torn in two directions.

Darach floated on his back and looked up at the dejected little figure perched on the craggy rock. She appeared so starkly alone, and he caught the glint of wetness on her cheeks. He experienced an aching in his chest; he felt impotent and angry. Why wouldn't she allow him to help her? He knew with every fiber of his being that she hurt, and yet she rejected his comfort.

"I thought you said you could swim," he challenged, not for one minute believing the assertion. He knew of no women who could swim. He also didn't know any other women who dressed quite so improperly and who could adeptly handle a variety of weapons, including a crossbow, bow and arrow, dagger, and throwing axe. He caught his breath when she launched herself into the air head first, arcing gracefully like a bird, before cutting cleanly into the water. He caught his breath again, this time with trepidation, when she didn't reappear, and he was afraid that she had hit her head on a submerged rock. Fear clawed through him, and he dove under the surface. His foot was caught by a mischievous hand as she swam under him like a playful otter.

Kat laughed joyously at his startled expression. She loved to catch him unaware. Then the stern planes of his face softened, and warmth tinged the cold silver of his eyes. She laughed again when his strong brown hands caught each side of her small waist, and he lifted her high and victoriously out of the water.

"Och, I've captured a water sprite!" He rejoiced, delighting in her lithe nakedness.

"Och, hae a care, for I may be the green *cailleach,* Peg Powler, or a wicked *glaistig,* or even *Nicneven* herself!" she gurgled.

"Nicneven?" he echoed soberly, his carefree happiness doused as their banter underlined the mystery of her identity.

"Aye, *Nicneven.* The *banrigh* of the demons!" she proclaimed, trying to retain the playful mood. She looked away from his set features and felt strong fingers dig cruelly into her tender flesh.

"Aye the queen of the demons, the thorn in my side!" he hissed harshly, flinging her from him. The water sprayed violently as she vanished beneath the surface. "Will this blasted torment ever end?" he snarled, swimming to shore.

They rode back to Duncreag in a stony silence that chilled Kat's whole being, and Hag Holly and Angus exchanged concerned glances. Calum MacKissock smirked with satisfaction, noting how his furious young master gripped the slender wrist of the ebony-haired witch, dragging her to their suite of rooms.

"She's but a common street urchin—or, even worse, a kelpie, a dark member of the host of the Unseelie Court," Calum snapped defensively, feeling the two old people's eyes boring into him, disapproving of his glee. "I've told the master again and again, but will anyone listen to me? Even tha' silly *auld* spinster sister of mine hae romantic notions about tha' green-eyed female," he chattered uneasily.

" 'Tis time to do something," hissed Cailleach Cuilleann. "Och, I wish I hae a wee poppet in tha' smug, sanctimonious mon's image so I could stick all manner of pins in him to deflate tha' pomposity," she yearned, glaring after the sturdy man.

"Wha' are you hatching, *auld* hag?" demanded Angus.

"The less you ken, the better," she retorted. "But I shall be overseeing the cooking of the dinner tonight, and the serving of it."

*   *   *

"We're going to Strathrannoch tomorrow," Darach stated, breaking the long silence. Kat didn't respond. It was the first thing he had said to her since he had flung her away from him, snarling that she was the thorn in his side. "We'll leave at first light," he added, stalking into the dressing room and slamming the door.

Kat sat on the bed trying to think. She knew where Strathrannoch was from having studied the maps in Angus's library. It was on Rannoch moor, clear across Scotland. She remembered the ride from Ballachulish five years before—the soaring majesty of the mountains and the stark awesomeness of the untamed countryside. At any other time, she would have rejoiced to be in Darach's company, riding through such magnificence, but now that she knew where she was in relation to Linnmanach, she had to make her escape. She couldn't wait. Somehow, she had to leave Duncreag before morning.

"But what about Sian?" she ventured, daring to open the door to his dressing room. "You told me that servants were bringing my hound from Edinburgh," she added. He didn't acknowledge her but just continued dressing quietly. "You promised me!" she shouted. Still, he didn't turn to face her but stared in the mirror, arranging his stock.

"Get dressed for dinner," he ordered, not deigning to raise his voice or to address her directly.

"Nay!" she spat. "I'll nae be treated this way! I'm not a *bairn*!"

"Then dinna act like such," he said witheringly.

"You promised me my hound, and now you suddenly decide that we're off to Strathrannoch."

"That's right," he snapped, his hard metallic eyes capturing hers in the glass. He sensed that she was tensed to fly. Premonitions of danger beat within his pulse, alerting him to the sharp change in her mood. Ever since they had been at the lake, when she had stared with such intensity into the distance, he had known that she was planning to escape.

"I'll not go wie you."

"You will go even if I have to tie you hand and foot," he remarked. His mirror shattered as Kat flung a boot at it, fragmenting his mocking reflection. She could not abide the tense smoldering silence or the wry twist to the mouth that could so lovingly drink from his lips and cause such wonderful sensations to flower.

"I hate you!" she screamed when he turned and she saw the same harsh mocking expression on his chiseled face.

"I know," he answered caressingly, staring at her heaving breasts. "But I have no time for a demonstration. There is a lot to prepare for the trip to Strathrannoch." He eyed her and the bed in a speculative manner. Goaded beyond reason, she picked up the nearest object and flung it with deadly accuracy. The amethyst geode cracked against his head. There was a moment of agonized shock when he stared at her with an expression of hurt bewilderment before he toppled slowly to the floor. She bit down on her clenched fist to stifle the dry sobs that burst from her throat.

"Darach?" She wept, falling to her knees and gathering his ebony head onto her thighs, her tears dropping freely on his still cheeks. "Och, my own true love. I'm so very, very sorry." She rocked back and forth, cradling him to her. How could she have used the precious amethyst geode to hurt him so? It was the only gift she had ever given him. On the day he had presented her with the young black stallion, she had found it in a mountain stream. It had been one of those wonderful, perfect times when she had been able to forget that she was a virtual captive. They had galloped through the verdant forest on the superb horses, delighting in each other's company and rejoicing in the burgeoning spring. They had lain together beneath the lacy canopy of tender green leaves on a blanket of fragrant blossoms. It had been in that sated, glowing aftermath of loving, when she had been curled happily against his relaxed strength, that she had spied the gleam of the jeweled rock, the morning sun causing the violet crystals to sparkle.

A sharp rapping at the bedchamber door froze her blood, and she gazed about at the stuffy darkness of the hot summer night. How long had she been sitting holding him? How long had he been lying so terribly still? Had she killed him?

"Wee-an?" the *cailleach*'s hoarse voice hissed urgently. Kat threw off her shocked inertia, gently laid Darach's head on the soft carpet, and scrambled to her feet to unlatch the door.

"Och, Cailleach Cuilleann, I think I've killed him, and I love him so!" she cried hysterically. The old woman shoved her roughly into the room and quickly bolted the door after looking furtively about for fear that the girl's impassioned words had been overheard.

"Guid thing tha' nosy steward, Calum MacKissock, is feeding his large belly," she rebuked. Then she knelt stiffly beside the prostrate man. "Och, tha' was nae a prissy blow you delivered, lass," she stated admiringly. "Tha' puir mon has a lump as big as a swan's egg and will hae an ache to match. Now, let's get him into bed. Take his shoulders. You're much younger and stronger than me," she stated. With great effort and a lot of panting and puffing, they finally managed to heave the large man onto the high mattress. "Now, lassie, get him oot of his boots and shirt while I clean up all tha' glass," she ordered, cocking a quizzical eye at the shattered mirror. "Hope you're nae as superstitious as me," she clucked dolefully.

"But will he be all right?" Kat worried tearfully, tugging off the gleaming boots.

"Campbells hae thick skulls. Now there's no time for idle prate. Just get his shirt off and tuck his legs under the covers, so when, or if, MacKissock comes by wie his fu' belly, 'twill seem tha' the young oak is sleeping."

"I maun leave." Kat sobbed, undoing the stock that Darach had arranged so elegantly and unbuttoning his snowy shirt. "I dinna want to, but I maun leave." She wept and her tears fell on his bare chest.

"Aye, my puir wee-an, I ken." The old woman sighed, sweeping the sharp splinters of glass under the wardrobe so that no signs of violence were apparent. "You dinna hae to trust me, but if you're ever in need, I hae a wee house on the eastern slope of Ben Vorlich. Ask any in Comrie and they'll direct you."

"Comrie?" echoed Kat, after the old crone named the town closest to Linnmanach.

"You ken Comrie?" the hag asked sharply, and the girl nodded. "Dinna say a word yet," Cailleach Cuilleann cautioned, placing a bent finger against her pleated lips. She fumbled through her layers of rainbow skirts and withdrew a small vial.

"What is it?" whispered Kat, but the old woman silently shook her gray head and motioned toward Darach. The girl watched as the hag poured the red liquid into the Campbell's mouth and then rubbed his throat, causing him to swallow.

" 'Tis a sleeping draft wie some other . . . embarrassing properties," she cackled. "Och, when he awakens he'll be wishing he was swaddled in hippens like a wee *bairn*." She giggled. "Or dead!" she added.

"You gave him rhubarb or damask?" inquired Kat, naming two herbal cures for bound bowels.

"Both!" the old woman boasted gleefully. "And horehound mixed wie a strong tincture of horse balm, jasmine, valerian, and a wee dab of hop oil. Och, the puir mon's going to be happily sleeping in his own muck! There's nothing better to humble an arrogant body!" she declared happily. "I gie even a stronger dose to that Calum MacKissock, the sanctimonious *mucker!*"

"You maun leave me now, for I maun hurry," Kat urged, not wanting the *cailleach* to witness her debasement as she searched her husband's pockets and chests. She had to steal as much money and jewelry as she could to ensure passage to France for her family. Hag Holly nodded sadly and patted the girl's cheek. She desperately wished that the dark child would confide in her.

"May all the forces of nature go wie you," she blessed. "Now, dinna forgie, I'm on the eastern slope of Ben Vorlich. Ask in Comrie."

Kat nodded silently, her teeth biting her lips painfully to stop her rash mouth from telling the old woman about Linnmanach. If it had only been her secret—but she had everyone to protect. Macaree, Robbie, Ailsa, and Aggie all relied on her.

"Thank you," she whispered inadequately. "But I maun hurry."

"You dinna hae to rush. Take care and your time. All here at Duncreag hae been dosed, so your escape and my departure will nae be observed," informed the crone. "I'm for my home, too, tonight. I've hae enow of Campbell hospitality."

"You dosed everyone? Even Angus!" exclaimed Kat, and the hag grinned toothlessly and cackled proudly. "But Angus doesna deserve such humbling," she said mournfully.

"And your handsome husband does?" Hag Holly probed wickedly. After a pensive pause, during which she thought over the many indignities she had suffered at the arrogant Campbell's hands, Kat nodded vehemently.

"Aye, as much as I love him, it'll do him no harm to hae

some belittling. I am pleased that Calum MacKissock is in for some embarrassment, but Angus dinna do me any harm. He's the sweetest man I have ever known."

"Dinna fret. All I gie him was a soothing draft of spearmint, rose leaves, and orrisroot. He'll just snore loudly tonight and tomorrow will be deaf to the great groans of Darach Campbell and his steward, who'll nae be setting a horse for several days," she chortled. Then she soundly kissed Kat's cheeks and hobbled out of the room after a long searching look into Kat's tearful green eyes. "East slope of Ben Vorlich," she reminded her huskily.

Kat listened to Cailleach Cuilleann's shuffling gait receding down the stone corridor, and then she dried her tears and helped herself to all the coins and jewels she could find. She stared at herself in the broken mirror for several moments. Then she unsheathed Darach's *skean dhu* and hacked off her lustrous hair to a boyish shoulder length. She placed a pillow beneath the bed covers and wrapped her husband's strong arms about the soft mass, arranging her ebony tresses so that it looked as though she lay within his embrace. She tenderly kissed him and rubbed her face in the fragrant warmth of his neck, filling her senses with him.

"I love you wie all my heart and soul, even though you be a Campbell, an enemy of my clan," she whispered. "I will always love you." Then she silently left the chamber where they had spent so many nights in passionate union.

Kat rode the young black stallion through the moonlit night, cantering the scant few miles between Duncreag and Linnmanach. Unwilling to enter through the main gates, she took another route through the forest. She edged the horse through the broken palings that bound the property and approached the rambling estate from the south. She was home, she thought dully, reining the young horse by the side of the still *loch* and staring up at the hulking ruin.

"Home," she stated bleakly, urging the stallion to a slow walk as she scanned the hollow-eyed windows for a sign of life. Only bats flickered about the broken eaves, and ravens shifted their cumbersome shapes in their roosts on the columns. She breathed deeply of the sultry aroma of the wild roses that strangled the crumbling gray stones. Then she rode to the stables. It was obvious that no other animals had been kept there since she and her father had left many months before. She ran practiced fingers through the dusty water troughs and kicked the powdery old manure. Unable to leave her vital young horse in such filthy decay, she led him back to the *loch* to drink and then left him to graze on the overgrown lawn.

Kat apprehensively mounted the gritty stone steps to the terrace, her boots rasping in the humid stillness. Her heart hammered painfully as she looked into the dank dimness of the house. She stood still, allowing her eyes to accustom themselves to the gloom. Then she walked into the rank darkness. Five years of living at Linnmanach without the comfort of lanterns and often without candles had made her adept at feeling her way through the maze of corridors. But the familiar sharp scrape of rats' claws in the shadows still made her spine shiver and filled her mind with nameless terrors.

Kat opened the door to Macaree's room, expecting to see her sister's golden hair gleaming on the pillow in the moonlight, but the bed was empty. It had been inhabited only by rodents, she realized, as her nervous hands found nuts and cherry pips beneath the chewed sheets and shredded pillow. Even more horrible was the sight of Macaree's ornate ballgowns hanging limply in the wardrobe. Something terrible had to have happened to cause her beautiful sister to abandon her prized gowns. Kat's pulses were pounding with dread, and her mind was desperately trying to invent plausible reasons for Macaree's absence. She blindly felt her way to Robbie's room only to find it also empty—as were Ailsa's, Aggie's, and that of the hostage, Riach Campbell. Sobbing aloud and painfully bumping her elbows and knees in her hysterical haste, Kat raced through every room of the sprawling stone mansion. She fell downstairs, screaming the names of her family. She knelt in the litter of torn books in the library, imagining all manner of horrendous fates. She searched every room, from the attic to the basement kitchens, where the hearths were cold. There was no sign of human life. Her family was gone. Everyone was gone. She was alone, totally and utterly alone. The dreadful enormity of that stark fact tore into Kat, and she screamed a raw animal howl of pure pain that echoed and reechoed through the crumbling ruin.

Kat staggered outside, unable to remain in the macabre mansion that seemed to mock her laments, throwing her cries back at her like jeering laughter, like Darach's sardonic mirth. She savagely battled the roses that clawed at her body and slashed at her face, impeding her escape, as she ran down the broken steps. She fled sobbing across the moonlit lawn and then stood still, scanning about her. She was clearly the only person who existed at Linnmanach. The sky was so vast, and everything was empty, a cold silver emptiness that stretched until time finished. She was in the middle of it, so very small, frightened and alone. The moonlight lay on the flat surface of the deep *loch* which appeared as impenetrable and enigmatic as the Campbell's metallic eyes. Would everything always remind her of him?

Kat trod numbly to the graveyard in the shadow of the ruined monastery. She stared listlessly at the two new mounds of earth beside the graves of Alisa's ancient band. Who had died in the intervening five months? Kat didn't want to know. She spun away as a grisly image of Macaree's gentle face smothered by death forced its way through her mind. She shook her head wildly from side to side, trying to dislodge the ghastly picture of her little brother's sweet features weighed down by the dirt of the grave.

"No!" she cried, fighting for control and gazing at *auld* Sebastian's marker, which she had carved when he'd been interred the previous October. "Oh, Sebastian," she lamented. How could she tell the old gatekeeper that Sian, the loyal wolfhound that he had entrusted to her care, was maimed and cruelly tethered in an Edinburgh stable away from all who loved him? She raised her eyes to the sky, desperately needing a mother's comfort. But how could she even think of Suibhan when the siblings that she had sworn to protect were lost —perhaps rotting beneath the earth? Another howl of raw pain burst from her throat and echoed over the still lake.

chapter 17

Robbie lay sweating in the static, humid night, unable to sleep for the heat and the irritating buzz of the midges. The parlor window was open in the hopes that even the faintest breeze would stir the heavy air and afford some relief. Macaree and Riach had long since climbed the wooden stairs to their bed, and there were no more creaks from above. The boy assumed they slept snugly in each other's arms. He felt alone. He stared up at the moon that mirrored his solitary state and thought sadly of Aggie and Kat, the two people on whom he had always depended. It had never occurred to him to think that they would die, and yet they were gone, leaving him and Macaree, the two less likely to survive. Aggie and Kat, who had always appeared invincible, as enduring as the mountains, were dead, and two wispy beings, who had never had much resilience, were still living. The irony of it nagged at Robbie's mind. God had made a terrible blunder.

A most terrible howl shattered the thick heat of the night. The boy shivered. Again it was repeated, echoing through the cloying stillness.

"Riach?" he screamed, struggling to sit. "Riach?" But there was no answer from upstairs. Maybe he had imagined the noise, he thought hopefully, but again came the unearthly howl. "Riach? Macaree? There's wolves!" he shouted, and he was relieved to hear the creak of movements overhead. A heavy tread came down the stairs and the young Campbell entered naked and yawning. "Riach, there's wolves! I heard them! There are wolves!" Robbie sobbed.

"Wolves? Och, you had a bad dream. There's no wolves left in Scotland."

"But I heard them. You must have heard them, too. Listen," the frightened boy begged. The young Campbell sat listening, but all was quiet.

"The last wolf was killed near Inverness more than twenty years ago. That is one of the few things I remember my father teaching me. Why he bothered to inform me of that fact, I dinna ken," Riach said sleepily. "Actually, I'm not being truthful wie you, Rob Roy. The reason my father pointedly told me about the last wolf being killed in Inverness in 1743 . . ."

"Was because he killed it?" Robbie guessed.

"Nay. Because I was too afraid to go hunting wie him for fear I'd be eaten by a wolf," Riach admitted ruefully.

"Then your father was wrong, because I heard a wolf. I did, and it wasna a dream, it was real. It sounded like this." And the boy tried to demonstrate.

"On hot nights like this one, ears can hear strange things. Maybe it was a stray dog on the road. Would you like me to go outside and see?" Riach offered, worried about the youngster's agitation.

"Aye, but take a gun and a dagger. I'd nae want you gone, too. Nay, dinna go . . . you could die, too." Robbie wept.

"What's the matter?" asked Macaree, appearing in the doorway.

"Stay wie Robbie while I get some trews on and take a look outside."

"No! Dinna let him go, Macaree. He'll be eaten by the wolf and he'll be gone, too!" The boy cried hysterically, holding on to the young Campbell. Riach gently extricated himself and lay the sobbing boy back against the pillows. He motioned to Macaree to take his place, and he swiftly ran upstairs. "Dinna let him go. There's a wolf out there. Really, I heard it. Listen!" begged the boy.

"I dinna hear anything but the whine of the midges," soothed Macaree after sitting quietly for a while. "Maybe it was an owl. You know we've more than six pairs now. There are pretty owlets trying their wings in the stables.''

"You think I'm away wie the fairies?'' shouted the boy.
"I'm nae daft! I ken the difference between an owl and a wolf,
and I heard a wolf!''

Riach returned dressed in his trews and carrying a gun and a
crossbow.

"There, young man, I think I am well protected, and I
promise you that no wolf will get the better of me,'' he joked.

"Your father would be very proud of you, but I think
you're *meikle* foolish,'' Robbie stated sullenly, wiping his wet
cheeks on the sheet and trying to stop his frightened tears.

Macaree and Robbie watched Riach from the open window
as he strode barefoot across the silvered grass, the moonlight
gilding his lean stripling figure. The air was heavy and still; it
seemed all nature held her breath. The golden-haired brother
and sister held each other tightly as they watched their only
protector disappear into thick shadows.

"What if he never comes back?'' whispered Robbie. "What
if he dies like everyone else?''

Macaree shook her head, unable to speak. The terrible
thought that Robbie was voicing was too much to contemplate. She started to rock soothingly, holding her brother like
a baby and singing a lullaby.

"Nay!'' The boy struggled to free himself. "Nay! Dinna
sing!'' he screamed when she continued. "You sicken me
when you sing!'' he spat, slapping her face. Macaree recoiled,
her eyes wide and frightened, holding her cheek and staring at
him with horror. "It sickens me!''

" 'Tis to comfort,'' she whispered.

"It sickens me to . . . my heart. It leaves me alone,'' he tried
to explain.

"But 'tis to comfort. Mother would comfort us. She'd sing
and rock when things went wrong.''

"I dinna remember my mother. All I remember is that
whenever I was afraid, you'd not talk to me, you'd not answer
me, you'd just sing!'' he shouted. "And I hate it! I hate it!''

Macaree turned away from her small brother's vehemence
and stared blindly out at the night. The moon caused great
ghostly shapes to loom from the dense rhododendron bushes,
and she wished Riach would reappear. What if he didn't come
back? What if he died like everyone else? She turned back and
gazed at her little brother, but she didn't recognize him. He

had hit her and screamed at her. He wasn't supposed to do that. She felt lost and frightened. She needed to sing, but she was afraid of being slapped again.

"You shouldna hit me," she stated, trying to control the sob in her voice.

"I dinna mean to," Robbie replied quietly, and as she stared at him, he became her small brother again. They clung to each other. "I'm sorry, Macaree. You can sing if it makes you feel better."

"Not if it doesna make you feel better," she replied.

Long minutes passed, and the silver-and-black night seemed laden with suspense. Macaree and Robbie watched silently, tensed for the slightest movement. Another howl of pure raw pain shattered the air.

"I told you I dinna dream it!" cried Robbie, clutching his sister and shaking her. "I told you there were wolves and you dinna believe me. We have to help Riach or we'll be alone forever," he stated. Before Macaree could stop him, he tried to leap off the bed, but his weak limbs buckled and he fell to the floor.

Macaree's ears were still ringing with the bloodcurdling howl when her brother collapsed. She knelt on the carpet, trying to rouse him, but he lay pale and still. She pulled him into her arms and sat on the floor, gently rocking and singing a soothing lullaby.

Riach was about to return to the gatehouse when he heard the lamenting howl. He stood still, trying to locate the source. Then he raced toward the *loch*. A beautiful black stallion grazed on the sloping lawn of the hulking house, and Riach stopped and caught his breath, not knowing if this was a figment of his imagination. The proud animal tossed his neck and whickered uneasily, pawing the turf and flicking frightened eyes toward the graveyard. Riach's heart pounded with terror, believing that somehow he had failed *auld* Ailsa and now she had returned to haunt him. The spine-shivering keening continued, dying to a low moan of sorrowful despair. He walked fearfully toward the eerie place of the dead, knowing that whatever was there had to be faced. The black stallion reluctantly walked beside him, nudging him forward and then prancing away like a messenger of doom.

Riach carefully edged between the fallen stones of the old

monastery, apprehensively approaching the gruesome graves, two of which he had dug himself. Had he inadvertently done something to offend? Not being well versed in the art of burials, it was very likely, he decided.

"Who's there?" he whispered, after a petrifying pause. He bravely decided to meet the phantom face to face, and he prepared what he would say to the dead Ailsa or Aggie. "Who's there?" he repeated loudly, his voice cracking.

Kat stopped sobbing, unsure whether she had heard something. She lay with her face on one of the earthen mounds, the gritty soil pitting her hot wet cheeks. Her stallion whinnied, and she sat up. A tall dark figure was silhouetted against the moonlit wall of the monastery, the features shadowed but the thick black hair gleaming.

"Darach!" she cried, and threw herself against the hard naked chest. Riach staggered back with the force of her assault. He gaped down at the small person who embraced him so fervently, keeping his arms held wide, still clutching his assortment of weapons.

Kat froze, realizing that she held an unfamiliar male. He did not have Darach's fragrance or his shape. She pushed herself away and stared up at the tall youth, brushing the blinding tears from her eyes.

"Katrine?" gasped Riach. "Katrine MacGregor?" he repeated when she stepped back in shock, her limbs turning to jelly and her belly heaving.

"You killed them!" she intoned. "You found out that we were MacGregors and you killed my brother and sister!"

"Nay," he denied, but she flew at him, biting and kicking, mad with grief and fear.

"You foul, filthy Campbell!" she screamed.

"They're alive!" he shouted, but she was deaf to him. Riach dropped his weapons and grasped her firmly by the forearms, but she continued fighting. "They're alive!" he bellowed. "Hear me! They are alive!" He shook her until his voice penetrated her hysteria.

"Alive?" Kat whispered hoarsely, staring up at him, panting for breath.

"Alive, Katrine," he stated. Then he pulled her against him and held her tightly, feeling her heart pound painfully. She allowed herself to be held, as her tortured mind tried desperately to understand what was happening.

"Where are they?" she asked fearfully. "I searched every room of Linnmanach."

"At the gatehouse."

"Who is buried there?" she demanded, pulling away from him and pointing to the new grave.

"Ailsa," replied Riach. He paused before he turned to the other mound. "And Aggie."

"Aggie? No, not Aggie?" Kat intoned. "Not Aggie," she wept, falling to her knees and pounding the earth with her clenched fists. "Och, Aggie, why dinna you wait for me?" she cried angrily.

Riach silently observed Kat MacGregor's grief, knowing there were no words to comfort her. Then he followed her down to the *loch*, where she plunged her sticky, tear-streaked face into the moonlit water. He grudgingly marveled at her strength when she turned her stubborn small face to him and stoically walked toward the gatehouse, ignoring his presence.

Kat didn't dare say a word to the Campbell youth. When she had left Linnmanach at the beginning of March, he had been a gangly, foppish sot unworthy of her attention. Now a lean, confident male strode beside her. She held her tongue, suppressing the many questions that burst into her aching head. How did the young Campbell know their identity? If he was so strong and healthy, why hadn't he escaped from Linnmanach and returned to his family? She couldn't afford to trust him, she decided.

A similar scramble of questions raced through Riach's brain. Why had the small dark girl called him by his brother's name? Where had she been? Where was her father? He glanced down at her, and, noting the obstinate set of her jaw and the rebelliousness that flashed from her green eyes, he was loath to break the silence.

They reached the gatehouse, and Kat hesitated, frightened by what she might discover inside. Had the Campbell youth exacted his revenge by inflicting tortures on her brother and sister? She snarled at him, noting his resemblance to his older brother, yet seeing that no harsh cynical lines marred his features. He was little more than a boy, she realized—older than she was in years, but still callow and immature. He opened the door and motioned her inside, but she silently indicated that he enter first, afraid to have him behind her. Riach acquiesced, noting her coiled tension and assuming that she was nervous about the reunion with her siblings after such a long absence. He frowned, hearing Macaree's singing, and quickened his step, throwing open the door to the parlor.

"What happened?" he cried with concern.

"What is it?" shouted Kat, pushing past him and staring at her older sister, who sat on the floor cradling the limp body of Robbie. "Dinna touch him!" she spat, when Riach reached down and lifted the inert boy from Macaree's arms. The young Campbell ignored her and laid the child on a small bed below the open window.

"What happened, Macaree?" he demanded, but her singing became louder and her rocking wilder.

"Tell her to stop singing, it sickens me so," whispered Robbie after a long, shuddering sigh. To Kat's great surprise, the Campbell youth laughed aloud and gathered the boy close. "Riach, she's your wife. Can you nae make her stop?" he pleaded wearily.

"Robbie?" Kat ventured tentatively. She felt like an intruder with her own family.

"Hush," ordered the Campbell, shaking his head. He was afraid that the boy couldn't take more shocks in his weakened condition. "That's right, Rob Roy MacGregor, close your eyes and go to sleep, and I'll shut your singing sister up," he crooned, placing the child against the pillows.

"If you canna stop her, you maun smack her." The child yawned, nestling cozily into his covers and drifting off to sleep.

"Smack her?" echoed Riach.

"Aye," Robbie murmured.

Macaree stared with disbelief at Kat. Her singing jerked to a stop and her rocking ceased.

"Robbie slapped my face. He said my singing sickened him," she said softly, her gentle face creased with bewilderment as she reached out and touched Kat's features.

"Let's go out of here—into the kitchen, so we don't disturb the boy further," said Riach forcefully, pulling Macaree to her feet and pushing her out of the room. Kat watched them go. She'd not be ordered about by that foppish youth, she thought angrily, crossing to gaze down at her sleeping brother. He was so thin and pale, the dark smudges beneath his large eyes accentuated by the eerie lighting. She tenderly stroked his soft cheek and softly traced his thin sensitive fingers, marveling that he was still alive. How tenaciously he held on to life. "Do not wake him. He has so little energy. The shock of seeing you might harm him," Riach's hoarse whisper grated on her nerves. She longed to spin about and tear at his face, but instead she nodded silently. She stood and stared out of the window, trying to control her jumbled emotions.

"Kat?" Macaree's quiet voice called. With a sigh, Kat walked into the kitchen, angry that Riach Campbell had triumphed. "Kat? I'm not dreaming. Is it really and truly you?" Kat allowed her sister to hug and kiss her before she sat down at the table and glowered at the tall youth. "Where have you been? Why were you gone so long?" But Kat wouldn't answer Macaree. She had to protect her family from the enemy. She didn't know how the Campbell had found out their true identities, but it no longer mattered. She had to get them away from him and escape to France. She was glad that the bulging saddlebag was safely hidden in the stables, and her fatigued mind tried frantically to plan. "We thought you were dead." Macaree wept, stroking the cropped ebony hair. "And then Aunt Ailsa and Aggie died."

Kat tolerated her sister's clutching hands and sobbing voice. She did not say anything, and she did not take her eyes off the lounging youth. She wished he would leave them alone, but he kept watching.

"Where have you been? Where is your father?" demanded Riach, when Macaree turned from her unresponsive sister and threw herself into his embracing arms.

"Why are you still here?" hissed Kat, glaring at the lean brown hands that held her sister.

"Would you have preferred I leave your family to die?" he asked bluntly.

"Did you kill Aggie?"

"No, Kat, no! Riach kept us alive! If it hadna been for him . . ." Macaree began to protest.

"Go up to our bed, my love. Go on, I shall be up soon," the youth ordered. To Kat's consternation, her sister kissed him lovingly, then obeyed. She stood in shock, hearing Macaree's nimble feet climb the stairs.

"You sleep wie my sister?"

"Aye," he replied.

"So Campbells rut wie MacGregors." She laughed harshly, turning away so that he couldn't see her tears.

"I consider Macaree to be my wife," he said stiffly, furious at her bitter words. He then gaped with amazement at her unexpected reaction. Kat MacGregor collapsed into hysterical laughter. "Maybe it would be better to talk in the morning. I know it is a shock to you, what wie Aggie's passing," he suggested awkwardly when she stopped for breath. But Kat didn't acknowledge his words; she resumed her uncontrollable mirth. "There are two unoccupied bedrooms upstairs," he stated tersely when she leaned back hiccoughing, tears of merriment streaming down her face. But she laughed all the harder.

Riach wanted to hit Katrine MacGregor for her derisive laughter. He wanted to quit the room, slam the kitchen door to drown out her demeaning mirth, and seek comfort in Macaree's soft arms. He glowered at Kat, furious with himself for wanting her to give him a chance. He knew how it must appear to her—she coming home to find him in her sister's bed, and he seeming to take advantage of her gentle innocence when he owed the MacGregor family so much money.

"Dinna let me keep you, my sister is waiting," she spat coldly, but he stared silently at her.

"I know when you left here I was . . ." He struggled to find the words to describe himself. "I was rather a pathetic . . . person."

"A debauched, drunken fop," she embellished.

"Aye, a debauched, drunken fop," he agreed. "But I have changed. I don't expect you to take me at my word, but I do hold your sister in the highest esteem, and I promise I shall pay back every penny that I owe your father," he vowed earnestly.

"Every penny you owe my father?" she repeated blankly.

"Every penny, and with interest if need be," he promised fervently. "Where is your father?" he asked when she didn't respond.

"Dead," she pronounced curtly, as her exhausted mind tried to sort out the new information. Riach Campbell didn't know that Gregor had been cheating him. He had no idea that the MacGregors had been trying to destroy both him and his older brother. He didn't even realize that he had been kept drunk and drugged as a virtual hostage.

"I'm sorry. Do you want to tell me how it happened?" he asked after a long silence, assuming that her muteness was due to grief. She shook her head. "I liked your father," he added awkwardly, and once again Kat roared with laughter. He waited for her to finish. It was obvious that she was over-wrought, he decided, trying to keep his temper in check. "If you could tell me where we are and let me borrow your horse, I could collect all the monies I owe your family and get a doctor for Rob Roy," he said quietly when her giggles had died away.

"Dinna call my brother by that name unless you mean his death," she snarled. "And I shall take care of my own family. We'll take nothing from a Campbell."

" 'Tis late. We shall talk tomorrow." Riach sighed, unable to cope with her anymore.

Kat watched him leave, listening dully to his heavy measured tread mount the stairs. She heard the creak of the floorboards overhead and imagined him getting into bed with her sister. Tears fell from her eyes as she remembered nights when she was safely held in Darach's strong arms.

"No more strong arms for me but my own," she whispered furiously, dashing her tears away. "I dinna need them," she tried to convince herself. Then she silently let herself out of the gatehouse. She had to hide the black stallion where the Campbell youth couldn't find him.

Kat returned as the smothering summer night lightened to a muggy gray dawn, with no relief from the oppressive humidity. She stood, gazing down fondly at her sleeping brother, noting the transparency of his pale skin and the bones that were clearly defined by his painful thinness. He was too weak to survive a journey across Scotland, let alone a grueling voyage to France. What should she do? Her head ached with fatigue and her guts roiled with anxiety. Leaving the decisions for a later time, she furtively tiptoed up the creaky stairs, seeking a bed. Two doors stood ajar, and the third was firmly closed. She listened outside, hearing the mingling of steady breaths. Then she selected the farthest room, the smallest of the remaining chambers. Fully dressed, she lay on top of the covers, unaware of the stifling heat. Instead, she felt cold, solitary and afraid. She thought of being securely tucked into Darach's firm belly as he curled his strength about her. It had been so long since she had been alone at night.

chapter 18

Kat awakened to thick molten sunlight hanging heavily in the airless room. She forced open swollen eyelids and stared at an unfamiliar ceiling. Muffled whispers mingled with the languid buzzing of a million insects and her skin felt stale and sticky. She sat up groggily, trying to pull her muddled thoughts together. She was home at Linnmanach, upstairs in *auld* Sebastian's gatehouse. Finally, she was home, she told herself, but there was no exultation, just a deadly, thudding pulse of anxiety and terror. She swung her legs off the bed and stood. The floorboards creaked and she immediately froze in panic. Her ears were strained, but there was no sound of movement within the house. Yet the whispers continued, seeping through the open window. Carefully, she placed one foot in front of the other, every muscle tensed, trying to cross the tiny room without being heard. Why was she creeping about? She was acting like an interloper in her own home, she berated herself angrily. It was the Campbell youth who was the usurper.

"You dinna belong here," she hissed under her breath. She stood at the window, watching him working bare-chested in the vegetable garden, in the sultry late-afternoon glow. She gaped with disbelief at the sight of Macaree dressed in trews, with a boy's smock straining over her voluptuous breasts. Was that the elegant, gentle, feminine Macaree? It was no wonder

Riach Campbell had wasted no time in taking her into his bed, she fumed. Her sister was even more beautiful than she had remembered. Her blond hair was streaked with silvery bands that rippled and curled freely down her back. Ever since her childhood, she had always worn it tightly braided and contained in a regal coronet. Her usually translucent skin was a creamy gold with a dusky pink tinging her glowing cheeks. Gone was the ethereal princess; in her place was a sensual earth goddess.

Kat watched Riach and Macaree play like two rambunctious puppies, teasing and nipping, hugging and kissing. She was confused by the violent emotions that flooded through her at witnessing their joyous happiness. Fury bubbled up as she recalled the youth's proprietary attitude toward Robbie. Something was very wrong. It was apparent that both her brother and sister trusted the young Campbell. She had to untangle the trespasser from their lives or they'd all be lost. She kept her eyes pinned on the loving couple and struggled to control her tumultuous thoughts so she could plan. Kat watched Macaree's joyous expression tense with indecision at seeing her staring from the bedroom window. She winced when the familiar doll-like mask replaced the previous glowing joy. Riach followed Macaree's frozen gaze, and Kat glowered defiantly back at him before turning her back and resolutely descending the stairs, determined to see Robbie. This time the arrogant Campbell youth would not interfere.

Kat heard the front door open and the soft pattering of bare feet, but she remained looking down at her sleeping brother, wishing he would wake and look at her.

"Katrine?" Macaree whispered hesitantly, but her dark sister didn't answer. "Katrine?" she pleaded.

"Dinna call me that," Kat said shortly, brushing by her and walking outside into the hot, mellow afternoon.

"Where are you going?"

"Let's go for a swim?" asked Kat. "Come along wie me. There's a lot we maun speak about," she invited, softening her tone as she remembered the difficulty of discussing anything unpleasant with the older girl. Macaree's eyes flickered uneasily from her sister to the lounging young Campbell, who leaned on his spade, watching them with interest.

"Speak about?" repeated Macaree, looking to Riach to see if he approved.

"You maun tell me about Aggie, and I maun tell you about

Father," Kat explained gently, trying not to notice her sister's hesitancy.

"Riach already told me about our father . . . being dead." Once more Kat felt rage screaming through her blood. How dare the trespassing Campbell meddle in their business! The way her sister kept looking to him, it seemed that he was more important than she.

"Who's that Campbell scum to you?" she spat venomously.

"My husband," replied Macaree, recoiling from her younger sister's blistering fury.

"You're nothing but his whore! He'll leave you! He doesna belong here!" shouted Kat, wanting to release the terrible pain that coursed through her. "How dare you let him have such control of you! He's the enemy! Do you hear me? He's the enemy!" she raged.

Riach dropped his spade and swiftly crossed to the two sisters, as soon as he heard Kat's bitter words. He saw Macaree's hurt bewilderment, and he shook Kat, spinning her around to face him.

"Don't speak to Macaree like that!" he yelled.

"Mind your own business!"

"Macaree and Rob Roy *are* my business!" he roared.

"No longer!" she spat. "My brother and sister are nothing to you! So go away and leave us alone!"

"Kat?" Robbie's high voice trilled. She turned to see him hanging out the open parlor window.

"Robbie?" She rejoiced, forgetting everything and running toward him. At last he was awake, and she could look into his solemn blue eyes.

"Riach is my brother!" the boy stated firmly, stopping Kat in her tracks. "And I'm *his* brother," he added for emphasis.

"Aren't you glad to see me?" she asked huskily after a shocked pause. "I'm home, Robbie. I've come home to you."

"You said that Macaree and I aren't anything to Riach, and you told him to go away," accused Robbie, his eyes brimming with tears.

"Aren't you glad to see me?"

"Not if you make him go away. Not if you make Macaree into a princess again. If you do that, I want you to go away and never come back."

Kat couldn't speak for the agony that welled up within her. She nodded silently and then walked away, past Macaree and

Riach, who stood quietly holding hands. She walked, feeling her feet hit the parched earth and then through her numbed body. She was unable to think. All the months of denying her love for Darach Campbell because of her commitment to her brother and sister had been a farce. She sat beside the *loch*, idly tossing pebbles and watching the circles widen. Then she stripped off her clothes and plunged into the limpid water.

Macaree stood in the shade of an oak tree and watched Kat swim strongly back and forth across the small *loch*. Both Robbie and Riach had insisted that she talk with Kat, but now she was afraid, not knowing what to say. She smoothed the long skirt of her gown and patted her neatly braided hair, waiting for Kat to get out of the water. Humming softly to herself for courage, she picked daisies from the grass and strung them together in a chain, as she used to do when she was a child living in the large château near Chartres.

Kat exhausted herself and then floated on her back, staring at the hot violet sky. Robbie's painful rejection echoed through her mind. A small movement above the rushes caught her eye, and she frowned, recognizing her sister, who was dressed neatly and elegantly. She watched her, knowing from the precise, measured movements that she was making a chain of buttercups or daisies. She knew that before she reached the shore and dressed, Macaree would be wearing a crown of flowers. Slowly, she swam to shore and waded through the shallow water, knowing sadly that the princess Macaree had returned. Would Robbie blame her? she wondered numbly.

"Tea is ready," Macaree said brightly with a gentle smile. "You maun be very hungry. You slept all day and havena eaten a thing." Kat didn't answer. She pulled her britches up her wet legs and tugged a shirt over her tousled hair. The thought of sitting down at a table with Riach Campbell caused her gorge to rise. How could she break bread with a man who had stolen her family? Again, she felt the enormity of her aloneness, and her eyes ached with unshed tears. "Talk to me, Katrine?" begged Macaree. Kat turned away, not wanting her sister to see her distress. She shook her head and walked into the woods. She had to feed and water her horse. "Kat?" shouted Macaree, but her dark sister just steadily walked into the dense forest until she was out of sight.

"You tried," soothed Riach. He hadn't meant to eavesdrop, but he had become worried when Macaree had not returned. He had been disturbed when she had dressed in the long, fitted gown and had bound her beautiful hair into rigid braids pinned tightly to her scalp. Now she sat beneath an oak tree with a coronet of daisies. But her face was not a mask; it was full of pain. Tears poured down her cheeks. "You're not singing," he whispered.

"Riach, she was crying." Macaree sobbed with awe. "My sister, Kat, was actually crying."

"Why are you so surprised?"

"She's not supposed to cry. She is *braw, bardach* Kat." She wept.

"Did you hear that terrible howl in the night? The one Rob Roy thought was wolves?" Riach asked, and Macaree nodded. "That was your little sister."

"No, that was an animal in pain," protested Macaree.

"That was Katrine. She lay on Aggie's grave and she thought both you and Rob were dead, and all her pain came out in those fearsome anguished cries."

"She never cried, even when our mother died. She got angry and mean—like Robbie was last night when he slapped my face and said my singing sickened him. Kat never cried, she was always brave and strong. Something's happened to her, and I don't know what to do. Do you?" she asked hopefully, clinging to his strength.

"No," he whispered into her hair, looking into the dappled darkness of the leafy forest where Kat had disappeared. "But maybe if your little sister can cry, you can be stronger," he dared to suggest.

"When she's not here I can be stronger. I can skin the rabbits and hares, pluck and draw the ducks and pigeons, put worms on the hook and gut the fish," she snapped defensively, then immediately looked shamefaced. "I'm sorry."

"What for?" he puzzled.

"I dinna mean to be waspish."

"You weren't. You could never be waspish."

"Nor shrewish?" She giggled.

"Nor shrewish," he assured, kissing her tenderly. "You are just right for me. Except I dinna much like all those clothes in this hot weather. Let me help you out of them and we'll have a little playful sport in the cool, caressing waters of the *loch*," he suggested, nuzzling her neck hungrily and undoing the little buttons on the bodice of her gown.

"What about Katrine?" Macaree asked nervously, covering her exposed breasts with her hands.

"I don't think your sister will be back for a while," he said huskily, trying to relax her by kissing one soft white shoulder, but Macaree scanned about apprehensively.

"If she came back to talk to me and found us . . ." She trailed away unhappily, remembering Kat's furious words about her being a whore. They were words her own father had said in a terrible dream many years before. She frantically hit out at his hands, and, gathering the two sides of her bodice together, she ran swiftly toward the gatehouse.

Riach watched her go, then turned and stared thoughtfully into the dense forest, wondering just where Katrine Mac-Gregor had concealed the young black horse. He had thoroughly searched the outbuildings and grounds but had found no trace. He shook his head in defeat, deciding not to follow either sister. It was too hot and sticky. He would indulge himself in a cooling swim and then deal with the two sisters.

Katrine and Macaree were like night and day, not only in appearance, but in temperament, he thought, as he lay on his back, floating in the refreshing water. It was not just that one was blond and the other dark, one gentle and one fierce and rebellious, but their very statures were unlike. The dark rebel was petite and lithe, and the golden madonna was tall and voluptuous, but both were as exquisite as the other. However, as beautiful as Katrine was, he infinitely preferred his Macaree. He hadn't the strength or confidence to handle such a strong female, he mused.

At the thought of those flashing green eyes, Riach turned on his stomach and started to swim across the lake, his violently kicking feet and stroking arms churning the serene surface. His newfound strength, his newfound manhood, and his newfound world were in danger. The healing rhythm of the golden summer days, filled with gratifying labor and joyous play, had turned discordant with the arrival of the tempestuous Katrine. He could lose all that had become important to him, he realized apprehensively.

Kat slipped between the broken palings and left Linnmanach. She made her way through the thick wilderness until she reached the hidden glen where she had hidden her horse. It was her secret place—not even Aggie or Simmie had known of its existence. It was her secret place where she had gone to be at peace with herself when the responsibility and decay of Linnmanach had become too much to bear—her secret place

where she could cry and gather together her ragged emotions
before returning to be strong for Robbie and Macaree. Only
auld Sebastian had known of the hidden glade with its roomy
cave, because it had been he who had introduced her to the
tranquil spot.

The sun was setting, the red molten rays seeming even hotter
as they stabbed through the still, tense air when Kat reached
the glen. The horse whickered a welcome and pranced up,
flicking his gleaming tail to scatter the clouds of buzzing insects. She rubbed her sweaty face against the stallion's satiny
girth, unable to think coherently. Robbie's intense little face
was searingly etched in her mind, his anguished words piercing
through numb layers of her brain. She wasn't wanted. She
wasn't needed, and her very presence had changed Macaree
from a glowing, happy woman back into the detached princess.

Kat swung herself onto her horse's back and kneed him into
a swaying walk through the tall, dry summer grasses. What
should she do? Where should she go? What was the use in
doing anything? She felt empty and devoid of purpose, and
she tried to dispel her hopelessness, but she had no energy.

"Och, Etalon Noir," she whispered sorrowfully. She had
not named the dark horse for fear that she would grow to love
him and he'd be taken from her, just like her hound, Sian—
and like countless other steeds she had been foolish enough to
love, only to lose when Gregor had needed money. "Etalon
Noir," she said again, unconsciously calling him Black Stallion in French. Sometimes she used the Gaelic, and he was
Eich Dubh and often just Black Horse, but now that the
young animal was all that stood between her and complete
aloneness, she reverted to the language of her early childhood,
when there had been someone stronger than herself to give
comfort.

Kat was unused to feeling sorry for herself. There had been
too many years of having to care for other people, and soon
she felt guilty and uncomfortable with her brooding apathy.
She dug her bare heels into her steed's ebony sides, forcing
him into a wild gallop across the dry moor land, trying to free
herself from her desolate inertia, trying to erase her brother's
earnest little face, trying to drown out his accusing words with
the thunder of Etalon Noir's hooves.

The young stallion stumbled and Kat nearly lost her seat,
bringing her back to reality. She could cause the horse grave

injury, racing him across the uneven ground in the strange shifting twilight. She reined in and looked about her, seeing the dying red rays spurting behind the looming craggy crest of Ben Vorlich, as Robbie's pale translucent face was superimposed upon it.

"That's it, Etalon Noir," she whispered. "I maun take my brother to Cailleach Cuilleann."

Kat rode the stallion back to the hidden glen and dismounted at the small mountain burn that rippled in the sunset. She lay flat on the springy moss and plunged her hot face into its crystal coolness as her horse drank thirstily. She then rolled onto her back and gazed thoughtfully up at the thickly treed slopes of Ben Vorlich that soared above her. Hope began to stir through her dark dejection. If anybody could cure Robbie, it would be Hag Holly, but how would she get him there? She thought of the old carriages rusting in the stables and wondered how long it would take to break the frisky, young stallion to a harness. She shook her head, realizing the trip was a grueling undertaking and one that could not be done secretly. Robbie would have to ride with her, she planned. She was strong enough to hold him in front of her. It was a rugged trek, but by no means impossible—no more than ten miles, if that, she decided, shading her eyes against the sun's last blinding rays and staring speculatively up the high mountain. But how would she get her brother away from Riach Campbell?

Ignoring the hunger pangs that clutched at her stomach, Kat fell asleep, lulled by the rippling burn that skipped liltingly over the rocks and pebbles. The air was heavy with the drone of many insects. The young horse rhythmically swished his tail and butted his head, idly scattering the insects that dared to land on him. Occasionally, he pawed the lush sod of the bottom land near the cool water. Frogs and toads peeped and croaked, and marauding owls hooted in the velvet darkness. It was a languid summer night filled with comforting common sounds, and Kat slept serenely for a while. But as the three-quarter moon climbed, bathing the world in an eerie sheen and twisting familiar shapes into spectral shadows, the nightmares descended.

Kat was locked in a tug-of-war with Riach Campbell, and Robbie was in the middle. She held one of the boy's painfully thin arms, and the strapping youth held the other. Each time they pulled, a stream of screaming curses flew out of Robbie's mouth, pitting Kat's skin so that she spurted blood as though pierced by darts.

"Cailleach Cuilleann will cure you," she tried to inform him, but all that bubbled from her was one of Macaree's nursery songs.

"Go away!" spat Robbie, and to Kat's horror she saw her sister embrace Riach Campbell, helping him so that now three pulled against one.

"No, no, you dinna ken! You maun understand," she tried to plead, but she just sang louder. She sobbed, refusing to relinquish her hold on her brother's arm, even though she saw it tearing away from his frail body. "Stop! Stop! You're breaking him!" She struggled to scream, but all that issued from her lips was Macaree's childish trills.

"Go away!" Go away!" hissed Robbie. To her further horror, she saw Darach's strong brown hands possessively cup Macaree's voluptuous breasts before sliding caressingly down to clasp her curvaceous hips, adding his strength against her in the human chain. There was a horrendous ripping sound, and she staggered backward, clutching her brother's detached limb.

"No! No!" she wanted to cry, but only French lullabies warbled mockingly from her mouth.

"Monster!" accused Robbie, maimed and bleeding. "Look what you've done to me! Look what you have done to Sian!" he added, and the large wolfhound limped toward her. "Look what you've done to Macaree." Her sister stood naked with a crown on her golden head, embraced by the older Campbell, while Riach howled with fury at her. All of nature was against Kat, rumbling and building and finally exploding. She cowered, cradling her brother's arm and wondering if Hag Holly could perform a miracle, as the disembodied hand reached up and grasped her neck in a strangling hold.

Kat awoke, fighting for breath, feeling the warm, heavy drops of blood still pitting her skin. She lay back panting, trying to sort through the jumbled, pounding terror as lightning slashed through the sky and the thunderclouds rolled ominously. The frightened horse screamed, panicking at the violence of the storm and pawing the ground near the prone figure of the girl. Kat struggled to understand where she was and if she was in a dream. The horse screamed again and butted, finally delivering a painful nip to the tender flesh of the girl's buttock.

Kat's scream joined the horse's as the stallion's teeth broke the skin. She leaped up, fully awake, and led the frenzied animal into the shelter of a large cave. She lit a torch, which she placed in a bracket on the wall. She sat down and stared about the familiar space, remembering all the times she had sought refuge there. Three years before, when she entered into womanhood with the onset of her monthly flow, she had crawled into the cave as though returning to the womb, needing to be alone with the mysterious, awesome knowledge that she was now capable of bearing a child. Each time one of the loyal ancient band had died, she had come to the cave after digging the grave and consoling the bereaved, needing her own solace.

Kat wished she had had the foresight to stock the cave with provisions, as she rolled back a heavy rock from a small niche to reexamine her treasures. Here was where she had hidden the jewels and money she had systematically stolen from her father over the long five years since coming to Scotland. She thought of the bulging saddlebag that she had concealed in the stables; she made a mental note to retrieve it and add its contents to her quite sizable fortune. There was more here than she recalled. If she could sell the rings, necklaces, and brooches, she would have more than enough money for passage to France—or maybe even to the Colonies. She tried to remember exactly what she had stolen from Duncreag, and a sense of uneasiness gnawed at her. After emptying Darach's pockets and chests of money and jewelry, she had crept into Angus's chambers to rifle through his possessions.

"I had no other choice, Etalon," she said defensively to the black stallion, whose eyes flickered uneasily in the dim light as he heard the violence of the storm outside. "When Cailleach Cuilleann has cured Robbie, we shall sail for another land where it is all right to be who we are—a land where there'll be no more secrets, where we can stand tall and say proudly that we are MacGregors, the children of the mist. Och, you miserable *baistie!*" she swore, when the frightened horse roughly butted the painful bite.

She stood and shimmied her trews down over her right hip and examined the angry wound, noting the deep teeth marks. "Och, that's an ugly mess you've made of my *derrière*,

Etalon, and I've nae salt nor yarrow to cleanse the dirt of your mouth." She sighed. "Och, dinna *fash,*" she said soothingly, stroking the fretting stallion. "The storm will pass and we'll survive. We've lots to do and promises to keep. Tomorrow, we maun plan how we're to spirit Robbie away from Linnmanach. I think we shall have to look to Hag Holly's devious ways," she reflected aloud. "I dinna think the Campbell runt will harm Macaree. He's too enamored of her shapely woman's frame. So if we brew a tisane of horse balm, yellow jasmine, valerian, and any of the mints, we can have them soundly sleeping in each other's arms," she plotted, while gently crooning to the horse and easing his fear with comforting caresses. "There is a wee problem, you devil's nag—there are no yellow jasmine flowers until next spring, no valerian nor horse balm. We're left wie mint, which would not put any to sleep," she despaired.

Then she remembered that *auld* Ailsa had had a special sleeping concoction for one of her ancient maids who was prone to convulsive seizures. Kat forced herself to recall the previous anguished night when she had arrived at Linnmanach and searched the crumbling ruin. *Auld* Aunt Ailsa's room had been intact, her cobweb-covered clothes still hanging eerily and her pots and jars still cluttering the dressing table. Kat remembered the dark green bottle and the pungent smell. The first time she had seen the tiny old maid lie jerking convulsively on the floor, she had backed away, thinking that the old woman was possessed with terrible demons. She had been appalled when her frail little aunt had roughly grasped the maid's gray hair, forcing open the grimacing mouth and pouring in several drops of potion. There had been one long cackling sigh and then many hours of slumber. As Ailsa had grown weaker and Aggie busier, it had fallen upon Kat to perform the ministrations on the stricken maid.

"So, Etalon, tomorrow I shall find Aunt Ailsa's green bottle, and I hope it will have enough drops to guarantee Macaree and her Campbell a deep sleep." With her mind planning and the storm abating until only low shuddering rumbles remained, Kat made herself comfortable and tried to sleep, ignoring her hunger and the throbbing wound caused by her horse's teeth. But sleep eluded her. Each time her eyes drooped and her senses whirled, she saw Darach's strong brown hands embracing Macaree, and she sat up, determined to dispel that insupportable image.

chapter 19

Darach glowered across the table. The thought of food after the discomfort and embarrassment of the previous two days was nauseating, and yet he knew he needed his strength. Angus glared back at his nephew. He had had none of that discomfort or embarrassment; nevertheless, he felt foolish —taken advantage of by a green-eyed little witch who had robbed him of several very sentimental tokens. The money and odd baubles were inconsequential, but there were some very personal mementos that could never be replaced; he felt violated.

"I dinna ken why you're looking daggers at me when it was your wife who's responsible," he snapped testily, squirming guiltily under the piercing silver gaze.

"It would seem to me that you're the one who conspired against me wie that *auld cailleach,*" retorted Darach.

"How many times do I hae to tell you tha' I knew nothing aboot this," the older man hissed. "I was poisoned, too," he added in aggrieved tones.

"A mild sleeping draft isna exactly poison! What I was dosed wie was pure, unadulterated venom, and I aim to exact vengeance," growled Darach, tenderly touching his still-throbbing head, and very conscious of his churning stomach.

"Would appear to me tha' the wee lass was a wee bit put out

wie you," Angus observed mildly. "And even more so wie tha' self-righteous steward of yours. Calum MacKissock got an even stronger dosage than you. What had the *gillie* done to deserve worse than his master?" he inquired wickedly.

"If I had but listened to Calum MacKissock in the first place, none of this would've happened," the young man lamented, doubling up as a spasm shuddered through his gut.

"The cook brewed this solely for you," stated Angus, feeling sorry for his ailing nephew. He pointed to a large tureen amid the many platters on the crowded table.

"What is it?" Darach inquired suspiciously, removing the cover and scrutinizing the steaming green contents, not at all tempted by its pungent aroma.

" 'Tis a potage of plantain, shepherd's purse, elder, potatoes, orrisroot, and garlic, wie a touch of stinging nettles and rosemary."

"Sounds remarkably like one of the *cailleach*'s potions," he remarked dryly.

"Och, I can guarantee this particular *bree*. 'Tis very binding and a wondrous tonic," Angus declared expansively. A sharp rap at the door stopped Darach's caustic retort, and Calum MacKissock popped a very green visage into the room. He blenched at the sight and scent of the steaming foods.

"What is it?" the Campbell barked brusquely.

"Your . . . your . . . your . . ." stammered the wan man, waving an explanatory hand, before he was rudely shoved aside. A woman stalked into the room, dressed in a voluminous black gown, her face entirely shrouded with layers of black lace. A very intricate, feathered hat perched on a very elaborate wig. She looked like a very large, strange raven, decided Angus, standing politely to welcome his unexpected guest.

"Felicity!" Darach exclaimed in horror. The sickening perfume she always wore released its aroma from her overheated body to mingle unappetizingly with the steaming dinner dishes. "Excuse me," he added hurriedly before dashing from the room, unable to deal with his clinging stepmother and her cloying odor. He desperately needed fresh air.

"Sir Angus," simpered Felicity, offering a black-gloved hand for him to kiss.

"Lady Felicity," he lamented, taking her hand and staring balefully after his departed nephew. "Calum, please see that another place setting is laid,'' he ordered. "You maun excuse your stepson, but he's been a trifle indisposed these last few days,'' he informed her awkwardly. "I understand that you also have been a trifle . . . inconvenienced. I was led to believe that you were . . . er . . . also indisposed,'' he ended unhappily, not knowing how to mention the woman's affliction delicately. He fervently wished that he hadn't broached the subject.

"He imprisoned me!'' Felicity spat bluntly. "Had me locked in Bedlam, just like your foul brother before him.''

"Oh, dear,'' sympathized Angus, not knowing how to cope.

"Have you met her?''

"Who?''

"Darach's wife?'' challenged the Englishwoman, throwing back her veil and reaching across the table to spear a succulent lamb chop and a stuffed partridge.

Angus's mouth drooped open. He smothered a shocked gasp at the sight of the terrible scar that traversed one painted cheek. It pulled down the corner of one eye and twisted up her top lip so that she had a permanent malevolent smirk. As much as he detested the grasping female, he was appalled by what had happened to her. Her only questionable attribute was gone—her prized pink-and-white English prettiness, an attractiveness he felt was grossly overrated, as it was too sickly sweet for his palate. He wondered for about the hundredth time exactly what had attracted his brother to this insipid female. He gaped, fascinated, yet repelled, by the livid, disfiguring scar, unable to add one morsel of conversation as Felicity avidly piled her plate with spiced apples, cauliflower, bean tart, and boiled mutton with lemons. He remained gaping as she crammed food into her mouth, heedless of the juices and grease that ran down her chin and beaded upon the rich brocade of her gown. When had the poor woman last eaten? he wondered.

"Excuse me,'' he muttered finally.

He felt extremely queasy and hastily quit the room, leaving several footmen sagging against the wall, looking extremely wan. "Where's my nephew?'' he demanded. Aware of the dangerous rage that simmered just beneath the surface of their usually mellow master, they quietly indicated the stable courtyard, where Darach gazed speculatively at a very large hound. "What the hell is happening to my tranquil retreat?" the elderly man bellowed. "First you arrive wie a nearly dead sprite dressed as an urchin who nearly kills us all and then absconds wie some of my most prized possessions. And then Felicity stalks in dressed like a giant raven wie her face near torn in two, while here you sit fondling a *meikle baistie*. Dinna I deserve an explanation?"

" 'Twas this wolfhound that nearly ripped Felicity's face in two," Darach stated bluntly.

"Nice pet."

"My stepmother was attempting to dispose of my wife wie a dagger. This creature received the wound instead."

"Then I take it that this is your . . . er . . . bride's wee pet?" Angus remarked, staring at the enormous hound with some trepidation.

"Och, he'll not harm you. He's as gentle as a lamb unless you mean to hurt his rogue mistress." Darach sighed, fondling one of the soft floppy ears. "He's a magnificent animal. My stepmother should be shot for maiming him so," he mourned.

"I hae a strange inkling that Felicity might share those feelings about him," his uncle remarked wryly. "But that doesna tell me what they are both doing here at Duncreag, my peaceful retreat."

"Och, now, now, *auld* mon, dinna gie me that outraged act. This *schlorich* is all your fault, so dinna try and make me feel guilty for the chaos that you find your house in!"

"My fault?" Angus echoed indignantly.

"This'll teach you to meddle in what doesna concern you. You and Cailleach Cuilleann deserve whatever you received," snapped Darach. "Is Iolair saddled yet?" he roared into the depths of the stables.

"Iolair saddled? Where are you going?" the older man squeaked. "You're nae leaving me wie . . . wie that woman?" he uttered with disbelief. "You canna be so cruel, Darach Campbell!"

"Och, it'll teach you to be true to your own flesh and blood!"

"You truly mean to abandon me? Leave me wie that female who you just said tried to murder your wife?"

"Aye, and I suggest that you lock your bedchamber door at

night because she has an irritating habit of crawling between the sheets, like a succubus," the dark young man remarked with savage mirth.

"A succubus?" repeated Angus. "But where are you going?" he pleaded, when an ostler led the large spirited stallion out of the dim recesses of the stable.

"I'm going to find my wife and I'm using the hound to track her scent."

"The hound is maimed. It'll be slow going."

"I dinna think she went far."

"What'll you do when you find the wee-an?" Angus asked softly, recognizing the icy, uncompromising fury that froze his nephew's chiseled features.

"What does one usually do wie a common felon?"

"Och, dinna be rash," whispered Angus, gazing beseechingly up at the tall dark man mounted upon the magnificent golden stallion.

"Dinna be rash!" Darach echoed scornfully. "Have you forgotten your great-grandmother's ruby pendant? The jeweled miniature of your first love? The *skean dhu* wie the diamond-encrusted hilt that belonged to your boyhood friend who died on Culloden moor?" he challenged, naming but a few of the precious, sentimental items that Kat had stolen.

"Suddenly they dinna seem as valuable as a wee dark girl wie emerald eyes," Angus replied huskily. His words were drowned out by the impatient hooves of Iolair. The horse sprang forward, eager to gallop after three long days of inaction.

Angus slumped against the cold, gray stones of the stable, feeling his age seep achingly into his bent bones as he watched his handsome, virile nephew ride through the gates of Duncreag, followed by the valiant limping wolfhound. He knew instinctively where Darach was headed, and he fervently hoped that Cailleach Cuilleann was away from home, because he wouldn't wish his nephew's cold fury on anyone. He turned dejectedly and gazed at the imposing granite walls of his fortress home, remembering the grotesque Felicity stuffing her greedy mouth and the sanctimonious whining of Calum MacKissock. No, his home was definitely not the place to be, he decided. Anywhere else was preferable.

"Saddle *auld* MacGhee," he ordered. "And I want a saddlebag packed wie food for three days wie a flask or two of spirits,'' he added imperiously, sending several young ostlers rushing to the main house. "And hurry up!" he roared, feeling his age lift away from him. He felt younger than he had in years. "Get cracking!" he shouted impatiently, striding back and forth, rubbing his hands together with anticipation. He knew where his rash young nephew was headed, but he knew a shortcut to the old crone's *clachan*. He chortled aloud at the realization that Darach's progress would be hampered by the limping hound. "What's taking so long?" he bellowed, eager to be mounted on his old chestnut warhorse, plodding through the hot summer night away from the strident Felicity Campbell and the moaning Calum MacKissock.

Calum MacKissock reeled out of the main keep of Duncreag just as Angus trotted sedately toward the twin turrets that guarded the main gates.

"Sir Angus? The lady Felicity demands that you and Lord Strathrannoch attend her," he informed the old man unhappily.

"Unfortunately, 'tis not possible, but I'm sure you shall be able to attend to her every need in your usual inimitable manner!" the older man shouted merrily, urging his ancient battle-scarred warhorse into a lumbering canter. He laughed aloud, his gravelly voice slicing through the heavy darkness. Adventure and intrigue spiced his sluggish blood, and he acknowledged wryly to himself that he was eager to see old Hag Holly. There was a kindred spirit in the woman's sharp eyes that also stirred youthful fantasies.

Darach was by no means as inspired as his uncle. He cursed his impetuousness as Iolair's rhythm jolted his delicate stomach and throbbing head, but he savagely comforted himself with the thought of escaping Felicity. He knew he was embarking on the lesser of two evils. Anything was preferable to his stepmother's company, even the rebel wildcat to whom he was married. At the thought of the green-eyed little minx, he slowed his stallion's pace and stared down at the loyal hound that limped beside him. His large hands tightened on the reins, recalling the savagely thrown geode that had nearly broken his skull. She really must hate him, he forced himself to acknowledge. Her hatred of him had to be akin to Felicity's hatred of her—both were prepared to kill. Pain at this realization flooded through his sore body, combining with his physical ills. He hurt everywhere, in every way a person possibly could, and he was furious with himself for having been so vulnerable, especially when he had known better. How could he have made such a mistake? He actually had had the stupidity, the utter idiocy, to fall in love with that unscrupulous, unredeemable, incorrigible little female. To his horror, his uncle's departing words rang in his head. What had the old man so eloquently cried when he had listed some of the precious items stolen by his wild bride? "They dinna seem as valuable as a wee dark girl wie emerald eyes."

"Silly *auld* fool," Darach growled hoarsely. "Well, I'll nae be so entrapped," he vowed, brutally reminding himself of the amethyst rock smashing against his head. Yet a poignant little face haunted his mind, and his heart hurt. "No more!" he chided himself savagely. "No more sickening sentiment! I'll wring the truth from her even if it means her life!" he resolved. How could he have been so callow and naïve? She had been caught entrenched in a plot to extort money and land, and she was also an accessory to his own brother's abduction. And what had he done? Fallen in love with the dissolute young felon! Thinking of this, he buried his emotions beneath layers of cold, vengeful logic. What would he do when he found her?

Darach sat comfortably back in his saddle; he derived great pleasure thinking of all the debasing tortures he would exact upon Kat's small, despicable body. One way or another, he would wrest the truth from her sweet, lying mouth. He snorted with impatience, furious with his traitorous mind, which kept sneaking her little endearing traits into his thoughts. He suddenly understood the male weakness that had been written about for hundreds of years. He had studied literature, yet he had never truly realized the power of the sirens who had tempted Odysseus or the myriads of mermaids that had lured many a brave seaman to his death. Suddenly, he understood the struggle between Adam and Eve, Antony and Cleopatra, Othello and Desdemona, and countless other poor men who had been ensnared by the opposite sex. He had always been cautious when dealing with women, but he hadn't really known about that inexplicable magic that could surreptitiously worm its way beneath a man's firm resolve, undermining even his faith in himself. He had actually had the

CHILDREN OF THE MIST

effrontery to believe that he was above and beyond all those other intelligent men, who from the beginning of time had been bedazzled and ensnared. How pompously naïve he had been!

Darach broke free of his brooding thoughts and stared about him, trying to locate the limping hound, but there was no sign of the animal in the shifting shadows of the quiet night. He whistled and keenly listened. Hearing nothing, he loudly cursed the green-eyed minx; the mere thought of her had caused him to lose sight of his objectives. He savagely turned Iolair about and retraced his way. Half a mile down the road, a smaller path bisected the main route. He peered down each overgrown, rutted lane, not knowing which route to take. He whistled again and there was a faint answering bark. He kneed Iolair forward, carefully picking his way, until once again he found himself behind Sian. The shaggy dog had perked up and was making little grunts of excitement, his heavy tail wagging as he busily sniffed the bracken. For nearly a mile through dense forest they traveled, the hound picking up pace until he broke into a halting run, rejoicing with eerie howls and whimpers. He tried to gambol like a rambunctious puppy, until he suddenly stopped and sat, baying at the moon.

Tall, majestic wrought-iron gates soared out of the tangled undergrowth, and Darach reined in and gazed with amazement at the incongruous sight. The moonlight limned the shiny leaves of the rhododendron bushes that bordered the carriageway, glinting on the diamond-patterned panes of a stone gatehouse that was nearly hidden by a thick tangle of wild roses. Sian stuck his large head through the palings of the imposing gates and then tried to wriggle between the measured spaces, only to retreat with a lamenting bark.

"You've grown a bit since you were last able to do that, Sian," Darach sympathized as he dismounted. "What estate is this?" he pondered aloud, noting the shape of a coat of arms that had once been proudly emblazoned across the entryway —all that was left was the rusty void. He stared appreciatively at the impressive gates and wondered at the size of the gracious home tucked deep within the private park. He grasped a long metal rod that dangled from the clapper of a large brass bell and rang it loudly. The sharp sound shattered the stillness, and the hound sat with his shaggy head cocked expectantly, whining with excited anticipation. The only movement was several twittering clouds of bats that rose from the ominous thickness of the shrubbery.

Angus allowed his old horse to pick his way at his own leisurely pace up the steep, wooded slopes of Ben Vorlich. He was lulled by the serene, warm night and *auld* MacGhee's steady rhythm. He frowned, hearing an echo of his travail shuffling behind, and he reined his steed. There was another weary traveler abroad, and he wondered if it was his nephew who was approaching so laboriously. He debated whether to race toward the *cailleach*'s *clachan* to warn her of Darach's presence, but instead, there was something that made him furtively back his horse under the concealing fronds of a juniper tree. *Auld* MacGhee waited patiently without making a sound, just as he had done years ago fighting the English. Angus's blood sang with exhilaration as the hoofbeats approached. Sometimes they slipped on the wet carpet of leaves beneath the trees that still dripped from the violent thunderstorms of the previous night.

"Hang on, Robbie, it canna be far now," whispered a well-known voice. Great consternation was apparent in the young breathless tone, and Angus gasped at the sight of the skittish black stallion that struggled up the sheer, slippery mountainside, carrying what appeared to be two riders.

"Well, now, lassie," Angus growled, kneeing his old horse out of hiding and blocking the way. For a brief moment, he envisioned himself a knight in shining armor or a *braw* Highland warrior instead of a middle-aged man.

Kat fought to control her inexperienced mount, which reared and screamed in terror, and also to hold on to Robbie's dead weight that made her arms ache unbearably.

"Help me!" she cried, knowing there was no way she could stop her young brother from falling, as she held on to the frenzied animal. Instinctively, she wrapped both arms about Robbie's fragile frame and launched herself off the frightened stallion's high back, thrusting away from the sharp, slashing hooves and cushioning the boy with her own body. She landed heavily and the breath was knocked out of her, stifling the scream of agony caused by the punishing blow to the bite wound that had swelled and inflamed her right buttock. She

lay back in the wet leaves as pain streaked through her, not
knowing if her brother was dead or alive. She felt his inert
weight suffocating her, and she was unable to release herself.
She heard the white-haired man dismount heavily, and his feet
hurriedly approached them. He loomed above her, silhouetted
against the dappled moonlit sky. She smiled wanly.

"Guid evening, Sir Angus," she panted, unable to catch her
breath and using mischievousness to hide her terror.

Angus frowned at the boy who Kat cradled so protectively.
A flaxen head lolled limply against her shoulder and the eyes
were closed. It was a pretty lad of no more than nine or ten, he
ascertained from the small stature and the thin, hairless cheek.
He knelt stiffly and felt the slender neck for a pulse, before
lifting the child's weight from the dark-haired lass.

"And who have we here, minx?" he asked bluntly, holding
the limp boy easily in his arms. "Another patient for the
callieach?" he surmised, and Kat nodded as she scrambled
painfully to her feet, biting back the cries of agony. "And who
is this wee lad?"

"My brother. Is he . . . is he . . . ?" She couldn't say the
word.

"He's alive, wee-an," Angus croaked huskily. "And luckily we're near. Catch the bridles and follow me," he ordered
tersely, striding up the slope. He sensed that time was of the
essence as he stared down at the almost ethereal beauty of the
unconscious child in his arms. The boy's pale fragility was like
fine bone china, and his stillness was frightening.

"If he dies it will be my fault," sobbed Kat, plodding behind and pulling the two horses. She slipped and fell, unable
to display her usual graceful agility as her right leg throbbed
and stiffened. "I shouldna have moved him."

"I canna walk and talk," panted Angus. The small boy felt
heavier by the step, and Angus's newfound youth was rapidly
departing. He scanned ahead, praying for sight of Hag Holly's
humble stone house, hoping that his heart, lungs, and limbs
would hold out. "Keep going," he directed, leaning back
against a tree for a few moments, while summoning a new
spurt of energy.

"Who's there?" a feral voice snarled, and the colorful
cailleach pranced out from behind a woodpile, pointing an an-
tique weapon. She reminded Kat nostalgically of a time years

before when *auld* Aunt Ailsa and her ancient band had futilely attempted to protect Linnmanach from Gregor's invasion. Now they were all dead.

" 'Tis me," she said with tears coursing down her cheeks. "I've brought my brother, and, please . . . please dinna let him die, too. Och, please dinna let him die. He's the hope of my clan—all the man that is left. Please dinna let him die." She was nearly incoherent. Angus staggered into sight carrying the unconscious child. "If he dies it will be my fault. It should be me who dies, not him," she babbled wildly. The two old people paid no attention as they carried the boy into the small stone house, leaving the grieving girl to tend to the two horses.

Kat sat in a pile of fragrant hay. She rocked back and forth, reliving the long tension-filled day, not daring to enter the *cailleach*'s *clachan* for fear of what she would find. She shouldn't have moved Robbie, she fretted, convinced that she had killed him. At daybreak that morning she had crept to the gatehouse at Linnmanach and dosed all the food and drink she could find with Ailsa's sleeping potion from the green bottle. She had then hidden herself within the thick rhododendron bushes to catch a little more sleep. She had been roused by Robbie's voice, a treble demand building to a screaming intensity, and when it was obvious that neither Macaree or Riach was able to stir to see to the boy's needs, she had left the shrubbery and had stealthily entered the house. Etalon had been tethered outside the main gates, so the distance she would have to carry her brother would be as short as possible. But heaving him onto the skittish stallion's back had been an agonizing, muscle-straining experience. Robbie had been frightened and upset, sobbing and crying for Riach Campbell and refusing to listen to her.

Kat curled on her left side as her right side throbbed. Her head ached, and she tried to summon the courage to enter the *cailleach*'s house before returning to Linnmanach to inform her sister that Robbie was safe. But was he safe? Was he still alive? Or was she responsible for his death? The question gnawed at her. Unable to lie still, she pulled herself to her feet, taking pleasure in her stabbing pain—she felt she deserved even worse. Maybe she should take Angus's old warhorse instead of her callow young stallion, she debated, knowing that the seasoned campaigner was a surer steed than her unpredictable colt. Why was she going back to Linnmanach? she puzzled dully, hanging over the split-rail fence and watching the animals graze. She was returning to reassure her sister that their brother was being cured. But why should she reassure Macaree and that Campbell trespasser? She remembered how they resented her very presence. No one there had cared that she was alive and well. Maybe she should let them suffer and never know what had happened to the boy. No, she had enough guilt, she mused sadly. She had to return to Linnmanach and face her sister so that she could be free. If the *cailleach* could cure Robbie, then she and her brother could go to France or America, or anywhere, leaving Macaree and Riach to lead their own lives. But if the hag couldn't heal her brother? That horrific question caused pitiful cries to burst from her mouth.

Kat spun about, feeling that she was watched, and her eyes widened with terrified anticipation at seeing Angus's worried face. He frowned, seeing her grimace of pain, and he put out a steady hand when she staggered.

"Och, please dinna say it," she entreated. "Och, please dinna say that he's gone, too! He canna be dead . . . he canna."

chapter 20

Darach questioned his sanity as he followed the limping wolf-hound away from the formal entrance gates, off the beaten track and into dense wilderness. Unable to ride due to the low-hanging branches and entangling vines, he led Iolair, while loudly cursing the showers he received from the moisture-laden trees. He swatted wildly at the gnats and midges that flew noisily into his ears and face. He was about to give up and retrace his steps, intent on scaling the tall gates, when familiar wrought-iron palings brought him up short. They appeared so suddenly in the thick underbrush that he very neary walked straight into them. He watched Sian snuffle about, his heavy tail waving like a happy flag before he gave a comical hop and flopped through an uneven gap in the symmetry. There was a rusty groan of metal and a portion of the railings shifted. A section had been conveniently sawed through, creating an improvised wicket that could be swung aside, allowing egress.

Less than a quarter of a mile from the surrounding palisade, the forest thinned. Darach halted at the edge, overcome by the beauty of the scene before him. He gazed across a tranquil lake, where regal swans glided in the silver moonlight, to an enormous house set upon a rolling lawn. Great columns rose impressively, and wide sweeping steps led to a central terrace with huge Italian urns supporting each corner. Completing the idyllic picture was a stag and his harem, grazing on the grass that sloped gently to the water. Darach mounted Iolair, keeping his eyes pinned to the majestic house, as Sian, unappreciative of this beauty, limped stoically toward the edifice, scattering the deer.

Seeing Linnmanach from a misty distance gilded by a nearly full moon did not prepare Darach. What had appeared so breathtakingly glorious from afar looked grotesquely decayed as he approached. The windows were hollow and haunted by roosting ravens; the stately columns were cracked and crumbling. Ivy and rambling roses clutched the whole disintegrating ruin in a strangling embrace, like a parasite feeding off the very mortar that bonded the great granite blocks.

The wolfhound slowly pulled himself up the broken steps to the vast terrace and disappeared through French doors that hung crookedly ajar, creaking in the faint breeze. Leaving Iolair to graze upon the overgrown lawn, Darach cautiously followed Sian.

"Nobody could live in here, beast," he remarked. "And nobody could've lived here for many a long year," he added, staring about at the ghostly, rotting remains of the great hall where cobweb banners still hung. "Halloo!" he called between cupped hands. His deep voice reverberated off the oozing dank stones, scattering squeaking rats and bats. Unable to abide the stench of rodents and damp decay, Darach strode back onto the terrace and gazed over the moonlit vista, wondering what tragedy could have occurred to bring such magnificence to such shameful ruin. Much love and thought had gone into the design of the house and its placement amid the verdant property. What hatred, greed, or catastrophe was responsible for its demise? he wondered.

Sian hobbled out of the house and limped painfully down the crumbling steps, his shaggy coat catching on the clawing brambles. Darach watched him set off purposefully toward the overgrown carriageway, and after several moments he whistled for his stallion and resignedly followed the long-suffering hound.

After there was no answer to his cursory rapping, Darach warily opened the gatehouse door. The wolfhound leaped in, whining with excitement, but even though there were definite signs of recent habitation, the downstairs rooms were empty. Was this Kat's home? he mused, not finding anything in the cozy neatness that reminded him of his wild bride. He had to stoop, as the ceiling was low and beamed in the tiny rooms. He walked into the clean little kitchen and helped himself to a long drink of water from a jug. It had a slightly bitter aftertaste, but it was cool and refreshing. He sat at the table, gazing about at the precise order of the pretty room, hearing the dog's halting progress up the narrow, wooden stairs. Then a frantic scratching and barking caused him to leap up, nearly cracking his head.

Sian was in a frenzy, pawing and baying. Darach grinned triumphantly. Finally, he had run his rogue wife to earth, he grimly rejoiced, taking his time before pressing down on the latch, as a pulsating white-hot fury melded with his joy. He gently touched the still-tender place on his head, as though to remind himself of her treachery, and thrust open the door. The sight that met his eyes made his jaw drop open with shock, and he slumped against the jamb. His long-lost brother, Riach, naked to the waist and bronzed from the sun, lay peacefully sleeping with one of the most beautiful women he had ever seen. Voluptuous breasts and curvaceous hips were seductively arranged against the youth's leanness. Lustrous spun-gold hair fanned across his young brother's tanned chest, and one long bare feminine leg was intimately curled about his thigh.

Darach's head started to spin and everything took on a strange semblance of unreality. He rubbed his eyes, expecting the romantic vision of the embracing lovers to vanish, but when he looked again, there they were, lying motionless in the revolving room, highlighted by the eerie moonlight. He thought they were dead, and he staggered closer, trying to focus his eyes, but the walls and floor spun about alarmingly. He reached out a hand to touch his brother, but he had no distance or depth perception, and it seemed the sleeping couple twirled about at the bottom of a whirlpool, becoming smaller and smaller. He clutched at the bedpost for support as his legs buckled. He fought to stay conscious, but suddenly it didn't seem to be worth the effort. He sagged slowly to the floor, where he curled up on the braided rag rug and drifted into a sound slumber. Sian moaned mournfully before circling and flopping next to the sleeping man. He sighed loudly and rested a doleful face on his shaggy paws, his soft brown eyes drooping sadly.

Hot, late-morning sunshine streamed in the window, and with it came the drone of the bumblebees and the demanding peeps of the martin nestlings in their mud nests under the eaves. Macaree stirred and cuddled closer to Riach, wrapping her arms about his chest, but he tossed fretfully and moaned loudly. She rolled onto her back and opened her eyes. Her head pounded and her mouth and throat were dry and scratchy.

"I dinna feel well," she whispered hoarsely, the bright light making her eyes ache. Riach moaned again and attempted to sit; he fell back onto the pillows, holding his head. The chirping of the birds and buzzing of the bees were too loud to bear, and he wished the wretched dog would stop its irritating whine. What wretched dog? his painfully thumping brain wondered.

"Riach, I dinna feel well," whimpered Macaree, and Riach struggled again to sit up.

"I dinna feel too well myself, love," he groaned. "And I think I'm hearing things that aren't there," he added, staring blearily around. "Oh, my God!" he gasped.

"What is it?"

Riach could not utter a word. He leaned back against the headboard with his mouth hanging open, gaping at the floor. He closed his eyes, expecting the impossible vision to disappear, but it remained constant.

"Riach, what's the matter?" whispered Macaree, resting her aching head on his thigh and staring up at him. The youth didn't answer; he sat still, gawking across the room. She pulled herself into a sitting position and turned fearfully, following Riach's gaze. "Sian!" she exclaimed, and immediately regretted her loud tone, as she and Riach sagged together, clutching their aching heads. The hound barked joyously, causing the couple more stabbing pain, and he wagged his heavy tail with such exuberance that he toppled over with excitement. "Riach, there's a strange man on the floor," she whispered, but Riach couldn't answer. All he could do was nod, make guttural sounds of agony and disbelief, and hold his pounding head. "Riach?" she cried loudly, tugging on his bare arms, trying to make him react.

"It's my brother, Darach," the youth intoned. "Macaree, are we really seeing the same thing, or are we dreaming? Is there a large, black-haired man and a great big beast in here wie us?" Macaree nodded, then whimpered.

"Och, my puir head hurts so," she complained.

"I've seen that dog before," puzzled Riach.

"Aye, 'tis my sister Kat's hound, Sian. You maun remember him."

"Dimly," he replied. Through the whirling mists of pain and the distortion of the days since arriving at Linnmanach, he vaguely recalled some large hairy beast.

"What's your brother doing here?" Macaree asked fearfully, and Riach shrugged. "Is he dead?" she ventured.

"Dead? Why would my brother be dead?"

"Why is he lying on the floor? Why is he so still?"

"Oh, my God!" he exclaimed, as Macaree's pertinent questions finally pierced the throbbing layers of his brain. He swung his long legs off the bed and stood up; the room revolved, and he hung on to the bedpost for several moments before lowering himself gingerly to the floor and crawling to his brother's inert body. "Darach?" he called urgently, shaking his brother's shoulder.

Darach heard Riach's voice from a great distance, and then it zoomed in loudly with excruciating clarity. He angrily tried to tell the boy to be quiet, but his tongue was thick and unwieldy. He tried to burrow more comfortably into the softness of his bed, but someone kept shaking him and a rasping wetness slobbered about his ear. He rolled onto his back and groaned loudly as the bright, hot sunlight pried beneath his eyelids and his head pounded.

"Darach?" the irritating young voice insisted. He forced open his protesting eyes and glared groggily into his brother's face. There was a still moment as they surveyed each other. Each was thankful that the other lived, but neither showed any emotion.

"Well, little brother, you've led me on the very devil of a chase," Darach remarked mildly, pulling himself into a sitting position and bracing himself against the bedroom wall. "I have the very devil of a hangover, with none of the previous pleasure," he added, looking past Riach's wan face to the incredibly beautiful girl who reclined seductively upon the bed, watching the proceedings with wide bright blue eyes. Her spun-gold tresses shimmered down to catch the mellow afternoon sunlight in rippling waves.

Macaree recoiled from the piercing gray eyes. They were lacerating and judgmental, stripping her naked and dismissing her mockingly. She was frozen, unable to move. Darach Campbell was an older, larger, more intimidating version of Riach. They shared the same fine chiseled features and thick black hair, but the eyes were very different. She shivered at the harsh coldness of the Campbell's steely eyes and turned to plead silently with Riach, preferring the warmth of his amber depths, but he knelt on the floor with his back to her.

"I maun see to Robbie," she muttered, needing to escape from the Campbell's mocking scrutiny. As she attempted to stand, she staggered and would have fallen, but Riach leaped up to steady her with such haste that they both fell back onto the bed.

"Who is Robbie?" the stern man snapped. For some reason, he was angered by the sight of their entangled limbs.

"My brother . . ." stammered Macaree, when Riach didn't answer. Riach just sat, clutching her arm tightly. "You must have seen him when you entered. He's sick and sleeps on a bed in the parlor."

"There was nobody here except the two of you," Darach informed. "And who are you?"

"Nobody here? But that's impossible . . . he sleeps on his little bed by the window in the parlor," she fretted. "What is the matter wie us sleeping all day? Riach? Help me?" she entreated, not knowing how to cope. "He says Robbie isna there and what's he doing here. And 'tis like we're in some nightmare," she ranted. To Darach's wry amusement, his usually indifferent younger sibling took charge, soothing the distraught female like a fond parent.

"It will be all right, Macaree. Robbie cannot have gone far," he comforted, holding her close for a moment.

"But he canna have gone anywhere at all. Not by hisself. He was too weak." She wept.

"Stop it!" ordered Riach. "Hysterics willna help. Pull yourself together and let's go downstairs and see what we can find. Maybe my brother was mistaken, and Robbie slept so peacefully he didna notice him," he suggested, leading her out of the room.

Darach hauled himself to his feet, wincing as the sudden movement caused pain to stab through his head. He couldn't credit the change in appearance and manner of his younger brother. He followed them down the stairs at a more leisurely pace. He hung back when the blond female's screams became more piercing as she found the empty cot in the parlor. His many questions could wait until Riach had calmed her hysteria, he decided, letting himself out into the hot afternoon sunshine, needing to relieve himself. Sian limped after him, seeming to have a similar intention.

Darach stared about, trying to rid himself of the last vestiges of the excruciating headache. Then he gazed speculatively down at the large shaggy dog that sat companionably by his side. He knew without a doubt that the valiant animal would eventually lead him to his vicious, wild mistress. In the meantime, he needed to know why his younger brother was living on this decaying estate with the incredibly beautiful girl whose anguished cries still disturbed the languid summer day. Whistling for the dog, he let himself back into the house, searching about until he found a length of sturdy twine. Sian whined his objections, but Darach ignored them and firmly tethered the wolfhound to a tree before summoning his energy and striding back to confront his brother.

"I wouldna drink that if I were you," Darach advised dryly, leaning against the kitchen doorway, watching Riach pour himself some water from a large jug. The golden girl sat quietly with her head pillowed on her arms, which were on the table. "Unless, of course, you mean to drug yourself into oblivion again—which, now that I come to think of it, is what you seem to have been doing to yourself for several years," he added sardonically. Riach looked at him with consternation, which swiftly turned to sullen rebellion. "Smell it?" Darach suggested mildly, and the youth reluctantly sniffed the contents of the pitcher. Then he looked with alarm at the still girl.

"Macaree drank some," Riach whispered, reaching for her limp hands. "Oh, my God," he lamented. "She's asleep again."

"All to the guid!" snapped Darach. "Take her to bed and then we maun have a talk."

Riach glowered at his older brother, furious with his dictatorial tone, but he recognized the intense fury that smoldered in the silver eyes and he picked up the unconscious girl. He set her down gently on the couch in the parlor and returned to his brother. Sitting silently opposite him at the table, he refused to open the conversation.

"Who is she?" demanded Darach.

"My wife," replied Riach after a very long pause. He sensed that his newfound world could come smashing about his feet if he wasn't careful. Then he would be returned to his mother like a recalcitrant truant abased by his older brother's chastisements.

"And who is she?"

"My wife," repeated Riach. He was not going to tell the Campbell chieftain that he had actually taken a MacGregor for his bride. It was his secret, his small victory against his clan, who had always made him feel inferior—his brother, to whom he could never measure up, and his father, whom he could never please.

"I have spent the last eight months worrying and searching for you."

"And now you've found me, and you see I am quite happy and well. So you can return about your own business and leave me to mine," retorted Riach.

"Aye, I find you playing house wie a beautiful woman on a rotting estate in Perthshire, after I received an invitation from a well-known swindler to a card party of which your life was to be wagered against Strathrannoch and Glengrian," Darach stated, leaning back nonchalantly in his chair and idly perusing his brother's shocked expression.

"Wagering my life?" the youth repeated dazedly. "But I was safely here."

"You had not been seen for several months, and the invitation implied you were held hostage."

"That's ridiculous! I am here of my own free will!" Riach spat defensively. "And who is this supposed infamous swindler?" he challenged truculently, after an uncomfortable pause.

"A totally immoral charlatan who unfortunately did not just confine his heinous activities to the gaming tables. He was also an unconscionable libertine who preyed off lonely old women, stupefying them with noxious substances such as opium and hashish, bleeding them of monies and jewelry . . ."

"You're making all this up!" the youth accused vehemently, the reference to drugs jarring him discordantly. "I tell you that I am perfectly all right. I am here of my own free will and dinna need your help. I am quite able to take care of myself!"

Darach nodded his ebony head. "Aye, everything is perfectly all right in this little Eden of yours," he remarked dryly. "Except someone poisons your water. And where is this little brother for whom your concubine wails so loudly?"

"Dinna call her that!" Riach screamed petulantly. Then he shook his aching head as he heard his childish tones, wanting to burst into tears. After all the months of feeling mature and capable, he was now reduced to impotence, to a whining, defensive boy instead of the confident man. "Did you?" he shouted angrily. "Did you poison it? Did you take Robbie?"

"Dinna be foolish!" Darach snapped impatiently.

"Is it so foolish?" demanded Riach, his voice cracking with emotion. "Everything was wonderful until you appeared, and now everything is falling apart, and Robbie is missing."

"Who is Robbie . . . and your extraordinarily beautiful woman?" asked the older man, softening his tone upon seeing his brother's agitation and looking toward the parlor, where Macaree slept.

"Robbie is a small boy. He's very weak and seems to be dying of consumption or some such malady," explained Riach. He did not mention Macaree, deciding that he didn't want Darach to know anything about her. He was well aware of his brother's reputation with beautiful women. "But he seemed to be getting better since I moved him from the big house."

"The big house? You mean that hulking ruin wie the crumbling columns?" Darach exclaimed with disbelief, waving a vague hand toward the manse. The youth nodded sullenly. "He lived in there? Och, 'tis no wonder the puir *bairn*'s languishing. And the woman?" he prompted.

"So you thought my life was endangered? That I was held hostage?" Riach laughed derisively. "And what is the name of this infamous charlatan?" he asked, pacing back and forth in the tiny space. Then he savagely wrenched open a cupboard to take down a stone whiskey jug.

"Tell me."

"You think I dinna ken the name of my host?" Riach asked evasively, uncorking the bottle and offering a drink to his brother, who declined it. "Rory MacNiall." He sighed, before taking a long swallow of the burning liquor. That was all he would tell his interfering sibling, he decided. He would figure out his own life for himself. "Where is he?"

"Dead."

"Did you kill him?"

"Aye," Darach replied shortly, not wanting to go into a long defensive explanation.

"And that's where you obtained the hound?"

"Aye."

"And the dark girl?" ventured Riach, after scrutinizing his brother's tired face. He took another punishing swig and grinned maliciously, seeing the tightening about Darach's thin lips. "An elfin, green-eyed female?" he expanded roguishly, leaning back in his chair with a satisfied smirk, remembering how Kat had called him by his brother's name when he had found her lamenting in the graveyard.

"What do you know of her?" Darach asked tersely.

"Tell me all that you know first," Riach bartered, finally feeling that he could regain some of his lost dignity. He took another drink and settled back comfortably.

"She is my wife."

Riach's look of incredulity caused a flicker of cynical mirth to cross his older brother's brooding features. "And you dinna ken who she is?" He chortled with delight, choking on the strong spirits.

"And you do?"

"I canna credit it! The great, rational, august Lord Rannoch of Strathrannoch and Glengrian, magistrate and member of the House of Lords, has actually married a green-eyed, undisciplined wench—whom I've yet to see dressed in female attire—and he doesna even know who she is!" The youth chuckled, tears of merriment streaming from his brown eyes. "I think your well-regulated days are over!" he spluttered.

"Who is she?"

"Och, I dinna think it is my place to inform you, big brother. If you canna deal wie and control your own woman . . ." He broke off in the midst of his gloating, and a puzzled frown crossed his face. "The room is spinning like before," he lamented, looking with horror at the whiskey jug.

"Who would drug everything within reach?" demanded Darach, watching Riach try desperately to remain awake. His eyeballs rolled wildly and his mouth sagged open.

"Your . . . wife," the youth uttered, before slumping onto the table and cracking his head against the stone jug.

Darach sat for several minutes, examining his younger brother's relaxed features, noting the change in his face since he had last seen him many months ago. Gone was the puffy pallor caused by nights of dissipation and days used to sleep away excesses. One hand lay open, and he noted the calluses and short blunt nails. It was a hand that had finally known hard work. The torso was lean and hard, with no spare flab, and nicely bronzed from hours spent in the sun. He approved of this metamorphosis—the debauched, spoiled youth had become a responsible young man. Darach strode into the parlor and gazed down upon the sleeping golden-haired woman.

Who was this new sister-in-law who had wrought such a miracle, and what was her relationship, if any, to Kat? She was the opposite in every conceivable way from his own defiant bride, and not just in stature and coloring. In the brief time he had observed his brother's tall, voluptuous wife, it was apparent that she was as docile and timorous as petite Kat was fierce and unmanageable.

Darach systematically searched every chest and drawer in the gatehouse, but he found nothing that enlightened him as to Kat's identity. In fact, he found nothing at all that seemed remotely to belong to her, and he concluded that she had never lived there. Everything was too well ordered and precise. Prettily embroidered doilies and cushions, delicate arrangements of flowers and grasses, cozy patchwork quilts and fussy ornaments—certainly not a setting for the unprincipled little rebel. Yet, the wolfhound had led him there, and his own brother had confirmed that Kat was responsible for contaminating the food and drink in the kitchen. Why? The question nagged him. His stomach ached with hunger; he gazed longingly at the tempting array of dishes in the larder, but he turned resolutely away. He had spent quite enough time flat on his back due to the amoral female's predilection for preparing embarrassing and stupor-causing concoctions; he would not even trust the innocent-looking loaf of bread. He wanted to shake his brother roughly awake, demanding answers to all his questions, but he recognized the futility of that idea.

Sian's frantic whines and barks penetrated his seething thoughts, and Darach strode out of the tiny house into the hot, lazy afternoon. He would release the protesting animal and follow him wherever he went. He knew without a shadow of a doubt that the loyal animal would lead him to his dark mistress. When he found her he would exact full payment for all the pain, embarrassment, thievery, deceit, and other vicious acts that she had inflicted upon him and his family. His burning rage welded with his gnawing hunger, and his palm itched with the thought of the well-deserved thrashing he planned to deposit upon a certain part of her anatomy. He swung himself onto Iolair's high back and urged him into a canter, and they followed the limping dog up the carriageway.

chapter 21

Kat lay awake in the cool dimness of the cave. Outside she could hear the lilting trickle of the rippling mountain burn and the low, mellow hum of the hot afternoon. She wondered fearfully if her little brother was still alive. She wished she was with him, but Angus had informed her that there was nothing more she could do for the boy and that the enraged Campbell was on his way to the Cailleach Cuilleann's *clachan*, intent on finding her. So she had fled, trusting that the two old people would not betray her by divulging the nature of Robbie's relationship to her. They would say he was the sick son of poor shepherds from a nearby *shieling*.

After guiltily remembering what she had already taken, and seeing the great affection that existed between the two old campaigners, Kat hadn't been able to steal *auld* MacGhee. Why hadn't Angus confronted her about her abuse of his hospitality instead of giving her food and kindness and lifting her tenderly onto her horse's back? She deserved his anger and contempt, not his loving help. But, then, he had smartly slapped Etalon's rump, sending him careening down the wooded slopes of Ben Vorlich, and each hoofbeat had jarred her agonizingly. She had stoically borne the intense suffering, hoarding it as the punishment that she so richly deserved. She had arrived back at the hidden glen before sunrise and had fallen off the young black stallion, unable to dismount properly. She had slowly crawled to the icy stream and tried to numb the throbbing wound by sitting in the crystal water, but it hadn't eased the pain. As the day wore on and the air had become hot and heavy, she had sought the coolness of the dark cave, where she lay flat on her stomach, attempting to stem the frightening images that tortured her brain.

Kat was dozing fitfully when she heard Etalon's treble whinny shattering the lazy afternoon, and the sound of him savagely pawing the ground reverberated through her prone body. She lay groggily listening, not sure of what was a dream and what was real, her heart thumping achingly in time with her throbbing wound. Then her blood froze at a joyful bark.

"Sian," she whispered, rearing back on her haunches and stifling screams of agony. She cursed herself roundly for not having had the foresight to hide the distinctive-looking stallion in the cave with her, but then she realized wearily that her wolfhound would have tracked her no matter where she was concealed. Quickly, she crawled to the back of the cave, knowing it would be just a matter of minutes before the dog led the Campbell to her. She fervently prayed that she was still small enough to wriggle down the long, narrow tunnel to freedom in the forest. The last time she had ventured through that frightening passage, she had been an undernourished fourteen-year-old.

Darach's saturnine expression shifted to savage satisfaction at the sight of the spirited young horse that snorted and reared nervously at seeing the wolfhound, pawing the lush grass of the verdant glade to warn the trespassers away. The vibrant sunlight glinted off the glossy ebony coat and winked and sparkled off the bubbling water of the swift-flowing stream where the dog drank thirstily, ignoring the posturing stallion. Darach urged Iolair toward the crystal-clear burn, his face set in a mirthless smile, his silver eyes hard and cruel. He dismounted and knelt to drink upstream from the animals before casually and confidently following the enthusiastic hound to the outcropping of rocks amid the tangled brush. At last he had run the vixen to earth, he rejoiced grimly, enjoying each measured moment of anticipation, but suddenly it seemed that the wolfhound had disappeared into thin air. One minute he had been noisily whining and snuffling, his great shaggy tail wagging wildly, and the next he was nowhere to be seen.

Kat had painfully managed to pull herself several yards into the long narrow fissure when she heard Sian bound into the cave behind her, his paws scraping on the hard rock floor. She felt so abandoned and scared in the close darkness that she was tempted to slither backward. She wanted to fling her arms about her pet's shaggy neck, burying her face in the dog musk for comfort, as she had done so many times over the long five years, but she forced herself to keep edging forward, hoping he would loyally follow where the large Campbell couldn't possibly fit. What if she didn't fit? she wondered, panicking as the passage seemed to get narrower. She took a breath to whistle, summoning Sian, and for a long terrible moment it felt as though she were wedged. But, to her relief, she was able to inch ahead. To be trapped forever beneath the earth was too horrendous a thing to imagine, and her heart pounded so loudly she feared the beating noise would dislodge loose shale and bury her. She forced herself to think positively. She and Sian would reach the end of the shaft, and the Campbell would never be able to find the exit in the woods. They would escape. To where? Her skeptical mind probed. Once more, panic flared up, but she doggedly continued to inch her way through the tight darkness, her hipbones scraping on the rock, her eyes glued to the pinprick of light ahead.

Darach fought his way through the prickly branches of the thick holly bush and into the large cave. He stared about him, and his eyes slowly became accustomed to the gloom after the bright sunshine. Hearing a whine, he just managed to grab the rope that trailed from the wolfhound's neck before the animal was out of reach, down a long dark tunnel. Darach exerted all his strength and hauled back the loudly protesting dog. Sian barked and howled, snarling menacingly, trying to loosen the man's strong hold, but he was dragged inexorably back into the cave, his four paws splayed, attempting to dig into the hard rock. He bayed mournfully to his young mistress, who was finally so near after the long months apart. Darach knelt and peered into the small dark hole. He shuddered, reluctantly acknowledging the girl's valor as well as her stupidity, as the thought of being so entombed gave him a cold sweat.

Kat knew she had not much time to formulate a plan. With the aid of her hound, the Campbell would now be able to find the exit to the shaft in a matter of minutes. Should she stay in the tunnel, or make a run for it? Either way, she had an even chance, she decided, preferring to race in the fresh air, no matter how painful or futile the chase would be, rather than be confined in the underground tunnel. She painstakingly wriggled, rejoicing as the end finally loomed into sight. In her excitement at the thought of thrusting her face into the air after nearly a half hour of smothering, tight darkness, she was careless. Terror stabbed through her when she realized that her shoulders were securely stuck in the small orifice. She couldn't move either forward or backward. She tried to calm the hysteria that threatened to consume her totally. At least her head was out, she comforted herself, as she desperately tried to get a good enough grip on the smooth ledge to haul herself forward. But it was futile and she clawed wildly at the rock, painfully tearing her nails. Ignoring the excruciating agony that shot through her right leg from hip to knee, she flexed her feet, trying to get a firm toehold to propel herself out of the narrow fissure; all that happened was that she got more firmly wedged. Angry, frustrated whimpers burst from her mouth. She was trying too hard, and all the blood was rushing to her shoulders, which were being torn by the imprisoning rock. She forced herself to relax and lie limply, hoping that she'd somehow shrink, but she remembered the approaching Campbell and was once more desperately struggling to free herself.

Kat was nearly hysterical and so obsessed by her nightmarish dilemma that she was oblivious to the moment she so dreaded. She was only made conscious of their presences when her hot, tear-streaked face was lovingly licked by a rasping tongue. She stopped battling to escape and collapsed wearily, allowing Sian to welcome her while she waited tensely for the harsh, sarcastic words. When none was forthcoming, she dared hope that by some miracle the insufferable man hadn't had the intelligence to follow her pet. She cautiously raised her head and scanned about. Her heart sank when she saw him at a distance, leaning nonchalantly against a tree, grinning sardonically at her predicament. She glowered back, hoping that her expression was as eloquent as his and that he'd know how much she truly despised him. He eased himself away from his resting place and strode toward her at a leisurely pace, seeming to derive great pleasure from the surrounding scenery. Kat then had to suffer the further indignity of staring at his booted feet because she couldn't swivel her neck to glare up at him. Then he slowly knelt so that she gazed at his muscular thighs. She squeezed her eyes shut, hoping to eradicate the sensuous memories that flashed into her perfidious mind. How could she think of those ecstatic, intimate couplings when she was so firmly wedged?

"Do you need assistance?" he asked mildly. Fortunately, she couldn't see the amusement that danced in his gray eyes. Kat's fury filled her to bursting and she felt herself expand, becoming even more hopelessly embedded in the impenetrable rock.

"I need nothing from a Campbell *muc!*" she spat, trying to wriggle backward. Even the almost unthinkable feat of sliding feet-first back through the underground passage seemed preferable to having the man's company. Why did his very presence wreak such havoc on her senses? Just the sight of him, the smell of him, the feel of him, somehow filled her with an aching pain. She pressed her cheek against the gritty rock, trying to still her hammering pulses.

Kat yelped with indignant surprise when the Campbell's large hands shimmied intimately past her breasts and then dug brutally under her arms. She pursed her lips stubbornly together, refusing to allow another weak whimper to escape her as she was unceremoniously dragged out of the cleft of rock. The smock was torn from her back, and then she dangled, imprisoned by his unrelenting grip, less than six inches from his critical gaze. She could feel the breath from his flaring nostrils on her hot cheek and was searingly aware of the censure and contempt that emanated from him. She glared back, refusing to show that she was the least intimidated or disadvantaged by being half naked and hanging several feet off the ground. Her right side throbbed, and she used that discomfort as fuel to fire her fear into white-hot fury, hoping to match the rage that blazed from his silver eyes.

Was he ever going to say anything? Was he ever going to set her on her feet? Did he propose to keep her dangling forever? The anticipation of violence was too much for Kat to bear. She was unable to remain glowering at his handsome features, which were distorted with abhorrence and disdain for her. She spat full in his face. The next instant, she gasped when the air was brutally forced from her lungs as she was roughly thrown face down across his thighs and a hard hand descended to smite her hurt buttock. She was being spanked like a recalcitrant child in a nursery. She bit the insides of her mouth, refusing to scream as agony flared, but she was unable to remain quite so stoic as the blows continued. A howl of pure, unadulterated pain burst from her lips, and then she sagged limply across his lap.

Darach had wanted to throw back his head and shout with laughter when he had discovered her stuck in the narrow fissure in the rock. The laughter contained as much relief at seeing her alive as it did pleasure in her mortifying predicament. He dreaded to imagine her wedged deeper in the underground tunnel, out of reach; he pushed that nightmarish thought away and concentrated on the gratifying vision of her embarrassment. He had a fairly accurate idea of the furious thoughts that seethed through her mind at being caught in so humiliating a position, and he took a savage delight in it, remembering the amethyst rock that had been smashed over his head and the nearly lethal concoction that had turned his belly to liquid. He had callously watched her snarling little face, wanting to prolong her discomfort, but a certain feverishness about the flashing green eyes had caused a twinge of concern and he had hauled her out. He had scrutinized her, trying to discern what gave him this anxiety, and she had resorted to her indefensible, feral behavior, spitting into his face with her usual accuracy. The fury he had fought so hard to contain had erupted. He consoled and congratulated himself on his forbearance in not losing all control and striking her insolent little face, which had been his instinctive reaction.

Darach's large hand descended four times, and he was determined to continue until he had wrested at least one sound of pain or remorse from her willful, undisciplined mouth. When the cry came out and she arched in agony before collapsing limply, it ripped through him, causing an inexplicable, hollow aching. His palm rested on her small rounded rump, and he felt heat emanating from it. For a moment he wasn't sure whether it was only a reaction to the thrashing he had just administered. But he felt an unevenness, and he pulled down her trews and discovered the festering wound. He frowned at the angry red lines that radiated from the distinct teeth marks, realizing what he had observed in her flashing eyes—they had been glazed by sickness as the poison spread throughout her body.

"Och, you are determined to kill yourself one way or another, you unmanageable rebel!" he chided, gently turning her to face him and staring down at her poignant little face, which was beaded with perspiration. "Well, I'll nae have your death on my conscience, so 'tis back to Cailleach Cuilleann wie you." He sighed, cradling her in his arms and striding through the woods to the suspended glen where Iolair grazed peacefully with the black stallion. Sian limped beside them, whining his concern for his inert young mistress.

Kat regained consciousness and wished she hadn't. She awoke and had no idea where she was. She kept her eyes firmly closed and whimpered with pain as the rhythmic beat of horses' hooves stabbed through her.

"It won't be long, brat," Darach snapped tersely, allowing no tenderness or compassion to be evident in his voice. Kat's eyes flew open, and her mouth closed stubbornly, smothering her shameful sobbing sounds. She stared up at his stern, dark features and shivered. "Seems your backside got what it so richly deserved," he added harshly, stung by her shudder.

"Go to hell, you Campbell *mucker!*" she shouted defiantly, and then her green eyes widened in panic. "Where are you taking me?"

"To the *cailleach.*"

"No! You canna!" Kat struggled wildly. Somehow she either had to escape, or make him go somewhere else so that Robbie would be safe. "No! Take me back to Duncreag!" she begged.

"The *cailleach* is at her *clachan.*"

"No! I dinna want to go wie you!" she shouted, kicking her legs despite the searing agony. She was trying to make the golden stallion panic so the Campbell would release his hold on her in order to bring the giant animal under control, but Iolair was too well trained and he kept his steady rhythm. Kat twisted her head and tried to sink her sharp teeth into Darach's muscular arm.

"That's enough! Unless you're wanting another thrashing!" he roared, placing a finger and thumb on each side of her mouth and digging painfully, forcing her jaws to part and release his flesh. He pulled her face up roughly and glared down at her, but Kat was battling for her little brother's life. She spat again, hoping to goad him into carelessness so she could free herself from his hard arms, but he pointedly wrenched his gaze away from her, ignoring her struggles and curses and urging Iolair into a punishing canter. The breath was bounced out of her by the jolting tempo.

Darach dismounted at the *cailleach*'s *clachan*, taking Kat with him like an unwieldy sack of laundry. Without so much as a cursory knock, he flung open the door and strode into the small stone house. Kat realized the futility of any further struggle and she sagged limply, pretending to lose consciousness as she looked furtively between her thick lashes for sight and sound of her small brother. The air was redolent with herbs and spices. Several cauldrons steamed over the merrily blazing hearth, and despite the summer heat outside, the stone house was comfortable. Great bunches of mints, honeysuckle, borage, nettles, milkweed, and mallow hung from the rafters, and the walls were lined with shelves containing every color, size, and shape of bottle. They were filled with different tinctures, essences, and infusions. The afternoon sun shone through the tinted glass, causing rainbows to shimmer on the gray stones.

"And why am I not the least surprised to see you here?" Darach asked dryly, staring at his uncle, who sheepishly got up from the scrubbed kitchen table.

"What took you so long?" rejoined Angus, swiftly recovering his relaxed manner. "I expected you last night. And where's the ferocious wolfhound?" He chatted sociably, scanning about for the shaggy animal and making no mention of the dark-haired girl who lay limply in his nephew's strong arms.

"Where's Hag Holly?" Darach demanded curtly.

"Tending to a wee patient. A young shepherd lad," explained Angus, waving a vague hand in no particular direction.

"What are you doing here?"

"Dinna be thick, lad! Do you honestly think I'd stay at Duncreag wie your stepmother, Felicity?" the white-haired man asked evasively, reseating himself and staring shrewdly at Kat. "Well, I see you found your wife. Did you have pleasure in wreaking your revenge?" he asked idly, pretending casualness to hide his concern for the flushed, docile girl.

"Wha' is all this?" demanded the *cailleach*, briskly bustling into the room and pointedly closing a curtained doorway behind her. "Well, 'tis the young Campbell chief wie his puir wee wife. Wha' is amiss this time?''

"It would seem her unbridled behavior either provoked some puir dumb animal to violence, or the creature mistook her *derrière* for a toothsome morsel and took a not too healthy bite, which appears to have festered," Darach remarked mildly, gazing down at the mutinous little face. He grinned as he noted the furious flaring of Kat's small nose.

"She looks a mite feverish, too," the *cailleach* noted, stroking the flushed cheeks with a coarse, gnarled hand.

"And angry enow to explode," Angus added dourly.

"Och, I just healed this lass. Wha's the matter wie you, Strathrannoch? You canna keep one sma' wife safe from harm, and you, so big and *braw?*" the hag chided sourly. "You maun love and cherish your bride, not cause her to flee from you and near perish every few months or so. Set her over there," she directed, pointing to a small cot. Darach stubbornly shook his dark head, goaded by the woman's scolding words. He pulled a straightback chair away from the table and sat, keeping Kat pinned across his lap.

"Dinna fear, old woman, she'll nae flee from me again," he stated, holding her firmly to him.

"How can I heal her wie your great paws all over the puir wee child?" admonished the *cailleach*.

Kat was just about to pretend to wake up when she was rudely turned onto her belly across Darach's thighs and had her buttocks embarrassingly displayed to Angus and the *cailleach*. She lay in that mortifying, degrading position while the three people remarked on the nature of her wound; she was unable to protest for fear that Robbie would recognize her voice and call out to her.

Darach felt Kat stiffen with rage. Thinking that she might resume her wild struggles, he planted an imprisoning hand in the small of her back and encircled her thighs with his other arm.

"Needs hot poulticing to draw the poisons up, and then a lancing," muttered the old woman. "But it has been caught in time. I dinna think the venom has fouled her bluid." She sighed. "Tha's a pretty wee bottie, isna it, Angus?" She chuckled wickedly, cunningly noting the jealous glares that the young Campbell directed at his older relative, who gazed sympathetically at Kat's small rump.

"Aye, 'tis tha'. I dinna care for big, flabby haunches on a

female, but firm, pert cheeks that snugly span a mon's broad hand," Angus agreed roguishly, and the old crone cackled mischievously.

"Then you dinna care for my generous curves?" she challenged as she tossed clean rags into the smaller of the cauldrons and stirred them about with a large wooden *spurtle*.

"Who can discern your generous curves under your layers of skirts?" Angus returned flirtatiously, standing back and surveying the swinging colorful flounces as the *cailleach* wiggled her hips coquettishly.

"Gie the lassie a wee drappie of spirits to take the edge off the pain," ordered the hag, waving her wooden stick at some jugs. Kat shook her head. She didn't want to be rendered incapable. She didn't trust the *cailleach*'s concoctions, and she wanted to keep her wits about her.

"Then bite doon on this, lass," the old woman directed, thrusting a hard piece of wood between the girl's teeth. Then she bustled back to ladle the hot compresses into a smaller bowl. Kat was terrified that she would scream and that Robbie would recognize her voice and betray himself. Was he alive? Was he able to speak? Her mind worried frantically, as she stared at the Campbell's large booted feet, which were planted firmly on the stone floor. She strained her ears to detect the slightest sound from behind the curtained doorway of the small room where she had seen her brother the previous night.

"Brace yourself," Darach warned tersely, holding her tightly as the *cailleach* lowered the steaming poultice onto the angry wound. Kat bit down on the wood, but a strangled scream burst out of her mouth and her whole body bucked in agony. Once more, merciful darkness closed in, and she drooped with a long sigh.

Darach tried to tell himself that the untamed, vicious female was receiving exactly what she deserved, but he felt her searing pain cut through him; he was oblivious to the tears that ran down his high cheekbones. He was thankful when she sank into oblivion. He held her close, fervently praying that she would not awaken until the painful treatment was completed. He winced when the *cailleach* thrust a long slender dirk into the burning embers of the fire.

"I hae to open the wound. It has sealed shut, trapping the venom inside," she explained, answering his silent query. "And 'twould be best to do it quickly, while she still sleeps."

Although Darach's attention was riveted to the boiling poultices and the red-hot knife that threatened to mar Kat's tender flesh, a furtive movement caught his eye. He glanced away in time to see his uncle disappear through the curtained doorway.

"There," the hag said with relief, placing a dressing of red moss on the cleansed wound. " 'Tis an awkward spot to bandage, so just set her face down on the cot." Darach silently obeyed and his arms felt strangely bereft and empty. He smoothed the riotous curls away from Kat's hot face, remembering the horror of waking up to the pile of shorn ebony tresses in their cold bed. He had reached for her, only to find an inanimate pillow and long black strands. For several long minutes, his aching head believed that she had somehow disintegrated and all that was left were the glossy, raven locks; then a violent indignation had consumed him. She had no right to mutilate herself so, he had fumed. She belonged to him. It was as though one of his prized possessions had been defaced. It was criminal and blasphemous. Then the excruciating stomach cramps had started, and he remembered the amethyst geode and ruthlessly wished her further disfigured. When he found her, he would do more than shear off her hair, he had vowed. Now he stared at his fingers that were lovingly entwined in her soft, black curls and wished that he could suffer in her stead.

"Puir lass," murmured Angus, noting his nephew's tenderness.

"Puir lass? That unprincipled little heathen has got precisely what her behavior merited," Darach snapped curtly, straightening up and staring suspiciously at the older man. He then crossed to the swinging curtain and paused with his hand upon it.

"Dinna be nosy," Angus scolded crossly. "Where are your manners? 'Tis nae your home and you shouldna be poking about that which dinna concern you." His words were useless, and Darach looked curiously into the adjoining room.

"That wouldna be a boy by the name of Robbie, would it?" Darach asked thoughtfully, stepping into the room and gazing down at the frail blond child.

"Robbie, Bobbie, Tammie, Jemmie. Och, I dinna ken wha' the *bagrel*'s name is. 'Tis but some shepherd's brat from one of the summer pastures on the slopes," dismissed Angus.

"And what is the matter wie him?" Darach asked quietly, noting the flaxen hair so much like that of the beautiful, voluptuous woman he had discovered in his brother's arms.

"I dinna ken . . . but could be the plague or the pox, so I would keep my distance if I was you," lied the older man.

"I found Riach," the young Campbell stated, turning piercing eyes on his uncle, wanting to gauge his reaction. He didn't trust him. Everywhere he looked there seemed to be a conspiracy. Everything was shrouded in mystery, elusive and infuriating.

"You found Riach!" exclaimed Angus. "Where? When? How? Is he well? Unharmed? How is he?" he stammered, overjoyed and then suddenly sober when he saw his nephew's intense expression. "Och, he's nae dead, is he?" he mourned.

"Nay, he's well. In fact, he's in better shape than I have ever seen him before," Darach assured hastily, satisfied that the older man knew nothing of Riach's whereabouts.

"Then why are you staring at me so strangely? You're making my hackles rise," Angus accused testily. "Och, you dinna think I was party to Riach's disappearance?" he added with disbelief.

"At this point, dear Uncle Angus, I dinna ken what to think."

"Riach?" the child muttered fitfully, and both tall Campbells stared down at the boy. "Riach?" repeated Robbie, blinking up at Darach in the dim light. "Och, I'm so glad you're here." He sighed, smiling trustingly up at the dark man and reaching for his hand. Darach looked down into the solemn blue eyes and was unexpectedly moved by the small fingers that clasped his. "Dinna leave me, Riach," he begged sleepily.

"I'll nae leave you, Robbie," whispered Darach, tucking the child's hand under the coverlet and turning to his uncle. Maybe now he would have some answers.

chapter 22

Riach opened his eyes to pitch blackness. He remained motionless, trying to establish where he was and what had happened, as discordant fragments jarred within his memory, causing him a nightmarish panic. His head pounded painfully and his neck was twisted at an uncomfortable angle. His cheek rested on a hard, flat plane. The air was hot and still, and outside he could hear the continuous rasping chirp and whir of crickets and cockchafers. An occasional eerie screech of a marauding owl and the sudden treble squeal of frightened bats, punctuated the constant monotony. A cold bluish shimmer reflected in the diamond panes, wavering in the contortions of thick glass. He was in the kitchen with his head pillowed on the table, staring toward the window that was slightly ajar, he methodically discerned. Without lifting his aching head, he blindly felt about the table until his fingers connected with the stone whiskey jug, and he remembered his futile struggle to stay awake. A long, shuddering sigh slipped from his mouth. For several months he hadn't wanted or even thought about liquor, yet within a few moments of his older brother's oppressive and dominating company, he was resorting to his old weak ways, using the spirits for false courage to make himself feel strong and confident.

"Darach?" he whispered hoarsely, and when there was no answer, he gingerly sat up and stiffly scanned about the room.

He groaned aloud as his neck felt inflexible. "Darach?" he repeated. He was evidently alone. His conversation with his condescending brother roiled in his brain, and he slowly rotated his head, trying to loosen his set muscles. It couldn't possibly be true, he decided angrily. He wasn't a stupid, gullible pup who could be so easily duped. He would have known if he had been cheated at the gaming table by Rory MacNiall, alias Gregor MacGregor, and surely he would have been aware if he had been held hostage for ransom. Yet the whirl of drug-warped days tore into his churning mind. He had not been held against his will! He could not have been, unless someone had acted as his jailer. Then he recalled being lashed to the bedposts in the filthy decay of the rotting mansion, and he heard Macaree's sweet voice singing as she sat by the window serenely sewing. He tipped back in his chair and tried to sort through the nightmarish muddle of memories.

"Riach?" Macaree's frightened voice called softly. He didn't answer. If what his brother had said was true, then the beautiful golden girl he had taken for his wife was the jailer, the conspirator. No, the mere idea of the gentle maiden being a scheming accessory was insupportable, yet what was he doing on the crumbling estate?

Riach forced his spinning thoughts back to his first meetings with Rory MacNiall and then to his arrival at Linnmanach. From the distorted haze of the Christmas festivities to the daft days that culminated in *Hogmanay*, he tried to unravel feelings and impressions. He had not been a hostage but a feted guest. He could recall Macaree's graceful, swanlike movements and her melodic voice, her slender white arms linked lovingly with his, her ethereal face smiling at him as she danced and sang pretty carols, beguiling him into a romantic daze.

"And what do you think of my beautiful princess?" Rory MacNiall's oily voice insinuated itself into his furious thoughts. The man had constantly kept asking, and Riach had been so very enamored with the exquisite Macaree that he remembered stammering like a callow adolescent, falling over his feet to pay court and dance attendance.

"And what do you think of my gentle princess?" Riach pictured the man's dissolute, sagging features. He blinked, trying to see the man as he really had been, not letting himself be unduly influenced by his brother's words, but the face remained the same—a fat, heavily painted and powdered mask, the smile false and ingratiating. He saw the three of them —himself, Macaree, and Rory MacNiall—all resplendent in costly clothes, drenched in expensive perfumes, glutting themselves on extravagant delicacies. They had been observed from the shadows by the dark, green-eyed girl garbed in rags and the large shaggy hound, and he had heard the languishing boy's weak cries spiraling through the rat-infested corridors.

What was real and what had been an illusion? In the beginning Linnmanach had appeared to be a majestic, gracious house, but that was when it had been surrounded by an opium mist. The MacGregor had been Rory MacNiall, a most generous host, so generous as to make no mention of the more than twenty thousand crowns. It had been the thought of that debt and Ailsa's deathbed threat that had first stirred his conscience to help Robbie and Macaree, he remembered, and then his fury was fired. He had been cheated! The cards had obviously been rigged! Why hadn't that occurred to him before? At the time, he had felt he was having a streak of bad luck, but that streak had never ended. Everything had been a lie, a swindle, a fake! Was anything true?

"Riach?" Macaree stood in the kitchen doorway looking like a goddess. She was lit by the warm flickering glow of the lantern she held, and silvery moths fluttered frantically about her golden hair. Riach stared silently at her, emanating a brittle hostility, keeping her at a distance. "I dinna ken what is happening," she whispered brokenly. "Robbie isna here, and I keep falling asleep and then waken wie my head hurting to either bright hot afternoon or dark stifling night." She stopped talking and gazed pleadingly at him, but he remained silent. "I remember that there was a man here. Your brother? And my sister's hound, Sian, was wie him. Was it so, or was it but an unco dream?" she asked, looking hurt and puzzled by his detachment. "Riach, speak to me. I feel I am going mad!" she cried piteously, but the youth kept his mouth closed in a thin stern line. "Have I done something to displease you?"

"Did your father wish me harm?" He attacked suddenly.

"My father wish you harm?" she repeated numbly.

"Did he?" insisted Riach, standing so roughly that the chair fell over with a crash. Macaree winced.

"My father is dead."

"Aye, and my brother killed him!" he stated brutally.

"Your brother killed my father?"

"Aye."

"Why?"

"Och, dinna play the innocent, weepy maiden wie me!" the youth snarled. "Well, are you nae going to sing a French tune? Pretend you are afeared and fey?" he challenged cruelly. Macaree wanted to sing, but she couldn't recall any songs.

"J'ai oublié les chansons," she explained.

"Quiet!" he shouted. "I'm nae a gullible lout to be cozened by a strumpet like you!"

Suddenly, Macaree was utterly vulnerable. Once again she was a little girl in a white lace dress. A tall, intense-looking man was coming toward her, but she had forgotten her pretty dance steps and the charming songs her mother had taught her.

"Bonjour, monsieur," she said politely, edging away from him.

"Give it up, Macaree MacGregor. I know it all. You're nothing but a conniving extortionist!" screamed Riach. "Did your father tell you to pander to me? Was that part of the scheme?"

"Oui, monsieur," she whispered, not knowing what to do or say to placate the enraged man. What was he doing in the nursery, and where was Katrine? She put down the lamp and curtsied prettily, as she had been taught to do.

"Dinna mock me, you filthy trull!" Riach cried, and Macaree backed farther away, not daring to look into his face. She kept her eyes unfocused on his chest.

"Pardonnez-moi, monsieur," she apologized, hoping he would forgive her and go away, but he kept advancing until her back was pressed against the wall. She closed her eyes tightly and whimpered, waiting for the tearing pain.

The youth glowered down into Macaree's terrified face and laughed harshly. "Och, you have guid reason to be afraid, you filthy whore!" His voice cracked with fury and pain. She had tricked him, made a complete mockery of his love. He had been so patient, putting his own aching needs aside in deference to her virginal terror, while she was nothing but a common felon. Oh, how she must have laughed at him! he thought in disgust.

"Monsieur, ne me faites pas mal! Je vous en pris." She sobbed. She screamed as her face was viciously slapped.

"Shut your lying mouth! Dinna waste your breath begging for mercy, for I have none, you foul bitch! You *saidhe*! You filthy whore! You disgust me!'' he shouted, oblivious to the tears that streamed down his face.

Macaree slid down the wall and collapsed, sobbing, on the floor. *"Maman?"* she cried, hugging her knees very tightly so the loud, abusive man wouldn't tear her legs apart and attempt to rip her in two by plunging into the tender depths of her body. *"Maman? Aides-moi!"* she pleaded, but no mother came.

"Get up, you lying slut!" Riach screamed. But she sat hunched, clinging desperately to herself. When he forcibly picked her up, she was caught in a tight ball, her forehead pressed to her knees. He threw her onto the sofa and knelt beside her, towering over her. "Look at me!" he howled. When she didn't respond, he mercilessly wrenched her bent head upward and glared venomously into her terror-filled blue eyes. "How can such a sly *futret* still manage to appear like an innocent angel? There's no guid staring so beseechingly wie those hurt eyes, playing the wrongly accused fair maiden! Give up your game, you cunning MacGregor! I have no pity!"

Riach flung her away from him, not trusting the murderous rage that made his pulses throb violently. He wanted to pound her to a pulp, wipe the guilt-provoking terror from her beautiful face, eradicate every vestige of love and tenderness from his naïve, stupid head. He paced back and forth, kicking the furniture and sweeping the shelves and the mantel clear. Delicate ornaments and fragile vases of flowers smashed to the floor, as he tried to ignore the cowering female.

"Which way is Perth?" he demanded suddenly. Through his blinding rage, he remembered his brother's words of that morning. "Where the hell are we? Where is this godforsaken hellhole?" he shouted, picking her up and shaking her. She stared at him as though she was a trembling little child who didn't understand his language. "Where are we?"

"Je ne sais pas." She sobbed.

"It doesna matter, because anywhere is preferable to being here wie you!" he shouted, dropping her. She scurried to a corner of the sofa, where she cowered with her legs drawn up and her arms fiercely clutching them. "I'd sooner sleep in the forest wie the insects and newts than wie you, you lying, filthy slut!"

Riach slammed out of the gatehouse, and, using all his energy, he undid the corroded hasps and bolts of the tall wrought-iron gates. He stared speculatively along the beaten path, trying to remember in which direction the sun set. He would traverse west and hope by some miracle to reach a hamlet. If he was in the vicinity of Perth, then he could not be too far from his Uncle Angus at Duncreag. He set off down the road, leaving the gates of Linnmanach standing open for the first time in nearly three-quarters of a century.

The little stone house shook with the violence of the slamming door. Windows rattled and broken shards of crockery and glass littered the hearth. The agonized screech of the rusty gates being swung open ripped through the stillness, and Macaree realized she was truly alone. Her arms dropped away from her legs and she sat up, listening, but once again the monotonous vibration of the crickets and frogs descended like a mantle.

Macaree frowned and stared about her with bewilderment. She was no longer in the sunny, airy nursery of the château by the river in France. She ran her hands down her body, feeling her breasts, realizing that she was no longer a formless little girl. The dim flicker of the lantern shone on the shattered mess about the hearth, and she gazed at the disorder, remembering who and where she was, hearing Riach's harsh, hateful names joining with her father's accusations of long ago.

"Riach," she mouthed numbly, looking toward the front door. The sharp sound of it closing still echoed in her mind.

Macaree stood in the moonlight looking steadily at the open gates. She then sat on the coarse gravel of the carriageway with her chin on her knees, perusing the space. The world was out there, she thought dispassionately. All the people who wrote the books that were rotting in the library were out there in one form or another. All the people who welded metal to make the tall pointed palings that had surrounded her for so long were out there living their lives. She stared behind her at the dense, ominous bushes that lined the carriageway like sentries guarding the inmates, warning trespassers away from the manse of Linnmanach. Then she turned back thoughtfully to the beckoning gates.

Angus rode *auld* MacGhee slowly along the overgrown road, thankful for the full moon that lit the unfamiliar way and cast long playful shadows from the encroaching forest. Darach had described a large neglected estate and had entrusted him to fetch Riach and return him to his mother at Duncreag.

"Puir lad," Angus sympathized, scrutinizing the tangled undergrowth on each side of the narrow road for sight of the tall palings. If he was correct, his nephew had described Linnmanach. He rode, lost in thought about the tragedy that had befallen the MacIans more than seventy years before at the hands of English government troops and his clan, the Campbells. Alisdair MacIan and his three sons had all been slaughtered at Glencoe, leaving his wife and four daughters. Legend had it that four of the five females never again set foot outside their home of Linnmanach. Angus recalled his father rhapsodizing about the beauty of the MacIan women and the shame against nature that it was for them to be so entombed. "What were their names?" Angus pondered aloud, needing to hear a human voice—if only his own—in the quiet darkness. There was no sign of human life. Not a croft or cottage, not a glimmer of lantern light broke the endless wilderness. "They all began wie the letter aye, *auld* MacGhee," he told his horse. "There was Allison and Ailis, Aileen and Ailsa. E'en the puir lads all began wie that same letter. Alisdair was the father, and then there was Artair, Alpin, and Aindrea. It was said that Ailsa was a fiery rebel and wouldna obey her mother and remain in mourning for all her puir life. She ran off wie a MacGregor, son of the rogue Rob Roy," he informed his horse excitedly. "So, you see, *auld* nag, I am right about the wee dark lass, if it be Linnmanach where Riach is hid."

Angus stopped muttering to himself and became lost in his brooding thoughts, lulled by his horse's plodding rhythm. It still didn't make sense, unless Kat and her small brother were Ailsa MacIan MacGregor's children. But Ailsa had never returned, or had she? But even if she had, she would have been more than seventy-five. Maybe she was their grandmother, he reasoned. It made sense. All Rob Roy MacGregor's five sons were reputed to be dead. They had either been executed by the English after the battle of Culloden, or had died in poverty after escaping to France. Maybe Ailsa had returned home after she was widowed, bringing her children with her. And they in turn had had children.

The tall gates of Linnmanach suddenly appeared before him, and he reined in *auld* MacGhee when he saw the stark majesty of the cold moonlight gleaming off the rigid black palings. The strip of gravel that snaked between dense, shiny-leafed shrubs shone silver in the moonlight. There was something ominous about the open entryway, and then he gasped, seeing the still figure who sat silently regarding him. He urged his horse to walk slowly between the gates, and he shivered at the sharp rasp beneath the hooves that seared through the humidity.

"I am Sir Angus Campbell, Riach's uncle." He introduced himself after a long pause in which he had gaped down at the exquisitely beautiful woman, waiting for her either to say something or to acknowledge his presence in some way. If this was a granddaughter of Ailsa MacIan, his father's praises of the legendary MacIan females were by no means exaggerated. "Is Riach about?" he asked conversationally, but the girl just kept staring beyond him to the open gates. "Riach?" he finally bellowed, looking toward the stone gatehouse and seeing the warm glow of a lantern through the mullioned panes.

The deep tones broke through Macaree's detachment, and she stared up curiously at the white-haired man on the stocky chestnut horse. She had seen him approach from afar, but it hadn't seemed to matter. She stood up and absently brushed the gravel from her shift, keeping her eyes on him. Why wasn't she afraid? she wondered, and then she sighed and shrugged. Nothing mattered, nothing hurt, all pain and fear were safely locked away under layers of numbness.

"Riach has gone back—out there," she said simply, pointing beyond the wrought-iron palisade.

"Where is Ailsa?" asked Angus, knowing as soon as the words left his mouth that he was being ridiculous.

"Aunt Ailsa is still in here," replied Macaree, turning and pointing along the winding carriageway. "Shall I show you?"

Angus nodded and the glorious, golden-haired female, garbed only in a modest nightrail, smiled absently and proceeded to walk gracefully between the looming rhododendron bushes. She was one of the most exquisite examples of womanhood he had ever had the good fortune to see. He marveled at her as he urged *auld* MacGhee into a slow walk and followed behind her, appreciating the sensuous sway of her rounded hips that undulated beneath the worn cotton. Her legs were long and shapely, and her feet were bare, as were her arms, which swung gracefully beside her. Her shimmering blond hair cascaded down her back, its sun streaks illuminated by the moonlight. She had the same coloring as the boy, Robbie. Could she also be a sibling of the spirited green-eyed Kat?

They rounded a bend, and Angus gasped as the enormous crumbling ruin loomed before him. The barefoot young woman walked steadily past it and then stopped, looking down a lawn that sloped to a *loch*.

"Ailsa doesna live in there still?" He shuddered.

"Nay, she doesna live, but she's still here."

Angus slowly followed Macaree to the graveyard in the shadow of the ruined monastery. Out of respect for the dead, he dismounted and left MacGhee to graze on the lush grass beside the serene waters of the lake.

"So, Ailsa is buried here?" he remarked awkwardly, not knowing why he had asked about the old woman whom he had never met. "My father spoke of her when I was a boy," he added, looking at the unmarked plot. "So she was your aunt?"

"Riach buried her," Macaree stated proudly. "And this is Aggie Fletcher, she was our *nurreych, notre bonne d'enfant,*" she stammered, not knowing which language to use.

"Your nurse, Aggie Fletcher," repeated Angus with a satisfied nod. Clan Fletcher had been allied with the MacGregors of Glenlyon for generations, first as arrow makers and then as henchmen against the Campbells, who were given title of Glenlyon when the MacGregors were outlawed. "And these other graves?"

"Sebastian, the gatekeeper, and my Aunt Ailsa's steward and maids," Macaree explained absently. She watched the tall stranger wandering about, reading the inscriptions on the mossy stones of the graves that were marked.

"Aileen, Ailis, and Allison MacIan—they maun hae all died *auld* maids. Och, what a terrible waste of womanhood," Angus stated mournfully. "Now, young lady," he said, straightening up after perusing the stones, conscious of the solemn girl at his elbow.

"Waste of womanhood?" echoed Macaree. "Old maids? Like me," she stated dully.

"Nay, lass, you might be a lot of things, but an *auld* maid isna one of them," he said with a chuckle. "How old are you?"

"Nineteen."

"You dinna look so *auld*, and, granted, nineteen isna a green *bairn* out of the schoolroom, but there doesna seem to hae been much opportunity for you to meet eligible bachelors hereabouts," Angus remarked dryly.

"Riach called me his wife." She sighed and stared blankly across the *loch*. Angus stared frowningly at her profile, silhouetted against the moonlit water, deliberating over the information that the girl had so casually stated. "But now he has gone back out there," she intoned hollowly. "He doesna want me more."

"My name is Sir Angus—"

"Campbell," Macaree interrupted wearily, without looking at him.

"Aye, Campbell. And what's your name?" he probed, but there was no answer. "I've met your sister . . . er . . . Katrine," he dared to say, and was gratified to see that he had managed to penetrate her defenses. Surprise and fear flickered across her fine features. "And your brother, Robbie, and I are great friends," he continued confidently.

"You ken where Robbie is?"

"Aye."

"Where? Where?" Macaree screamed. Without a thought, she savagely flew at him, hitting him and tearing at his clothes, much as her sister would have done. "Why did you steal my brother? Why?" Then she stared aghast at her pummeling fists. What was she doing? She was the gentle daughter.

Angus imprisoned her small fists in his large hands and stroked them reassuringly. "I dinna steal young Robbie. It was your sister, Katrine, who brought him to my friend, the Cailleach Cuilleann. He is sick, and she hoped my friend could heal the lad."

"Kat took Robbie out there?"

"Aye," murmured Angus, watching the girl look fearfully in the direction of the gates.

"But she had no right to do such a terrible thing. We maun not leave Linnmanach," the girl whispered distractedly.

"Why?"

"We maun never leave Linnmanach."

"Who said so?"

"No one had to. It is just so. It will mean our deaths."

"It would've meant your young brother's death to stay," Angus said softly. "Surely you could see he was slowly *dwyning?* Fading awa' to nothing. He was dying here."

"I think . . . maybe we were all supposed to."

"Och, nay, pretty lass, you were nae meant to die in this drear place fu' of sorrow and tragedy," he said gruffly.

"Robbie can get better? He doesna have to die?" Macaree asked incredulously.

"It has only been two days and already I can see improvement."

"Linnmanach was killing him?"

"I believe so."

"But how can a house kill a person?" Macaree puzzled.

"There are sad, tragic places where bitter spirits canna rest. They rise from the cold earth and sap the strength of the living to avenge the cruel injustices of their own lives," explained Angus, putting a fatherly arm about the young woman's shoulders and leading her out of the graveyard. "Once upon a time in my grandfather's day that drear ruin up there was a handsome mansion filled wie laughter and brimming wie happy children." He sighed, staring across the graceful slope of the lawn to the desolate gray manse.

"And there was a tragedy?" Macaree prompted after a long, brooding silence. She had waited for him to continue, but he had just gazed sorrowfully at the hollow windows.

"Aye. It was the year 1692, and the Laird of Linnmanach, Alisdair MacIan, and his three sons were murdered. They were visiting the MacDonald chieftain of their clan at Glencoe—"

"And so were the Campbells," Macaree interrupted, remembering the nightmarish journey from Ballachulish nearly six years before. "My father said that they were guests of the MacIans, and the Campbells abused their hospitality by killing them all," she recounted. "The Glen of Weeping," she whispered, recalling the awesome starkness that had caused her soul to shiver.

"Aye, the Glen of Weeping. It was a terrible thing, and it is to my shame that my forebear, Robert Campbell of Glenlyon, led the slaughter," he acknowledged, stalking past the hulking, crumbling house and crunching along the graveled carriageway, followed by *auld* MacGhee. "The puir MacIan widow, distraught at losing her husband and all her sons, locked herself and her four daughters behind Linnmanach's tall gates and vowed never to set foot in the outside world again. Rumor has it that only her youngest daughter, Ailsa, dared rebel. Apparently, she ran away and married a MacGregor, an outlaw who was betrayed to the English redcoats by his ain brother after the last uprising at Culloden," he continued, shrewdly watching her reaction.

"Betrayed by his own brother?" echoed Macaree, remembering her Aunt Ailsa's contempt for her father. "I dinna want to hear more of your drear stories," she whispered uneasily. What was she doing with the tall white-haired stranger? Why was she talking to him? Why was he touching her? she fretted, as they walked between the high, sinister bushes and bats flitted against the eerie sky.

"You'll nae tell me your name?" asked Angus as she roughly pushed his arm from her shoulders. She shook her head. "But, lassie, I ken that you're a MacGregor," he stated softly. "Does my nephew, Riach, ken that you're Mac-Gregor?" There was a long pause, and then she nodded. "Is that maybe why he left?" She shrugged sadly, not wanting to recall his ugly words or the discordant smashing of their pretty little house.

"My name is . . . Macaree."

"Aye, I can see why you'd be reticent to use such a MacGregor name wie your clan outlawed. What name do you use outside of Linnmanach?"

"I don't ever go outside the gates."

"But I detect a slight accent that is nae a Scottish brogue. Were you born in France?" he probed. Her heart began to beat frantically. Why was the man asking her so many questions? What did he want from her?

"I never go outside, and neither should Robbie! You maun bring him back to me at once!" Macaree shouted as the open gates loomed in the moonlight. "They should be closed and locked!"

"Robbie isna returning here. He's going to live free of the wasting hands of the past and grow straight and true into a *braw* mon," declared Angus.

"How? By living a lie? He can never be himself!" she cried. "He can never grow straight and true outside, never be able to be himself. He'll always have to call himself by another name. How can that be straight and true?"

" 'Tis how a mon lives, not what he calls himself," Angus growled, recognizing the truth in her furious words.

"Robbie belongs here wie me and Kat."

"Katrine willna be returning."

"But she promised our mother that she would take care of us. She maun return. It was a deathbed promise, a solemn vow." Macaree sobbed in great distress, realizing that she would be utterly alone when the white-haired man rode away from Linnmanach.

"Katrine is older than you?" Angus asked with surprise.

"She's two years younger, but she is the strong one who maun take care of us. She promised our dying mother!" she shouted.

"When did your mother die?"

"It has been more than five years."

"Tha's a *meikle* big burden for a puir wee lass of no more than twelve years!" Angus gasped, suddenly understanding the defiance and wildness of the petite, green-eyed girl. "But 'tis surely time for that burden to be shared. Your sister understood that, and 'tis why she took your ailing brother to the Cailleach Cuilleann," explained Angus, but Macaree silently shook her blond head as tears streamed down her smooth cheeks from her wide blue eyes. " 'Tis time that you grew up, Macaree MacGregor, and left fearful childhood behind! You are nineteen years old, a woman! Walk oot of those gates!" he ordered, but she continued to sob and shake her head. "Leave the past, Macaree, go oot there and face the future."

"I canna! I canna! Kat will come back, and so will Robbie, and I maun be here for them," she insisted.

"Nay, neither your brother nor sister will ever return to Linnmanach!"

"They will! They will!" she cried. "Kat will never leave me! She promised our mother!"

"Her husband will nae allow her to return here." Macaree's wild weeping stopped and she stared up at Angus in shock.

"Her husband'll nae allow it? But Kat isna married."

"Aye, she's married and has been for nigh on six months," Angus informed gently.

"That's where she's been?" she asked. He nodded silently. "Well, that doesna matter! No mon can stop my sister when her mind is made up to something. If she wants to return to Linnmanach, she'll return, and not even a husband can prevent her!" she stated fiercely.

"Granted, your wee wildcat sister will make a valiant effort, but I dinna think she'll succeed. For stubborn and determined though she is, so is her husband, and he's a mite larger and stronger." Angus sighed, thinking ruefully of the many battles that were destined to occur between Darach and his bride before they found harmony.

Macaree heard this, and the words caused a hollow dread. She looked longingly toward the safety of the snug little gatehouse, but then remembered the chaos of broken glass and crockery and the empty rooms. There was no Robbie or Riach. She then turned to the yawning gates. She was paralyzed, unable to decide. There was no comfort for her anywhere.

Angus scowled with consternation as a low disjointed humming picked up momentum until the blond girl was merrily chanting a French lullaby, her voice high and tremulous like a tiny child's. Her exquisite face was devoid of all feeling, appearing like a porcelain doll in the cold moonlight.

"That's a very pretty song, but I dinna think it quite appropriate," he said awkwardly, not knowing how to deal with her sudden change in behavior. The girl continued singing. "Maun be the effects of the fu' moon turning her lunatic," he muttered, and expecting furious resistance, he placed his hands firmly on each side of her slender waist and hoisted her onto his horse. She was as docile as a little child. He sighed with relief and swung himself wearily into the saddle.

Macaree wrapped her arms about Angus's girth and laid her cheek restfully against his broad back. She closed her eyes, remembering the far-off, carefree days when her father had been a handsome, dashing soldier, a member of the elite Garde Ecossais of the French royal court, and he'd take her on his destrier for rides through the elegantly cultivated parks.

Angus gently urged MacGhee through the gaping gates of Linnmanach, tensed for a struggle from his passenger, but she just hugged him tightly and continued singing.

part three

chapter 23

Kat lay on her stomach on the narrow cot, watching the lambent reflections of the flames flickering across the stone floor, causing a kaleidoscope of shimmering rainbows as they lightly touched upon the colored glass bottles and vials that lined the walls. She listened to the incessant brittle chirruping of the night insects, the dry crackle of the fire, and the rhythmic creak of the *cailleach*'s rocking chair. The *clachan* door was wide open, and the Campbell filled the threshold as he stood smoking a pipe and gazing over the tranquil, moonlit vista of soaring mountains and lush wooded valleys. The air was redolent with rich tobacco, aromatic herbs, and the resinous pine that sizzled upon the hearth. Keeping her green eyes pinned to the tall man's broad back, Kat cautiously shimmied into her trews and wriggled off the cot, biting her lips to stifle her protesting whimpers of pain. She tiptoed across the room to the curtained alcove where her brother slept, grateful for the firm stone floor that muffled the sound of her feet. The Cailleach Cuilleann watched shrewdly beneath hooded lids, but she maintained her constant rocking and the clicking of her knitting needles, so the Campbell would not be alerted to his small bride's endeavors.

Kat swiftly ducked behind the thick wool blanket that served as a curtain. She stood for a moment allowing her eyes to accustom themselves to the dimness, before reaching down and shaking the boy awake. She placed a hand over his mouth in case he cried out in alarm; she stared pleadingly into his startled blue eyes.

"Robbie, do you hear me?" she whispered, and he nodded. "Now you maun listen very carefully. 'Tis very, very important. No matter what happens, we are NacNialls, do you ken?" He glared hostile. "We are Caree, Robert, and Katherine MacNiall. We maun not trust any!"

"What about Riach?" queried the boy, his face set warily.

"We maun not trust any!" she repeated firmly.

"But you dinna ken Riach. He is fine, really he is. He'd not do anything to harm us."

"Hush yourself!" she whispered.

"But you dinna gie him a chance!"

"Hush!"

The curtain was suddenly wrenched open, and both young MacGregors gasped. Robbie blinked in the dancing lantern light and struggled to sit up. He looked blearily up at the tall, dark man and then frowned with bewilderment.

"You are not Riach, but you have the look of him about you," he puzzled. "Were you here before? Was that you wie the white-haired Angus?"

"Riach is my brother," Darach informed him, smiling down at the frail boy. "Aye, and we met before."

"Remember, Rob, we dinna trust any," insisted Kat, worried by the apparent warmth that existed between the two males. "Dinna say any more, or it could mean our deaths!" she warned urgently.

"*Vos noms veulent dire le mort?*" Darach remarked acidly, recalling Kat's anguished words in Edinburgh. "So your names mean death. Why?" he demanded harshly. "What are your names?"

"I am Katherine, and this is my brother, Robert."

"And your family name?" he continued, noting the similarities of the finely etched features despite the difference in coloring. He wondered why he hadn't realized the relationship before. Now he knew; it was obvious.

"MacNiall."

"Och, are we to go through that again?" he lamented. "If not MacNiall, maybe Clarke, Wilson, Fletcher, or Smith?"

"Our name is MacNiall," Kat repeated stubbornly.

"Dinna weary me wie more lies!" the Campbell snapped impatiently. "Robbie, you've nothing to fear from me," he said, softening his tone and sitting on the bed. "Dinna allow your sister's female paranoia to influence you." There was a long, ticking silence, and Kat's pulses pounded with suspense, not knowing how her brother would respond.

"My name is Robert MacNiall," the boy finally stated. Kat sagged with relief.

"So, you are siblings?" remarked Darach after a pause. "What is your other sister's name?" he probed, racking his brain to remember what Riach had called the breathtakingly beautiful woman.

"What other sister?" Robbie queried solemnly. Kat grinned victoriously at Darach.

"She was wie Riach on that neglected estate. She's tall, curvaceous, and extremely comely," he described, shaking his head as he pretended to disparage Kat's lean petiteness. "Has glorious hair the color of spun gold, and eyes as blue as cornflowers," he rapturized.

"That is my sister Caree," the boy said nervously, staring with dismay at Kat's furious face.

"Aye, that is our sister, Caree MacNiall," Kat spat, choking with jealousy.

"Nay, it was not Caree," denied Darach, scowling as he tried to recall exactly what his brother had called his young wife. "That was definitely not her Christian name! And I know for a fact that her surname is not MacNiall," he declared. Both Robbie and Kat froze, staring expectantly up at the dark Campbell.

"Our sister's name is Caree MacNiall," Kat croaked, breaking the tense silence.

"Not according to my brother."

"And according to your brother?" the girl challenged bravely.

"Her name is now Campbell."

"*Tous les Campbell sont malfaiteurs,*" Robbie cried, repeating his own father's impassioned words. Kat clasped his hand tightly to reassure him.

"*Oui, mon petit frère tous les Campbell sont malfaiteurs,*" she agreed. "*Toute la lignée de Diarmid est vénimeuse!*" she added savagely.

"I wouldna be so vindictive against the clan that you are a part of," Darach observed mildly, and he was gratified to see the blond boy look questioningly at his sister.

"What is he saying?"

"I dinna ken. Anyway 'tis not important right now," she returned, struggling to keep up the lie.

"I am married to your sister. Her name is now Katherine Campbell of Strathrannoch. Or should I say Lady Katherine?" he stated derisively, gazing witheringly at her ragged, male attire. "Though I'll admit, judging from her appearance and behavior, 'tis hard to gie credence."

"Is he lying, Kat?"

"It was not of my choosing, Robbie," she protested.

"You are married to him?" the boy gasped, pulling his hand free of his sister's. "He's not lying?"

"Any strong bully of a man can force a frail female into his ... bed ... but ... but 'tis not a true wedding of the flesh," Kat explained defensively.

"Och, I dinna recall that I had to force you into my bed. And as for a true wedding of the flesh, I couldna have used a better way to describe our equally shared lust!" Darach laughed. He did not reveal how very much her words stung. Kat blushed hotly and tried desperately to think of a cutting retort as the Campbell lifted a quizzical eyebrow at her obvious discomfiture. "Robert, did it ever occur to you to think of your sister as a 'frail female'?" he added wickedly. The bewildered boy looked from his sister to the tall man, not understanding the prickly unease that stretched between the dark couple. Absolute, impotent fury flashed from Kat's green eyes, and her small body was coiled to pounce, while the larger Campbell lounged nonchalantly, daring her to attack.

Angus's distinctive deep brogue and the *cailleach's* squeal of surprise shattered the crackling tension and saved Kat from losing complete control. She had wanted to fly at the sardonic man, scratching the mocking smirk from his all too handsome features.

"Kat, 'tis Caree," Rob whispered fearfully, as a shrill, childlike singing broke through the continuous night sounds. Kat started to rush into the main room, but she was swiftly stopped by Darach's strong arm encircling her waist. She winced as he drew her sharply to him. Unconsciously, she clutched at his clothing.

Darach felt the frantic pounding of her heart as she trembled against him. Her head barely reached his shoulder, and he could smell the heatherlike fragrance of her glossy ebony hair. He held her closely, listening to her sister's eerie French lullaby. He frowned, remembering that Kat had sung the very same nursery song when she had been so lost and afraid in Edinburgh.

"I maun go to my sister. She's upset, or she wouldna be singing," Kat begged, trying to free herself from the grip of his strong arms. She was afraid of the temptation to relax against him, seeking solace. "She always sings when she's afraid and canna cope."

Darach quietly drew back the curtain. He stared at the stunning woman who prettily sang her simple Gallic air, as though she were performing at a polite drawing room gathering. Still tightly holding Kat, he strode out of the alcove, and Robbie noiselessly slipped out of his bed and followed in his little nightshirt.

"Caree?" called Kat, but then the Campbell's large hand firmly covered her mouth. She tried to bite his fingers and remove his gagging grip, but he increased his pressure.

"Caree MacNiall?" shouted Robbie. His voice was pitched high with terror as he desperately tried to warn her not to give them away. "Caree MacNiall, where's Riach?" he screamed, hoping the youth would enter and prove to Kat that he was their friend.

"Get your bare feet off these cold stones, you wee *bagrel!*" the *cailleach* scolded. The boy scampered across the room and jumped onto the cot that Kat had vacated earlier. He peered anxiously out the window, but there was no sign of anyone outside.

"Uncle Angus, you were supposed to return to Duncreag wie Riach," Darach snapped testily, trying to be heard above the piping song.

"Riach wasna anywhere to be found, and I certainly wasna going to return to Duncreag wie your stepmother, Felicity, in residence," Angus replied tartly, seating himself wearily at the table and surveying the three MacGregor children and his irate nephew. He exchanged conspiratorial glances with Hag Holly and then poured himself a generous portion of whiskey. "Attractive *bairns,* aren't they?" he declared conversationally.

"Caree MacNiall, stop that singing at once, it sickens me!" shouted Robbie. "Stop it or I'll smack your face!" he threatened. Macaree came haltingly to a stop, her masklike expression slowly changing to one of pure terror. She attempted to politely curtsy as she stared about the unfamiliar room, her mouth silently mouthing various phrases. She backed away from the sight of Darach, who had caught her sister in a punishing hold, one large brown hand nearly obscuring her whole face. All she could see were Kat's green eyes gleaming, warning her of danger. "Caree, where's Riach?" demanded Robbie, hoping to hear that he was outside stabling the horses.

"Riach's gone," Macaree replied dully. "He left me all alone."

"At Linnmanach? He left you all alone at Linnmanach?" Robbie asked, aghast. His oldest sister nodded sadly. Darach noted the unfamiliar name and wondered if they were speaking of the rotting estate. "But he called you 'wife,' so that means he'll return for you," the boy continued eagerly, not wanting to believe that his hero would abandon them. "Father always returned to Mother."

"Nay, he'll not return. He knows what I am. He called me 'whore,' just like Papa did," Macaree stated sorrowfully. Then she turned furiously on Kat. "But 'tis all your fault! You left the nursery door open, and the man came in and hurt me, and *maman* was very cross because my pretty dress was soiled!" she shouted. "I had forgotten all about that terrible time but when Riach was screaming so fiercely and telling me that he knew what I was ... I remembered. I remembered that horrible time when everything changed. Papa said *maman* was never to know because I was supposed to be the guid daughter, the gentle princess, and it would kill her to know that I had been despoiled. Oh, Kat, because of you I am spoiled forever!" she keened. "Maybe *maman* found out, and that is why she died," she wailed.

Kat struggled to break free of the Campbell's grasp, but it was futile. She kicked wildly at his shins and butted her head, hoping to connect to his chin. He tightened his hold, not wanting anyone to stop the frenzied flow of words from the distressed beauty. He was determined to learn the truth about the three youngsters.

"It was all your fault, Kat! You were meant to stay wie me in the nursery, but you went out and left the door open. It was all your fault! You were the bad one, and I was the guid one. You should've been spoiled, nae me," she lamented.

"Och, you puir MacNiall *bairns*," mourned Angus, deciding to keep their identities a secret from his oldest nephew. If the marriage between Katrine and Darach was to work—and he sincerely wished for it—then the wild lass had to learn to trust her mate. It was for her to confide in the young Campbell chieftain, and no one else should interfere in the process. "Puir Caree MacNiall, none can be spoiled forever," he comforted, taking a clean linen handkerchief from his pocket and gently mopping her tears. "Cuilleann, are there any victuals? For not only is my belly rudely grumbling, but I think this sad lass is also very hungry. Isna tha' right, wee-an?" he asked, leading her to the table and seating her.

Gnawing guilt hollowed Kat's stomach and dug at the center of her bones as she listened to her older sister's accusations. A nightmarish image of Macaree's masklike face spiraled back through time to the château by the serene river, and she heard the faint ghostly screams before the lullaby. Everything had changed from that time. Kat sank against Darach, her eyes wide and haunted, understanding for the first time her responsibility in the rape of her sister.

"Och, why all these long, gloomy faces?" chided Angus. "Do you three *bairns* know the tale of one of your ancestors at the time of the Great Flood?" He laughed, trying to lighten the morose atmosphere.

"Aye, if you are really MacNialls, you'd ken what was said by your forebear when Noah invited him onto the Ark," challenged Darach. Angus scowled at him.

"Here am I, trying to cheer up these glum *baichies*, nae continue your cruel inquisition," he snapped. "And how do you expect your wee wife to answer wie your great paw smothering her?"

"Tell me what your ancestor said to Noah," Darach repeated, removing his hand from her mouth.

"He said 'The MacNiall has a boat of his ain!' " spat Kat, thankful for her mother's reminiscences about her clan.

"Och, and you're as proud and stubborn as your ancestor," chuckled Angus, clapping with delight.

"Aye, you'd prefer to drown than accept a helping hand," Darach remarked dourly.

"Why did you leave the door open?" Macaree sobbed. "If I werena spoiled, Riach wouldna hae been so angry."

"Where is Riach?" demanded the Campbell, releasing his wife. Kat made no motion to approach her weeping sister, but instead stared at her sorrowfully, loath to leave the safe shadow of the tall man.

"When I arrived at Linnmanach, the gates were wide open, and Caree, the puir lass, was sitting on the ground all alone in that drear place," Angus recounted as the *cailleach* bustled about, filling wooden bowls with steaming rabbit stew and clay mugs with rich homemade ale.

"I warned you that no Campbell was to be trusted!" cried Kat, finding her voice and hastily moving away from the Campbell.

"If you had been guid and not left the door open, he wouldna have left me!" accused Macaree. "Then I wouldna be spoiled forever, and Riach would still want me for his wife."

"The gates were open? The door was open?" Robbie queried distractedly. "What door? Where? When?"

"It was a very long time ago, and I dinna think we should be speaking of our private affairs wie the Campbells about," Kat stated severely.

"But why did Riach go away? Maybe he went looking for me. Maybe it is all your fault, Kat? You shouldna have taken me from Linnmanach! Riach's probably out searching for me!" shouted Robbie.

Kat looked from Robbie's hostile little face to Macaree's angry tear-streaked one. She shrugged, not knowing what to say. She turned away and stared into the crackling fire, willing her own tears to stay concealed.

Angus ached with sorrow, knowing the terrible burden that the small dark girl had to bear. She was responsible for an older and a younger sibling who leaned on her too heavily, yet they also seemed very quick to blame.

"I dinna think Riach left Linnmanach looking for you, Robbie-lad," Angus defended gruffly, forgetting his resolve not to interfere. "It appears that he left due to a disagreement between Caree and himself. Isna that right, lass?" he asked of Macaree, who sat sadly picking at her food.

"Riach wouldna have left if I were still at Linnmanach. We were brothers! He promised we were, so it is all her fault!" the boy yelled angrily, stabbing an accusatory finger at Kat's stiff back. " 'Tis always her fault! She always spoils things!"

"I was spoiled," Macaree whispered, plaintively.

Darach furrowed his thick dark eyebrows, listening to Robbie's strident hostility, but he kept his gaze pinned speculatively on his proud wife, wondering what was going on in her mind. Her poignant little face was set defiantly as though she didn't care about her siblings' words.

"Och, I am thoroughly ashamed of both of you!" roared Angus, once more forgetting his resolution. "Two spoilt brats, tha's wha' you both are! Your wee sister, Kat, has been taking care of you since your mother died, and this is how you show your gratitude?'' Darach wrenched his gaze from Kat and turned suspiciously to his uncle.

"What is this, old mon? How much do you know about these three?'' he demanded.

"Nothing! I ken nothing!'' lied Angus, quickly filling his mouth with rabbit stew and a hunk of bread so he could not answer.

"But you dinna ken! Everything was wonderful, and then she came back and spoiled it all. She screamed at Riach and told him to go away! Maybe that's why he left. And Caree changed back to the gentle princess always singing when she was afeared, leaving me lonely!'' ranted Robbie.

"If you had stayed wie-in the crumbling walls of Linn-manach much longer, my wee mon, you'd nae be alive to be so fractious!'' scolded the *cailleach*. "Your wee dark sister saved your wretched life, and you owe her a mite mair than the wrong side of your hurtfu' tongue!''

"Aye!'' Angus agreed vehemently.

Robbie glared truculently up at the irate old man and woman, his thin face flushed with embarrassment from their harsh chastisements. "Caree, they dinna ken. Tell them?'' he pleaded but his older sister gently hummed and delicately ate. "Look at her! See her? When Kat isna about, she's nae like that!'' he screamed in frustration.

"And you blame Kat for it?'' Darach asked quietly.

"Who else?''

"I was a guid girl. I did as I was bid. I stayed in the nursery. It was Kat who disobeyed. She went out and left the door open,'' tattled Macaree.

"And how *auld* was she when she committed such a terrible sin?'' Cailleach Cuilleann queried dryly.

" 'Tis not their business!'' Kat's determined young voice stopped the conversation. She spun about and surveyed everyone in the room, trying to appear controlled and unafraid, even though she was caught in a nightmarish coil of memories. "I dinna need any to answer for me!'' she stated coldly, glowering belligerently at the old couple, whose loving looks caused aching tears to well and weaken her resolve. "I dinna need any to defend me!'' she added ferociously.

"You were naughty and left the door open for a man to hurt me, and I was only a little girl,'' Macaree lamented piteously.

"I am so very sorry, and we shall speak of it another time,''

Kat answered stiffly, conscious of the Campbell's searing silver eyes.

"If you were a little girl, your wee sister couldna hae been more than a babe, for isna she two years younger?" Angus stressed. Darach sighed and made himself comfortable with a dram of whiskey. Maybe if he was patient, everything would soon unfold with the assistance of his meddling uncle.

"Two years younger?" echoed Macaree, suddenly realizing how very young her sister must have been—no more than seven or eight years old. She carefully laid her spoon on the table and turned to scrutinize Kat. For the very first time, she saw how small and young she really was.

" 'Tis not your business!" howled Kat, looking so valiant and at the same time so desolate that Darach had to resist the temptation to pull her onto his lap. Who exactly was this fierce little vixen to whom he was married? He glared at his uncle, convinced that the wily old fox knew everything. "Robbie? Caree? I dinna mean to hurt either of you, but it is not the time to squabble among ourselves. We are a family and owe allegiance to each other," she begged.

"A wife owes allegiance to her husband," Darach remarked roguishly.

"Who else are you going to trust but me?" pleaded Kat, pointedly ignoring him.

"I trust Riach!" Robbie stated.

"He's gone."

"Because you drove him away!" the boy accused. "You were jealous because you knew Caree and I loved him! You were jealous because I needed him and not you! I am sick of being smothered by women!"

"I drove him away," Macaree admitted. "I did, not Kat."

"I dinna care who drove him away! I dinna care who's to blame or who's at fault, or what drove him away!" Kat yelled. "We have one another to take care of, and that's all that's important!"

There was a welcoming bark. The petite girl turned and stared bemusedly at Sian, who hobbled wearily into the *clachan,* limped across the uneven stone floor, and collapsed at his young mistress's feet, where he lay wagging his heavy tail in ecstasy. Forgetting her anger and her injury, Kat dropped to her knees, yelping loudly with agony. Then she sagged, burying her face into the hound's shaggy, burr-snarled coat, while she waited for the pain to ebb.

"Well, I'm glad to see there's one true loyal friend for our Scottish lass," growled Angus. He took one of the untouched bowls of stew and removed the splintery rabbit's bones from it. Then he placed it on the floor for the hungry dog, while the *cailleach* poured a deep dish full of spring water.

"I'm hungry, too," Robbie complained.

"Pity!" snapped the hag. "For you'll nae get one bite until I hear an apology to your sister!"

"You dinna hae to humble yourself, Rob," whispered Kat. "I wish you'd all mind your own business!"

"If'n he wants to eat my food in my modest *clachan,* he maun obey my rules and nae yours, wee *banrigh.* So 'tis my business," the feisty crone retorted.

"What guid is an apology if it is not meant?" challenged Kat, wishing that she had some magical way to stand up painlessly. Darach sipped his drink and watched her, moved by her wise words. He knew the deep anguish she must be feeling, both from her sibling's accusations and from her sore haunch.

"I'll nae eat, then, because I'm nae sorry for one thing that I've said," Robbie replied sullenly.

" 'Tis important that you eat," protested Macaree.

"I dinna care if I starve to death," the boy added dramatically.

"At this point I dinna care if you do, either, but just die a wee bit quieter, for you're gieing me a headache," Angus snarled heartlessly. "Sit down! He's smothered by women, remember?" he said, stopping Macaree when she tried to rush to her little brother's side. "What that pup needs is a guid *skelping!*"

"That means I really maun be getting better," the boy gurgled happily. Despite himself, Angus bellowed with laughter.

"Och, you young rascal, I think you were right, you need to be about *braw* males; you've been coddled by females long enow!"

"Tell me about Linnmanach," ordered Darach. He then took advantage of the stunned pause to lift Kat to her feet. He debated pulling her onto his lap, but he felt her resistance. He reasoned that if he had his way, he would soon have all the time he needed to sort through their many difficulties, and he firmly set her away from him. "Whose estate is this Linnmanach?" he demanded when nobody answered. "Och, use your gray matter, Uncle Angus! It'll take less than five min-

utes and a pint of cheap stout in any tavern between here and
Perth, and I'll have all there is to know about the dreary place
now that I know the name."

Kat rubbed her forearms, still feeling the imprint of
Darach's warm fingers. She felt strangely bereft at his curt
rejection of her, and stared pleadingly at the white-haired
Angus.

"Dinna tell him. Let him go begging about the *howffs* buy-
ing the gossiping *gillies* and *billies* their cheap stout," she
urged spitefully.

"I hae to tell him, lass." Angus sighed. "Linnmanach
belonged to Alisdair MacIan," he stated sadly.

"MacIan?" echoed Darach. "Part of the MacDonald
clan?"

"Aye, the puir MacIans who were slaughtered by you rough
Campbells at Glencoe," the *cailleach* embellished.

"Of course, you're MacIans!" Darach gasped. "So that's
it! Is that why you have such animosity toward the Campbell
clan?" he exclaimed. "Is that why Riach was abducted? Was
your father continuing an ancient feud that ended more than
seventy-three years ago?"

Kat gaped at him with astonishment, not knowing how to
respond to the swift change of events.

"So you've found us out!" yelled Macaree with such unaccustomed alacrity that she shocked herself. Her siblings stared
at her with stunned amazement.

"MacIans?" whispered Robbie.

"Aye, we're MacIans, and the foul Campbells abused our
clan's hospitality and massacred our forebears at Glencoe!"
Macaree continued, thoroughly enjoying her role of ag-
gressor.

"MacIans?" Darach repeated wonderingly, scrutinizing
Kat's stupefied expression and interpreting it as dismay for
having at last been found out. "But why would having the
name MacIan mean death for the three of you?" he pondered
aloud.

"I dinna want to appear as inhospitable as you Campbells
were to the puir MacIans at Glencoe, but my wee *clachan* isna
big enow for all of you, so I suggest we hitch the horses to my
wagon and all trundle back to Duncreag, where there's plenty
of room, servants, beds, and food," announced the *cailleach*.

"But Felicity is there," Angus protested.

"Och, there's enow of us to take care of one puny Englishwoman," the crone declared confidently.

"What's Duncreag?" asked Robbie.

"My home—at least it used to be," Angus replied glumly.

"And Felicity?"

"Riach's mother." The white-haired man sighed mournfully.

"Do you think Riach will be at Duncreag?" the boy asked eagerly, his blue eyes lighting up with excitement. Macaree looked hopefully at Angus, holding her breath for his answer.

"Maybe."

"But I canna go to your home dressed like this!" she cried, looking down with dismay at her shabby cotton shift. The *cailleach* cackled and threw open a large cedar chest, exhibiting piles of gaily colored gypsy skirts and blouses.

"Help yourself, lass," she invited.

"And what of me?" demanded Robbie. "I need some trews."

Darach watched Kat. She stood apart from her chattering brother and sister, silently watching their happiness as they related lovingly to the fussing older couple.

"You've taken care of them since your mother died?" he asked softly, noting her sad detachment, but she didn't seem to hear. "That's a long time. More than five years."

"How do you know when my mother died?" Kat backed away from him, her exquisite face full of fear and sorrow, reminding him of that cold, stormy night in Paris. The bright green eyes of the small waif had been as eloquent then, their hollow depths of pain sparking in him an aching need to comfort her, despite his disillusionment with women.

" 'Tis time to let go of them. They have Angus and the *cailleach* to help them fend without you," he observed gently.

"Without me?"

"Aye, you're my wife and belong wie me."

"Never!" she retorted defiantly.

chapter 24

It was well after midnight. Lady Felicity had indulged in Sir Angus's excellent cellar. She was sleeping soundly when the motley assortment of people and animals clattered into the courtyard of Duncreag. Only Darach appeared to maintain some semblance of dignity, choosing to ride Iolair, leaving his vexed uncle to crowd into the rickety farm cart with Cailleach Cuilleann, the bedraggled youngsters, and the large shaggy hound. The noble destrier, *auld* MacGhee, suffered the worst affront, having to pull the laden dray, the hag's donkey trotting placidly behind them, contentedly munching on the feed that had been strategically placed to ensure against her usual stubbornness. The sleepy *gillies* and ostlers staggered from their comfortable beds and gaped with disbelief at Sir Angus, their lord and master, who uncurled his tall, rangy body from the cramped quarters of the humble farm cart. He climbed out stiffly, wisps of straw sticking to his tangled white hair and rumpled clothes. The eyes of the bemused servants bulged with further amazement at the glorious sight of a beautiful, voluptuous woman with a halo of spun-gold hair. She was dressed in a colorful gypsy costume, the blouse cut tantalizingly low, exposing the creamy orbs of her seductive breasts. The swirling layered skirt provocatively framed long, bare legs, as Sir Angus gallantly lifted her to the ground, and she stood smiling shyly at the stunned array of servants.

"Stop gawking like a gaggle of *gomerils* and carry that wee lad into the house!" Sir Angus snapped testily. He was irritated both by the adoring throng and by his silent nephew, who had curtly dismounted and led his stallion into the stable, as though he wished to disassociate himself from the confusion. With a throaty chuckle and a warning screech, Hag Holly confidently launched herself into the air, depending on Angus's chivalry to catch her, which he just managed to do. He staggered backward and the breath wheezed out of him like a rusty old gate, a demeaning sound that belied his virile fantasy and made him ruefully admit to his true middle age.

Kat huddled silently, trying to be as unobtrusive as possible. She studied her brother's and sister's excited faces and listened to their bubbling chatter at the sight of the graceful lawns and manicured gardens that surrounded the impressive castle. Every inch of Duncreag was lovingly nurtured. Both Rob Roy and Macaree positively glowed with joy and happy anticipation. It was as though the shrouding cobwebs of Linnmanach had been ripped away and both youngsters were vibrant and animated, ready to seize the future hungrily, making up for the long years of deprivation. They had either completely forgotten her existence or were conveniently ignoring her presence, Kat brooded, sinking farther into the dark shadows of the farm wagon. She kept her eyes pinned to their retreating backs as Sir Angus ushered Macaree and the *cailleach* toward the main entrance. A footman carried Robbie, whose blond head bobbed this way and that as he tried to see everything around him. The enormous door opened, and welcoming golden light spilled onto the cobblestones. The group entered, chattering gaily, and then the door was firmly closed. Once more, the bluish shimmer of the moon covered the cobblestones with cool light. Kat felt that her siblings didn't seem to need or want her anymore, and her belly filled with panic.

The Campbell's deep voice reverberated through the hollow dimness of the stable, disturbing Kat's morose introspection. She stared with trepidation in his direction. She heard him curtly barking orders, knowing from his harsh tones that he was sorely out of temper. She sighed and gazed toward the orchard, smelling the ripening fruits wafting in the summer night, remembering how he had claimed her beneath the lacy, spring boughs. Would there be such ecstatic interludes again?

Would there be delicious nights spent curled against the hard
safety of his body? She absently rubbed her forearms, still
feeling the imprint of his strong hands and remembering the
time that he firmly set her away from him as though he could
no longer bear to touch her. She sighed wistfully and snuggled
closer to her dog, not knowing what to do. It seemed that she
was not needed or wanted by anybody except her loyal pet.

"Er . . . 'cuse me . . . er Lady Rannoch, yer ladyship?'' an
awkward, husky voice whispered. Kat was startled to see a
young stableboy nervously twisting his leather apron and staring up at her with consternation. "Will ye be gettin' doon?
Will ye be needin' assistance?'' he inquired. She silently shook
her head and impatiently motioned him away, not wishing
Darach's attention to be drawn to her. "But I hae to unhar-
ness *auld* MacGhee and take the wagon 'round back, yer ladyship,'' the boy explained unhappily.

"I'll drive the dray about the back of the stables,'' hissed
Kat. She ignored the pain in her buttock and clambered onto
the driving bench, picking up the reins.

"Allow the puir lad to do his job so he can crawl back to his
bed,'' the Campbell snapped, looming out of the shadows and
plucking her from her high perch. He set her curtly on her feet
and then reached up to lift down the crippled hound.

Katrine limped beside her hobbling dog, following the tall
silent man across the courtyard. Her heart beat painfully, and
tears made her eyes ache. What was going to happen? Would
they be as before? Would she share his bed? She didn't dare
look up at his face—she was too afraid of the contempt and
hatred that she might see there. His cold fury was evident in
the decisive clip of his boots and the crackling tension that
emanated from him. She felt cowed by his shadow, but she
lifted up her chin.

"Welcome to Duncreag, Lady Rannoch.'' The footman's
servile tones caused Kat to stare with startled confusion into
his blank face. If he had any censorious thoughts about her
unorthodox garb, he was too well trained to show them. Kat's
usual agility was hampered by her bewilderment, her fatigue,
and her throbbing wound, and she tripped as she stepped into
the vast entrance hall. Darach made no motion to assist her. In
fact, he seemed to recoil, making sure that there was a distance
of several feet between them. The front door slammed behind
her, making a dreadful, ominous sound as it echoed about the

high vaulted ceiling. Kat wanted to sink into a dark corner and hide.

"Please see that a hot herbal bath is taken to her ladyship's chamber," the Campbell ordered tersely. "Good night, *madame*. I trust you'll sleep well," he added cordially, coldly inclining his head in her direction before striding off toward the library. Kat stood stock-still, her hand clutching her hound's shaggy mane, watching her husband's tall figure disappear down one of the long corridors. Then she wearily followed the housekeeper and her clinking keys up the wide, sweeping staircase.

Kat impatiently waved the sleepy maids out of her chamber, preferring to be alone with her sad thoughts. She firmly closed the door after them and leaned backward, surveying the steaming tub that was set up before a crackling hearth in the strange room. One of the beautiful lacy nightgowns that Darach had bought for her was draped carelessly across a virginal single bed, and a tray laden with wine, cheese, biscuits, and soft fruits was on a table by the bath. Kat undressed slowly, numbly letting her stableboy attire fall to the floor. Then she stepped into the scented water. She leaned back and closed her eyes, feeling the warmth seep in and soothe her sore muscles. But it did not reach the cold, hollow void deep inside of her. Sian whined dolefully, sensing her sorrow before curling up on the hearth rug to sleep.

The connecting door burst open and Macaree whirled in, twirling about in an elegant robe of silk edged with egret feathers that clung seductively to her curvaceous body.

"Sir Angus said you'd nae mind me borrowing this gorgeous peignoir. 'Tis a wee bit short and snug, but it doesna matter. I love it, Kat." She laughed. "Och, I've never seen such beautiful clothes, not even when we lived near Chartres, before anything bad happened. Not even our mother's wardrobe was as impressive, not even her court gowns! Why dinna you tell me of the exquisite wardrobe that your generous husband had purchased for you?" She chattered on, oblivious to her younger sister's dejection as she posed and preened in front of the looking glass. "I counted at least twenty gowns wie matching shoes, and according to Sir Angus that isna all, for you hae a town house in Edinburgh wie bulging dressing rooms. Kat, you're rich! You're a lady! Lady Campbell of

Strathrannoch and Glengrian!'' she sang out.

Kat allowed her sister's animated chatter to wash over her. She had no interest in title, wardrobe, or riches. She just wanted to rid herself of the cold, hollow dread, the icy desolation that filled her.

"Well, at least our father would have been very happy,'' Macaree said sharply after a long, pensive pause. She had been forced to note her younger sibling's glum preoccupation, and it had doused her own enthusiasm, causing her pain and sadness.

"What has our father to do wie anything?'' snapped Kat, sitting up so suddenly that the tepid water spilled over the sides of the enameled bath and formed puddles on the thick carpet.

"He achieved his goal!'' the blond girl declared with a bitter laugh.

"I dinna ken.''

"At last a MacGregor is mistress of the MacGregor lands!''

"The Campbell maun never know that we are MacGregors,'' Kat whispered hoarsely, looking anxiously toward the door, hoping no one had heard her sister's strident voice. "And you'd better pray for your own sake that he never finds out, or we'll be back in the slums of Paris.''

"But Sir Angus knows, and so does Riach,'' Macaree stated fearfully, staring with horror at her sister.

"Sir Angus'll nae tell, but I canna say the same for Riach. Why did you tell him?'' berated Kat.

"It wasna me, but Aunt Ailsa, on her deathbed.''

"Do you think he'll tell?''

"I dinna ken. He was so very angry, shouting and screaming, breaking all the pretty ornaments from the mantelpiece. I dinna recognize him for my gentle, caring lover who held me so tenderly each night,'' she confessed. Tears brimmed in her blue eyes. "Och, Kat, what are we going to do?''

Kat numbly shook her wet head and stood up. She stepped out of the water and reached for the fluffy towel that was warming by the fire.

"I dinna ken.''

"What happened to you?'' cried Macaree, seeing the inflamed wound on her sister's haunch.

"Och, 'tis nothing. My horse bit me.''

"What horse? You have a horse?''

"No more. I left him near the cave." Kat sighed, all her worries and sorrows bursting through her tired brain. They seemed out of proportion, insolvable.

"What cave? What horse?"

"My cave! My horse!" shouted Kat, fighting the nightmare feelings that clawed at her. "Where's Robbie?" she demanded.

"Downstairs wie the *cailleach*. He has a beautiful big chamber that opens onto a balcony, and a room full of toys and books. He loves it here! He loves Angus and Cailleach Cuilleann, and so do I." Macaree sobbed petulantly. "Can't we stay?"

"What happens when Riach Campbell arrives?" Kat snarled angrily, impatient with her sister. "Then what? He'll tell, and we'll be arrested and thrown into jail or deported—if we're not hanged from the closest gibbet!"

"But we've done nothing wrong," protested Macaree, blanching at the hideous thought and pulling the silk peignoir tightly about her shivering body.

"We are outlaws!" Kat stated baldly. "And we have done something wrong. Our father kidnapped Riach Campbell!"

"But that was our father, not us."

"We were accessories. We knew what he was doing."

"You might have, but I dinna ken what was happening." Macaree whimpered. Kat didn't answer as she recognized the truth in the reply. Her sister had chosen not to be aware of what was going on about her. "I didn't know what Father was planning," she insisted.

"I know. I'm sorry. It wasna your fault."

"Then why canna I stay here?"

"We are MacGregors."

"But if we are now married to Campbells, we're nae MacGregors anymore." Macaree sobbed hysterically.

"It will be their word against ours."

"I dinna ken."

"Have you papers to prove that you're married?" Kat asked. Her sister tearfully shook her blond head. "Were you wed in a church where records were kept?" Again came the dismal denial. "By declaration?" There was a hopeful nod of assent. "Where are your witnesses?"

"There's Robbie."

"A MacGregor outlaw who just happens to be your own brother?" Kat scoffed. "Do you seriously think that he would be believed?"

"There was Aggie, but now she's dead." Macaree wept. Kat sat beside her and wrapped her arms around her sister's shaking shoulders, trying to comfort her. "Och, Kat, I wish I was as strong as you. What are we going to do?"

"Pray that Riach doesna turn up until Robbie has had a chance to heal a bit, and then we maun leave," replied Kat, not feeling the least bit strong and wishing that she had a stalwart shoulder on which to cry.

"And go where?" Macaree whispered. The thought of living without Riach seemed bleak and uninviting. Kat gently untangled herself from her sister's clutching arms and walked to the fire.

"Maybe to America," she said. She paused to control her own tearful emotion.

"America?" Macaree lamented. "That is so far away. How will we get there? We need a lot of money."

"I have money hidden."

"Enough?"

"Enough to get us to America."

"Where did you get such a sum?"

"It doesna matter," Kat replied evasively, unwilling to admit that she had stolen, especially from Angus, who had been so kind.

"So we'll book passage to America," Macaree stated dully.

"We'll start a new life—start afresh."

"Can we have just a wee while to heal? A little happy time here at Duncreag wie the beautiful clothes and cared-for rooms? Please, Kat, 'tis not too much to want. Just a few days to enjoy this sort of life again?" Macaree begged. "A few days of speaking wie other people? A few days of scented baths and different foods? A few days of comfort and happiness, like when we were children at the château?"

"Well, 'tis too late tonight to do anything but sleep here at Duncreag," Kat relented wearily.

"No, not to sleep, but to enjoy every second of this lovely luxury!" Macaree giggled, a little too excitedly. "Just look at this tray of food, and it isna even a proper meal but a wee bedtime snack! Chablis, grapes, peaches, and gages, four sorts of biscuits and three cheeses. I have the same in my chamber next door. I'll fetch it, and we shall have a picnic." She bounced out of the room, and Kat didn't have the heart to stop her, although she would have much preferred to be alone with her tumultuous thoughts. Macaree was soon back with her own tray. She was dressed in another provocative robe—this one edged in sable. The two sisters sat on large velvet pillows in front of the blazing hearth, sipping the crisp, dry wine and nibbling the biscuits, fruit, and cheese. The petite dark girl was silent, lost in her brooding, painful thoughts. The tall blond one chattered gaily, so as not to dwell on her own sadness and the frightening future that loomed ahead.

Darach stalked grimly back and forth in the library. He was furious with his uncle, who declared stubbornly that he knew nothing whatsoever about the three MacIan children.

"Dinna be a bore, nephew!" Angus blustered. "I hae told you all I know and now I'm off to my bed."

"You've told me nothing!" •

"Because I know nothing," retorted the white-haired gentleman, keeping his hand on the ornate doorknob. "Och, by the bye. I have had to change your suite of rooms. Or, rather, your man, Calum MacKissock, took it upon hisself to change your suite of rooms," he added casually with a roguish glint in his eye.

"What the hell for?"

"Because it would seem the Lady Felicity has availed herself of your bed," he informed his nephew airily. "Your possessions have been moved to the west tower."

"And where's my wife?" Darach demanded, his voice dangerously low.

"In the east tower wie her sister."

"I am in the west tower and my wife is in the east tower?" Darach repeated with stunned outrage.

"I dinna want Lady Felicity's murderous jealousy to be aroused again, so I presumed to put the two lassies together in the east tower wie servants guarding the stairs."

"You presumed too much!"

"You informed me of your stepmother's attack on your wee bride, so I sought to thwart another such attempt until plans are made to return the demented female to the asylum in Edinburgh," Angus explained defensively.

"I am in the west tower and my wife is in the east?" repeated Darach, unable to come to terms with their separation.

"Besides, the puir wee lass is injured, and the *cailleach* advises that she not be bounced about upon a bridal bed until she's mended a bit." With that last wicked riposte, the white-haired man agilely ducked out of the room and quickly slammed the heavy oak door, muffling any rejoinder his irate nephew might make.

Darach glared at the door for several long moments before pouring himself a generous glass of his uncle's favorite cognac. Muttering furiously to himself, he glowered at the dying embers in the fireplace. How long would it be before he could set his affairs in order so that he could take his rebellious young bride to Strathrannoch, where he hoped to reach some sort of agreement with her? Whether he could bridge the rift that yawned between them, he did not know, but Kat was his wife, for better or for worse. He was determined to hold her to that contract. Why? his churning mind probed. He settled in his uncle's favorite chair and stretched his long legs. Whether or not he had planned for it, his emotions were intricately entangled—in fact, he was securely bound to the heathenish little wildcat, he mused. She tormented his nights and days, making a ruinous mockery of his sanity and the measured order of his life. Since he had first gazed into her haunting emerald eyes on that dark, cold Parisian backstreet more than five years before, she had wound her way into his life, becoming an integral part of his whole being.

"Bewitching little siren," he murmured gruffly, wishing that she was curled like a sleepy kitten within his grasp. Maybe it was as well that she was out of reach at the opposite end of the large castle, he ruminated, helping himself to another generous portion of the superb cognac.

Angus had just drifted off into a deep, pleasant slumber. He was lithely gamboling on a verdant plain with several nubile nymphs when he was rudely awakened by his valet, MacNab.

"Aroint ye!" he roared, flailing his arms, hoping to scare away the usurper of his halcyon dream. He tugged the pillow over his tousled white head and tried to recapture his virile youth.

"But, Sir Angus, you left strict word tha' only you were to be awakened if'n master Riach arrived at Duncreag," the poor valet protested, wishing he were back in his snug bed. Despite the hot summer night, the stone fortress was drafty and chill, and his thin, bare legs were cold.

"Begone! Avaunt ye, thou churlish poltroon!"

"But, Sir Angus . . ." objected the miserable man.

"I am not Sir Angus, I am Zeus!" The proclamation issued from beneath the mound of bedcovers.

"But you said tha' none was to permit the lad into the castle until you had spoken wie him. Said it was a matter of life and death, you did. Said any disobeying your command would hae terrible things happen to certain unmentionable parts of their anatomies, you did," wailed the valet.

"Och, MacNab, has anyone ever told you tha' your voice has a very irritating whine?" Angus snapped, resignedly pulling himself into a sitting position and blearily surveying his dim chamber. "Where is the lad?" He yawned.

"At the gates."

"Then why are you dithering aboot like a headless biddy? Light the lamps! I canna e'en see my ain shadow in this darkness! And where's my trews! I canna gae prancing aboot near naked, as you are fond to do!" he roared, scowling down at his servant's knocking knees. "And when you've helped me wie my dressing, you're to tippy-toe up to the east tower and bring the two lassies down to the chapel. Do you ken?" The skinny little man nodded his understanding. "And none's to know of it, except maybe you and me. Do you ken? If any others are roused, you'll be singing wie the choirboys next Yuletide!" he threatened.

"But Cailleach Cuilleann kens something's afoot. She's been prowling aboot the corridors wie her herbs and spells, mumbling and muttering pagan incantations. The housekeeper's packing to go back to her sister's in Perth, for fear we're all to be struck down again like before, even though the witch says she's just trying to keep the Englishwoman at bay," whimpered MacNab. "And I canna fetch the lassies from the east tower wie-oot waking more, because you've posted guards and they're sprawled across the stairs."

"Och, stop your whining and *fashin'*, you silly mon. 'Tis guid that the *cailleach* is still up and aboot. She can go wie you to fetch the lassies," he planned, impatiently slapping at his servant's fumbling cold hands. "And dinna fret aboot the *gillies* on the stairs. They can accompany you, too; just be sure there's no noise. 'Tis imperative that the lassies be taken quietly to the chapel wie-oot anyone else knowing. Do you ken?''

''But what if others wake up and we havena made a peep?'' MacNab worried. In his anxious confusion, he held Sir Angus's coat upside down.

''Och, leave me be, you nincompoop! I can dress myself!'' he blustered, struggling to remove the tangled jacket. ''Where's my nephew?''

''I told you, he's at the gates wie the lodge keeper.''

''Not that nephew! The other? The Campbell? The young chieftain. Where is he?''

''I dinna ken, but his mon MacKissock is setting ootside the south library.''

''Och, I am a shrewd mon, MacNab!'' Angus rejoiced gleefully. ''That means Darach Campbell is helping hisself to my very best cognac. Unable to avail hisself of his winsome young bride, he's drowning his sorrows, just as I planned!'' He stamped his feet into gleaming boots and surveyed himself in the mirror. He combed his hair and then nodded his approval. ''It doesna matter what unearthly time of night or ungodly time of morning, it is beholden to a gentleman to look the part,'' he stated solemnly.

''You look very fine, sir.''

''Why the hell are you dawdling aboot? Fetch Hag Holly and collect the lassies, MacNab!''

''Can I get dressed?''

''No time, my mon, no time!''

Half an hour later, a confounded Kat and Macaree stood clutching each other in the cold, dark chapel. The air was scented with jasmine and honeysuckle, but as there was no light, it was impossible to see if any flowers were actually there.

''Is this a jail?'' Macaree whispered. Kat shrugged and stared about, trying to pierce the gloom to see where they were, not knowing what to make of their rude awakening or the armed men who clustered in the shadows. The two girls had fallen asleep on the pillows in front of the hearth. It had been one of the few times in their lives that they had achieved a closeness, due in part to the consumption of both bottles of wine and their combined miseries. ''My head is swimming,'' Macaree complained. She swayed, and Kat held her tighter.

"Am I dreaming? Where are we? Do you think we'll be hanged?"

"Hush yourselves!" warned a skinny little man in a strange short nightshirt who brandished a flickering candlestick. In the weird half light, he appeared ghoulish and grotesque.

"Cailleach?" called Kat, ignoring the officious little man. The hag didn't hear her as she pranced in and out of the columns waving bunches of herbs. "Cailleach?" she yelled, and MacNab squealed with fright.

"Hush, hush, hush yourselves. Make them hush up!" he begged three sleepy servants who were slumped in a dark pew. "If you dinna get them to button their lips, we'll all be libbed, and I dinna want to be a eunuch," he lamented. The three younger men gaped at him in consternation.

"Shut your mouths!" one of the louts ordered, waving a large claymore menacingly. Macaree stifled a frightened squeak and cowered against her sister.

"Dinna threaten us, you *mucker!*" snarled Kat, standing on tiptoes and puffing out her petite frame. She felt at a decided disadvantage garbed in the filmy, frothy nightgown.

"I'm freezing," Macaree said as her teeth chattered. She was dressed in a similar inappropriate fashion, but with a frivolous edging of ermine about her wrists and calves.

"Och, this dreary place certainly puts me in a foul humor," the *cailleach* declared, prancing up to the two shivering girls and painfully barking her shins on a carved pew. A loud stream of colorful Gaelic curses spewed from her mouth, causing MacNab to bang his head in distress.

"And what is this drear place?" asked Kat.

"And why are we here?" whispered Macaree. "And who are those horrid men wie weapons? And who's tha' goblin—the one who looks like a gargoyle?"

"Goblin? Gargoyle? Where?" the hag queried. She followed Macaree's wavering finger and cackled loudly with merriment. "Och, tha's none but MacNab. Where's your trews, wee mannikin?"

"Och, please, please hush yourselves! Sir Angus said we maun be very quiet," the valet fretted, wringing his thin hands and sinking dismally into the darkness between two pews.

"But where are we?" demanded Kat.

"Och, be quiet, I beg you," MacNab pleaded. "If anyone hears, there'll be the very de'il to pay."

"Have we been arrested?" Kat inquired loudly.

"Arrested? Of course not. What a silly question," chuckled the *cailleach*. "Why would we be arrested?" she added sharply, suddenly losing her bright smile.

"If we've nae been arrested, then why are we being held in this dark, cold dungeon in the middle of the night? And why are those men armed wie guns and claymores? And why does that wee goblin keep hissing and threatening us, ordering us to be quiet?" Macaree sobbed, looking fearfully at the group of men.

"Och, dinna get yourself in a tizzy. Tha' pitiful quivering creature is none but MacNab, Sir Angus's puny valet. He daren't say boo to a goose. Watch this!" she cackled. "Boo!" she shouted, and the little man scurried into the darkness between two pews.

"Och, please, please dinna make noise!" he pleaded.

"And this is no dungeon, though it might as well be," the *cailleach* continued, ignoring the poor valet. " 'Tis supposedly a hoose of worship, but what God in his right mind would be found in such an unwelcoming spot? This is the Duncreag chapel, and what we're doing here in the middle of the night is quite beyond my ken," she ranted, her eyes narrowing with speculation. She was unable to come up with a plausible reason for their assemblage. "MacNab, come here!" There was no answer—just a furtive scuffling and several shuddering sobs.

"Someone's coming," whimpered Macaree. Everyone stiffened and stared apprehensively through the thick gloom, toward the ominous sound of rhythmic boot steps. Eyes fixed on the bouncing light that approached, causing great shadows to loom, distorting each object into eerie shapes that busily filled the small chapel. Macaree's beautiful face gaped with horror. The approaching lanterns illuminated sightless stone faces adorning the vaulted walls; it played across carved prone figures with clasped praying hands in the likeness of the corpses interred beneath the raised tombs. "We are in a burial chamber!" she gasped.

" 'Tis Sir Angus and a younger mon," the *cailleach* hissed, impatiently nudging the whimpering girl. Macaree turned her frightened blue eyes in another direction and saw the tall white-haired man resolutely closing and barring the heavy studded door.

"It's Riach," Macaree mouthed, taking an involuntary step back when she recognized the youth who strode solemnly beside his uncle. Was it really Riach? He had changed since the last time she saw him. Had it really been earlier that day? It seemed a lifetime ago, and he looked like a stranger. His hair was trimmed, and he was freshly shaven. What was different? What was it that made her want to slink away and hide from him? Was she intimidated by his perfectly tailored clothes and gleaming boots? Or was it the masklike molding of his features that made him appear so alien? Unable to say a word, Macaree blindly felt for her sister's hand as she became filled with an awesome dread.

"I am sure you are all wondering what we're doing down here in Duncreag chapel at this unco hour of not yet morning and not quite night?" Angus orated, thoroughly enjoying being the center of attention as he stood before the assembled puzzled people much like a priest in the pulpit. "We are gathered here to witness a marriage by declaration between my nephew and *heir* . . ."—he stressed stentorially, inclining his head toward the tall youth, who didn't acknowledge his words —". . . *and* my newly acquired ward, Caree MacIan."

Everyone with the exception of Riach looked expectantly at the blond girl who stood clutching her small, dark sister and shivering convulsively. The young man glowered furiously at his uncle, but said nothing to contradict or protest.

"Come here, Caree," Angus invited. "Dinna be afeared. I ken that you're already man and wife. This is just a formality."

Many disjointed images flashed through Riach's befuddled brain as he stared straight ahead at the round window above the simple altar. The window had just begun to show the emergence of the new day by the barest glimmer of color through its stained glass. He had arrived at the gates of Duncreag, nearly dropping with exhaustion, only to be rudely denied entrance. No amount of posturing, indignant remonstrations, and threats had swayed the hefty gatekeeper, who had dispatched a sleepy lad to the castle, leaving him to cool his heels outside the walls on the dusty thoroughfare like a common peddler. He had finally been granted admission, but then only into the gatehouse. There he had met his uncle, who had made him feel like a callow truant instead of a prodigal son. The ensuing conversation—if, in fact, it had been a conversation, because Riach couldn't recall saying much—spun about in his aching head. His uncle had expounded about duty and manhood, and he had been too weary and astounded to be defensive. His uncle had also warned him that no one was to know the identity of the MacGregor trio, particularly his mother, Felicity, or his brother, Darach.

Darach and Felicity were at Duncreag? At this strange news, Riach had allowed himself to be stripped, washed, shaved, and then dressed. He had felt dazed and overwhelmed, unable to comprehend all that he was being told. Not only Darach and his mother, but also Macaree and her two siblings, had somehow miraculously been transported here. Nothing had seemed real, so Riach had pretended he was in a dream and had comforted himself with the knowledge that eventually he would awaken. Then he had followed his uncle through the handsome castle to the chapel.

"This will all be yours, my boy," Angus had stated. "Darach has the title and the Campbell lands of Strathrannoch and Glengrian, so Duncreag shall be yours—*if* you fulfill your obligations." Just what those obligations might entail was too much for his fatigued brain to unravel.

"Riach Campbell?" His sharply pronounced name cut through his detached reverie, and he stared about in confusion. Then he scowled at the scandalous spectacle of Macaree half naked in a diaphanous scrap of lace edged with fur. She was being lasciviously eyed by several burly *gillies* who leaned comfortably on their claymores, virtually drooling. Her dark sister was similarly clad but had the modesty to stand in the shadows. A wild-haired old crone shuffled about waving clumps of dried weeds and muttering strange incantations.

"Riach Campbell?" Angus boomed impatiently.

"Aye," he answered tersely, unable to wrench his furious gaze from Macaree. She stood motionless, draped in the shred of a nightgown that molded seductively to her voluptuous figure. She looked like a Greek statue.

"Did you claim Caree for your wife?"

"I did," Riach replied acidly, and then he snorted derisively. What a gullible, naïve idiot he had been to think of her as pure and virginal, when it was obvious that she was as conniving and corrupt as his own mother. Even after realizing that he had been duped by the golden girl, who had been pandering to him at her father's behest much like a common whore, he had been obsessed with her. Every dusty inch of the long rugged trek from Linnmanach to Duncreag had been filled with thoughts of her. Even the rhythm of his stride had echoed her name. Macaree, Macaree, Macaree. Och, she was a cunning wench.

The irony of Riach's tone and the sardonic sneer that marred his handsome face caused Kat's stomach to lurch, and she was afraid for her gentle sister.

"Caree, love, did you claim Riach for your husband?" Angus asked softly, in awe of the young woman's breathtaking beauty and unaware of his nephew's antagonism. Macaree nodded silently, keeping her eyes pinned to his kindly, comforting features. "Then, in front of the witnesses gathered here in Duncreag chapel, I declare that Riach and Caree are husband and wife," he announced triumphantly. Only then did Riach turn to stare at him with pure incredulity.

Many responses streamed through the shocked youth's head. He wanted to scream that it was all a farce, a nightmare, but there was a tremendous buzzing in his ears. All he could do was to gape at his uncle and at the people who clustered about, putting their signs to the large registry. Hysterical laughter bubbled within him and burst out in harsh spurts, silencing the assembled people.

Kat looked from Riach's contemptuous expression to her sister's sad confusion. The youth's raucous mirth died away, and the silence and the space yawned unbearably. She wanted to scream and snap the tension. She reached out shyly and tugged at his arm.

"I thought you loved my sister," she murmured.

"That was before I found out about the role I was assigned to play in your father's little plot," he retorted, steeling himself against her luminous eyes.

"You canna blame Caree for that."

"Och, I most certainly can!" he countered. "Oh, I can also look to myself and acknowledge that I was a prime fool—weak, artless, a perfect pigeon, too gullible and innocent to recognize your sister for the conniving whore that she is!" he snarled.

"Dinna call her a whore! 'Tis not true! If any is to blame, it's me!" But Riach Campbell roughly shoved her aside and walked away. "Believe me, she didn't know what was going on," she pleaded. He stalked to the chapel door without a backward glance, removed the heavy bar, and flung it savagely aside so that it crashed sharply against the granite walls. Then he quit his marriage ceremony, leaving the door gaping hollowly, its hinges laboriously creaking. Everyone stared mutely as his footsteps receded along the stone passageways, echoing into silence.

"He hates me." Macaree's plaintive whisper finally broke the suspended stillness. Kat wrapped a comforting arm about her quaking sister and glowered accusingly at Angus, who had lost his happy confidence. He sagged against the pulpit, seeming lost and much older than his middle years. He stared with sad confusion at the young sisters.

"I dinna ken," he muttered disjointedly.

"You dinna ken!" the hag cried, shaking her gray head with disbelief.

"The lad maun be tired. He needs his rest, and then he'll come to his senses. It'll be all right, lassies. Wie a new, fresh day everything will be mended. Aye, he just needs a guid night's sleep," he added.

"Ha!" Cailleach Cuilleann snorted disparagingly.

"Aye, and he needs a guid talking to," Angus amended, unable to deal with the three distraught women. He hurried after his younger nephew.

chapter 25

Macaree's musical voice drifted over the rolling velvet lawns of Duncreag. It mingled with the merrily singing birds and the gentle breeze that wafted through the surrounding pines, tinkling the wind chimes that Angus had brought back from one of his numerous trips to the Orient. Kat stood at an open window of her bedchamber in the east tower, gazing down at her older sister and marveling at her happy resilience. She nostalgically recalled their carefree childhood days when they had lived an idyllic life in the beautiful château near Chartres. Macaree's periwinkle gown mirrored the infinite, cloudless sky and floated about her elegant figure as she moved gracefully from hoop to hoop with her croquet mallet. The ribbons of her impudent bonnet streamed gaily with her spun-gold curls.

"So beautiful." Kat sighed, envious of her sister's melodic laughter. She felt that she had stepped back in time and was watching her own mother, who had often been the center of an admiring throng of men. Angus and a veritable army of male servants bordered the lawn, their eyes pinned to the enchanting young woman, who seemed to blossom from their worshipping attention. Suibhan, their mother, whether she wished for it or not, had been constantly surrounded by uniformed soldiers from Gregor's regiment, the prestigious Garde Ecossais from the French royal court. The doting males would stand about, much like Angus and his liveried minions, each poised to be the first to gallantly retrieve a ball or a carelessly dropped fan or glove. But just like Suibhan, Macaree's happiness was slightly false, a little awkward as her blue eyes anxiously scanned the grounds, hoping for a glimpse of Riach, who was not in attendance.

"Childhood wasna really so carefree," murmured Kat, realizing that there had been sad shadows even before Macaree's rape. She remembered being at the nursery window, kneeling on the toychest so that she could peer out at her beautiful mother. Suibhan's blue eyes would also search anxiously, avoiding the adoration of other men, desperately seeking the love that she craved from her own husband. He was usually dallying with other women. Kat leaned on the windowsill, recalling the many outrageous stories and activities she had invented to divert her mother's attention from her father's embarrassing behavior. Even though she had been only four or five when she had first become aware of her father's unfaithfulness, she knew how very hurt it would make her mother. Kat frowned, suddenly comprehending that Suibhan must have been aware of her husband's numerous and blatant infidelities.

At the searing thought of infidelity, Kat felt physically ill. The sickening picture of Felicity Campbell sprawled seductively across Darach's bed, draped in the merest whisper of black lace, clawed its way into her mind. Darach's bed! Their bed! Their very special haven, where they had spent intimate days and nights—the place where each had laid claim to every inch of the other. Felicity's delicate profile blazed itself in Kat's memory. The horrendous scar had not been apparent, but the sated smirk was even more nightmarish. What ever had possessed her to seek Darach's help? Kat berated herself angrily, furiously wiping the tears from her cheeks.

"I hate him!" She sobbed, turning her back on the pastoral scene and staring blankly into the interior of her chaste chamber. She saw white blobs dance teasingly before her eyes as she remembered the agonizing chain of events that had occurred after the mockery of her sister's wedding. When Riach had coldly stalked out to be followed by the distressed Angus, Macaree had retreated behind her doll-like mask and childish nursery songs, but there had been a terrifying difference.

When Kat had reached out to comfort, her sister had attacked her, viciously scratching, and hitting. She had screeched her French ditty with such strident ferocity as she clawed at Kat's face that even the burly menservants had backed away, hastily crossing themselves for fear that she was possessed by evil spirits. Cailleach Cuilleann had taken charge, leading the screaming girl away, followed by a fearful MacNab and the armed guards, leaving Kat alone in the gloomy shadows of the grim chapel. She had tucked her legs beneath her and huddled numbly on a cold hard pew. The new day had slowly unfolded, turning the thick darkness to a dismal gray. Then the hot sun rose, causing rainbow beams to stab through the stained-glass panes, piercing the sepulchral gloom and Kat's detachment. She had stood stiffly, and in her fatigue had foolishly resolved to entrust the Campbell chieftain with the truth of their MacGregor identities. She had hoped that he would allow them to leave if she promised to return the articles she had stolen and quit Scotland, never to return. After the traumatic events of the preceding days and a long night without sleep, it seemed to be a sensible, plausible plan. Unconsciously, in the dim recesses of her confused mind, there was an unmentionable fantasy that perhaps Darach would declare his undying love for her. Then everything would turn out happily ever after, just like the bedtime stories her mother had recounted in a bygone golden time when a kiss could make everything better.

"How could I have been so stupid?" she spat aloud, recalling the sight of her dusty bare feet moving slowly and steadily across the cold gray granite slabs of the chapel floor. She had methodically placed one foot in front of the other as she walked along the warmer, polished flags of the winding corridors, smelling the nurturing wax of the well-kept castle. One foot in front of the other, as she saw the cozy glints and flickering shadows cast by the bracketed torches on the high vaulted walls. One foot in front of the other, as she climbed up the steep steps of the west tower, remembering how she had been carried to her bridal bed and how the strong beat of his heart had resounded in her ear, as she nestled against his broad chest. One foot in front of the other, as she was remotely conscious of her own heart thudding. One foot in front of the other, never faltering, as her hand slipped up the coolness of the shining copper banister. One foot in front of the other, as she approached the place that promised love, safety, and enchantment. She felt like a small, lost child yearning for comfort, but she hadn't allowed herself to picture what she cherished in her mind.

Kat put her hand on the ornate handle of the heavy oak door, letting it rest for a brief moment before confidently flinging it open. She didn't know that she expected to see him sleeping in all his naked, male majesty, his thick, ebony hair rebelliously falling across his chiseled face, softening the stern handsome lines so that he appeared boyish and vulnerable. She didn't know that she expected to see one brown arm outstretched and empty, as though reaching for her compliant warmth—outstretched and empty, seeming incomplete without her petite complement. But, instead, there was another woman in her place—one with a delicate pink-and-white complexion. Was she perhaps a more ideal contrast for his dark perfection?

Kat had fled from the sight, but not before the chiding violet sparks from the amethyst geode had stabbed through the intimacy of the bedchamber and she was reminded of the awful sound when it had cracked against the Campbell's temple. It had not been until late the following day—after hours of convincing herself that she didn't care, after hours of burying her wounds beneath layers of icy detachment, after hours spent dressing herself in a severe, concealing gown and harnessing her unruly hair so that she appeared to be a prim governess—that she discovered the identity of her replacement. She had swept haughtily into the dining hall after being summoned for dinner, firmly convinced that she didn't mind who the *mucker* slept with, and then she was introduced by Angus to the Campbell's mistress, his own stepmother, Riach's birth mother! Kat had forgotten her resolve to be distant and cool. She had leaped to her feet, knocking over several dishes of food in her haste to escape, and had been humiliatingly and violently ill in the corridor. This had given rise to the speculation that she was with child. At first she had been horrified and was about to deny the assumption hotly, but at the sight of the Campbell's tall lounging figure standing at a distance with a sardonic sneer on his handsome face, she had realized that she could use the misconception to her own advantage. She had supposedly taken to her bed and, because of her delicate condition, had not been expected to socialize with any of the other occupants of Duncreag Castle. She had refused access to her bedchamber to all but one maid, the smallest, most insignificant servant, not trusting the shrewd *cailleach*, whose practiced eye would surely guess the truth. How the Campbell chieftain must hate her, she fumed. Even believing her pregnant, he kept her prisoner in her tower room, posting armed guards outside her door. For seven long days, she had paced the confines of the small suite of rooms, desperately trying to formulate a plan for the future. She had spent the nights edging along the narrow stone parapet outside her windows, eluding the jailers who blocked the corridor to the stairs. Then she had systematically explored Duncreag, locating weapons and money, and studying the best routes from the stables into the surrounding forest. It was obvious to her that Darach Campbell hated her, and so he had made no attempt to speak with her. Unaware that he had gone to Edinburgh to arrange for Felicity's return to the asylum, Kat assumed that he was busy with the Englishwoman and disgusted by the thought that his child grew in Kat's belly.

Rob's husky young voice broke through Kat's anger and pain, and she thrust the bitter memories aside and turned back to the open window. There was no time for regrets and self-pity—she had to logically and rationally plan their escape. Her brother reclined on the terrace, playing a card game with Cailleach Cuilleann, as he watched their older sister's graceful but inept attempts at croquet. In the short week since coming to Duncreag, Robbie had visibly strengthened, losing his frightening fragility and delicate pallor. He was impatient to be up and about. His happy voice rang out, good-naturedly teasing Macaree about her poor ball sense and causing loud merriment with his impish wittiness.

Even though it had been just a week, the lonely time she had spent at Duncreag seemed like an eternity. Each morning Kat awoke and braced herself for a confrontation with the Campbell, and each evening she sighed and sagged with relief when another healing day for her brother had passed without incident. Soon Robbie would be strong enough to sit a horse, and she could lead him far away to safety. They would ride across Scotland to Ballachulish and buy passage on a vessel for the New World, where they could proudly regain their clan name without fear of death or imprisonment. But the prospect engendered no joyful anticipation; for her, the thought of leaving Duncreag and the Campbell was tinged with unadmitted regret.

Kat leaned on the window ledge, breathing appreciatively of the warm fragrances. It was a sultry summer afternoon, conjuring up nostalgic reminiscences of her childhood.

"I was never a child!" Kat hissed, impatient with herself for her rosy reverie. "Nothing has ever been perfect!" It had all been a lie, a veneer, just like everything she now glared down upon, she mused bitterly. Great banks of lush flowers bloomed, perfuming the air and tempting the languid butterflies. They floated idly from the profusion of pastel petals to the vibrant clashing reds and yellows shimmering in the hazy heat. All appeared to be lazy and tranquil, but underneath there was a grating unease, as though concealed under the pretty stillness was an evil coiled to attack.

Kat scowled as a slight movement caught her eye. She half expected to see her father tumbling a chambermaid amid the regal hollyhocks, but her hysterical laughter caught in her throat when instead she spied Felicity hovering like an avenging bat in the long shadows of the evergreens. The strange, disturbing woman was arrayed in her usual layers of black lace, shedding an ominous foreboding across the bright landscape. She was staring intently at Macaree, and even from a distance, Kat could feel her icy hatred and was afraid for her sister. Another movement distracted her, and she glanced sharply across to the north turret. Riach stood there at an open window, also staring down at the beautiful Macaree, his gaze as intense and unwavering as his mother's.

Riach was lost in his own confusion of thoughts and emotions as he watched his graceful wife. He admired her flowing gown, but he wistfully recalled her dressed in tight trews and a skimpy smock that strained across her ample breasts. He remembered the dirt smudges on her exquisite face as she knelt in the garden pulling weeds, her sweet breath puffing with exertion through her pursed lips. He had barely spoken two words to her since arriving at Duncreag, yet they slept in adjacent rooms in the same suite. He pointedly avoided her eyes, knowing that he would weaken. He would drown in their limpid blue depths, yet he would feel callow at being gulled by their pathetic mute appeal, or callous for ignoring it. Was Macaree a consummate actress, able to manipulate his emotions deftly and hoodwink even the cunning, wordly Angus?

Or was what his uncle repeatedly insisted true? Was Macaree MacGregor an innocent pawn, a hapless victim of an amoral father? At the thought of her brutal ravishment as a mere child, fury pounded through his veins. Yet, at the same time, he was suspicious. What better way for her to explain the loss of her maidenhood? he seethed. What should he believe? What should he do?

Every night was torture as he tossed and turned, all too aware of her presence in the adjoining room, her heady perfume drifting under the door and into his nostrils, beckoning, seducing. He was hard-pressed not to throw his doubts aside and seek her bed. At the thought of his weakness, anger would surge and he wanted to ravage her cruelly. He wanted to punish her, but he was afraid—afraid of being made a fool by being loving and gentle, and afraid of violating her further. Did he want to be an object of ridicule or an object of loathing? Did he love her or hate her? Did he want to make love to her passionately, or violently possess her? He didn't know what he wanted or what he felt, and he wished that his older brother was around so that he could ask his advice. At that thought, he snorted with impatience.

"It is as well that Darach is not about to do his usual interfering," he muttered, furious with himself for entertaining the idea of asking for his brother's assistance. He glowered down at his pretty young wife, trying to unravel his conflicting feelings. Every day he was determined to ignore her, but he was achingly aware of her every move. Each nuance was riveting for him—a blink, a shy smile, a reproachful tear, the faint rustle of her skirts that conjured up a delightful picture of her long, slender legs underneath, a golden curl shimmering, tempting his fingers to caress it. He was so burningly aware of her that he scarcely noticed his own mother's very uncharacteristic behavior. She hovered in the peripheral shadows, intently scrutinizing Macaree instead of ensuring that she herself was the focus of everyone's attention.

Macaree's breathtaking beauty and melodious voice grated upon Felicity's nerves. She glared at the young woman with a jaundiced eye, silently and malevolently heaping curses upon her. They ranged from total loss of the spun-gold curls to dire diseases that would rot the firm flesh and ravage the seductive curves, bringing about premature old age. Bitter hatred seared through her as she recognized the tall slenderness of her son at the window. She was all too aware of what consumed his mind. How dare he stare so hungrily at the brassy chit! Riach was a mere child, too young for carnal desires. He was just a little boy—she certainly wasn't old enough to be a mother to a full-grown man. She was a child—a little girl.

Felicity thrust her way through the prickly branches of the juniper tree and leaned against it, heedless of the coarse, hairy bark that snagged the layers of her Valencia lace. Misery and self-pity bubbled up achingly in every part of her. She was lonely and unloved because of the three crass intruders who hadn't the right to venture near her family. It was so very obvious that they did not belong in her exalted sphere of polite, well-born society; it was also evident that they must be disposed of, the sooner the better. Darach, Riach, and even Angus would eventually come to their senses and thank her for her foresight after the gory, inevitable deed was done. Who the three conniving adventurers were and where they came from was of no interest to Felicity; she simply wanted them removed forever.

Felicity absentmindedly caressed her mutilated cheek as she turned her burning eyes to the east tower and saw the glossy raven hair of the slight girl at the open window.

"Die!" she cursed, as hatred roiled within her. "Die!" she repeated vehemently, stabbing a finger in that direction. Four times she had crept up the steps to the east tower, intent on murder. But she had been thwarted by the sight of sprawled armed guards and by the vicious hound's warning growl.

Robbie's youthful merriment caused Felicity's hands to claw into avenging talons as rage contorted her coiled body. Her face grew even more grotesque as malice further twisted the disfiguring scar caused by Sian's protecting fangs. She jealously regarded Sir Angus striding across the manicured lawn and bending over the skinny runt of a boy, giving him the attention that she so desperately craved.

"Die!" she spat, fingering the sharp point of the ornate dagger that she had concealed among the folds of her skirts. "They have usurped what is mine! Relegated me to obscurity! Cast me into the shadows to be ignored! I'll teach them to look right through me as though I didn't exist!" she vowed. Then she shook with laughter, leaning against the trunk of the tree as cackles of hoarse mirth burst through her veils. "I am invisible!" she rejoiced. "They cannot see me because I am invisible!" she proclaimed joyously, suddenly whirling out from the sheltering gray-green boughs of the juniper, her black cob-webbed layers swirling about her. "I am the breeze, elusive and invisible! I am the winds of revenge, intangible and deadly!" she proclaimed insanely. In her exultant delirium, she was deaf to the gasps of fear from the servants and the busy trundle of wheels and clatter of hooves in the courtyard as Darach galloped in, followed by two enclosed carriages. "I am invisible and deadly!" she sang, blind to the consternation that was evident upon everyone's face as she dramatically pro-duced the lethal dagger from beneath her tiers of black lace. She lifted it high above her shrouded head; it gleamed wickedly in the bright light before lunging at Macaree, who stood frozen with terror in the very center of the grass.

Sharp reports tore through the shimmering humidity. For several seconds they seemed to silence the lazy drone of the sultry afternoon. Felicity and Macaree clasped each other and wavered, caught in an eerie embrace, before slowly spiraling apart and toppling to the ground, where they lay motionless, their fingers still touching.

Kat gaped with shock at the macabre scene. Then she looked down at the smoking pistol in her numb clasp. She gazed back at the greensward with the two fallen females in the center, one dressed in somber black lace, and the other in celestial blue. Liveried servants were frozen in various at-titudes of alarm. It was a tableau—nothing moved except a lone yellow butterfly and the flicker of a mischievous breeze that imperceptibly ruffled the full skirts of the black and blue gowns. Minutes ticked by, and then there was a spurt of fran-tic activity. A babble of voices crescendoed to a cacophony of hysterical screams and then diminished to a low roar. Darach Campbell appeared from the direction of the stables followed by several strange men attired in identical dour frock coats and gray periwigs. Angus and Cailleach Cuilleann leaped into action, racing across the lawn, followed by Robbie. An end-less stream of servants gushed from castle, orchard, garden, and field, converging upon the limp forms in a rumbling mass.

A terrible howl of anguish ripped through the thunderous chaos, and Riach, with a gun in both hands, streaked from the castle, keening. He furiously shoved the clustering people aside and knelt between his wife and mother.

"Caree, my love?" he whispered hoarsely, tears streaming

down his tanned cheeks. She lay so still and pale, seeming to be made of crystal. Her closed eyelids were white and bloodless, a horrific contrast to the blaze of red that stained the delicate silk of her bodice. "Och, my Caree," he mourned, fearfully picking up her limp hand and feeling the frightening coldness of her fingers. "Wake up, my darling," he begged. He held his breath at seeing a faint fluttering movement in her long graceful neck.

Irritating hands plucked at him. Without looking at the source, he slapped them away much as he would an annoying insect.

"Riach?" moaned Felicity, unable to move anything but one arm and her head. It felt as though she had been nailed to the earth, crucified with red-hot spikes driven through her, pinning her to the ground. "Son? 'Tis me, your mother, Felicity." She tossed her head impotently from side to side and clawed at his back. The fabric of his shirt was pulled tightly across his flexed muscles, and her long nails scraped futilely, unable to catch a hold. With an anguished snarl, Riach blindly flailed one arm, savagely smacking her hand away; he cradled Macaree in his other arm. Laying his dark head against her bloodied chest, he strained intently to hear a heartbeat. "Riach? Riach? I'm your mother," Felicity whined.

"For God's sake, silence her!" Riach screamed with frustration.

"Help me, son," whimpered the woman, balling her fist and pummeling him in a bid for his attention. The youth swore with rage before staggering to his feet with the girl in his arms.

"Cailleach, for God's sake help me!" he entreated, elbowing his way through the buzzing throng and carrying Macaree into the castle, away from the evil woman in black.

"No! I'm your mother, you unnatural bastard!" screeched Felicity, summoning all her energy and grasping one of his legs, nearly tripping him. At an autocratic signal from the Campbell, several servants gingerly closed around the cursing, writhing woman, forcing her to release her son.

Kat was unable to wrench her horrified eyes from the milling scene below. Felicity's vitriolic screams consigning everyone to purgatory attested to the fact that she was very much alive, but Macaree's stillness and silence convinced her that she had inadvertently killed her sister. It was too terrible a thought. Kat was vaguely aware of the weight of the gun in her hand, and distantly she smelled the acrid stench of the gunpowder. She dully remembered the explosion that jarred her tense body.

She absently watched the tiny figures converging far beneath her. Then they diffused in different directions like busy ants around spilled honey. The hive of activity dissipated until only one figure stood, staring up at her. Somewhere in her shocked mind she recognized Darach, but the horror of shooting her own sister had paralyzed her. In a strange suspension with her eyes half focused, she watched him stride toward her and then disappear out of her range of vision as he entered the castle. She dimly knew that he was coming for her, and she waited for the sound of his distinct footsteps, hearing the rhythmic tread in the pulse of her blood before his boots were discernible on the stone steps. Still, she did not remove her blank gaze from the now tranquil garden. She still could see the spectral shadows of the two women imprinted on the empty lawn. The door handle was impatiently tried.

"Open this door immediately!" Darach's imperious voice and heavy fist shuddered through the thick oak. Only then did Kat turn in that direction.

"She's not set one foot ootside that there room since you left for Edinburgh, your lordship," a guard volunteered, eager to please. "And she'd let no one in to share company wie 'cept Morag, the youngest scullery maid. Not Sir Angus nor even Miss Caree nor young master Rob. Och, but she's been eating real guid, sir. Real guid. Aye, I keep an eye on the empty platters and ken tha' she's feeding your *bairn*, so 'tis sure to be a fine healthy babe," the sycophant continued. Darach made no sign that he had heard. He hammered on the door again, and Sian growled warningly.

"Kat, open this door at once!" he ordered.

Kat moved slowly across the chamber like a sleep walker and obediently slid back the stiff bolts. She stepped away as the door was wrenched open and stared blankly into the Campbell chieftain's chiseled features, noting with detachment how the aquiline nostrils flared and the silver eyes gleamed with barely suppressed fury.

Many conflicting impulses and emotions churned through Darach's brain as he looked into those wide emerald eyes. He ached to gather her against his heart, to hold her close and run his possessive hands over every inch of her, laying claim and exulting in her safety. It could easily have been she lying motionless on the lawn, bloodied and ripped by Felicity's murderous jealousy. Kat stood poised like a startled fawn, so achingly beautiful, so petite and young, that it was difficult to believe that she was soon to be a mother. His seed grew within her perfect little body. He scanned her trim litheness, seeking an indication of their impending parenthood, in awe of that age-old process. There was no sign. He scowled, seeing that she still opted to wear the stable lad smock and trews that accentuated her boyish leanness, rather than the expensive gowns that he had chosen to complement her rare beauty. He quelled the desire to shake her thoroughly until her teeth rattled. His eyes narrowed with speculation at smelling the acrid fumes and seeing the blue smoke that still hung in the dense summer air. Tearing his gaze from her confused green eyes, he focused on the dueling pistol in her hand.

"How the hell did you obtain that!" he exclaimed, recognizing the weapon as one of a treasured pair that his uncle kept under lock and key in a desk within his private study. He snorted and rolled his eyes heavenward as he spied its mate tucked snugly into her waistband. Before leaving for Edinburgh, he had given implicit orders that his wife was to be kept under constant surveillance, not only to protect her from Felicity's madness, but also from her own wildness, especially in her delicate condition. He shook his dark head with defeat as he spotted the telltale outline of a dagger strapped to her thigh and another one across her breasts. Obviously, Angus and the staff of Duncreag Castle were no match for the devious little wench to whom he was married.

Kat took an involuntary step backward, shocked by Darach's loud voice, before following his smoldering eyes to the gun that dangled in her grasp. She wanted to ask him about her sister but was too afraid of the answer. Had she shot Macaree? All she could do was to stare at the Campbell mutely, waiting for his simmering rage to erupt into violence. The gun dropped from her hand and thudded onto the carpeted floor, narrowly missing her small bare feet. He made no motion to pick it up or to disarm her. He just kept his searing gaze pinned to her face. The tension was unbearable, burning painfully through her protective layers until she was exposed and vulnerable, agonized by her turbulent emotions. Silently, she spun on her heel and stared blindly out the window over the formal gardens of Duncreag. Maybe none of it had happened. Maybe it had all been in her imagination. She would focus her eyes and see Robbie lying on a chaise on the sunny terrace playing cards with Cailleach Cuilleann, while Macaree and Angus played croquet. Slowly, the gardens came into focus, but the golden sunshine was gone and long mournful shadows dissected the ominous stillness. Macaree's bonnet lay forlornly on the lawn, and a respectful hush seemed to smother everything.

"Och, I canna trust you out of my sight," Darach muttered beneath his breath, infuriated by her apparent rejection and resisting the temptation to force her to face him. "I dinna ken how you managed to spirit yourself out of this room without the guards being any the wiser, but I strongly recommend you remain in here until Felicity has been transported back to the sanitarium in Edinburgh," he stated.

Kat was too intent on trying to formulate the dreadful question in her mind to allow the full import of his words to penetrate her consciousness. She vaguely heard that he planned to return to Edinburgh with Felicity, but she thrust the painful knowledge aside and summoned up her courage.

"Is she dead?" she finally dared to whisper. The words stuck to her dry lips, and she did not dare to look at him, fearing the sardonic condemnation on his face. But the only answer she received was the decisive slamming of the door as he curtly left the room. The emphatic sound echoed hollowly, and she interpreted it to be a confirmation of her worst fear. Her sister was dead.

Kat stared down at the discarded gun, hearing the Campbell's brisk footsteps diminish as a terrible ache welled within her. Slowly, she sagged to the floor, where she sat hugging her legs like a lost child, remembering the promise she had made to her dying mother in the squalid attic in Paris. It had been a lifetime ago. She had been a twelve-year-old girl, and now she was nearly an eighteen-year-old woman.

"Oh, *maman*," she intoned, wishing that she could weep and release the burning pain between her eyes. She had solemnly vowed to protect her weaker siblings, but instead she was responsible for the gentle Macaree's death. She had failed completely. She rocked numbly back and forth with her forehead pressed against her bent knees, recalling the pervasive decay of Linnmanach that had slowly and inexorably sapped Robbie's youth and strength. "Oh, *maman,* I am so sorry."

Unaware of the extent of Kat's distress, Darach strode through Duncreag with her poignant face pressed in his mind. Despite the awesome array of weapons that she had amassed, she had appeared extremely vulnerable, and her image gnawed at him. He slapped his broad palm against his muscular thigh, chiding himself for uncharacteristic sentimentality, and he resisted the temptation to return to comfort her. He laughed harshly, imagining her reaction. She would probably use the infernal gun on him. He rubbed his ebony head reflectively, remembering the amethyst geode's punishing blow to his skull and to his male pride. No, he'd not leave his guard down again. He'd leave his small rebel wife in her lonely tower room until he had set his affairs in order. Then he'd carry her away to Strathrannoch, away from her demanding siblings and his interfering family. They would deal together one to one, he determined. He would strip away the lies, the subterfuge, the aggression. He whistled tunelessly, lost in thought. Kat's distinctive features, imprisoned in his mind's eye, suddenly melted into a wiser, more mature face. He frowned, recalling dusty beams of light bouncing off the taut, flat plane of a cracked oil painting. Bright green eyes with a myriad of crinkly laugh lines seemed to mock him.

"Who the hell are you, Kat Campbell?" Darach wondered.

chapter 26

Macaree gradually awakened and snuggled her cheek into the soft pillow. She opened her eyes and smiled tenderly at the incongruous sight of Riach asleep in a dainty chair. His gangly legs sprawled, and his willowy leanness folded uncomfortably into the miniature confines of the pink satin upholstery. His thick black hair fell across his face. One arm dangled, his long sensitive fingers gently brushing the thick pile of the floral-patterned carpet.

Morning sunlight filtered through pastel draperies, bathing the pretty, feminine room in a rosy glow. It had not been a dream. Riach was really there, his clothes soiled and rumpled. Macaree ached to reach out and run her fingers over his prickly unshaven cheeks, smoothing away the dark smudges of fatigue beneath his closed eyes, but she contented herself with the beloved sight of him. She didn't know how long she had been incapacitated since Felicity's murderous attack, but she had become more and more aware during the last three days and two nights. In the beginning everything had been murky and nightmarish. She had drifted in and out of dark pain and terror, but through the widening, clearing circles, she had heard his voice comforting her and felt his strong arms cradling her. She had smelled the reassuring scent of him as he had saved her from being submerged in insane panic. Through thick, unreal layers that muffled and distorted her world, she had recognized the voices of Angus and the *cailleach* remonstrating, but Riach had refused to leave her, refused to relinquish the care of her to another.

"She is mine!" he had declared so possessively that the phrase still echoed in her mind, causing thrill upon thrill to ripple through her.

Macaree quietly watched him sleep as she explored her own body for signs of hurt. She was completely naked. She frowned when her fingertips rasped against a scaly coarseness that marred her silky-smooth skin. A sickening coldness streaked through her belly, and for several tense moments she was afraid to trace the extent of the puckered wound. Her trembling touch froze midway between her shoulder and the swell of her left breast. Fearfully, she followed the scab of the jagged gash as it dissected her bosom, taking deep breaths to calm herself. Felicity had tried to stab her in the heart, but had instead carved a long disfiguring mark.

Carefully, Macaree sat up, wincing from the pain as her healing flesh stretched. She tugged the sheets about her neck, not wanting to see how she had been mutilated. French lullabies bubbled into her mind, but they became muddled and irritating, serving to aggravate rather than soothe. She tried to force away her overwhelming terror by concentrating on the elegant château and the serenely flowing river of her childhood, but all she could envision was Duncreag's exquisite gardens. She tried desperately to evoke her mother's calming voice and beautiful face, but Riach's tired unshaven features and husky voice obstructed other images.

Tightly clasping the sheets about her chin, Macaree sat blindly staring at the play of sunlight on the patterned wallpaper, struggling against the desire to burrow beneath the cozy bedclothes like a frightened child. Suddenly, she flung the covers aside and swung her legs to the floor. She stood up resolutely, clinging to the ornate headboard as the room spun alarmingly, before fixing her eyes across the room to the bottom of the carved frame of a full-length mirror. She took a breath and walked slowly toward it, not quite brave enough to raise her eyes above the reflection of her bare feet.

Riach watched bemusedly from beneath half-closed, heavy lids. He was not sure whether he was awake, because in the rosy suspension of the soft filtered light and his own sleepiness, Macaree appeared to be a celestial being, golden and glorious, naked and graceful, floating across the dappled carpet toward her misty image in the looking glass.

Suddenly, the ethereal mood was shattered by a spine-chilling scream that hung in the air and then trailed away into a low moan of pure misery. The fluid, swanlike movements became jerky and awkward, and then Macaree huddled in a dark corner like a wretched hurt animal, her arms clutching her legs to hide her nakedness, her long tangled hair rippling about her.

"Wha' is it? Wha' is amiss?" Loud voices called out and knuckles rapped sharply at the door. The latch was frantically tried. "Is something wrong?" Again there was a noisy hammering at the door, bringing Riach to total consciousness.

"Caree, what are you doing? You shouldna be out of bed!" he cried, leaping out of the dainty chair and nearly falling flat on his face as his cramped muscles rebelled.

"So ugly. So ugly. So ugly," the girl intoned, hugging her knees and rocking back and forth, trying to erase the shocking image of the mutilating wound from her mind. "So ugly. So ugly. So ugly."

Riach limped toward her and then knelt beside her, not quite knowing what to say. He couldn't see her face because her long blond hair cascaded about her curled, rocking body. Tentatively, he reached out and stroked her bent head, but she rocked more furiously, frantically intoning the two words. He grasped her bowed shoulders, and she screamed, trying to shrug off his strong hands.

"Dinna touch me! I am ugly and spoiled!" She wept, drumming her heels with rage as he plucked her off the floor, exerting all his energy. "Put me down! Leave me alone!" He carried her across the room to the bed, where he sat cradling her against his chest, imprisoning her arms by her sides.

"You could never be ugly and spoiled to me," he said huskily.

"Caree? Caree?" Kat's voice screamed. The door latch was furiously rattled.

"Go away!" shouted Riach.

"No! What are you doing to my sister?" shouted Kat, bruising her fists and bare feet on the unyielding oak of the heavy door.

" 'Tis none of your business," Darach remarked idly, standing at a distance and staring quizzically at the cluster of people in the corridor.

"Also none of yours," Kat retorted rudely, turning away

from the attractive sight of him in his well-cut riding clothes.
She proceeded to hammer away at the door with the butt of a
pistol. Angus gaped and then groaned as he recognized one of
his prized weapons.

Inside the securely bolted chamber, Riach smoothed Caree's
hair back from her hot, tear-stained face and vainly attempted
to ignore the clamor.

"Listen, my love, maybe if you were to tell your ferocious
young sister to go away, she'd know I wasna doing violence to
you," he suggested mischievously, kissing one salty cheek.

"You'll never want to do violence to me now that I'm so
ugly and spoiled," she sobbed.

"But I'd never want to do such a thing!" protested Riach,
frowning with confusion.

"So you do think I am spoiled and ugly!" Macaree howled,
and the crashing at the door was renewed with fervor. Riach
gaped at her. He was completely perplexed. "Let me alone!
Go away!" she wailed, struggling to free herself and opening
part of the healing gash.

"No, I won't! I love you! You're my wife!" shouted Riach,
tears of anger and frustration flooding his brown eyes.

"Then why don't you want to possess me like a man is
meant to possess a woman?" she snapped angrily. Then she
fell silent, appalled at her immodesty. She glanced fearfully up
at his face, seeing his embarrassed blush and the wetness on
his unshaven cheeks. "I'm sorry," she whispered, hanging her
head with shame. "My father said I was a whore. So did you.
Maybe you both were right."

"Goddammit! Open this door, you Campbell *mucker!*"
Kat screeched, denting the polished oak with the ivory butt of
the pistol. The Campbell's heavy hands grasped her shoulders,
spinning her around as Angus swiftly took advantage of the
opportunity to wrest his prized possession from her clasp.

"If I were you, I should also take the mate," Darach suggested, imprisoning her arms and indicating the other pistol.

"Och, I believe I shall," agreed his uncle, plucking the twin
from her belt. "And now I think our presence here is definitely superfluous. Come along, Cailleach," he added after a
shrewd evaluation of his older nephew's thunderous expression as he held his wildly struggling young wife. Kat was hissing a stream of very colorful and imaginative curses. Angus
and Cailleach Cuilleann ushered the curious cluster of mutter-

ing servants away, leaving the two dark brothers to cope with their wives.

"Och, so it takes two great bullying Campbells to disarm one puir wee lass," Kat mocked, viciously kicking and hoping to wound a vulnerable part of Darach's anatomy. She was absolutely determined to see her sister. She had spent a long, torturous night believing that she had killed Macaree before finding out that Macaree, though badly injured, was still alive. She had promised their dying mother that she would protect her siblings, and no one was going to prevent her from fulfilling her duty. "I shall see and speak with my sister!" she stated, glaring up at him with all the belligerence she could muster. "Now!" she emphasized.

Darach gazed thoughtfully into her mutinous little face. He nodded silently, noting the fear that flickered in her emerald eyes despite the bravado that blazed from them. He released her, set her firmly to one side, and tapped courteously at the door. "Be still," he warned quietly, raising an autocratic finger when he noticed her tensing to spring. She nodded tersely and leaned against the wall. Only then did he address his brother through the oak barrier. "Riach? I apologize for the rude disturbance, but my wife should like to speak with her sister. If it isna convenient, I am sure she will understand," he added after a pause; he felt her rage crackle through the charged atmosphere.

"I willna understand!" she snarled. "I willna! Open this door!" she ordered, ducking beneath his arm and cracking her small fists against the damaged wood. Darach heard the desperation and near hysteria in her voice, and he stared down at her with concern.

"Is it your delicate condition causing you to be even more unreasonable than usual?" he asked mildly, his casual tone belying his anxiety. She pointedly ignored him and continued her frantic assault on the door.

"Caree? Caree? Are you all right?" she screamed.

"No! I'm ugly and spoiled!" Macaree's muffled lament drifted through the bolted wood and into the corridor. "Oh, Kat? Kat?" she called pathetically. Kat stood poised, feeling the vibration of a heavy tread approach. Then she heard the harsh rasp of bolts being pulled back and the sharp rattle of the latch, and the door was flung open. Riach stood on the threshold, fatigued and unshaven. Gone was the golden supple youth; in his stead was an ashen, stooping older man, his clothes rumpled and soiled with fresh blood. At the gory sight, Kat was goaded into action. She gasped and pushed past him into the bedchamber.

"Caree?" she whispered, afraid to approach the bed, where her sister sat braced against the headboard, clutching the covers tightly to her neck with both hands. "Caree?" she repeated. There was no answer, and she saw that her sister was trembling violently. "Caree, are you all right?" she asked lamely, not knowing what to say. Fearfully, she approached the bed, her eyes pinned to the bright drops of red that bled through the white sheet that was drawn tautly across Macaree's heaving breasts. "Are you all right?" Her sister shook her head silently, her long tangled hair covering her face and sticking to her streaming tears. "Did Riach Campbell hurt you?" Macaree continued shaking her head, her movements gaining momentum. "Because if he did, I shall kill him! I promise you, Caree, I shall kill him!" Macaree shook her head even faster until she was flinging it from side to side in a frenzy.

"You will kill no one," sighed Darach patronizingly, as though dealing with a recalcitrant child.

"I shall do what I have to do!" Kat replied savagely. "Did you harm my sister?" she demanded loudly, turning like a vengeful inquisitor and glaring at Riach. Her own guilt for having inadvertently shot her sister gnawed in her belly.

"I love your sister," was Riach's simple reply.

"But now I am so ugly, so very ugly," Macaree lamented.

"You are beautiful," Riach countered.

"Look at me!" she commanded. With both hands she wrenched off the sheet, exposing herself to the waist.

Kat stepped back and gaped with horror at the enormous bloody gash that slashed across her sister's whiteness from her shoulder to below her cleavage, nearly bisecting the left breast.

"Och, Caree, I am so sorry . . . So very sorry," she croaked, her throat achingly restricted. "I dinna mean to hurt you. I wasna aiming at you. I was trying to save you." Riach and Darach turned together and stared with astonishment at the petite girl.

"Am I really so very, very ugly?" Macaree gasped, petrified at the horror of Kat's expression and deaf to her words. Her own sister, who usually comforted her, was backing away from her, repelled by the horrendous sight of her disfigurement.

"I was trying to shoot . . . to shoot . . . to . . ." Kat's voice trailed away. She was unable to name the Campbell chieftain's pink-and-white mistress, who was also Riach's mother. "I was just trying to shoot . . . to shoot . . . shoot . . ." she babbled. She had to somehow fill the awful ticking silence or she would drown. She was conscious of Macaree's accusing eyes burning into the core of her. "I dinna mean to shoot you!" she screamed, transported back to a nightmare time when once before she had been responsible for hurting her sister. Her father, his friends, Aggie, and Simmie had circled about the wounded Macaree, who had screamed and screamed. "I'm sorry. I dinna mean to," she mouthed, her appalled gaze fixed on the bright blood that marred her sister's white lace dress and pantalets.

Katrine's distress penetrated Macaree's self-absorption. "Shoot me?" she repeated, confusion evident on her face.

"I hurt you wie-out meaning to. I am so sorry," Kat whispered miserably. She winced and ducked when Darach expelled his breath loudly as realization dawned.

Shocked by Kat's involuntary movement to defend herself, the Campbell swore beneath his breath. He strode to the window, where he wrenched back the delicate draperies and scowled out at the tranquil order of the gardens, trying to collect his thoughts. His young wife seriously believed that she was responsible for her sister's injuries. What hell she must have writhed in during the five days and nights since Felicity's brutal attack. He swore again, misting the windowpanes with his hot breath, furious with himself for not having been aware of her dilemma. But how could he have been, when there was no communication between them? All that existed was a crackling void. When they happened to be near each other, it seemed she tried to goad him to violence, and he was equally determined that he would remain in steely control of his emotions. She was with child, his child, and he sought to keep her calm.

For the most part, she had kept to herself, locked in the pristine chamber in the east tower, choosing to eat her meals alone and take long walks in the twilit hours with her lame hound. She had made it clear that she was fully aware of the guards who followed her at a respectful distance. Her eloquent

language, more suitable to a tavern, had in no way indicated
the terrible turmoil that she was feeling. Darach had purposefully left her alone, though adequately protected from Felicity's insanity, until the murderous woman had sufficiently
healed to be removed to a more secure asylum. Then he had
planned to carry his savage bride away to Strathrannoch,
where the rugged, untamed countryside was a perfect setting
for her wild spirit.

"I wasna shot!" Macaree's voice broke through Darach's
seething recriminations.

"Not shot?" Kat echoed.

"No pistol did this," the blond girl mused sadly, gently
touching the long, jagged cut. "It was a knife. A dagger."

"Not shot?" Kat repeated, stunned. Riach moved closer to
the bed, intrigued by the exchange.

"No, I was carved like a plump pheasant," responded Macaree. She gave a watery chuckle, but her younger sister continued to stare at her incredulously.

"I'm no *bairn*. You dinna hae to spare my sensibilities,"
she stated stiffly. "I'm strong enow to deal wie whatever the
truth be."

"I am speaking the truth. Felicity had a dagger," Macaree
insisted, as Riach tenderly tucked the sheet about her nakedness. Kat was mesmerized by his brown hands against her
sister's soft white skin.

"Dinna speak that evil *saidhe*'s name!" she spat, tearing
her jealous eyes from the nurturing caresses that stirred an
unbearable aching need in her. "Och, I ken that evil bitch is
your dam, Riach Campbell, but I am not sorry for shooting at
her. I am just very sorry I dinna kill her!" She hissed viciously
before spinning on her heel and stalking out of the room. She
did not want to say anything she would live to regret. She
wanted desperately to rid herself of the pain and anger that
roiled inside her by telling Riach that his mother was his half
brother's mistress. But she knew that such an outburst would
create pain and embarrassment for Macaree and her husband.
The Campbell chieftain, whom she really longed to wound,
would remain unscathed. He'd probably not be the least
disconcerted about the airing of such a fact. Instead, he'd be
proud of his virility. He was no better than her father, no better than a barnyard rooster strutting amid his harem of hens.
Her small bare feet slapped against the polished stone flags of
the castle corridor as she put as much distance as she could

between herself and the imposing dark man.

When Kat stormed out of the room, Macaree whimpered with distress and struggled against Riach's cradling arms.

"I maun go to her. She's hurting. She dinna mean to speak so irreverently against your mother." She sobbed, collapsing against his strong chest, appalled by her sister's crude bluntness. "We were not raised to be so rude. She forgot herself and dinna ken what she was saying." Darach raised a wry eyebrow at the girl's anguish over Kat's lack of etiquette. It was not an opportune time to worry about such trivialities, he mused.

"Hush, my darling," Riach crooned. "She dinna say anything I havena thought myself," he admitted, rubbing his bristly cheek against her silky hair and kissing her ear.

Darach knew that his presence in the pink bedchamber was impolitic, but he lingered there, fascinated by the strength and honesty of his young half brother.

"But she shouldna say such terrible things aloud. She knows better, truly she does," Macaree complained. "And no matter what the provocation, she knows that no well-bred young lady should go about shooting people," she continued. Darach shook his head in amazement.

"It wasna your sister who shot my mother, but me," confessed Riach.

"You shot your own mother!?"

"When I saw she meant to harm you, my love, I had no other choice."

"Oh, Riach!" cried Macaree, bursting into a fresh flood of tears and burrowing into her young husband's chest.

"Actually, it is nearly impossible to ascertain which of the two of you managed to hit the unfortunate female," the Campbell interjected dryly. He privately held the opinion that his savage bride was by far the more superior shot. But he did not want to damage his sibling's newfound sense of masculinity.

"But what's going to happen to my sister?" wailed Macaree.

"Dinna *fash* yourself about my reckless wife. She is my concern. I shall deal wie her." Darach sighed, scowling ruefully at the cozily entwined couple on the bed. He was more than a little envious of the loving, albeit soggy, trust that was evident between the two.

"Oh, dinna be too angry wie her. She doesna ken. 'Tis just

that she is used to being . . . to being." Macaree's pleading stopped. She was too embarrassed to continue.

"Aye?" coaxed the Campbell, poised in the doorway with his large hand on the handle. "She is too used to being . . . what?" he urged when she didn't speak. Macaree shook her head mutely. He was so tall and formidable, looming on the threshold of the dainty bedchamber, that he appeared to dwarf everything. She was afraid for her petite sister. "My wife is too used to being . . . what?"

"Too used to being in charge," Macaree stated bravely, her voice squeaking with the effort. Riach clasped her tightly, shaking with uncontrollable laughter.

"Och, big brother, I wouldna trade places wie you for all your titles and lands," he howled. "Och, the marriage of two people who are both used to being in charge!" He saw that Darach was not amused. Riach tried to stem his bubbling mirth, but it was too much of an effort. The thunderous expression on his big brother's face served to increase his laughter. "I'm sorry, but I dinna think your marriage promises much . . . much . . ." The door was pointedly slammed, and Darach strode away in search of his wife.

"Promises much what?" queried Macaree after his merriment had abated and he lay sighing happily with her in his arms.

"Promises much harmony," he answered with a chuckle.

"I wish for harmony in our marriage," she said wistfully after a long pause.

"And what else?" he asked, softly tracing her aristocratic nose and well-shaped mouth.

"Gentleness and . . . gentility. Serenity and music. Prettiness and the fragrance of flowers—in fact, everything that Duncreag epitomizes," she said pensively, shivering at the thought of the stench and decay of Linnmanach. "I want our children to be safe and loved, playing on the soft, nurtured lawns, with no dark shadows or cloying cobwebs from the past to frighten and ensnare them."

"And they shall, my darling," Riach promised.

Kat glowered resentfully at the manicured gardens of Duncreag, feeling harnessed and confined by the neat arrangement of flower beds and clipped hedges. She wanted to scream and disturb the strict order, but instead she gazed longingly away into the distance to the snow-capped rugged mountains that rose majestically above the treetops. Her sad eyes followed a hawk that spiraled higher and higher and then appeared to drift idly with the air currents. She watched breathlessly, waiting for him to stoop upon his prey. She yearned for such unfettered freedom.

Robbie's complaints and the clatter of hooves brought Kat down to earth, and she hurried to the stableyard in time to see him mounted on a plump, piebald pony.

"Och, Uncle Angus, this fat *baistie* is a wee *bairn*'s steed. 'Tis more fit for a vaporous female. 'Tis an embarrassment to be so poorly mounted. You said I was near a mon," he grumbled petulantly. Kat smiled, recalling a time when he had fervently clung to his little pony, terrified of a larger horse, much to their father's derisive fury.

"Aye, you're near a mon, but 'tis best to take things a wee bit at a time. Today the chubby sholtie, and maybe tomorrow the old gray nag, and soon you'll be astride a winged stallion," chortled Angus.

"It's bloody humiliating to be riding such a miserable creature," the boy lamented gracelessly.

"Now, dinna be hurtin' the puir animal's feelings," Angus chided good-naturedly. "Och, look who's come to see us off on our way," he added cheerfully, doffing his hat at Kat as she stepped into the yard.

"Good morning," she said politely, before turning to her brother and gesturing for him to stop. "Robbie! I need a few words wie you!" she shouted, but the boy glared furiously at her and roughly tugged at the reins, yanking the pony about. He drummed his booted heels into the plump girth, and the pony lumbered away. His rude rejection stung and Kat stood motionless, fighting to control her raw emotions as hot blinding tears welled in her eyes. Angus looked down compassionately from *auld* MacGhee's stalwart back, searching for comforting words, but before he could attempt to voice them, the girl had angrily dashed away the salty evidence and was glowering up at him, as though daring him to make a sound. He silently nodded his understanding, and, allowing her the dignity she mutely demanded, he cantered away, determined to catch up with the truculent youth and severely reprimand him for his uncouth behavior.

Kat gazed after the two riders, feeling very abandoned. Gone was the dear little boy who had once regarded her with such love and worshipful trust. He was now a hostile stranger.

It had been Macaree who had chosen to stand apart in her own, safe little world of nursery rhymes. Now she was the one alone, but not out of choice. What had happened to change everything? Maybe her little brother was growing to manhood. When she had returned to Linnmanach to find him living at the gatehouse with Riach, his loyalty had already switched to the younger Campbell. Now at Duncreag it was the older Campbell who had become his mentor. Once she had held that exalted position, she recalled sadly. Now her brother pointedly ignored her, as though fervently guarding himself from her influence. Several times she had crept to his bedchamber, determined to discuss plans with him, but he wouldn't listen. No amount of logic, cajoling, or threats swayed him. No matter how rosy the picture she painted of a country where they could use their clan name without fear of reprisal, he remained adamant. He wanted to stay at Duncreag with Angus.

From a distance, Kat had watched the older Campbell and the blond youth together, and she had to acknowledge grudgingly the rightness of the bond that existed between the two. At last Robbie had the strong father whom they all had been denied. At that realization, she felt lonelier and more afraid than ever before. The closer the bond, the more painful their departure would be, and they had to leave Scotland; their MacGregor lives depended on it. Would Robbie ever understand? Or was she destined to be hated?

Lost in her brooding thoughts, Kat was unaware of the Campbell's approach until his tall shadow fell across her. She shivered, oppressed by the weight of his presence. She knew who it was without turning.

"My uncle has hired a tutor for your brother," he stated conversationally, knowing why she gazed so forlornly down the bridle path through the orchard. He had watched the exchange and had seen Robbie's curt rejection. "A personable young man, not a dry old Latin relic who'd bore the curiosity out of the boy," he continued. She made no sign that she had heard him.

"We dinna need your charity, Lord Rannoch," she stated witheringly.

"Och, yes, you do, Lady Rannoch," he parried, running an idle finger along the curve of her stubborn jaw. "You need every vestige of charity I can muster."

"We shall see about that!" she retorted, jerking away from him, as though burned.

"Aye, we shall see because it is becoming increasingly difficult to have any charity. You, my vixen, would try the patience of a saint."

"And you regard yourself as a saint?" she jeered acidly.

"Far from it," he countered roguishly.

"If you will excuse me?" she said with an excess of civility, sensing danger in his lounging nonchalance. He reminded her of a soaring hawk, seeming to float lazily on the wind currents, though his sharp, predatory eyes were ever alert.

"But I will not excuse you," he objected, reaching out in one swift movement and grasping her forearm. Kat curbed her fiery temper with a long, contemptuous sigh, tolerating his touch with obvious distaste and tapping one bare foot in intense irritation.

"Well?" she was goaded to ask after a ticking silence. She waited in vain for him to explain why he had detained her. "Well?" she repeated, keeping her eyes unfocused on her tapping foot. The silence yawned. She summoned her courage and glared challengingly up at him, only to be unnerved by the twinkling humor in the silver eyes. "What is it you want?" she rasped, trying to disguise her bewilderment at his playful tenderness.

"What is it I want?" he murmured huskily, letting his gaze slowly and impudently caress her tense body. He raised a wicked eyebrow and grinned suggestively into her upturned face, enjoying her evident discomfort.

Kat didn't trust herself to speak. His deep voice sent tremulous thrills coursing through her, and she wrenched her gaze from his compelling features, trying to still her wildly racing heart, only to focus on the orchard where he had first possessed her. She smelled the warm musk of the ripening fruits, which intensified the bittersweet need that ached within her. His large brown hand still grasped her slim arm, and she could feel a hot pulse radiating from his touch, streaking to the soft core of her.

Darach was by no means insensitive to the powerful tension that crackled between them. He had never wanted to claim a woman as much as he did the petite, dark girl who stubbornly refused to look at him. He, too, was painfully conscious of the seductive aroma of the maturing fruits, and he achingly recalled that springtime passion. He resisted the temptation to caress her flushed cheek, fearing he would lose all control. Soon he would have all the time he needed, free from interference and interruption.

Darach firmly set Kat away from him, releasing her arm and rubbing his palms together, as if to erase the very feel of her.

"The scullery maid, Morag, whom it seems you have taken a liking to, is packing your gowns," he stated brusquely. "And as soon as Felicity is safely dispatched to Edinburgh, we shall be on our way to Strathrannoch."

Felicity's name had the same effect as a pail of icy water, successfully dousing her smoldering ardor. Kat fought against her overwhelming desire to spin about and slap the Campbell's autocratic face, calling him every foul name she knew. She kept her furious eyes pinned to the rustling leaves of the orchard as she vowed never to weaken again. How dare the pompous man callously dispose of one mistress and have the gall to expect her to be waiting? Was she a mistreated bitch, fawning and cowering, so devoid of pride and so hungry for love that she would consent to such treatment in return for a few crumbs of affection? And they would not even be crumbs of affection, but dregs of lust. What was the matter with her? Despite years of fervent resolutions to the contrary, she was behaving like her mother.

"Morag is packing my gowns?" she intoned, not daring to look at him.

"Aye, Morag is packing your gowns," he affirmed, conscious of her sudden change and instinctively on his guard. The passion that had smoldered less than a minute before had been extinguished; in its place was frigid calculation.

"So Morag is packing my gowns." Kat sighed, feeling in enough control of herself to turn and face him. "Then I should go and help dear Morag," she added sweetly. "So if you'd be so kind as to excuse me?" she asked, her emerald eyes wide and guileless. Darach nodded stiffly, his own eyes narrowing with speculation.

Darach watched Kat mincing sedately into the castle, knowing that he was being mocked and that she indubitably planned mischief. He longed to detain her forcibly, plying her with kisses and caresses until she melted in his arms and became one with him. How he missed the fiery sweetness of their union! He regretted that their savage embraces would have to wait just a little while longer until he had taken care of Felicity.

"Felicity," he groaned aloud, not enjoying the prospect of another encounter with his stepmother, even though it promised to be the last. Since her son's rejection, when Riach had chosen his bride and left his mother to bleed on the croquet lawn, the unfortunate woman had lost her tenuous hold on reality. She had become helplessly infantile, totally dependent, unable to talk, walk, and feed herself. No matter what spiteful destruction she had caused, it was horrendous to see the once beautiful woman crawling about in soiled rags, babbling incoherently as food drooled from her slack mouth. Maybe she had regressed to a time of innocence, he mused, for the first time feeling compassion for the devious, manipulative female who had been responsible for so much pain and turmoil in his life.

Darach cast a regretful glance up at the east tower and caught a glimpse of Kat before she ducked out of sight. He grinned mischievously, knowing that she must have quickened her sedate walk to an inelegant scamper to have reached her bedchamber so swiftly. His smile broadened as he fondly imagined her fleet progress up the steep stone steps and the sinuous movement of her flanks under the tight trews. Well, it wouldn't be long before he could take her away to his ancestral home of Strathrannoch, he comforted himself, curbing his lusty impatience. He'd take her there by force if need be, he amended grimly, losing his humor as a ballgown of French lace that he had ordered especially for her at great expense was savagely flung from her window. It sailed incongruously across the topiary garden, the full skirt belling gracefully in the morning breeze. It was followed by a motley assortment of shoes, nightwear, undergarments, and brushes.

"So much for *puir* Morag's packing." He sighed resignedly.

chapter 27

Kat scowled out the carriage window, impervious to the wild beauty of the passing countryside as she tried desperately to channel her rising terror into a cold, calculating rage. She was irritated by the monotonous lumbering pace, and her smoldering eyes fixed unwaveringly on the Campbell's chiseled profile as he rode leisurely beside her on Iolair. She cursed herself for her rash impulse in allowing him to believe her pregnant. If not for that lie, she would be riding a horse, and in a much better position to make her escape, she fumed. If only she had both a horse and her hound, she wouldn't feel so alone. But Sian had been left behind at Duncreag, and for all she knew, Etalon was still in the hidden glen by the cave. Kat was in a quandary, and she fought against the waves of panic that threatened to submerge her completely. She tugged the itchy blanket about her nakedness, feeling perspiration sting her chafed skin. They had been traveling at a painfully slow pace since before daybreak, and now the afternoon sun cruelly blazed down upon the roof of the stuffy carriage, as no protection was afforded by the treeless moor.

"That bloody Campbell is trying to roast us alive," she muttered, consigning him to the fiery pits of purgatory in very unladylike language.

"There's cool wine and water," the drab maid sitting opposite her suggested timidly. "Maybe you should eat something, laik his lordship suggested?''

"Like his lordship suggested?'' Kat attacked. "Like his bloody lordship suggested! That rutting whoremonger dinna suggest! He *ordered!*''

"Hush!'' Morag squeaked, turning fearful eyes to her master, who rode beside them.

"Och, the very next village we pass through, I hae a guid mind to leap naked from this vehicle,'' Kat declared vehemently. The little maid's eyes widened with alarm before she hurriedly concentrated on her embroidery, only to stab her trembling fingers and bleed copiously over the white linen that she was decorating. "Well, Morag Glennie, what do you think of a mon who abducts a pregnant woman against her will and strips her as bare as the moment of birth, so she canna escape his lecherous clutches?'' Kat challenged, hoping to inspire outrage in the timorous little maid and somehow gain an ally.

"But he's your husband.''

"Not by the kirk!''

"Declaration is binding,'' Morag whispered unhappily, bending studiously over her sewing.

"Whether the bastard is my husband or not, he doesna have the right to tear me from my only family and carry me off against my will!'' spat Kat, feeling dangerously close to tears. "He dinna even allow me to make my farewells, but stole me away in the dark of night. My own sister . . . my little brother . . . it isna right,'' she said angrily.

"A mon can do wha'ever he wants wie his ain wife,'' the maid piously stated. "My puir mither was beat black and blue just aboot every day of the week, and usually twice on Saturdays.''

"And you think that's right!'' exclaimed Kat, horrified by her matter-of-fact disclosure.

" 'Taint one of those things a person thinks aboot. 'Taint wrong or right but . . . just so. Canna do nothin' aboot it. 'Tis laik night and day, sun and the moon, just so,'' answered the maid with an awkward shrug of her thin shoulders. "You maybe should thank your lucky stars tha' his lordship ain't laik my da.''

"Well, he's just like mine, the rutting, pox-ridden, whoremonger!'' Kat cursed. Once more the meek maid peered anxiously out at her master for fear that he'd heard his wife's insults.

"You wouldna really jump oot his carriage wie-out a stitch

on, would you?" asked Morag after a long, brooding silence. She was vainly attempting to untangle her damp, knotted embroidery silk, but she only managed to make it worse.

"Nay." Kat sighed ruefully. "I'd nae trust that great bully. It would be just like him to turn it to his advantage and parade me about naked like some wretched creature he has just purchased."

"Och, his lordship isna like tha'. He'd nae do such a thing."

"If he'd nae do such a thing, then where are my clothes, Morag Glennie?" Kat charged triumphantly, hoping that she had finally won the diffident girl to her side. Morag shrugged miserably and didn't answer. "If his lordship isna like that, then why am I being dragged across the breadth of Scotland as naked as the day I was born?"

"If you dinna mind me sayin' so, your ladyship, it was you yourself who wouldna put your clothes on," the girl whispered bravely, sinking back into the soft upholstery and anticipating Kat's fury.

"It was the middle of the night. I was asleep. I dinna expect to be dragged from my bed!"

"You cut up all those beautiful gowns," Morag lamented. "Threw some out of the window, even," she continued mournfully. "Such bonny, bonny things."

"Whore's clothes! Fussy frills and flounces!"

"Och, tha' elegant traveling dress of velvet, the selfsame color as your pretty eyes, all cut up into weeny pieces and thrown to the four winds," the girl remarked enviously, staring down at the drab brown of her frock and smoothing the coarse nubbed material. "All them lovely, lovely clothes his lordship bought for you."

"He canna buy me wie such trappings!" Kat shouted defensively, feeling ashamed of the waste. She fortified herself with the memory of the expensive presents that her father had showered upon his many mistresses, while his family had huddled together, cold and hungry. "But if 'tis pretty clothes you want, Morag Glennie, take anything you wish, for I'll not accept anything from that foul Campbell *muc*, except my freedom!"

"Dinna speak so loud; he'll hear you calling him a pig," cautioned Morag fearfully.

"I dinna care a tinker's fart if he hears me or not," Kat retorted crudely. It was imperative that she escape. Perhaps if she completely disgusted him—shamed him in front of the coachmen and outriders—he would be relieved to be rid of her. "Darach Campbell kens that he's a filthy, rutting *muc*, but I'm no doxy to be bought wie his trinkets and baubles!" she screeched, scouring her seething, frightened brain for other choice epithets and fueling her anger with thoughts of Felicity. "Filthy *muc!* De'il's dung!" Her small nostrils flared with savage satisfaction as she noted the tightening of his lean cheek, but in no other way did he acknowledge her insults. "The son of a *sassanach saidhe* comes crawling drunkenly into my bed drenched wie the stench of an Edinburgh bawdy house!" she continued wildly. Morag Glennie gasped and sank even farther into the soft leather upholstery, desperately trying to seem invisible.

"Och, my ladyship, now you've gone and done it," she keened when the rumbling chatter of the coachmen ceased. The silence was ominous. All that existed was the steady trundle of wheels and the muted rhythm of the hooves. All eyes except Kat's stared expectantly at the tall dark man on the golden stallion.

"If the lecherous *mucker* doesna care to hear my opinion of his base character, he kens just what he can do about it," Kat goaded recklessly, using the awed hush to her own advantage.

"Och, please, please, please, I beg you dinna rile his lordship mair. 'Tis said he has a wicked temper—not often shown but *meikle* wicked when raised." Poor Morag whimpered, wishing that she had the courage to hide under the seat.

Kat rolled her eyes disdainfully, showing how very unimpressed she was to hear about her husband's temper, but her heart lurched in panic when the carriage came to a sudden jarring halt and the door was wrenched open. She managed to smother a squeal of fright at being unceremoniously hauled out of the dim, stuffy interior into the hot, blinding sunlight. She concentrated on keeping the woollen blanket clutched modestly about herself, and on walking with some vestige of dignity. She was very conscious of the gawking array of servants as the Campbell roughly propelled her toward a concealing cairn.

"I wager four pints of porter tha' his lordship's going to flay her naked backside," chuckled one of the men.

"Aye, *bairn* or no *bairn*," another agreed.

"Aye, a man can only taik so much of a woman's mouth."

"I'd do worse if'n tha' was my wife," another chimed in.

Kat flushed scarlet upon overhearing their words, but she raised her chin haughtily. She stubbed her bare toes painfully on the hot rocky ground as she tried to keep up with Darach's long strides. Out of earshot of the carriage and the cluster of horsemen, he stopped, his hard fingers still digging into her shoulders. He took several deep, shuddering breaths, trying to control his fury. His silver eyes icily scanned her face.

"Hae you no breeding?" he demanded finally.

"You ken only too well that I hae no breeding," she responded, sneering scornfully into his thunderous face.

"Then I shall hae to give you some," he threatened.

"Put your mark on me," she dared. "It'll do no guid! Och, aye, you can hurt me. You're twice my height and weight, so you can easily break my bones and bruise my flesh, but you canna make me what I am not," she stated derisively. "Except maybe dead," she added thoughtfully.

"Why do you want me to beat you?" asked Darach. "Do you want a sound thrashing? Is that what your vulgar display has been about?" he added cuttingly. She glared at him silently, not knowing what to say.

"I want nothing from you," Kat spat finally, feeling that she was losing ground, and clinging desperately to her rage. "But my freedom!"

"Then you'd better listen to me and pay close attention, or you'll receive a bloody sight more," snapped Darach. "You are my wife, Katherine Campbell, whether you like it or no, and I'll not have my clan name sullied and disgraced by your outrageous behavior," he continued, his voice low and dangerous.

"Your name is already sullied and disgraced with the filthy, murderous deeds of your clan!" she responded belligerently.

"I am responsible for my own actions, not those of my ancestors," Darach stated stiffly, willing his mounting rage to diminish. "The massacre of Glencoe happened long before either of us was born. I regret that it happened, but I canna do anything to change that sorrowful episode in history. I am deeply sorry for what happened to your clansmen, the MacIans, at the hands of my forebears, but canna we bridge that hatred?" he pleaded. He softened his tone and his touch, and his fingers caressed her tense shoulders. "It increases bitterness and does no good to live so entrenched in the sadness of the past," he added after she refused to answer. She stared stubbornly across the heather-covered moor toward the gray mountains that soared to meet and meld with the shimmering heat of the sky.

"Have you quite finished wie your chastisement?" she asked coldly, not daring to look at him for fear of weakening. Such an enormous lie yawned between them, too enormous ever to be bridged. What would he do when he found out that she was not a MacIan, but a MacGregor? What would happen to Macaree? What would happen to Rob Roy?

"If you canna think of yourself wie any respect, at least consider your unborn child," he clipped angrily, his face contorted with barely suppressed rage, and his fingers once again dug uncomfortably into her soft flesh. "For I gie you fair warning, Kat Campbell. If you indulge in any more vulgar tantrums, I shall not remove you to a discreet distance to patiently scold, but I shall administer the thrashing that you seem to be begging for—and in front of the very people you would use to humiliate me! Do you ken?" Kat nodded curtly, wishing an end to the blistering encounter. "Do you ken?" he insisted, not content with her silent assent. He savagely needed to bend her defiant will by hearing her voice. This would somehow prove to him that he had some control over the little hellion. There ensued a long crackling silence during which Darach refused to repeat his command, and Kat's mouth remained stubbornly closed. Gray and green eyes clashed without blinking. Beads of perspiration gathered on Kat's mutinous face. They trickled in muddied rivulets down her flushed cheeks, matting the unruly tendrils of ebony hair. They disappeared beneath the coarse blanket, burning a prickly channel between her small breasts. She kept her rebellious gaze pinned to his searing eyes, and to her horror, she recognized the intimate sparks of love lights pulsing deep within their molten depths. The furious intensity of his censorous glare had been magically transformed, sending an aching need tingling through her taut body. The thin cruel line of his lips had subtly softened to a seductive curl, and an intoxicating male musk whirled her senses. Involuntarily, she arched toward him.

"For the sake of our unborn child, let us heal the breach between us?" he murmured hoarsely, noting her labored breathing which puffed out of her parted lips. He pulled her relentlessly toward him, craving the feel of her litheness. Kat struggled against the surge of traitorous emotions. Suddenly, she understood the terrible battle that her mother had lost. She would not be so debased. She could not kiss him and ignore the taste of other women on his lips.

"There is no child!" she shouted angrily, summoning all her strength and hitting out at him with the only weapon he afforded her. "Do you really believe I'd let a bastard Campbell seed grow in my womb?" she cried savagely, desperately taking advantage of his stunned inertia to tear free of his grip.

"No *bairn?*" he repeated. She was appalled by the swift change of expression. He became a looming, menacing stranger. He showed no emotion whatsoever—no humanity, no anger, no pain. His finely hewn features seemed like a mask, hard and impenetrable, like the gray outcroppings of weathered granite that dotted the stark landscape. His eyes were hooded and as icy as a descending hawk's when it mercilessly stooped upon its prey.

Kat backed away, knowing she had gone too far, but he relentlessly advanced until her spine was pressed against the sharp, jagged cairn. The balanced boulders seesawed and shifted, raining loose shale and dirt, and she feared she would be crushed and buried alive.

"There is no *bairn?*" he coldly repeated. Kat shook her head, waiting for the blows to descend, but the granite blocks resettled and the Campbell chieftain just loomed before her, making no effort to touch her. He kept her imprisoned by his shadow.

Darach felt mortal terror streak through him, weakening his limbs as he recalled Missie MacKissock's stories about his mother's many miscarriages before the miracle of his birth. And his arrival had killed his poor mother, allowing her finally to rest in peace. He glared down into Kat's mutinous face, searching for an answer. He knew her fierce independence. She had endured unspeakable agony alone, believing that she had killed her own sister. Had the stiff-necked little vixen suffered even further by losing their child in the isolation of the east tower? Had she writhed in pain, too willful and proud to cry out for help?

"Did you miscarry?" he asked, his harsh clipped tone concealing his concern. Again she shook her head, the sweat-dampened hair whipping her hot cheeks.

"There never was a child," she proclaimed huskily, making a desperate attempt to be victorious and contemptuous. "I lied!"

"Then I maun remedy that," he stated, brutally grasping

her small chin and wrenching her face upward, forcing her to look at him. She fought her inclination to close her eyes and instead met his scathing glare without flinching.

Darach could almost smell her fear, yet she made no sound, nor did she soften her arrogant little features. Only her eyes betrayed her. Deep in the unfathomable emerald depths, he saw the frightened waif of the Parisian back streets. He battled against the compassion that threatened to temper his wrath, yearning to bend her to his will, aching to break her defiant independence by savagely claiming her on the parched earth of the barren moor, yet he knew that by surrendering to such primitive tactics he would lose her forever.

Every muscle and sinew in Kat's body was taut with anticipation, waiting, almost hoping for the violence to be unleashed. It was that breathless, simmering suspension before a storm. She was poised, reveling in the gathering rumbles. Long, tense moments passed, and then he suddenly released her and stalked away. The sun blazed down on her upturned face, but she still felt his hard fingers digging into her jawbone, forcing her to look into the thunderous shadows of his rage. She closed her burning eyes as a cold desolation shivered through her.

The rasp of his boots caused her to turn and gaze after him, and she noted with detachment the clenched fists that swung beside his long legs and saw the constant ticking in his lean brown cheek. He was still in suspension, still building toward an explosion. She forced herself to try to think rationally. Was he going to mount up and gallop away, leaving her unclothed and unarmed on the vast wasteland? Why didn't the thought make her happy? It was what she had carefully contrived, yet the prospect was bleak and she wondered dully about her ability to survive. She watched the rigid lines of his stiffly held shoulders and the play of strong muscles across the span of his broad back, remembering the hard, satiny feel of his flesh beneath her splayed palms. She angrily tried to eradicate the sensuous reminiscences. He strode away from her without a backward glance, and she spat contemptuously on the crumbly earth. Did he expect her to run after him, tugging at his clothes, weeping and begging for forgiveness? A weak, loathsome part of her longed to do just that, and she sneered disdainfully, hating herself and refusing to contemplate such a form of humiliation.

It wasn't until the Campbell was out of sight that Kat abandoned her rebellious stance and sank dejectedly onto the parched earth. She huddled in the shadow of the cairn, burying her muddled raw emotions beneath muffling layers, waiting for the vibrations of the departing horses and carriage to jar through her. She sighed and vaguely wished that she had swallowed some of her pride and accepted the offer of clothes, food, and water. She did not look forward to the long, arduous trek back to Rob Roy and Sian. The last village she remembered passing through—if, indeed, five tiny *clachans* and a mill could be called a village—had been more than ten miles on the other side of the endless moor. She gazed in each direction and was not able to locate a trace of civilization. There was not a croft or a wall in sight; there was not even a stray sheep cropping the coarse, sparse vegetation. The only signs of life were some lazily circling buzzards high above in the hot summer sky. Even if she reached a house or a farm, what good would it do her? She had no coins and no personal property—nothing except a sweaty blanket to trade for more appropriate clothing, some food, and a ride.

"Your ladyship?" Morag's timid voice pierced through Kat's numb glumness. "Are you all right, your ladyship?" inquired the maid, staggering toward her and lugging a small trunk. "His lordship says as how he thinks maybe you might've changed your mind aboot wearing . . . clothes," she explained awkwardly, stopping several yards from her mistress, deterred by her woeful expression and the dispirited slump of her shoulders. In all the time she had known the unconventional wife of the Campbell chieftain, she had never seen her so despondent. "Did he gie you a terrible *skelping?*" she asked, overcome with curiosity. She decided that the muddy streaks on Kat's cheeks were caused by tears, even though she and the rest of the entourage had vainly strained their ears to hear her frantic wails and screams. "Och, my puir lady, did he hurt you bad?" she probed, thinking of the avid wagering that had taken place. "Are you all right?" she whined, unnerved by her mistress's silence. "His lordship says as how I maun gie you this," she stated, edging closer and holding out the small trunk. "Shall I put it doon, then?" The huddled girl made no move to take it from her. "Here it be, then," Morag chattered unhappily, placing it carefully on the ground, then hovering uncertainly, her feet kicking the earth, filling the air with choking powder.

Kat sighed, irritated by the jerky nervous movements. She gazed balefully at the trunk, loath to touch it. But she knew that if she was to survive, she needed more than a blanket. Maybe she should pretend to be a contrite, obedient wife, biding her time until she had accumulated enough resources to escape.

"Go back to the carriage," she said, waving away the nail-biting maid. She did not want a witness to her debasement as she was forced to swallow her pride and wear the Campbell's clothes.

"I canna," muttered Morag, not removing her fingers from her mouth. She shuffled her feet more frantically until Kat was forced to stand, choking in the cloud of dust. "I canna. His lordship says as how I maun stay wie you . . . be a lady's maid . . . help you dress and tha' if'n you dinna hurry he'd . . . he'd . . ."

"He'd what?" snapped Kat.

"He'd be a lady's maid hisself, and you maun ken he's in a *meikle* evil temper," Morag wailed. "And if'n I dinna do as he says, maybe he'll *skelp* me, too, and leave me oot here in this awful place and—"

"Open the trunk, then," Kat interrupted, unable to deal with her rising hysteria. Morag's fingers dropped away from her mouth, and she snuffled noisily as she scurried to obey. She squatted on the ground, carefully wiped her hands on her bodice, then unhasped the gleaming brass latches of the blue leather trunk.

"Ooh, your ladyship!" The awed girl gasped, rocking back on her heels and gaping at the contents. "Ooh, your ladyship! Och, I havena ever in all my born days seen such fine . . . fineness," she gushed.

"What the hell is it?" snapped Kat, unable to see past the girl, and reluctant to show any curiosity.

"Fit for a queen, it is. Och, 'tis the most beautiful, beautiful fineness tha' my two eyes hae ever seen," she declared rapturously. "But I dinna ken wha' his lordship means by it, 'specially in this wild place in the middle of nowhere."

"What the hell is it?" repeated Kat, refusing to lower herself by approaching the trunk.

"Look," invited Morag, waving her hands and shaking her head, overcome by emotion.

"For God's sake, take it out and show me!"

"Och, I canna touch it! 'Tis much too fine," Morag replied indignantly. "Would nae be right to touch it. 'Tis like it's holy."

Unable to contain herself, Kat approached the open trunk and gazed down in absolute horror at the contents. It was a formal wedding gown of delicate filigree lace. Its tiny iridescent seed pearls seemed to wink derisively in the smoldering heat, hard and silver, like the sardonic glint of the Campbell's gray eyes.

"Nay! Nay! You canna kill it laik the others!" Morag screeched, behaving in a most uncharacteristic way. She roughly pushed her mistress to one side and snatched up the wedding gown. "You'll nae murder this'n by cutting it up in teeny-weeny bits!" she screamed, clutching the gown to her thin breasts as though it were a baby. "Och, I can see the murderous expression on your face, but you canna kill it. Please dinna kill it," she begged.

Kat glared at the exquisite lace-and-pearl creation as boiling fury pulsed through her body. Did the Campbell really believe that she was so desperate to be clothed that she would agree to wear the wedding gown and be dragged to Strathrannoch as the captive virgin bride? Never, she resolved, staring frantically in each direction, hoping to find a way out of her dilemma. The vast, inhospitable wasteland stretched into the distance, offering her no answer.

"His lordship probably wants to introduce you to the staff at Strathrannoch Castle as his bride, maybe laik a tradition?" Morag chattered, backing away from her enraged mistress and still protectively cradling the wedding dress. Kat glowered fiercely at the dress and the accompanying pristine accessories that still resided in the satin-lined trunk. When, where, for whom had the Campbell bought this ludicrous, virginal costume? The image of Felicity's pink-and-white countenance mocked her, and the frothy intimate underwear further infuriated her as her perfidious mind conjured up a vision of large brown hands gently touching the silken pantalets and petticoats, tenderly holding the sensuous scraps of hose and mischievous garters. Unconsciously, she made a feral growling sound deep in her throat as she advanced toward Morag, her green eyes flashing dangerously. Then they narrowed with speculation at the contrast of drab homespun and delicate lace.

"Och, please hae mercy, your ladyship! I beg you hae

mercy!'' the maid pleaded pathetically, as though begging for her very life. "You canna harm it. You canna!" She sobbed, her grubby bitten fingers lovingly caressing the expensive material. She was defending a dream that she had dreamed since she was a tiny child, a dream that her mother and grandmother had had before her, an impossible dream for the Glennie family, crowded together in their small croft with the dirt floor. They hadn't even had enough money for a spare frock for Sundays or funerals, let alone a special one that was only good for a marriage ceremony. The Glennie girls, all eight of them, had to be content with a change of apron or a wildflower plucked from the hedgerow. To be a bride in a glorious flowing white gown was a fantasy for Morag and her seven sisters. One by one they had fled the abysmal poverty of the croft and their father's drunken brutality by going into service or else escaping with the first man who would have them, no matter how old or toothless. "You canna kill it!" Morag sobbed, her muddy tears drizzling onto her cherished bundle. " 'Tis the most beautiful gown in the whole wide world. You canna kill it. I'll do anything, anything, but dinna harm it."

"Take off your clothes," ordered Kat.

"Take off my clothes?" Morag repeated after a long stunned pause.

"Aye, and hurry yourself," Kat directed, immodestly dropping her blanket. She was completely naked.

"Nay!" the incensed maid shouted. "I canna take off my clothes. 'Tisna proper!"

"Morag Glennie, if you dinna take these clothes off this minute, I'll tear tha' disgusting wedding dress into wee pieces and wipe the ground wie it!" she threatened savagely.

Impatient to resume the journey, Darach remounted Iolair. More then twenty minutes had elapsed since the timorous maid had trudged behind the cairn. He smiled mirthlessly, imagining Kat's reaction to the virginal bridal wear. She had a choice: either accept the fact that she was his wife, or to ride into the courtyard of Strathrannoch clad solely in a blanket. She had no alternative but to wear the gown that marked her as his bride. He felt victorious, confident that he had won the battle of wills without having to resort to the violence that she fanned in him. He gazed across the scrubby moorland, anticipating her appearance as a demure bride. He cursed his gullibility in believing her to be pregnant. But for that lie, they could have been at Strathrannoch hours ago. With her supposedly delicate condition in mind, he had planned a long circuitous route at a sedate pace. Now that there was no need for chivalrous consideration, he would take the rugged trails he much preferred and hope to reach his ancestral home within two hours.

Darach resisted the temptation to gallop to the cairn and forcibly collect his wife. He tempered his impatience, looking away from the shimmering heat of the moor and staring at the sparkling peaks of the distant mountains. He was aware of the sound of stumbling feet coming closer, and then he heard a sudden loud gasp. It seemed that all the members of his company had expelled their breath at the same time, and he grinned with satisfaction. He believed that the sight of his rebellious wife forced to submission, dutifully dressed as a virginal bride, had caused the audible sound of surprise. He savored the moment as he continued to stare toward Strathrannoch, but then he felt every eye pinned on him in coiled anticipation. The hair on his neck prickled, and for a few moments he was afraid to turn around, fearing that his impossible spouse was totally naked.

"Well?" her voice rang out challengingly. He set his expression on bored lines, preparing himself for anything and deciding whatever the provocation, he would not give her the satisfaction of a reaction.

Kat strode triumphantly toward him, feeling that she had managed to salvage some vestige of her tattered dignity. Poor Morag sniveled and cowered behind her victorious mistress, trying to be invisible despite the very conspicuous wedding dress, complete with jeweled tiara and flowing veil. It was the supreme moment that Morag had dreamed about, but it felt as if she was in the midst of a terrible nightmare. She could not stand tall. Instead, she hunched over, her sweaty hands clutching the beautiful flowing skirts, bunching them gracefully for fear that they would be soiled by the ground. She was alone. No handsome beau stood beside her promising to love and cherish her. And there was no kirk, just a frightening barren wilderness.

"Well?" repeated Kat. Giving an exultant chuckle, she posed smugly in Morag's shapeless, homespun frock. She brazenly lifted the drab skirts, exposing a long, lithe expanse of bare leg, impudently showing that she had also rejected the silken underclothes. "Is there anything you wish to say to me, your lordship?'' she asked, placing one hand audaciously on a thrusting hip in a saucy imitation of a common bawd, goading him to respond. She was thrillingly conscious of every eye, and she reveled in her moment of supreme victory.

Darach strove to remain detached, wanting to deflate her triumph by not reacting at all. Once again the minx had foiled him by turning what he had felt was his coup de grace into her own stroke of genius. He leaned back nonchalantly in the saddle, appreciating her gloriously defiant image. Garbed in the appalling drab rags of a scullery maid, she was still breathtakingly exquisite. Nothing could disguise her perfectly proportioned body, and no amount of sweat and grime could conceal her savage beauty. Emerald eyes sparkled with a provocative fire, and unruly ebony curls rioted about her bare shoulders. She had wickedly remodeled the homespun frock by tearing off several buttons to expose a daring cleavage between her thrusting breasts. She was a wild lusty wench, and she was his, he silently rejoiced, forgetting his resolve to appear bored and detached. He threw back his head and bellowed with unbridled joy and mirth.

At the Campbell's sudden violent sound, Morag frantically crossed her shaking legs, fervently praying that she wouldn't disgrace herself and soil the expensive bridal gown by the flood of nervous water that threatened. Surreptitiously, she sidled away from her mistress's shadow, seeking the more substantial cover of the carriage, but the voluminous skirts and the trunk that she clutched impeded her. Blinded by the wedding veil, she tripped and sprawled gracelessly in the arid earth, where she lay sobbing uncontrollably.

At the sound of the Campbell's sudden unrestrained laughter, Kat haughtily mounted the carriage steps, slamming the door firmly behind her, angered and puzzled by his unexpected response. She scanned about irritably, looking for Morag. Then she covertly peeked out the window. Upon seeing the forlorn figure in full bridal regalia sprawled sobbing in the dirt, a sense of shame made her stiffen. Forgetting her own predicament, Kat wrenched open the door and all but tumbled down the steep steps to kneel beside the prostrate little maid.

"I am so sorry, Morag. I had no right to use you so abominably,'' Kat admitted, awkwardly straightening the crooked tiara on the bobbing head. "I shouldna have embroiled you in my battle wie the Campbell *mucker,*'' she added, putting her hands under Morag's arms and attempting to haul her to her feet.

"No! No! I canna get up! I maun nae get up!" wailed the maid, scratching futilely at the ground, trying to dig her bitten nails into the hard dry earth to anchor herself more firmly. "No! Put me doon!" she begged wildly, but Kat relentlessly raised her. "Och, your ladyship, let me just lie doon and die on this very spot," she lamented, following Kat's quizzical gaze and squirming with embarrassment at the conspicuous puddle. "I ain't wet myself since I was a wee *bagrel,* and now I go and do it when I'm dressed laik the fairy bride of my dreams," she whimpered brokenly, wiping her streaming eyes and nose on the long veil.

"Just put your chin in the air and remember that there isna one person here who hasna pissed his trews at one time or another," Kat stated crudely, glaring about menacingly at the assembled men, tacitly warning them to wipe the derisive smirks from their faces.

"Och, your ladyship, now they all ken my shame!" howled Morag, furiously shaking herself free of her mistress's solicitous clasp and clambering hastily up the carriage steps, the long wet skirts clinging and hampering her frantic movements. Kat caught her when she tripped and pushed her roughly into the vehicle, where she collapsed across one of the leather seats, crying hysterically.

The very moment the door was shut, the horse sprang forward and they were off at such a rapid pace that both women were jostled violently. Kat thrust her legs across the space and braced them on the opposite seat to avoid being thrown onto the floor with Morag.

"Wha' the bloody hell does his lordship think he's doing?" Morag cursed, forgetting her previous debasement and crawling on hands and knees across the listing floor. She clawed her way up the wall and glared angrily out of the window at the Campbell, who galloped beside them, his saturnine face glowing with a savage exhilaration. "I think you've pushed him too far. He's gone mad. He'll make you lose the baby!" The words were brutally bounced out of her mouth by the jolts of the carriage bucking over the ruts and rocks. "Whoa! Slow doon!" she screamed to the coachman, hammering her small fists against the wall.

"Morag, there's no baby," Kat confessed. She was tenderly moved by the young maid's concern for her well-being despite the painful humiliation she had borne in order to save her mistress's pride.

"Oh, no! You dinna lose it?" mourned Morag. Kat shook her head.

"There was never a baby, Morag," she said softly. "I lied." The girl threw back the voluminous wedding veil and gaped with disbelief, her freckles and tear stains prominent on her pale face.

"You lied? There wasna ever a *bairn?*" she repeated. Once again Kat nodded, trying to squash her pangs of guilt. "But there has to be a baby! I sewed lots of wee dresses, and his lordship says as how I maun help you wie the *bairn* when it come oot, because I was the only person tha' you allow near. There has to be a *bairn* because tha's the only reason his lordship wanted to humor you. But now tha' he kens you lied and there isna any *bairn*, he'll nae want to humor you, but punish you, and I'll be sent back to the sculleries at Duncreag. And I'll never get to Edinburgh wie you one day to see the Royal Mile and all the shops," wailed Morag. The anguished words were bumped out of her thin body by each jolt of the wildly racing carriage. "There maun be a *bairn*, or I'll nae see Mr. Calum MacKissock again, and I did so hope tha' he would notice me—e'en though Sir Angus dinna laik Mr. Calum Mac-Kissock very much, called him sanctimonious, and Cailleach Cuilleann called him a fussy *auld* woman."

"Calum MacKissock?" Kat queried, trying to make sense of the long stream of bouncing chatter.

"Aye, Calum MacKissock, I dinna care tha' he's called a fussy *auld* maid. I laik tha' in a mon. 'Tis better than a dirty mon wie ugly big fists and a lusty appetite for whores and whiskey laik my da. Och, I ken tha' he's e'en *aulder* than my ain da, but I laik tha' in a mon. I laik an *auld* mon who's carefu', and particular, scrubbed clean and steady."

"You are in love wie Calum MacKissock!" Kat exclaimed incredulously.

"I dinna say tha' I was in love wie the mon. He's a likely prospect, tha's all!"

"But isn't he at Duncreag?"

"Nay, his lordship sent him to Strathrannoch more'n a week back to get everything ready for you, and to tell Sir Colin tha' you was coming."

"Sir Colin?" probed Kat.

"Aye, Sir Colin Campbell, his lordship's uncle, Sir Angus's

older brother. He lives at Strathrannoch—takes care of the place when his lordship isna there. But wha's the use? Now tha' there's no *bairn*, I shall be sent back and there'll nae be time to make a guid impression so I'll be noticed,'' she lamented.

"By Sir Colin Campbell?" struggled Kat.

"Nay, by Mr. Calum MacKissock!" mourned Morag, each word punctuated by snorts or gasps whenever the racing wheels bumped over ruts and rocks. Kat grinned wryly, thinking Calum MacKissock would have to be blind not to notice the incongruous sight of the maid dressed in the soiled but elaborate wedding ensemble. But she kept silent for fear that the distressed girl would demand the return of her homespun frock.

"Oh, well, maybe Mr. Calum MacKissock isna the marrying kind nohow, and the *cailleach* says tha' he has a bossy spinster sister, and two women under one roof doesna bode well. But I ken she stays in his lordship's town hoose in Edinburgh, but he could still be under her thumb, couldna he be? Och, there maun be a *bairn*, for I do so laik his scrubbed-clean look and the smell of strong soap aboot him. 'Tis a woman's duty to find a guid mon, and I did so want to be taken care of, though I dinna much care for the dirty part of marriage, do you? Oh, nae tha' I've had anything to do wie it, for I'm still a maid, but my ma says tha's a female's lot—says so in the Holy Bible, it does. A woman's lot is pain and suffering, it says. But my ma says after a while you forgie the dirty shamefu'ness of it and 'tis laik any other bothersome smutty chore—best got over wie the least fuss.''

Kat let Morag's constant stream of chatter flow about her as she lay braced across the width of the wildly bucking carriage, trying to devise a plan of action. She absently watched the nostalgically familiar scenery rush by them. For a while, she was transported back five years to the time when she and her father had ridden through MacGregor country. Her namesake, Loch Katrine, twinkled in the heavy afternoon sunlight, its serene surface ruffled by a warning breeze. Perhaps it was only her romantic imagination, but she thought she spied the sloping graceful lawns and turrets of Balquhidder, where her grandfather, the outlaw Rob Roy MacGregor, was buried.

"Tha's why I settled on Mr. Calum MacKissock, nae just 'cos he's scrubbed-clean, but *auld*. Och, I wouldna want the bother of a young lusty lad always throwing me doon and having his way. An *auld* mon doesna hae the strength to keep pushing and poking, and he soon stops his puffing and rolls off to sleep, so my ma says. My ma says tha' if she had hers to do over again, she'd gie herself an *auld, auld* mon," droned Morag as they sped through the small hamlets of Crianlarich and Tyndrum. The rugged tree-covered mountains soared on either side of the rough road. It was the part of Scotland that Kat loved, the part that joined inexplicably with her most basic pulses and rhythms, stirring within her the tremendous aching emotions of kinship. She shook her head angrily, trying to dispel the hypnotic allure of her native land. She closed her eyes, blocking out the beloved sight, knowing that for her brother to survive, she had to take him across the ocean to a new world where their clan, the MacGregors, could live without fear of death. The tantalizing perfumes of the pines and heather-covered slopes assailed her. She desperately tried to concentrate on other things, but she was nervous and irritated in the uncomfortable stickiness.

"There's a storm brewing," she muttered, feeling the menacing suspension of the still humidity despite the violent buffeting of the speeding coach.

" 'Tis said tha' *auld* men who still live wie their sisters oft prefer the company of men, if you ken wha' I mean. But I dinna think tha' Mr. Calum MacKissock is tha' sort of mon, do you? And e'en if he was, maybe 'twould be a blessing, for he'd nae want to do much poking and tumbling, so I wouldna complain. Mind you, I wouldna mind a *bairn* or two, but nae more'n tha'. My puir ma bore fourteen—eight live and six daid! Och, 'tis terrible to live under the same roof wie seven sisters," Morag continued. "Ooh! Look, your ladyship! Do you think tha's it? Over there? The only place the sun's still shining? Is tha' Strathrannoch?"

When Morag's monotonous drone changed into a strident screech, Kat opened her eyes and stared about her in confusion. She clawed her way along the bouncing slick leather seat and gazed out the window. Enormous purple and yellow stormclouds shed giant shadows over the landscape, but stark golden rays shone on a suspended glen where an ivy-covered castle nestled below gleaming, soaring mountains. The scene was reflected in the jewellike waters of a large tranquil lake. On the high verdant plateaus at the fringe of dense forests, herds of deer poised gracefully. Coveys of red grouse and pheasant exploded into the threatening sky, disturbed by the furious dust of the approaching travelers.

Kat had never imagined a more exquisite setting. There was an inexplicable richness and abundance—man and nature appeared to coexist harmoniously. On the lush green shoulders of the mountains, sheep and cattle grazed docilely, while rust-colored kestrels and golden eagles circled with their mates around the frosted peaks. Wild goats gamboled on the rocky slopes. Despite the dense humidity and the hush of the impending storm, the air was redolent with a crisp tang of exhilarating freedom, a heady mixture of crystal *loch* and burgeoning sky, resinous pine and musky oak, fertile lea and impenetrable stone, purple heather and blazing yellow broom—redolent with every color, sound, sight, and sense in existence.

The carriage barreled over a gray stone causeway that spanned a full moat and connected to an enormous courtyard with high buttresses that concealed the surrounding natural majesty. The menacing clouds finally shrouded the last intense rays of the sun, suspending everything in a portentous pall. Both Kat's and Morag's eyes widened with astonishment at an unexpected and awesome sight. Long formal lines of uniformed servants stood stiffly at attention with their eyes focused upon them. They hastily ducked their heads back through the carriage window and tugged down the blind.

"And that lying Campbell *mucker* said he lived a simple, unpretentious life at Strathrannoch!" hissed Kat with unbridled fury.

"Och, and tha' was Mr. Calum MacKissock hisself standing at the end, up the steps laik he was the laird hisself!" gasped Morag, collapsing onto the seat and bunching the voluminous wedding gown nervously in her lap. "Well, I dinna ken wha' you say, your ladyship, I'm nae setting one foot ootside dressed laik this!" she declared, defiantly folding her skinny arms across her flat chest.

Darach groaned loudly at the ludicrous display of pomp and ceremony that welcomed them. He glared toward the sturdy, self-satisfied figure of his steward, who pompously presided over the veritable army of immaculate servants. Where had the man found so many people? he pondered, scanning the long rows of shining faces that radiated from the main door of Strathrannoch. Everyone within a twenty-mile radius was in attendance. Calum MacKissock must have emptied every boat, farm, croft, lodge, hamlet, and shieling, he deduced. He recognized shepherds, falconers, gamekeepers, farmers, fishermen, weavers and their families, mixed together with his regular staff. The busy steward must have also raided the numerous attics to obtain so many matching old-fashioned uniforms. What was his man about? Darach wondered, knowing well Calum's fervent disapproval of his bride. Maybe he sought to frighten Kat away by the impressive spectacle? Or did he perhaps seek to ensure her discomfort, hoping to spark her rebellion and consequent humiliation? Whatever the steward planned, the Campbell was confident that his wayward wife would somehow be the victor.

Darach leaned back in his saddle, mesmerized by the unfolding scene. He ignored the hovering ostlers who patiently waited to stable Iolair, as his fatigued mind tried to come to terms with this spectacle. It seemed that he was in a bygone era when Strathrannoch had housed upward of five hundred people, an army to defend against marauding clans. And often they would attack those same clans to increase the Campbell holdings or to find new blood to breed with, strengthening their lines.

"Where's Sir Colin?" he barked suddenly, staring about for his oldest uncle. He felt that he needed an ally.

"Took oot for the hunting lodge when all the fuss started," replied an old groom, raising a grizzled eyebrow at the dusty carriage that started bouncing about wildly, as though a battle was being waged within it.

"Intelligent mon," Darach sighed, gazing up at the gathering stormclouds and resisting an overwhelming urge to quit the ridiculous scene and join his retiring uncle.

"Will you be dismounting, your lordship?"

"Nay, I've a much better view from here," Darach answered dryly as muffled squeals issued from the violently bucking carriage.

Two footmen stoically advanced, and Darach swiveled about to better witness the drama.

"Is there a wild animal in there?" whispered the old groom.

"Aye, my wife!" was the terse reply.

The liveried servants were too well trained to give one sign that they were disconcerted by the obviously raucous dispute that was taking place. They efficiently opened the carriage door, unfolded the steps, and stood at attention waiting for their new mistress to alight. There was a hushed pause. All eyes respectfully regarded the door, and necks craned eagerly.

Darach urged Iolair forward, not wanting to miss one fraction of the performance.

A loud protesting squawk shattered the suspense and a beveiled bride with a tiara hurtled out of the coach. She was fortunately caught and steadied by the hovering footmen, then she was greeted by polite applause from the long lines of nearly assembled people. The timorous bride faltered, her trembling knees nearly buckling under her. She would have fled back into the carriage, but she was swiftly followed by a perkly little maid laden with an assortment of luggage. The woman briskly propelled her diffident mistress forward with a well-placed parasol in the small of her back.

For one of the few times in his life, Darach Campbell did not know what to do. Tradition dictated that he gallantly escort his bride through the lines of welcoming servants to introduce them to their new mistress, but that was impossible without causing mayhem. He resisted the temptation to haul Kat up into the saddle with him and gallop off to join his Uncle Colin at the hunting lodge. Instead, he patiently walked his exhausted horse behind the two bedraggled women, anxious to witness Calum MacKissock's outraged expression when he recognized the bawdy little wench who strutted confidently behind the sagging bride.

Morag's feet felt so heavy that she was certain the ground was going to crumble beneath her, and in fact she prayed fervently that it would open up and swallow her before she reached the scrubbed figure of Mr. Calum MacKissock. Each time she stopped, she received a wicked prod from behind, propelling her forward. Fortunately, everything was blurred by the clouds of wedding veil that shrouded her vision, and she was only vaguely conscious of the army of people bowing on each side of her. When she finally arrived within touching distance of Mr. Calum MacKissock, he didn't appear to realize that anything was amiss. He couldn't help but frown at the appalling condition of the once pristine wedding gown, but then he shrugged, as if deciding that there had been a carriage mishap. He bowed respectfully, and Morag felt faint, smelling the fresh sting of his soap.

"Welcome to Strathrannoch, your ladyship," he proclaimed, barely concealing a contemptuous smirk of victory at seeing her obvious terror. He had been most satisfied as he observed her timorous approach, believing that his impressive display had at last made her realize the gravity and unsuitability of her position as wife of the Campbell chieftain. "Welcome," he repeated, taking her trembling gloved hand and bowing. The rebellious hellion was tamed, he rejoiced inwardly. She was now a docile wife who would obediently and uncomplainingly carry on the Campbell line. He smiled benevolently at the bowed shaking head and then scowled with confusion at seeing a reddish curl escaping from beneath the voluminous lace. There was a throaty chuckle. He looked over the cowering bride and gaped with incredulity at the impudent, ebony-haired maid who posed challengingly in the background.

"You!" he spluttered impotently.

"Och, Mr. Calum MacKissock, I'm ever so . . . ever so sorry, sir," wailed Morag.

"Well, I guarantee the mon's noticed you now," Kat said unsympathetically into the quaking maid's ear. Then she poked her brutally with the parasol, hurtling her against the man's barrel chest. "So very sorry, sir," Morag squealed. After an aghast peek at his apoplectic face, she promptly collapsed into a pathetic pile of limp lace between his sturdily braced feet.

Kat was now at a loss. She felt very lonely and small, dwarfed by the sheer castle walls and the surrounding soaring mountains. She kept her chin proudly lifted, knowing that every eye was fixed upon her, and none was friendly. On either side of her were endless ranks of gawking strangers; before her was the disapproving Calum MacKissock, who believed that she belonged in jail like a common felon; behind her, still mounted on his stallion, was the Campbell, the arch-enemy of her clan MacGregor.

The eerie stillness of the storm-charged atmosphere was oppressive, and Kat yearned for the dangerous calm to explode and shatter the unbearable tension. It was as if nature was poised to witness her destruction. She felt cornered, and there was no escape. What should she do? A traitorous part of her wanted to appeal to the Campbell for help, but the moment that thought came into her mind, she rejected it. She could stalk past the censorious steward and go into the castle, but then she would most certainly lose herself in the vast unknown building. That would just protract her mortification. She hoped that her intense fear wasn't apparent as she glared arrogantly at Calum MacKissock. Instinctively, she sensed he had designed the welcoming assembly for the express purpose of her humiliation, and that knowledge fired her rage. It was evident that she was Lady Rannoch, whether or not she wanted to be, so why not make use of the exalted position?

"MacKissock, pick up my puir maid and carry her inside," she ordered autocratically, her young voice ringing clearly across the hushed courtyard. There was a taut moment. The thunder rumbled ominously, and Calum's mouth sagged open with indignation. "Did you hear me, MacKissock?" she announced icily, and the outraged man turned beseeching eyes upward to his master. The Campbell made no sign or movement to aid him. The sky darkened and lightning slashed, but Kat kept her green eyes pinned to the squirming steward as large, heavy raindrops fell, mottling the dry gray stones.

"Aye, your ladyship," he finally acquiesced after a great sobbing breath. There was a gasp from the uniformed people. A gossiping whisper hissed through the long rows, building like the rising wind that keened about the towering peaks. Calum MacKissock picked up the bedraggled bride and carried her into the castle. Only then did the storm erupt in full fury, scattering the neat lines of welcomers in all directions.

Kat sighed and raised her hot face to the sheeting rain that scoured her exhausted, sticky body, molding the brown homespun frock about her lithe curves. She was so very weary, but she delighted in the violence that rent the sky. Great round clouds clustered together, shrouding the high peaks and crashing together in a wondrous display of power. She was dimly aware of the protesting squeak of wet leather as the Campbell swung his lean body out of the saddle. She braced herself for the onset of their stormy battle, but he just stood close to her—not quite touching—and raised his own face to the cleansing, stinging torrent.

chapter 28

Kat stood awkwardly in front of the roaring fire, where she had been deposited. The water streamed down her body and formed puddles on the thick fur rug. She heard the bustle of activity behind the closed door of the adjacent room, while she tried to ignore the silver eyes that assessed her saturated appearance. There was a constant muttering and the sound of many buckets clanging sharply together while being emptied. Kat concentrated on the leaping flames in the wide hearth and wrinkled her nose with distaste at the stale-smelling steam that rose from the borrowed woollen frock that sagged uncomfortably about her. Her back was pointedly turned to the large bed that dominated the intimate bedroom.

"It would be sensible to get out of those wet, foul-smelling rags," remarked the Campbell. Kat spun about, glaring silently but eloquently at him. "Suit yourself," he answered airily and proceeded to strip off his own soaked, travel-stained attire. Kat glowered with confusion. Then, to her horror, she found herself blushing at the sight of his bared brown chest as he unbuttoned his shirt and tugged it free of his tight riding britches. She was very conscious of the wry amusement in his ever watchful eyes, and she fought the temptation to avert her gaze like a modest virgin. Instead, she steeled her expression to match his own sardonic look, hoping to disconcert him. She unconsciously rubbed her arms, still feeling the imprint of his possessive hold when he had carried her from the courtyard and through the castle to the luxurious bedchamber, where she was now, tensed and ready to do battle once again. Darach chuckled and raised a roguish eyebrow. "Och, dinna tempt me, Lady Rannoch, there'll be plenty of time for a lusty marital wrestle after the banquet," he quipped wickedly. He gave a long regretful look at the wide bed.

"Banquet?" she echoed unhappily, choosing to ignore his suggestive words that caused her pulses to race.

"Aye, banquet," he affirmed, inserting his foot in a jack and pulling off one sopping boot.

"Och, so now the self-righteous Calum MacKissock has planned a banquet to show the Campbells of Strathrannoch the barbarian that their chieftain has captured for his wife? Och, she'll most likely use her hands and put her face in the platter to feed like an ignorant beast," she jeered bitterly.

"Lady Rannoch may eat in any manner she chooses, and I wouldna think an overly solicitous steward wie an overzealous sense of duty would faze her," Darach remarked idly, fitting his other foot in the jack and wrenching off the other boot. "The puir misguided man probably thinks that Lady Rannoch has not the courage to show her pretty face at the banquet," he goaded gently, hoping to fire her resistance. He was surprised to see a flicker of shy confusion.

"Banquet," Kat repeated, disconcerted by his referral to her pretty face. She wondered miserably what she had to wear to the feast, and her mouth filled with saliva as she remembered the delicious aromas that had assailed her nostrils when she had been carried so possessively through the castle. Why hadn't she struggled? Why had she allowed the Campbell to master her? Why had she allowed him to carry her wet and submissive, like a drowned cat, like a victor with the spoils? At the time it had seemed the only solution. She had been too weary to struggle against his obviously superior strength, and she didn't relish the thought of being lost in the maze of alien hallways or having to run at an undignified trot to keep up with his long legs. It had seemed to be the most expedient way to enter Strathrannoch. She had been able to relax in his arms, recouping her jangled, exhausted senses, closing her eyes, blind to the curious faces that peered out of the shadows to catch a glimpse of the Campbell's newest woman. "Banquet," she said again, her shoulders sagging with defeat.

"Aye, a banquet to honor our marriage, wishing us a long,

harmonious . . . fruitful union," he added with a wry laugh, striding barefoot across the room and flinging open the connecting door. Two steaming bathtubs were set up before a blazing hearth, and a valet and a maid stood waiting to give assistance. The Campbell impatiently waved them away and locked the door after them. "Well, my lady wife, I'll not dare presume to tell you what to do, for fear a suggestion will be misconstrued as an order, but if I were you, I should avail myself of the offered luxuries while you are able," he proclaimed, waving a hand to indicate the fluffy towels and steaming baths.

"While I am able?" whispered Kat. Panic clawed into her belly. She feared that finally she had gone too far with her rebellious ways and soon would be turned over to the authorities, charged with the abduction of Riach Campbell.

"Aye, tomorrow there'll be no more overzealous stewards, no maids, valets, cooks, demanding siblings, or interfering relatives."

"I dinna ken." She scowled, trying to cover her intense terror.

"It'll be just you and me, dear wife," he snapped, stung by her evident displeasure.

Kat silently watched him turn his back to her; without another glance in her direction, he stripped completely and stepped into the larger of the two baths. He lay back in the hot water and gave a long sigh of pure contentment. Closing his eyes, he left her to shiver with fear, cold, and barely suppressed fury. Outside, the storm continued to rage unabated, the screaming winds and driving rains lashing against the leaded panes as though demanding admittance. Kat suddenly turned her back on the Campbell, wanting to claw ferociously at his smooth golden body. But at the same time, she yearned to rub her cheek lovingly against the ebony hair that curled across his strong chest. Angrily, she yanked apart the lush velvet draperies and scraped her fingers in frustration against the misted, opaque glass. She was unable to see outside. Feeling stifled by her conflicting emotions and her overwhelming predicament, she unlatched the window, flinging it open. She knelt on the wide, cushioned casement. Ignoring the sheer, perilous drop to the churning waters in the moat below, she leaned out, taking perverse pleasure in the punishing pain of the hail and rain. Icy drops stung her face as she breathed deeply of the exhilarating air, trying to calm herself. She rocked with the violently bending trees, marveling that they didn't snap; her own fury was further fueled by the savagely slashing lightning and crashing thunder. She tried frantically to drown out the Campbell's disturbing presence, but the very limitless spectrum of grays—from the deepest purple of the rolling billowing clouds that dipped their fullness to the earth, to the searing silver shafts that rent the roiling seething vista—was reminiscent of his arresting eyes.

Kat was unaware of the mewing cries that burst from her mouth as she gazed out at the storm. A terrible painful battle raged within her. Part of her pulsed with an intensifying, all-consuming excitement, and she yearned to become an unthinking, inseparable piece of him, no longer standing so alone, no longer so strong and responsible for other lives. She achingly recalled their past intimacies of sharing a bath before another crackling hearth—she had fit so naturally and rightly between his long, strong legs, feeling special and feminine, cherished and chosen. But those treacherous sensuous cravings were the sharp, lethal teeth of a merciless trap that was inexorably closing, and she would never be able to free herself without leaving part of her soul behind. Enraged at her perfidious mind, she shook her wet head wildly from side to side, trying to erase the seductive thoughts. She was no better than her mother, weak and easily swayed, like the trees in the gale that were bent to the ground. And she was not even as resilient. She was about to snap, to break in two, to be conquered by the force of the Campbell's presence. No, she would not be like Suibhan! she screamed within herself. She would not sacrifice her name, her family, her peace of mind, her pride, even her own unborn children, for a man who so easily betrayed her love. A garish image of Felicity lolling obscenely across the bed where they had made love ripped into Kat's tortured brain, strengthening her resolve. She callously forced herself to recall the cloying stench of cheap perfume, reminding her of a nightmarish Edinburgh night and a pink brothel in Paris as her mother lay dying. No, she would never be so debased, she vowed.

Darach kept his expression blasé and his eyes half closed, feigning unconcern as he soaked in the bath by the crackling fire. Despite the deafening clamor of the raging storm, he had heard the faint, whimpering cry of a hurt animal. He listened intently, straining his ears, wondering if a kestrel or an eagle had been cruelly hurtled against the castle walls and was lying wounded on a ledge, battered by the storm. He kept his veiled gaze pinned to Kat's back and shrewdly noted the tremor that shuddered through her. He heard the plaintive cry again. He had always found it ironic that such a majestic, fearless bird of prey such as the golden eagle had such a vulnerable cry—the cry of a lost, hurt baby. It was equally ironic to realize that the mewing sound came from his savage young wife. He watched her struggling against the howling wind to close the window, and he knew that it wasn't only raindrops but also tears that trembled on her cheeks and long dark lashes. He felt helpless to comfort her, knowing her stubborn pride would be an impediment, and he wondered why she battled so furiously to maintain the distance between them when their mutual attraction was so evident.

Kat felt the Campbell's scrutiny but didn't glance in his direction. She brushed the wetness from her face and stared thoughtfully at the doors leading from the bedchamber. She had to find some clean dry clothing because the uncomfortable dampness and cloying staleness of Morag's woollen frock was making her flesh crawl. Tentatively, she opened a door and peeked in, hoping that she wouldn't come face to face with Calum MacKissock's condescending visage. A gasp of delight burst from her mouth at the sight of a pleasant lounge where yet another generous fire blazed and a light repast of fruits and wines rested on a shining oak table. Kat poured herself a glass of sparkling wine and drank thirstily, causing the Campbell to raise an eyebrow and wash hastily. He did not wish to have an inebriated bride. Kat heard the sudden splashing and poured herself another glass, which she leisurely sipped, trying to feign indifference. But, unable to remain calm under his constant wry scrutiny, she snorted with exasperation and rebelliously drained her glass, daring him to object before stalking toward him and slamming the door.

Darach swiftly finished his ablutions, hearing her systematically opening and closing drawers and doors and wondering what she was planning. There had been a disconcerting purposefulness of movement and a fierce glint in her eyes that he didn't trust. He reached for a towel to cover his loins, not wishing to be too exposed to his scheming spouse; he quietly entered the bedchamber anxious to observe her actions. He knew from the stiffening of her back that she was aware of him, but other than that there was no sign of recognition. He lounged in the doorway of her dressing room, watching gleefully as she gaped at the contents of a wardrobe filled with clothes that he had ordered, sparing no expense, from Paris and London. There were gowns and accessories for every conceivable occasion. He grinned, knowing that she longed to swirl around and attack, but to do so would mean that she had to acknowledge his presence. He chuckled, thoroughly enjoying himself, knowing that she had no option but to wear one of the exquisite gowns that he had carefully selected to complement her unusual beauty—unless, of course, she stubbornly decided to cling to the disgusting rag that she had coerced from the wretched little maid. Resisting the very strong temptation to rip the offensive article violently off her body and hurl it out into the raging storm, he padded barefoot into the salon to fortify himself with an earthy glass of burgundy. It was sure to be a long arduous night, he surmised with a shrewd glance at her warlike stance.

Kat was relieved to be free of his presence. The fact that she was forced to accept his largesse rankled, shredding her dignity, and she chose a somber black gown more appropriate for a funeral than for a joyful wedding feast. She even tore off the few ribbons and lace that adorned the modest bodice, hoping to make it as staid and insignificant as possible. Taking advantage of her privacy, she hastily grabbed some undergarments and the gown and scampered into the bathing room. She cursed loudly at not finding a key or bolt, and to ensure her seclusion, she placed a chair beneath the knob. She groaned, knowing that the flimsy obstacle would prove ineffectual if the Campbell really wanted to enter. With resignation, she stripped off the ugly brown frock and stepped into the bath. The water had cooled considerably, but the scented cleanness of it soothed her. Kat lay back, staring at the crackling fire, willing her aching body to relax, but the anticipation of expecting at any moment the door to be forcibly flung open was not conducive to repose, so she quickly and efficiently scrubbed herself from top to toe.

Darach dressed leisurely, sipping the excellent burgundy and listening to the domestic sounds of his young wife splashing in her bath. He enjoyed the intimate noises and vividly imagined her lithe naked body, satiny and slippery with soap, reflecting the hungry licking tongues of fire from the hearth. He drained his glass, impatient to smash the frustrating barriers that Kat had erected between them. He perused his image in the mirror as he ran a careless hand through his still-damp hair. He straightened his jabot, wondering what terrible secret she could be hiding. A furtive tapping at the door broke through his introspection.

"Aye?" he answered absently, and Calum MacKissock's ruddy face popped into the lounge, his eyes flickering nervously as he looked to see if his master was alone. "Well, what is it, Calum?" Darach snapped impatiently.

"Where's the wench?" whispered the steward, nodding his head conspiratorially toward the bedroom and raising his sandy eyebrows questioningly.

"My wife is dressing for dinner," replied the Campbell, his tone dangerously low, tacitly warning the steward against impertinence.

"Och, laddie, dinna be incensed wie me. 'Tis only your guid name I'm thinking aboot. I've only your well-being at heart, as you well ken," Calum hissed, sidling into the room and quietly closing the connecting door to the bedchamber.

"What the hell do you think you're doing, MacKissock?" roared Darach, furious at the man's presumption.

"Hush yourself, lad," the earnest steward warned. "I wouldna disturb you unless it was very, very important."

"It had better be!"

"I ken who she is," Calum pronounced ponderously with an air of doom.

Kat pressed her ear to the door, her heart beating in triple time. There was a long silence after MacKissock's ominous announcement, and she wondered what the Campbell was doing. She held her breath, waiting to hear the steward state her true name, but all she could detect for several minutes was the sound of wine being poured.

"I assume you are referring to my wife?"

"Aye. Who else?" returned Calum. "You ken it has always teased and bothered my mind. 'Twas so haunting, laik I had seen the conniving wench before, but I couldna fathom where. Then *auld* Granny Denoon, your ain father's *auld nurreych*, recognized her," Calum proclaimed.

Kat leaned her hot cheek against the cool polished wood, remembering her Aunt Ailsa's warning to Aggie Fletcher: "Dinna let an *auld* Campbell see the wee dark lass, or they'll ken who she is." The words repeated themselves like a dirge within her pounding pulses.

"And who is she?" demanded Darach. He hated himself for asking anything of the manservant, who obviously detested the new Lady Rannoch and seemed prepared to go to any lengths to humiliate and discredit her. Kat was tensed to hear herself exposed, and she splayed her hands against the door, standing on tiptoes in suspense.

"I canna rightly say for sure, as *auld* Granny Denoon is in her dotage and slips in and oot, but she cackled and pointed and chattered aboot a painting here at Strathrannoch. Went on and on aboot green eyes and black hair. Carried on laik a lunatic, clapping her hands and screaming tha' another was back at Strathrannoch," Calum narrated awkwardly, not knowing if he was being heard because his young master had turned broodingly away.

Kat sagged against the door, feeling that she had been given a reprieve.

"Where is this painting?" barked the Campbell, his dark brow furrowing as he recalled the smooth, shiny surface with myriads of cracks.

"Come wie me, lad, and I'll show you," Calum offered eagerly. Then he spun about at the sound of a door opening and stared with dismay into Kat's haunted face.

Kat stood on the threshold of the bedchamber wearing the austere black gown. Her emerald eyes were wide and luminous, and her cheeks were rosy from her bath by the fire. Her unruly mane was still wet, and droplets of water sparkled like jewels among her gleaming jet curls. Calum was unaccountably very ashamed. She looked so young and vulnerable that he felt like a murderous bully.

"If you'll excuse us," he muttered, unable to meet her direct gaze or call her by her title. She was nothing more than a common felon, the daughter of a known criminal, and she'd not seduce him with her innocent demeanor, he strove to convince himself.

"Lady Rannoch will accompany us," the Campbell stated.

"But . . ."

"You will await us outside," he ordered tersely, and the steward backed unhappily out of the room.

Kat stared steadily at Darach. Dread beat heavily in every cold corner of her proudly held body. She bravely kept her stubborn chin raised, refusing to look away from his penetrating glare. He had never appeared so handsome as at that moment, she thought, appreciating with detachment his perfectly tailored but unfussy clothes. The only adornment was the snowy-white lace jabot at his throat, an ideal contrast to the hard, tanned planes of his face. He also looked more forbidding and dangerous than ever before, she decided numbly, noting the coiled tension about his tall frame.

"Do you have something to tell me?" he asked roughly, breaking the long taut silence. He wanted to learn her identity from her own mouth, not from an obsequious, jealous servant. Kat didn't answer or avert her eyes from his chiseled features. She found herself thinking of powdered hair and periwigs.

"I'm glad you don't follow the dictates of fashion," she stated simply, enjoying the way his dark hair curled about his ears. "But I suppose wigs are convenient for bald men," she added thoughtfully. Then she scowled with confusion, not understanding why she was expressing such inane thoughts. The Campbell's expression became even more thunderous, so Kat listened for the storm outside, only to realize sadly that, like herself, its ferocious rage was spent. All that was left was the plaintive patter of the gently weeping rain.

"Put some shoes on!" he ordered unaccountably, infuriated by the touching sight of her defenseless pink toes peeking out from beneath the severe black gown. She made no move to obey but remained mutely gazing up at him. "Well, it seems that you follow some of the dictates of fashion. Are you plotting my demise? Is that why you choose to garb yourself in widow's weeds?" he gibed savagely.

"I feel like I'm dressed for my own funeral."

The Campbell took her small hand in a punishing grip and strode out of their suite of rooms. Kat bit back her protests and concentrated on keeping up with his long legs, knowing that if she faltered, he would most likely drag her behind him. The humiliation of having to trot beside him like a small puppy on a leash fed her anger.

"There!" proclaimed Calum, lifting a lantern to illuminate the painting. The light hit the varnished surface in such a way that all Kat could see was a glare.

"That'll be all," dismissed the Campbell.

"Who is she?" the steward probed.

"Leave us, MacKissock."

Kat glued her eyes to the sturdy back of the stalwart steward as he sullenly plodded back along the gallery. The swinging lantern he held in his hand caused eerie shapes to dance rhythmically across the highly polished floor and vaulted ceiling. She kept looking at him, even after he had been absorbed by the thick shadows and she could no longer hear the echo of his reluctant feet. She was too terrified to scrutinize the portrait at which the Campbell gazed so intently. Feigning boredom, she idly scanned the other paintings that were hung at regular intervals on either side of the gallery. She saw them as hollow squares on an impenetrable wall, becoming smaller and smaller and finally melding together as they faded into the distance. The Campbell still held her hand, though not as tightly, and her fingers nestled against his warm, hard palm, sending strange sensations tingling through her.

Darach gazed up into the wide, mischievous eyes that had been captured on canvas by a deft artist many years before. Then he looked down into the truculent emerald orbs of his rebellious wife. He sighed, remembering how as a little boy he had been mesmerized by the portrait, and he struggled to recall what he knew about this beautiful woman.

"Are you afraid to look at your own ghost?" he challenged.

"Afraid of my own ghost?" Kat retorted caustically, raising her chin and glowering disdainfully at the painting. She was prepared to be totally unmoved, but her mouth dropped open with astonishment. It was like looking into a mirror and seeing how she would appear in another ten years. Her own eyes, older and more worldly, playfully mocked her; her own mouth curled roguishly, as though sharing a delicious jest. Ebony tresses just like her own cascaded down in orderly ringlets from a lacy little cap.

"Who is she?" whispered Kat, fear clutching at her heart.

"Who are you?" demanded the Campbell, giving her one last chance to entrust him with the truth, but she stubbornly shook her head. It wasn't just her secret—she had a small brother to protect. He had to be allowed to grow to manhood, the last surviving male of her family. A horrible silence yawned. Kat was painfully aware of the searing silver eyes, but she kept her own gaze fixed to the constantly smiling painting. She fervently wished that the unknown replica of herself would understand the awful gravity of the moment and alter her expression, but the green eyes maintained their mischievous twinkle, seeming to thoroughly enjoy the battle of wills. "Who are you?" he repeated. Kat yearned to unburden herself and defuse his inexorably mounting fury, but she remained mute.

"That is Mairghread Campbell," he finally stated, and she

gaped at him in amazement, not quite certain if she had heard him correctly.

"Mairghread Campbell?" she repeated incredulously, pulling her hand free from his and moving closer to read the inscription on the brass plaque on the ornately carved frame. "Mairghread Campbell, born 1646, died 1685," she pronounced. Then she giggled, sheer relief making her giddy. She had expected to be brutally exposed, and the anticlimax was nearly too much for her overwrought, fatigued state. "Mairghread Campbell! Well, I am charmed to make your acquaintance, milady," she mocked, sinking into a deep curtsy. "Mairghread Campbell, I'll be damned! I maun be a bloody Campbell, then," she spluttered, sagging against the paneled wall and surrendering to great gales of laughter.

Once more her hand was caught in a punishing grip, her arm nearly yanked from its socket. Still in the throes of helpless giggles, she was forced to an undignified scamper in order to keep abreast of Darach as he strode purposefully through the torch-lit corridors of the castle.

Kat's hysterical giggles came to a sputtering stop when she was dragged into a somber library. The door was slammed with an ominous crash that echoed about the stone walls, and she was forcibly seated in a cold leather chair at a long polished table. No fire blazed in the hollow hearth to cheer the cavernous, gloomy room. The only illumination was the distorting flame of the torch that the Campbell had angrily wrenched from a bracket on their headlong rush from the portrait gallery. Kat sat stiffly where she had been thrust and anxiously watched him scour the bookshelves, his long fingers running across rounded spines, causing a brushing sound that chilled her spine.

The streaming, smoky light contorted his already harsh features into satanic angles, increasing her fear. With a triumphant snort, he roughly hauled down a dusty ledger and crashed it onto the table in front of her, causing her to shudder. He then swooped over her, and she felt the devastating weight of his looming shadow. His seductive male scent curled through her, mingling with her pulsating terror. Desperately trying to calm herself, she gazed at the strong arms that were extended to each side of her, so near and yet not touching—not touching, yet she could feel the heat of his blood making her skin tingle. If she moved her head an inch to either side, she could close her eyes and nestle against his strength, but the furious rustle of paper that ensued as he leafed through the large pages and the furious muttering that hissed from his lips deterred her.

"Aye, of course!" he roared suddenly after expelling his breath in a loud exasperated sigh that curdled Kat's blood. "Of course!" he bellowed again, slapping his hand forcefully onto the opened page. She winced as though it were she who was struck. "No wonder all the lies! No wonder all the hatred! No wonder all the subterfuge!" he muttered, appalled and infuriated by his own stupidity. It was so blatantly obvious, yet he hadn't been able to see what was under his nose. "Read it!" he commanded. When she didn't obey, he viciously slapped the ledger again. "Read it!"

Kat could neither move nor speak. Her throat was painfully constricted, and her heart hammered wildly. She stared at the page where his large splayed hand was poised, but her eyes couldn't focus. She impotently shook her head from side to side in an attempt to clear her vision and stop herself from spiraling into a pit of panic.

Darach was so consumed by his own ineptitude that he was unaware of the depths of Kat's distress. All he could see was the top of her glossy head. Taking her frantic trembling for emphatic defiance, he became even more enraged.

"Read it!" he insisted, crashing his clenched fist onto the opened page. Kat gripped the arms of the chair, bracing herself for the violent blows to descend. "Then I maun read it for you," he pronounced stiffly, appalled by her convulsive shudder. Realizing that she was expecting to be beaten, he stalked away from her, trying to calm himself. There was a maelstrom of conflicting emotions surging through him. He wished that she'd leap up and battle him in her usual feral manner instead of sitting like a small waif in an absurd black gown awaiting her doom. He gazed thoughtfully out of the window, watching the gentle rain ruffle the now serene surface of the *loch* and seeing the shimmering echoes of the storm in the night sky.

Memories of her poignant little face when she opened the door of number 14 Comyn Square that fateful night her father died tore into his mind. He clearly saw the cruel imprint of the fat ringed hand marring her soft cheek and splitting her tremulous lips. He remembered the brutal bruises that marked her slim limbs, and now she sat dwarfed by the ponderous

carved back of the chair, expecting the same abuse from him.
The knowledge stung him, melding with the fury he had with
himself.

"Mairghread Campbell, born 1646." Kat's husky halting
voice broke through his brooding thoughts, and he slowly
turned to face her.

"Go on," he encouraged softly, hoping finally that the last
barrier was about to be hurdled.

"Mairghread Campbell married Domhnull . . . Mac . . .
Grioghair," she continued bravely, somehow expecting great
claps of thunder. "In 1671, her son, Raibeart Ruadh Mac-
Grioghair, was born."

Kat pressed her back against the uncomfortable carvings of
the thronelike chair as the Gaelic name ripped through her
tense body. Raibeart Ruadh MacGrioghair, the notorious Rob
Roy MacGregor, her little brother's namesake, her own
grandfather. The woman in the painting was her own great-
grandmother. It was the first time she had seen the likeness of
any of her ancestors. She was so immersed in her own whirl of
thoughts that she wasn't aware of the Campbell's approach
until a warm hand grasped her chin and gently forced her to
look up.

"Katrine MacGregor?" he pronounced softly, remembering Angus's hastily covered slip of the tongue when he had
first brought the rebellious girl to Duncreag. There had been
so many clues, and he hadn't picked up on one of them. He
snorted with impatience.

Kat was blinded by the flickering torch that mercifully
shadowed the Campbell's stern face. She was aware of his fury
and didn't have the energy to confront the searing condemnation she knew would beam from his eyes.

"I dinna ken what you're inferring!" she retorted.

"I'm not inferring anything, but stating a fact, Katrine
MacGregor."

"Just because you happened to have an ancestor who con-
sorted wie a known outlaw, and for some strange quirk of
nature I hae an unco resemblance to the . . . indiscriminating
female, doesna necessarily mean that I am . . . who you imagine I am," she said lamely, glowering savagely up into his
face, thankful that his disgusted expression was shrouded. She
couldn't see the tenderness and empathy that softened his
chiseled features, but something emanated from him that confused and frightened her even more than the expected rage.

"Och, my kitten, no more lies," he pleaded, his voice soft and caressing, no more than a whisper.

"Dinna call me a liar, you Campbell *mucker!*" she spat, fighting against the threatening flood of tears and the overwhelming urge to fling herself into his arms.

"Trust me, Katrine MacGregor Campbell," he begged. He gazed down into her flashing green eyes and watched as they gradually welled with tears that brimmed tremulously before spilling slowly down her defiant little face. Unable to help himself, he groaned aloud and gathered her to him.

Kat held herself stiffly, determined to battle her overpowering desire to submerge unthinkingly into his seductive strength, knowing that if she surrendered she would never be free from him. She would be as open and defenseless as her mother had been, an abject slave to her love.

"Och, my wee Wild Kat, 'tis time you trusted," the Campbell murmured, resting his cheek against the top of her glossy head and feeling her rapidly thudding heart jarring through him.

Kat yearned to howl with pain and confusion. How dare he use her mother's pet name for her and unfairly assail her resolve that way? How could she ever trust him, even if she wanted to? What about his own stepmother, Felicity? At the thought of the insanely jealous woman, she felt physically ill. The cloying stench of cheap perfume clawed into her consciousness, reminding her of countless nightmarish times during childhood—and another more recently in Edinburgh. If she couldn't trust him to be true to her, how could he be trusted with the secret of her own brother?

Kat splayed her small hands against the hard muscles of the Campbell's broad chest and fiercely pushed herself away from his enticing safety. She stared up into his face, searching for answers, only to become more confused by the incredible tenderness that softened his usually ruthless, enigmatic features. She wanted to trust him with every fiber of her being, but sadly she couldn't. If she were solely responsible for only one life, her own, she might consider taking the risk, but what if she submitted to her consuming weakness and merged with the Campbell, costing her little brother his freedom or his life?

"Well, my love?" Darach asked huskily, breaking a long silence in which he had patiently submitted to her intense scrutiny. He understood her inner conflict. He had wrestled against his own cynicism and experience before ruefully and joyfully realizing that he had no choice. He loved her. She was firmly and irrevocably entrenched in every part of his being. She tormented his nights, haunted his dreams, and destroyed his emotions during every waking minute. "Well?" he prompted.

"I am hungry," she pronounced nonchalantly, too weary to engage in any more confrontations. She'd not admit to anything except the need for food and sleep. "There was to be a banquet?" she challenged. He stared sorrowfully down at her, and she felt his cradling arms tense against her ribs.

"Aye, a wedding feast awaits." He sighed, reluctantly setting her on her bare feet. "My lady?" he mocked icily, formally offering his hand.

They walked through the castle at a sedate pace, side by side, not saying a word. Then they heard a merry bustle and clatter and smelled the mouth-watering aromas. Kat was very conscious of the Campbell's silence and wished she could scurry away and hide in the shadows to sort through her tumultuous fears and feelings. All too soon, they stepped into the great banquet hall to be met by loud cheers and a profusion of rose petals. If the people of Strathrannoch were taken aback by a young barefoot bride dressed entirely in black, they were either too well bred to make mention or too well fortified with spirits to notice.

Kat's face ached from the forced smile she politely bestowed upon each of the merry revelers who filed past, paying homage. She was seated beside the Campbell, high above the milling crowd on a raised table at the head of the vast, torchlit hall. Fires blazed in several enormous hearths, each roasting carcasses of mutton, lamb, pork, and beef. They were turned on spits by impish lads who risked burned fingers while sneaking crispy tidbits. A steady stream of happily chattering people carrying laden trenchers dripping with meat juices wended in and out, serving the crowded tables. Large wooden and clay bowls of vegetables and fruits, flagons of wines and porter, and salvers of bread and cheeses were already resting there. Kat fervently wished that she was part of the bustling anonymity in the main part of the hall. She was too weary and self-conscious to chew under the constant stares of two hundred curious people. There was not one familiar face—not even Calum MacKissock's disapproving features were discernible in the sea of people. Her eyes blurred while she attempted to transform the ravenously munching throng into an inani-

mate textured tapestry, and she sagged tiredly against the immovable strength of the Campbell, who stolidly ate. Soon she
was fast asleep.

Kat was unaware of being gently cradled across the Campbell's lap, where she slept peacefully while he finished his
meal. She was unaware of the fond looks and gentle murmuring prayers as he carried her out of the banquet hall. She was
unaware of the sprigs of white heather and rowan that were
reverently placed upon her sleeping breast to ensure happiness, good luck, and a long life. She was unaware of the hush
as all the people stood for them, and of the noisy clamor that
resumed with renewed fervor when the great carved door
closed after them.

Darach carried Kat through the castle, hearing the joyous
revelry of their wedding feast fade into the distance. He felt
lonely, and instead of going directly to their suite of rooms, he
made a detour through the portrait gallery, where several hundred years of ancestors stared down lugubriously. He sat on a
wooden bench with Kat cradled against his chest, gazing up
into Mairghread Campbell's whimsical green eyes, remembering lonely rainy afternoons as a small motherless boy. He
would play in the long shadowy gallery, sliding along the
highly polished floor, kept company by his multitude of forebears. After his father's marriage to Felicity, he had been
shunted off to boarding schools and the house in Edinburgh.
His old companions had been forgotten, especially his first
love, Mairghread Campbell. He had hidden his vulnerable
childhood memory of her until a small tatterdemalion in a
Parisian back street had barreled into him and ever after
changed his life.

Kat opened her eyes and sleepily surveyed the impressive
collection of paintings. She was not quite awake but suspended in a safe warmth, lulled by the steady beat of the
Campbell's heart beneath her ear. She dimly recalled the portrait gallery at Linnmanach, the squares of dirt etched in the
grime where pictures had once hung, and the imperative absence of ancestors in her own life.

"I have spaces instead of faces." She yawned. "And you
have frames and frames and frames, with names," she mumbled with an infectious giggle before snuggling back against
his chest.

chapter 29

Kat was rudely awakened by a sharp slap on her bottom as the warm covers were roughly stripped off her. Bright sunlight pried under her heavy eyelids.

"Up and get dressed. 'Tis nearly noon," ordered a cheery voice, accompanied by an eager bark. Kat kept her eyes firmly closed. It couldn't be the Campbell sounding so devil-may-care. And it could not possibly be Sian. She was obviously still dreaming, yearning for things she could never have. She lay still, trying to collect her muddled thoughts. In a daze, she recalled sitting high above the rest of the people in the humming, bustling banquet hall. Her stomach rumbled as she remembered the aromatic, succulent meats that she had been too weary to eat. It had been night, and there had been the rhythmic patter of rain against the dark windows mingling with the crackling hearths and chattering people. Now it felt like a crystal morning, and she could hear the clear piping songs of the mistle thrush and wren. The oppressive stickiness of the previous day had evidently been dispersed by the violent storm. Now there was a decided chill in the air. Kat shivered and blindly groped about for blankets to cover her nakedness.

A lamenting howl and a frantic scratching caused her to turn toward the sound and apprehensively open one eye, expecting to see nothing except a forbidding glare or an empty

room. She opened both eyes with amazement at the sight of
the Campbell looking devastatingly handsome in tight riding
britches and high jockey boots, his plain white shirt, unbuttoned, revealing the golden skin and jet-black curls of his
broad chest. His usual stern face was open, and he laughed at
the clumsy antics of her large shaggy hound, who futilely
scrambled to get up on the high bed. Kat blinked, expecting
the vision to be a figment of her imagination, but the smiling
man and the excited dog were real. She slowly pulled herself
into a sitting position and leaned back against the headboard,
still not believing her eyes. She didn't know what was more
astonishing: the presence of her pet, the expression on the
Campbell's face, or the wonderful timbre of his deep laughter
that sent waves of excitement vibrating through her as he lifted
the exuberant animal onto the bed. Kat sat dazed, numbly
allowing her sleepy face to be thoroughly licked by a wet,
rough tongue.

Beneath his thick dark brows, Darach's gray eyes twinkled
with warm satisfaction as he watched the joyful reunion. He
ruefully admitted to a twinge of jealousy, wishing that the
lithe arms would hug him as ecstatically as they did the rambunctious, shaggy beast. But Kat's glowing happiness was infinitely worth the long wet ride through the night to Duncreag
and back to collect her large hound. And the ride had been infinitely preferable to the unbearable torture of a long night
lying close to the dark girl and being unable to possess her. It
would have been too easy to have taken advantage of her complete exhaustion, knowing how quickly her sensuous body
became aroused. He had tenderly undressed her and tucked
her into the wide bed before roughly throwing the funereal
black gown out the window. There would be no more gloomy
remnants, no more mourning shadows of the past, he had
determined, aching to lie beside her. He yearned for the feel of
her cool skin against the length of his body, craved to taste her
fiery sweet passion. But he had stoically resisted, remembering
how quickly the fires of lust could be ignited between them
and how desolate and cold the morning ashes often were.
Until she trusted him, there could be no reciprocal love. He
had watched her sleep, wondering how he could accomplish
the seemingly impossible task of gaining her confidence.

Kat watched the Campbell's brooding expression. He was
staring at her, lost in thought. His usually austere face ap-

peared wistful and boyish. Sian lay happily and heavily across her legs, his speckled tongue dangling as he panted, exhausted by his vigorous wrestling. As the Campbell became aware of her gaze, Kat saw his features harden into their usual sardonic lines, and he raised a quizzical eyebrow.

"Good morning," she said shyly, hoping to coax gentleness back into his eyes.

"Good morning, Katrine," he murmured. Instantly, he regretted his choice of words when he saw terror flicker across her exquisite face. Then her small nostrils flared and she glowered defiantly. "Och, pax," he pleaded, holding out his hands in mock surrender, but she continued to glare. "No more battles, my love," he begged with an engaging grin. She looked away, blushing with confusion.

"Dinna call me that," she muttered furiously.

"Dinna call you what?" he asked mischievously. "Dinna call you 'Katrine'? Or dinna call you 'my love'?"

"Dinna call me either!" she snarled, pulling the sheet tightly about her nakedness and nervously entwining her fingers in Sian's shaggy mane.

"Sad, it is, that you canna be called by your rightful names," he said softly and seriously. "But I am amenable, kitten," he quipped.

"I am not a kitten!" she spat, her emotions muddled by his loving banter.

"Nay, you're a wildcat. My Wild Kat," he said claimingly, and before she could guess what he was about, he grasped her chin and kissed her snarling mouth. "Now, get dressed," he ordered, huskily stepping back from the temptation of her quivering body. She gaped up at him, her face a study of delicious confusion. "Here are clothes," he added, throwing a bundle onto the bed. "Your own, you will note." Then he strode out of the room.

Kat stared suspiciously at the closed door and then at the bundle of clothing. She recognized the familiar materials. She pulled the bundle toward her and was surprised by its weight. She unrolled her modest stableboy clothes—trews, smock, jerkin, and boots—and then gaped with astonishment at the weapons that had been concealed in the center. There was a *skean dhu* to be worn down her boot, a dirk to be carried by her heart, and a pistol to be tucked at her waist.

What was the Campbell planning? she pondered, as she

quickly took advantage of her privacy and donned the clothes
She hesitated with her hand on the door that led to the
lounge, hearing the clink of cutlery and rattle of crockery
Tempting aromas of crisp bacon and newly baked bread
firmed her resolve, and she thrust the door open and stood
belligerently on the threshold, prepared to meet Calum Mac
Kissock's disapproving visage. Only the Campbell was in
evidence. He looked up from his breakfast and smiled, disre
garding her warlike stance but noting astutely that she was
fully armed. "You maun be hungry," he remarked softly, in
dicating the sumptuous array of dishes on the table. She
hesitated, unsure of how to react to the gentle side of this im
posing man. Why was he trying to disarm her?

Sian bounded awkwardly into the room, effusively wagging
his tail, his wet black nose appreciatively sniffing the delicious
scents. Darach calmly ate, while watching the play of emo
tions cross her expressive face. He knew that she was torn be
tween suspicion and delight at having her hound once more by
her side. She felt safe with the daggers against her skin, and he
understood the need. He had spent several hours with Angus
and the *cailleach,* hearing about his willful, wild bride, who
had been totally responsible for two siblings since at least the
age of twelve, if the tales of Gregor MacGregor's sybaritic
selfish, and irresponsible appetite were true. Riach had also
shared all he had learned from Macaree, and Darach had been
appalled and touched to his very core at finally comprehend
ing the incredible dimensions of his seemingly rebellious bride
He was totally in awe of the pain, loneliness, commitment
courage, and strength of Katrine MacGregor. She was more
valiant than an army of Highland warriors, and so very small
and young. He stared long and lovingly at her, comparing her
favorably to the simpering society women with whom he had
associated during his adult life.

"Where's Calum MacKissock?" demanded Kat, somehow
too shy of the fondly smiling man to step into the room with
out a display of force.

"Och, I sent that bothersome man back to Edinburgh
'Twas the only way to coax my uncle Colin out of the hunt
ing lodge so we could have it to ourselves." The Campbell
laughed. He stood up and gallantly held out a chair for her.

"But what about Morag?" she exclaimed with dismay.

"What about Morag? Surely you'll not be needing her a

the lodge? I can be a most adept lady's maid," he offered impishly.

"Aye, I'm sure you've had plenty of practice," she snapped caustically, viciously spearing a slice of ham. Darach raised one eyebrow speculatively at her jealous retort. "Morag was planning to marry Calum MacKissock," she added, irritated by his smug knowing grin.

"Then I shall send Morag to Edinburgh posthaste." She gave him a skeptical glare, suspecting mockery, but she was unable to deal with the warm laughter in his eyes. She concentrated furiously on her breakfast, determined to ignore him. "When you are quite finished, there is another beast nearly as anxious to see you again as that gluttonous creature," the Campbell informed after she had stolidly eaten her fill. She fed the remains to the apparently ravenous hound, which, unbeknownst to her, had already devoured a leg of lamb left over from the wedding feast.

"Etalon?" she whispered tentatively, and he nodded smilingly. Kat pushed herself away from the table and stalked to the open window. She found it easier to cope with him when he was her adversary; she was now at a loss, having had no experience with his gentler side. She gazed out across the serene loch, watching the moorhens and ducks scud back and forth, and attempted to sort through her tumult of raw feelings. She took great shuddering breaths of the chill air, marveling that yesterday could have been so sultry while today was so exhilaratingly crisp, like the contrasting moods of the disturbing man in the room behind her. Her green eyes climbed the slopes of the soaring mountains to the intense blue sky, following the golden eagles that circled lazily about the frosted peaks, knowing they were also like the Campbell—cunning, merciless, and deceptive in their apparent nonchalance. She spun about to face him, sensing that his astute silver eyes had never left her.

"Why?" she demanded savagely. He shrugged casually, not understanding her sudden question. "Why? Why Sian? Why Etalon? Why these clothes?" she shouted, tugging at the leather jerkin. "Why this?" she spat, wrenching the pistol from her waistband and aiming it at him.

"Aren't they yours?" he asked idly, leaning back in his chair, seeming unperturbed by the weapon she brandished. Kat hastily tucked the stolen pistol away and looked embarrassed. "I had no right to deprive you of your possessions. I am sorry," he continued when she didn't answer.

"Dinna apologize!" she screamed, feeling extremely guilty.

"I was hoping that if I did, then you might also," he quipped roguishly, rubbing his temple and idly spinning the amethyst geode that resided on the polished table amid the breakfast platters. Kat blushed again, remembering their sensuous lovemaking in the lush grass beside the rushing mountain stream. The geode was the only present she had ever given him, yet she had used it as a weapon against him.

"I'm sorry," she mumbled, scratching behind her dog's floppy ears.

"I would've brought two other creatures back wie me, but your sister, Macaree, is very happily occupied wie her husband," Darach informed her softly. "And Rob isna quite strong enough, but he promises that he'll visit you as soon as he can ride a decent piece of horseflesh and not be transported in a carriage like an invalid or a vaporous female. He also said to tell you that he loves you, and he is also sorry."

"For what? He's done nothing to apologize for! You've no right to make him feel guilty and beholden," she attacked. "You went to Duncreag last night?" she asked incredulously, after a long brooding pause during which her curiosity overcame her indignation.

"Aye."

"While I was asleep?"

"Aye."

"Why?" she probed as a pang of rejection shot through her. She had naturally assumed that he had slept intimately beside her in the wide bed.

"I hoped to undo some of the hurt I have caused you," he replied simply. "I wish I could undo all the hurt you've received in the past but that is near impossible. I can, however, try to ensure that the future for you and your siblings is less painful. Hear what I have to say first," he begged when he saw her tensing to protest.

"Speak," she snapped tersely.

"If it meets wie your approval, Angus would like to make Robbie his ward. He would also like to restore Linnmanach to its former glory so your brother has an estate to pass on to his own sons."

"Under what name? Campbell?" Kat jeered savagely. "Och, you *muckers* steal a clan's land, cause it to be a crime

:ven to use one's own name, coldbloodedly slaughter all the male heirs, and now hae the bloody gall to offer charity!''

"All right, Katrine MacGregor, let us deal wie your accusaions," Darach responded, losing his lounging benevolence and abruptly standing. His imposing height blocked the sunight that streamed through the open window, and a cold brooding shadow fell across the defiant girl. "First, the lands supposedly stolen from your clan?''

"Glenorchy, Glenstrae, Glenlyon, and Glengyle," she chanted triumphantly. The four names were like a litany, repeated so often throughout her childhood by her embittered father.

"Glenorchy, Glenstrae, Glenlyon, and Glengyle all belonged to clan Campbell long before the MacGregors were given them by Alexander in 1222 after the defeat of Argyle. Your clan kept those lands by the right of the sword until 1296, when a chieftain, Iain MacGregor of Glenorchy, was captured by the English and his property was passed to his own son-in-law, a Campbell. It would seem that MacGregor women were partial to Campbell men even in the thirteenth century," he observed whimsically, trying to lighten the crackling tension.

"And it would seem the Campbells fought on the side of the English," she retorted with disgust.

"Aye, sadly sometimes they did, and so did the MacGregors when it suited them. Neither clan was particularly noble when it meant their very survival. Both were equally to blame for many generations of bloodshed," he admitted.

"And yet it isna against the law to bear the name Campbell! Why is it just clan MacGregor that is outlawed?" she challenged.

"Aye, it is an injustice that clan MacGregor is proscribed."

"And has been since the fourteenth century, thanks to you bloody Campbells," she accused snarlingly.

"I dinna ken where you learned your history, but 'tis erroneous. It was not the fourteenth century, but the seventeenth. It was after the battle of Glenfruin in 1603, and it wasna the Campbells but the Colquhouns," corrected the Campbell. Kat was at a loss. Was all the history her father had taught her just tiny grains of truth embellished and exaggerated by his hatred and jealousy? "If you dinna believe me, there are many history books in the library downstairs," Darach stated.

"Aye, probably all written by Campbells!" she accuse
lamely. "But it doesna change the facts!"

"Which are?"

"My clan has been unfairly deprived of everything!"

"Dinna sell your ancestors short, Kat; they werena innocer
victims."

"Neither am I! Oppressed people are forced to resort t
many immoral acts in order to survive. But to die in povert
filth, and degradation is the most immoral act of all. 'T
against all nature."

"I agree."

"My clan was forced to be thieves and cheats but that is be
ter than being beggars."

"Am I to understand from all this that you dinna approv
of Angus's guardianship? I assure you that it isna charity c
pity for an oppressed child that prompts Angus's offer, bu
pure unadulterated selfishness. He loves Robbie as the son h
couldna have, and the lad loves and respects Angus as th
father he was denied, even though he is a Campbell," ex
plained Darach. "Kat, dinna let your father's bitterness bligh
your brother's life more than it has already," he pleade
noticing indecision flicker in her emerald depths.

"I was planning to take Robbie to America, where we coul
be proud of our name and use it without fear," she stated be
ligerently.

"But the boy doesna want to leave Scotland. He doesn
want to leave Angus. Will you tear him from his native lanc
away from the first real security he's ever experienced? Ay
'tis a terrible crime that he canna be known by his rightf
name, but hopefully by the time he's a man the laws again
the MacGregors will be repealed."

"And if they're not? Would you be content to give up yo
clan name? Would you be content to gie your children anoth
man's name? Would you be content to have your sons live
lie?"

"Will we have sons, Katrine?" he asked huskily. St
blushed but forced herself to continue to glare challengingly a
him. "You are my wife, the only one I shall ever have. Th
mother of my unborn sons and daughters," he murmure
noting her heightened color and pressing his advantage.

"And if I bear your sons, doesn' it bother you that they ca
admit to only half of themselves? Our sons and daughter

whether you care for it or not, will be both Campbell and MacGregor—"

"Aye, two great clans," he interrupted, trying to defuse her building fury. "The merging of the race of Diarmid wie the children of the mist."

"Aye, but one half will always be shrouded in the mist, will have to be kept a secret! Are you content wie that?" she shouted, attempting to ignore the smoldering desire that she recognized in his gray eyes. "Would you be so complacent if it was the Campbell part of them that always had to be hidden? The Campbell half that was illegal?"

"I am never complacent about injustice, but I'd certainly not run to America wie my tail between my legs, sacrificing my native land as well as my name. I'd stay and fight."

"How?"

"In Parliament."

"Och, aye, the English Parliament," she scoffed.

"Until we regain some rule, 'tis all Scotland has right now," he answered sadly.

"And you think the English care enough about the barbaric Scots that they'll lift the proscription against clan Mac-Gregor?" she asked derisively.

"There is Scottish representation in the Houses of Parliament," he replied wearily, deciding tactfully to omit the fact that he was one such representative to the House of Lords. "We canna solve the problems of the world right now, but maybe we can try to solve the conflicts between the two of us, if you are willing," he suggested softly.

"Conflicts between us?" she echoed warily, uncomfortable with the abrupt change of subject and unnerved by the tenderness that once more emanated from him.

"You dinna think we have any conflict between us?" he teased playfully. "We are both very stubborn, extremely proud, and, as your astute sister, Macaree, says, 'both used to being in charge.' Now, what sort of marriage does that promise to be? Certainly by no means conventional and boring!" He laughed. Then his expression grew serious when he noted the fearful confusion that darkened her dear green eyes, turning them into unfathomable haunted pools. "I love you, Katrine MacGregor," he stated solemnly, realizing that he had to be the braver of the two and take the initiative. "I have never said that to any other woman," he admitted when she stood staring mutely up at him. "I love you, Kat," he repeated softly.

"What about Felicity?"

"What about Felicity?"

"What about Felicity?" Kat imitated viciously. "Och, you can spout so glibly of love. 'I love you,' he proclaims, throwing one woman aside and rutting wie the next one. Well, I'll not be deceived by lying words. I'll not have a man between my thighs who stinks of another woman! I'd rather be dead than be a slave to that kind of love!" she raged. "I'll not patiently lie there while you thrust into me the seed that you so generously bestow on any other puir panting bitch in heat! I'll not sit home like my mother, the meek, loyal wife, waiting, but I'll take as many lovers—if not more than you! For every woman you take, I'll have ten men! Och, maybe even twenty! I'll do anything but sit and wait day after day, night after night, pretending that nothing's amiss! Pretending I dinna ken that my children are fetching their drunken father from the nearest brothel! Pretending I am blind and canna see! Pretending I canna smell the stench of cheap perfume and unwashed bodies sticking to my man's clothes!" she ranted fiercely.

"I love you, Kat MacGregor," he repeated, when she stopped her diatribe and stood glowering at him, panting for breath. He longed to pull her into his arms to reassure and comfort her, but he knew it would be a grave mistake. She was a proud, defiant woman, not the hurt, frightened child from the Parisian backstreets of nearly six years ago. He was certain there were vestiges of that lost, wounded waif beneath her haughty, sensual exterior, but he hoped that they would have a long life together, allowing him to nurture every aspect of her glorious being. "I love you, Wild Kat MacGregor."

"No, you'll not deceive me wie pretty lies! I'll not be trapped and debased! I'll not be destroyed!"

"I love you," he reiterated. She stared helplessly at him, shaking her unruly ebony head, trying to deny her feelings.

"Och, why do I love you so much?" she suddenly howled, breaking a long, tense silence. "I tried so hard not to love you," she lamented. He laughed joyfully and pulled her compliant body against his.

"Now what is this nonsense about Felicity?" he murmured, kissing her hot salty cheeks. He felt her muscles stiffen, but he continued to gently and mischievously kiss her earlobes and soft velvet neck.

"Och, I dinna want to hear that *sassanach saidhe*'s foul name ever, ever again!" she spat vehemently, standing on tiptoes and straining to reach his mouth, yearning to submerge herself in blind passion. "But if I ever, ever find her in your bed—*our* bed—again, there'll be vital parts of you that'll never rise again," she threatened. She desperately tried to wriggle her lithe hips against his groin to clarify her point, but she wasn't tall enough.

"She was in my bed?!" he echoed innocently, with a teasing note of outrage in his tone. He obligingly lifted her so that she rested invitingly against his arousal. "And where was I?" he inquired casually, nibbling thoughtfully on her pouting bottom lip and sighing, appreciating her sensuous gyrations.

Kat pushed roughly against his chest and reared back in order to gaze suspiciously into his laughing silver eyes. "Where were you?" she repeated dazedly, very conscious of his warm, strong hands, which firmly cupped her buttocks, moving her so that she intimately and rhythmically rotated against him.

"Aye. Where was I?" he echoed, as he carried her into the bedroom.

"Weren't you there?" she asked, trying to think logically despite the waves of sensations that threatened to overwhelm her. He sank down with her on the wide bed and proceeded to unbutton her jerkin.

"Dinna you look?" he growled huskily, sliding his hands under her loose smock and cupping her quivering breasts.

"I dinna want to see," she confessed hoarsely. "She's not your mistress?"

"Is not," he stated emphatically, impatiently wrenching off one boot. He raised a quizzical eyebrow at the *skean dhu* that flew out and skittered across the room, narrowly missing the hound that slept peacefully in a patch of sunlight. "Has never been," he stressed, removing the other boot. "And shall never be," he punctuated, plucking the pistol from her tiny waist and adeptly shimmying her tight trews over her curved hips and down her shapely legs. "Felicity *was*, and *is*, solely my puir demented stepmother," he emphasized, deftly stripping her of the stableboy's smock, leaving her entirely naked except for the leather belt that crossed her chest. The sheathed dagger was tucked snugly between her thrusting young breasts. "You, my *bardach* Wild Kat, *are*, and shall *be*, my only love, my only mistress," he earnestly vowed, accentuating his solemn oath by kissing each of her trembling, tightly budded nipples. "You dinna believe me?" he inquired huskily. "You still dinna trust me, Katrine MacGregor Campbell?" he challenged, noticing that despite the convulsive tremors of passion that shuddered down her exquisite body, her shimmering emerald eyes had narrowed with a cunning speculation.

"I'll not be the only one exposed, Darach Campbell!" she stated savagely, frustrated at not being able to rub her length against his bare skin and feeling frighteningly vulnerable. "I'll not be the only one naked!" she resolved. Darach collapsed across the bed, overcome with joyous laughter, allowing her to tug off his boots. "There is *trust*, and there is downright *stupidity*," she informed him cynically. His mirth increased as, with great grunts of exertion, she strove ineptly to strip the britches from his long, heavy body. "*Now*, I trust you," she proclaimed wearily, when she had finally managed with enormous difficulty to divest him of all his clothes. "You are now as naked as I am!" She sighed happily, rubbing her silkiness against his warm, hard flesh.

"Not quite, you vixen," he chuckled, eyeing the lethal little dagger that dangled between her beckoning breasts. "You are still armed."

"Aye, and so are you," she purred mischievously. "And your weapon is a mite larger than my puir wee one," she added roguishly, after a slow suggestive assessment of his tanned virile body.

"Och, that is not a weapon, my love," he corrected huskily. "Never a weapon." He sighed, gently pulling her lithe sleekness against him but making no move to disarm her. They had a lifetime to work on each other's defenses.

Kat forgot her siblings, her clan, her country, and the multitude of other painful problems that she had battled alone for so many solitary years. Instead, she surrendered to the Campbell . . . for a while.

NOTE: The penal statutes against Clan MacGregor were not repealed until 1775.

Glossary of Gaelic and Scottish Words

argent	silver
auld	old
bagrel	child
baichie	child
bairn	child
baistie	beast
banrigh	queen
bardach	fearless
bawd	hare
beag	little
ben	mountain
biast	beast
billy(ies)	young man (men)
bothan	humble dwelling
bradan	salmon
braw	brave
breac	trout
bree	broth
brose	watery oatmeal
cailleach	hag
clach	stone
clachan	stone house
clavan	buzzard
columan	dove
creag	rock
cuilleann	holly
darach	oak
dawtie	darling
drookèd	drenched, saturated
dubh	black

dun	fortress
dwyning	declining, languishing, consumptive
eich, each	horse
fail	cliff
fash	fret, worry
fionn	white
futret	vermin, weasel
gillie	male servant
glastig	a water fairy, part seductive woman, part goat, with vampiric tendencies
gomeril	half-wit
gowan	daisy
gowkèd	stupid
grian	sun
hippens	diapers
hogmanay	New Year's Eve
howff	tavern
hubbley-jock	tom turkey
iolair	eagle
libbed	castrated
linn	pool
loch, lochan	lake
manach	monk
maun	must
meikle	great, large
muc	pig
mucker	euphemism for a person suspected of perverted practices
naithair	serpent
nickneven	Hecate, the mother witch
nighean	daughter, girl
nuckelavee	most awful of the Scottish sea fairies: a monstrous one-eyed horse
nurreych	nurse

oir, or	gold
righ	king
saidhe	bitch
sassanach	person from the south of the Scottish border
schlorich	messy chaos
scunnering	disgusting
shieling	summer pasture
sholtie	pony
sian	storm
skean dhu	small dagger
skelping	thrashing
slummock	lumpish slattern
spurtle	wooden stick for stirring porridge
stamash	blind fury
stite	nonsense
strath	valley
swick	sly cheat
uisque	water
unco	anything strange or prodigious
unseelie court	wicked fairies
urisk	satyrlike brownie
usquebaugh	whiskey

Highly Acclaimed
Historical Romances From Berkley

_____ 09333-6 **Blaze**
$3.95 by Susan Johnson
The beautiful, pampered daughter of a Boston millionaire is taken hostage by a proud Absarokee chief in this sweeping epic of the Montana frontier.

_____ 09079-5 **A Triumph of Roses**
$3.95 by Mary Pershall
"Five stars." —<u>Affaire de Coeur</u> From the author of <u>A Shield of Roses</u> comes a new novel about two lovers caught in a struggle where surrender means love.

_____ 08792-0 **Scarlet and Gold**
$3.95 by Ellen Tanner Marsh
From the <u>New York Times</u> bestselling author of <u>Wrap Me in Splendor</u> comes the dramatic tale of wild, beautiful Athena Courtland and silver-eyed sailor whose soul raged with desire.

_____ 09472-3 **Let No Man Divide**
$4.50 by Elizabeth Kary
An alluring belle and a handsome, wealthy ship-builder are drawn together amidst the turbulence of the Civil War's western front.

Available at your local bookstore or return this form to:

THE BERKLEY PUBLISHING GROUP
Berkley • Jove • Charter • Ace
THE BERKLEY PUBLISHING GROUP, Dept. B
390 Murray Hill Parkway, East Rutherford, NJ 07073

Please send me the titles checked above. I enclose _____ Include $1.00 for postage and handling if one book is ordered; add 25¢ per book for two or more not to exceed $1.75. CA, IL, NJ, NY, PA, and TN residents please add sales tax. Prices subject to change without notice and may be higher in Canada.

NAME_____

ADDRESS_____

CITY_____ STATE/ZIP_____

(Allow six weeks for delivery.)